The
Friday Tree

The
Friday Tree

SOPHIA HILLAN

WARD
RIVER
PRESS

Published 2014
by Ward River Press
123 Grange Hill, Baldoyle
Dublin 13, Ireland
www.wardriverpress.com

ISBN 978-1-78199-983-7

Author photograph, 2004, copyright Bobbie Hanvey,
reproduced with thanks to Bobbie Hanvey

Printed and bound by CPI Group (UK) Ltd, Croydon, CR0 4YY

www.wardriverpress.com

About the Author

Former Associate Director of Queen's University Belfast Institute of Irish Studies, Sophia Hillan returned to her first love, writing fiction, in 1999, when she was runner-up in the Royal Society of Literature's first VS Pritchett Memorial Prize. Her short story "The Cocktail Hour" was subsequently published in David Marcus's first *Faber Book of Best New Irish Short Stories*, and another short story, "Roses", was broadcast on BBC Radio 4 in 2007. In 2011 she received high praise for *May, Lou and Cass*, the untold true story of Jane Austen's nieces in Ireland. She lives in a hollow at the bottom of a hill, in a house filled with light and many, many books.

Contents

To the memory of David Marcus

> "Come, we will go forth together into the wide world."
> *Grimms' Household Tales*: "Brother and Sister"

Chapter 1: The Plot

"*Elle est absolument pure*," said Francis and, although she did not understand, Brigid laughed.

It was late summer, a bright day, the smell of cut grass stronger than the lingering must of the sun-curtain at the front door. Outside, the sky, moving across the top of the house in stripes of white and blue, led to seven trees at the back of the plot. Seven trees and seven days bounded the map of their lives and on this morning, given what had been happening, it seemed necessary to both children to find something to make them laugh.

Brigid and Francis Arthur lived in a time when men of a certain standing wore dark suits and hats, their wives soft wool with a single strand of pearls, and families aspired to modest comfort, to a house like the Arthurs' house, at the edge of the town, minutes from fields and the dark blue hill they called the Black Mountain. Brigid and Francis had careful parents, and Isobel, the girl, who was not a girl at all. Relatives and friends visited, the children spent a month each summer by the sea, their birthdays brought toys and handsome books. In the five and eleven years that Brigid and Francis had, respectively, lived, they had never known deprivation, until the night in August 1955 when their parents left them.

On that summer night, the children asleep, their parents crept away, instructing their taxi-driver to let the silent car roll down the passage slope, out on to the quiet road and, only then, out of earshot of their sleeping children, to start the engine and allow the headlamps to sweep ahead and show the way. As the light travelled across their darkened ceilings, the children turned, shuddered as if cold, then settled back into quiet sleep. Yet, when they woke, Brigid was conscious of emptiness in the morning and Francis, through the blinds, saw the pale beginning of the end of summer.

They asked questions that morning and all that day of Isobel who, without apparent interest or information, told them that their parents would not be long, and that they had no need to worry. Yet, when that day became night and their parents did not return, and another night and day passed, then another – when, slowly and inexplicably, days and nights accumulated, until their parents had been away for over a week, then the children's questions lessened and, finally, they ceased.

On the tenth morning, as they sat at the silent breakfast table, Francis reached across and opened the cage where his budgerigar lived. "Hello, Dicky," he said, as he stroked the bird's head. Dicky put his head on one side and looked hard at Francis; yet, as always, and despite the hopeful persistence of Francis, he said nothing. Isobel put before the children bacon and toast, for which both of them said, "Thank you, Isobel," and Isobel did not reply. She opened the window a little further as if it, too, had given offence, took up a basket of damp clothes, slanted it against her hip and walked away through the kitchen towards the back door.

It was then that Francis, twisting round from the budgerigar's cage, looked at the cold bacon and the hard and curling toast, checked to see that Isobel had gone, and reached to the sideboard for the bottle of brown sauce. "*Elle est absolument pure,*" he read aloud, and Brigid laughed.

Suddenly, before their eyes, in a flash of green and white, with a black, dismissive glance, and a purposeful pointing of his long tail, Dicky leapt from his cage and flew through the open window, flapping, then soaring through the summer morning.

Francis, in delighted surprise, said once more, "*Absolument pure*," then, stopping as if to listen, he pushed back his chair, stood up, listened again, took Brigid's hand, drew her after him through the kitchen doorway, through the shaft of light motes in the hall, beating past the front-door curtain and, jumping with her down the two steps from the small front garden, lifted her up to stand on the gate pillar. Then he stopped, and Brigid could hear the pounding of his heart.

"What are we looking for, Francis?" she asked. "Dicky? Is Dicky here? Would he go out on to the road?"

"Oh, no," said Francis, shading his eyes against the light. "Dicky's up at the back of the plot. He'll wait for us."

The plot, the large field of vegetables behind their house, was out of bounds to them. Yet, if Dicky was there, he was near enough home to be safe. Still, that did not tell Brigid why they had left their breakfast.

"Why are we out here, then, Francis?"

Francis, scanning the horizon, said: "I'm sure I heard a car door slam. Someone is coming."

Brigid's stomach jumped, turned over, jumped again. "Mama and Daddy?" she said.

Francis' face closed, his cheekbones suddenly sharp. "I doubt it," he said. "But it could be Rose."

Brigid's stomach sat empty, a flat balloon. "Rose," she said, thoughtfully. "Will she take care of us till Mama comes back? Not just Isobel?"

"Maybe," said Francis. "That could be the plan."

"Francis?"

"What?"

"I hate Isobel. She hates me back."

"Why don't you kill her then?" said a languid voice behind them. "By the way, I can see your pants."

Scrabbling at her dress, and so ripping it, Brigid looked down to see the next-door boy, their sometime friend.

"I hate you, too, Ned Silver," said Brigid.

3

"Hello, Ned," said Francis, without surprise. "You don't have a pair of binoculars about you, do you?"

"No," said Ned.

"I do." Out of somewhere came a deep, male voice. "What are you looking for?"

"Uncle Conor!" cried Brigid and Francis together, turning round just as Ned squeezed himself through a gap in the hedge between their front gardens. "Where did you come from?"

The man at the gate looked at them from sleepy eyes, one eyebrow slightly raised, one corner of his mouth turned up as in a private joke. One hand out as though to break her fall, he leaned into the pillar where Brigid stood. Brigid looked at the hand. It was square and strong. Her father's hands were narrow, the fingers long. Her father himself was narrow and long. Uncle Conor was high and broad, his shoulders wide.

"From nowhere," said their visitor. "Is your Aunt Rose here?"

Francis had opened his mouth to reply, when Isobel appeared through the summer curtain, red and angry.

"Get down from that, this minute, before I tell your mother!" Her voice was a hiss.

Brigid wanted to say, 'How can you, when she is not here?' but, hearing the hiss, she said nothing.

Francis, just as silent, reached to lift her down but, before he could, Uncle Conor scooped her up. He smelled of tobacco and tweed. One strand of his hair fell forward as he swung her to the ground and, when he smiled at her, she saw a crooked tooth at the side, which she had never noticed before. She was not sure she quite liked it.

"Don't be cross, Isobel," he said. "She's my best girl, and he's my best boy. Aren't you, children?"

They nodded, carefully, and then saw Isobel had become soft at his words, not like Isobel at all. Practised, they waited for her to come back to herself. In a few seconds, she turned to them and, hands on hips, eyes narrowed where Uncle Conor could not see, she said: "What were you doing, anyway, you villains?"

Her words sounded friendly: the children knew they were not.

Francis looked out from under his hair. "Watching for our Aunt Rose, Bella," he said. Only Francis was allowed to call Isobel by that name. "*Elle est absolument pure.*"

"Oh, your nonsense," said Isobel, but she had softened again. "She'll be here, a bit later. Come in now till we get Mr Todd a cup of tea."

"Can we have tea, Isobel?" asked Brigid, thinking of her lost breakfast.

"Waste not, want not," said Isobel, sharp as before. "You've torn your dress. Get upstairs and change."

Brigid, thinking how little adults could be relied upon, went angrily upstairs, past the silent room where her parents should be and began, as best she could, to change out of her clothes. Downstairs, she could hear the clinking of cups. There would probably be something nice with the tea. Isobel would leave her out, just because.

I should really kill her, thought Brigid, but left the thought as she heard footsteps on the stairs, heard a bumping knock on the door and, awkwardly pulling on another dress, scrambled to open it. There stood Francis, with tea in the blue-rimmed cup she liked and, beside it, on a saucer, a piece of buttered, floury white soda bread. In his mouth he held another piece of bread.

"Oh, Francis!" said Brigid. "Snow bread! The breadman came? I didn't hear the van."

"Mm," said Francis, taking the piece of bread from his mouth. "You need to listen more carefully. Please adjust your clothing."

Brigid pulled and stretched at the cloth, and then gave up. She began to gobble up her bread and gulp down her tea.

"Who's down there now?" she said then. "Did Rose come?"

"Not yet. There's nobody down there now, except Isobel."

"Has Uncle Conor gone?"

"Yes," said Francis. "I think he wanted to see Rose."

"Oh," said Brigid, disappointed. "I wanted to talk to him. I thought he might tell us about Mama and Daddy."

"I doubt that," said Francis. He was silent for a moment. Then he shook himself, like a swimmer. "Anyway, Uncle Conor will be back. Now," he stood up, and brushed floury handprints on his shorts, "up you get."

"Why? What are we doing?"

"We're going to get Dicky, of course. He'll be ready for us by now."

"What about Isobel? She'll be so cross."

"Too busy to be cross at the moment. Come on."

Brigid followed him, trying to talk through a whisper: "But if he's in the trees, that's the plot. We're not allowed in the plot."

Francis stopped on the stairs, and looked up at her, his face crossed by the bars of the landing rail: "I'm going to bring Dicky in. Are you coming?"

Brigid thought, looking down at him: I'm taller than you now. She said, "Yes. Wait. Wait for me," but she had to run to catch him, ducking past the sitting room where Isobel was now sweeping, sidling through the kitchen, careful not to slip on the damp patches of mopped tiles, and even more careful not to leave sandal marks, out after him through the backyard, past the narrow coalhouse, up the steps into the high bushy garden. She crept along the path by the next-door fence, making sure over her shoulder that Ned was not there to tell tales, then bumping up against Francis' warm shoulder at the hidden place behind the broom tree, the one little place where it was possible to climb over into the plot.

Francis was waiting easily, calmly, as if they were not forbidden to go into the plot. It belonged to Ned's family, but it was used by other people to grow vegetables. Some neighbours had bought parts of it. One man had made a house for his plants from an old tram. The part of the plot directly behind their house was let to two policemen from the barracks at the end of the road. The children knew them as Mr Doughty and Mr Steele, and Brigid had an idea that they kept house together in the barracks, until the day Francis told her, to her disappointment, that they each had their own houses, and families. Brigid pointed out to him that they grew flowers – roses – at the front of the barracks, which to her mind meant it was their house, but Francis did not see the importance of this. When Mr Doughty and Mr Steele worked in the plot they wore no collars on their shirts. Their trousers, sitting just under their arms, were held up by braces with shiny clasps and leather buttonholes. Mr Doughty wore wellingtons, their toes turned up like clown shoes, but Mr Steele wore great leather boots with steel caps on the toes. Sometimes, when Brigid was by herself in the garden, Mr Doughty would come to the fence and give her large heads of cabbage, or a bunch of rhubarb tall as herself and say, "Bring that in to your mammy," which Brigid, with some difficulty and much anxiety – there were creeping things in the leaves – usually did. Mr Steele did not hand her things to bring in. He raised a straight hand to them sometimes, from a distance, but he did not come up to the fence, and he did not speak.

Today, no one was in the plot. Brigid and Francis looked at each other and, with easy accord, broke the rules. Francis took the piece of grass he was chewing out of his mouth, and lifted Brigid over the fence. "Don't step in the nettles," he said, and handed her a large, springy docken leaf.

"What's that for?" said Brigid, turning it over in her hand, all damp and furry.

"For when you step in the nettles. To rub on the sting. Hold on to it, and keep behind me," he said and, swinging himself quickly over the fence, landed beside her like a long-legged cat.

Facing him, in his cool shadow, Brigid could see their house as she had never seen it. Now, it seemed someone else's house, strangely angled and chimneyed, the television aerial a large surprising H. The pipes on the back wall were a crooked nose. The windows, their blinds pulled midway up, were half-closed eyes, looking their disapproval and, seeing them, Brigid hesitated. Then Francis took her hand and, threading a path through the chess-squares of vegetables, kept her close behind him. Here and there, he indicated hidden nettles and Brigid saw they did all have docken leaves beside them. She looked about her. The plot was much bigger when they were in it and, glancing back, Brigid saw the house had gone far away. It was not strange any more, but a lost warm place.

They made their way to the centre of the plot, quiet, watchful, as if the birds or the bushes would give them away, as if any moment they would hear a voice calling them back. Yet, no voice came. Somewhere, they could hear a contented insect browsing, a lazy summer sound. As they neared the seven trees, the high leaves about them brushed their cheeks, as though lifted by the light itself. The children stopped. High above them, in the sudden stillness, the birds sang out their joy. Francis, his head on one side, put his hand to his ear to listen. Close to, the trees were bigger, leafier. Now and again the sun darted through the dense summer leaves, light green, dark, light again, shining like diamonds in the cool hollows.

Brigid, fearful of heights, was not afraid of the trees. They were familiar to her, though this was the very first time she had been close to them and seen them clearly. They had the shapes and colours of all the days. Right ahead of them was the Wednesday Tree, fan-shaped, a dull orange, not like the warm brown of Saturday, or the bright apricot of narrow Tuesday, or the dark blue of Thursday. Over to the far left was the Sunday Tree, a green implacable square, and beside it the dun-coloured bulk of Monday. To the right, the far right, was the tree that Brigid loved most. Friday was leaf-shaped, a light blue day, and the Friday Tree was a haze of greys and greens against the moving sky. It lifted Brigid's heart to be near this tree, so close she could discern the whispering of its kindly leaves. She tugged Francis' sleeve to see if he heard it too, but Francis did not seem to notice. He was looking up, scanning the branches for Dicky.

In a sudden moment, Brigid could hear Dicky squawking, not far away, and could picture his black eye challenging them.

Francis reached a hand to Brigid. "Stay here," he said and moved forward, quietly, purposefully.

Dicky, his point made, seemed to be tiring, less in the mood to play. Letting Francis climb up to him, he stepped with delicacy from his branch on to the arm which was extended, and allowed himself to be covered, lightly and gently, in the cupped shade of Francis' hand. Brigid, afraid to breathe, watched their slow descent, Francis' softly cupped hand, Dicky's twitching dark tail, the leaves and the branches folding and releasing them as they slid towards the earth.

Halfway down Francis stopped, frowning, looking down.

Brigid, who could see nothing but a dark space below him, called softly: "What's wrong?"

Francis did not answer. He was still looking down, all the time holding Dicky in his cupped hand. After some moments, beginning once more to move, he said thoughtfully: "Someone's been here."

"Mr Doughty or Mr Steele?" said Brigid, alarmed. Quickly, she looked about her. Mr Doughty might not mind; she was not sure of Mr Steele.

Francis shook his head. "No. Someone's been sleeping here. Come and see."

Brigid did not move at first. "But Mr Doughty and Mr St–" she began, then stopped.

Francis was not listening. He was looking fixedly at something, and Brigid was curious to see what it was. She stepped over the roots and tangle of brambly shoots and there, at the foot of the Friday Tree, Brigid saw what looked like a nest, a small pile of possessions in a little branchy hut. Someone had made a place to stay here. Brigid thought: why not? A person might well want to live beneath the Friday Tree. It would be an obvious thing to want to do.

She shrugged her shoulders, took Francis' hand and, while he minded Dicky against his shirt, she led the way back through the plot. She felt strangely content. Their parents were gone without explanation, they would probably be in trouble with Isobel, but they had Dicky back, they had been to the end of the plot, they had walked right up to the Friday Tree and, best of all, they had a secret.

Chapter 2: Rose

When they were as far as the house, Francis paused uncertainly at the back door. He turned to Brigid and, dropping his eyes, said: "Strict truth. We were just outside in the back. Where were we?"

"Just outside in the back," said Brigid.

Francis nodded.

"In the plot," added Brigid.

Francis, who had turned away, stopped. His shoulders fell. He sighed, shook his head, turned back to her once more and, taking her shoulders, held her eyes: "That's not necessary, Brigid," he said. "Outside in the back will do."

Brigid, meeting his gaze, repeated: "Outside in the back," and made to follow him into the empty kitchen, until he stopped her.

"Stay out here for a bit," he said, "till I settle Dicky."

Brigid, about to protest, stayed quiet. Francis did not move.

"Please, Brigid," he said. "I do know what I'm doing."

Disconsolate, Brigid turned and went back out to the garden without him, the whole day suddenly darker and smaller. She thought: he only wants me with him when he has nothing better to do. She was pulling some leaves from the blackcurrant bush, shredding them, rolling them into green paint in the heart of her hand, when she heard a voice on the other side of the fence.

"Saw you," it said.

"Go away, Ned," said Brigid. "I told you I hate you."

"You can't hate me," said Ned. "I know too much."

Brigid stopped rolling the leaves. "Know too much what?"

"Saw you," said Ned again.

Despite the summer sun, Brigid felt suddenly cold. "Saw me what? This is our bush. It's our garden. You just stay in yours."

"It's not your plot," said Ned, his voice like honey on a spoon, a golden sticky drip.

Brigid felt her breath tighten. "We were getting our budgie," she said and she felt her voice shake.

"It's not your plot. I could tell the police. I could just run down now to the barracks and tell them."

Brigid spun round, but she still could not see him. "Ned!" she said, and suddenly, maddeningly, his face appeared, smiling and insolent, from behind the hollyhock.

"Unless," he said.

"Unless what?"

"Unless you do as I say."

Brigid looked round in despair. No Francis. No parents. No one to help her. She said nothing. She could say nothing.

"All right," said Ned. "I'll just run in now and telephone."

In that second Brigid was, in spite of herself, impressed. It was possible that Ned did know how to use the telephone, and that his father's housekeeper might just allow him to do it.

"I'll tell your daddy," she said.

"Will you?" he said, and examined his nails. "He's in Egypt. Are you going sometime soon? Or will you be telephoning long distance?"

"All right," she said. "All right. What is it you want me to do?"

Ned dropped his voice, as if he were on the wireless. "Kiss me, you little fool."

Brigid snickered.

"Naughty," said Ned, smoothly. "I could tell about that too. I could tell your Ma-*ma*."

"It's *Ma*-ma, stupid, not Ma-*ma*."

11

His face hardened. "Kiss me," he said, "or else."

"Ned Silver, I will hate you for ever."

"It'll be worth it," said Ned. "See you round the front."

"The front!" repeated Brigid, alarmed. "Here will do."

"Oh no," said Ned, in the wireless voice. "I don't want our love to be a secret," and Brigid could hear his triumphant crow as he ran down his steps and around to the front of the house.

She did not know what to do. There was no point at the moment in trying to find Francis, and she could not tell Isobel. She bit her lip. There was nothing to do but get it over with. She put her head down and ran to the top of the steps, where she stumbled, catching one plait in the rosebush that was being trained along a fence. It pulled taut. The thorns caught. To get away, she had to pull her hair hard, losing one ribbon and scratching her face, so that by the time she got round to the front of the house Ned had had leisure to compose himself, and was leaning easily against the pillar inside the gate.

"Oh," he said, "I like that wildcat look," and he pulled her toward him, bending her backward like a dancer, shimmying her with his arms sideways and forward so that her feet followed his, until the moment when, just as she was getting used to the sensation, he suddenly pressed his sticky mouth straight on top of hers.

Brigid could scarcely breathe. Just as she was thinking it was the way they put stamps on letters, she suddenly found herself sitting, surprised and sore, on the hard ground. Ned had dropped her, and was already halfway back to his own garden through the hedge.

"You pig, Ned!" she cried to his departing back.

His voice carried over the hedge: "You're not allowed to say 'pig', either. I'm telling."

That was when she heard Rose's car pull up.

There was no mistaking the arrival of Rose, their mother's sister. Her little red car, with its noisy horn and an engine too large for itself was, in Brigid's mind, a life-size clockwork toy. Ned had once pointed out, for no reason which satisfied Brigid, that that was impossible. Francis and Brigid loved Rose's car, and Rose's navy suitcase, neat and small, with triangles on it from places where she had been. Francis used to bend his head to read the names; Brigid looked at the tiny pictures of domes and towers and bridges. The case smelled of leather and flowers. Always, Rose carried about her a faint scent of flowers, which remained on everything she touched, even when she was gone. Rose was gentle, and she was kind. Once, Ned, appearing as usual out of nowhere, had sneered at Brigid, sitting in Rose's car, imagining she could drive, but Rose said, "Would you like a go, Ned?" and, to Brigid's surprise and annoyance, Ned got in, started steering and making engine noises and braking noises, and seemed, for a while, almost like anybody else.

Now, Rose's car came to its noisy halt as Brigid sat breathless and dishevelled at the front gate.

Rose, if surprised, did not say so. She helped Brigid up from the ground, her cool hand a relief after the outrage of Ned, and she simply said: "I didn't know you were a dancer, Brigid."

Brigid, wiping at her mouth, knew then that Rose had seen the kiss. She said just one word: "Ned." She was grateful that Rose did not press her and, as they went up the steps together and Rose rang the doorbell, Brigid missed her parents a little less. When the door was opened by Isobel, Francis behind her in the hall, it seemed to Brigid that she herself was arriving, with a suitcase and a car, like a visiting princess.

At the sight of Brigid, however, Isobel's initial smile of greeting vanished. It occurred to Brigid that, given the state of her hair and clothes she would, right now, have been in trouble again but for Rose. Brigid understood that having to mind the Arthur children was a trial for Isobel. The idea did not distress her. She had gathered from Isobel in the last ten days that, whatever hope there was for Francis, she, Brigid, was beyond help. Isobel read out to them, on mornings when she was friendly, advertisements for jobs she could have without children to upset her. In this moment, however, Rose's hand in hers, Rose carrying sunshine into the hall, Brigid believed in herself. And, as Isobel stepped back into the kitchen to turn down the kettle, the house itself seemed to relax, warmed and relieved by the arrival of Rose.

Yet, even as Francis stepped forward and pressed in close to Rose beside her, Brigid felt a shadow interpose itself between them and the kitchen. It was momentary, a second's coldness, and the children looked up to see not a dark shadow at all, but Uncle Conor, his smile as quizzical, his arms as wide as before. Wondering where he had come from, or how, having left earlier, he was suddenly in the kitchen with Isobel, Brigid saw that his smiles were directed not towards them, but towards Rose.

To Brigid, watching Rose's face, it was as if she had switched out all the lights, in her eyes, in her smile, even in her voice as she said: "Cornelius. What a surprise."

"Cornelius!" he said, one eyebrow raised, his arms absently extended to the children. "I'm usually Conor in this house, amn't I, children?" He dropped his voice, unexpectedly, almost frighteningly, as he added: "Except when I'm a grizzly bear!" He made his arms suddenly long, his face slack, eyes bulging, and he growled. He was suddenly a bear.

Brigid did not like it. Something heavy hanging from his neck swung towards her, like a live thing. She moved back, behind Francis.

Rose put out her hand to draw Brigid behind the circle of her skirt, and she said: "I don't believe in diminutives, Cornelius. In fact, as I think you may know, I don't much care for short cuts of any kind."

Uncle Conor looked towards the children: "My!" he said. "Is the grizzly bear in trouble?"

"Certainly not," said Isobel, smiling again, appearing from the kitchen with a tray. "Come all of you now and have some tea."

Brigid, remembering her earlier exclusion, whispered to Francis: "Does she mean us, too?" and Francis, just as urgently, whispered back: "She'd better. I'm starving. Say nothing. Just sidle behind me . . . no, sidle, Brigid, not shove . . ."

It was not, in the end, a very comfortable gathering. Rose's sudden coldness made it hard for Brigid and Francis to concentrate on the tray, though there were sandwiches.

After a time, which seemed very long, Uncle Conor, no longer a grizzly bear, got up to leave, and Francis, who had, for some time, been looking intently at the pendulum around Uncle Conor's neck, unexpectedly asked: "Uncle Conor, are they new, your binoculars?"

The ice broke. The big man smiled, and his shoulders eased as he loosened and swung from his neck the heavy object. He took out of a dark case something solid yet shining, angular and curved at the same time, glasses and a camera at the same time, to Brigid's eyes a large black letter M. "They are new," he said. "Well spotted." He looked at Francis for a moment, as though wondering about him. "Would you like to try?"

"Yes, please," said Francis, and looped the heavy weight about his neck, moving quickly to stand at the window, whistling below his breath as he swept the binoculars round.

Brigid, concentrating on the name of the black shiny glasses, did not even ask for a turn. Instead she repeated the word, slowly, in her head: *bin-oc-u-lars . . . bin-oc-u-lars*.

At last she said: "Francis asked Ned for some bin-oc-u-lars, for the plot."

"The plot?" said Uncle Conor. "I'm intrigued. Have you two been hatching a plot?"

Francis turned from the window, his eyes warning Brigid. "No, Uncle Conor. Dicky got out of his cage, and we were afraid he might fly away – or even go into the plot. I mean the plot behind the house." He handed back the binoculars.

Uncle Conor worked at placing them in their case for quite a long, careful time.

"And did he?"

"Did he what, Uncle Conor?" said Francis, his face shut down.

"Go into the plot," said the man, his eyes, looking down, little more than slits.

Isobel, collecting the tray, straightened up and answered for them: "It wouldn't have mattered if he had, Mr Todd. They're not allowed in there, and woe betide them if I find out they went in."

Uncle Conor snapped the case shut, half-opened his eyes and looked down at the children. He was the grizzly bear again, but not a friendly one. "Woe betide them indeed," he said. The silence sat uncomfortably in the air. "Woe betide them if they disobey Isobel." He smiled, showing his crooked tooth. Yet his eyes remained watchful as, with one swift, sharp twist of his hand, he fastened the lock of the binocular case. "Well," he said, "Dicky's in his cage now, isn't he? I think I can hear him."

Indeed, they could all hear Dicky, squabbling to himself, crossly reminding anyone listening that he was on his own in the other room.

"And that surely means he can't have gone anywhere very far, can he?" continued Uncle Conor, and he looked directly again at Francis.

Francis met his eyes and said: "Not very, no."

Uncle Conor watched Francis, straight and hard, for a little longer, then turned to Rose, standing quietly with her hands folded. "Who is Ned?" he said.

"Next-door child," replied Rose, not yet warm, but not quite as frozen as before. "Nine years old. Precocious, but, well . . . Prep school, comes next door for holidays."

"Parents?"

Rose dropped her voice and turned a little away. Brigid heard only the words "The Silvers . . . *Princess Victoria* . . . You must have heard at the time."

There was a long pause before Uncle Conor replied: "Ah, yes. The *Princess Victoria*." He paused again: "Do little pitchers . . . ?" His head inclined toward the children and back again to Rose.

Brigid heard Rose say, in her newly distant voice: "More than one house bore that loss," and then, shaking Cornelius Todd's hand civilly, distantly, she walked with him to the front door, and stood there with the children behind her until he was out of sight.

Only Isobel seemed sorry to see him go, and the children stayed subdued and careful until Rose became herself once more. Once she did, she answered the questions which Isobel had not. They learned that their parents were well, would return in a very few days and that she, Rose, would be here with them until they arrived. Rose was quiet and reassuring. Yet, there was in her face and her voice something which told them not to ask too much, so that neither Brigid nor Francis asked why their parents had gone without telling them. They knew enough for now. They went quietly and with something of their old content about their day and their evening and, when it was time for bed, climbed the stairs without protest.

Still, they did not go straight to their rooms. Francis was brushing his teeth when Brigid came in and settled herself on the edge of the bath.

"What happened to privacy?" said Francis.

"Francis. Tell me. Is that the same Princess Victoria we aren't supposed to talk about when Granda Arthur comes?"

Francis rinsed his mouth. "Come over and clean your teeth, seeing as you're here." He spread the toothpaste on her brush and handed it to her. "Yes, it is."

"Who is Princess Victoria?" asked Brigid, foaming.

"Don't do that. Spit out. No, here, Brigid, not there. The *Princess Victoria* is not a person. It was a ship, a ferry that went down off the coast two years ago, in a winter storm. Someone Granda and Daddy knew well was lost on it. He was sort of an uncle. I called him Uncle Laurence. Or Laurie."

Brigid could not imagine why, if he was lost, they did not just go on the ship and find him, but she had another question, which she could not ask without spitting and foaming again. She brushed. She rinsed. She spat. Francis, watching her, sat where she had, on the edge of the bath.

"Before you ask me, yes, that is what happened to Ned's mother too – but I don't know much about that – and I can't ask, and you're not to, either."

"She got lost on the *Princess Victoria*?"

"Yes," said Francis. "She did."

"But Francis, if a person is lost why doesn't someone just go and –"

Francis stood up. "Brigid, please. I'm tired. Leave it for tonight. I'll do the *Princess Victoria* with you another time."

Brigid, who was tired herself, decided to let it be, but she still wondered why no one simply went and found Ned's mother. Brigid shook her head. She was tired, and she'd had enough of the Silvers, lost or found, for one night.

If Francis or Brigid had not been so relieved that night that they slept almost immediately, and if they had looked through the banister railings from the landing, they might have seen Rose, sitting by the fire, in her hand an envelope on which was written, in a bold, black hand, her name: *Miss Rose Durrant*. They might have seen her, after a few moments, tear up the envelope and toss it on the fire, watching it curl, watching it catch in the dying tongues of fire, ignoring its last leaps and sallies in the grate. They might, if they had had patience, have seen her sit a long while with her head in her hands and then rouse herself, smooth her clothes, rise from the chair and, slowly, climb the stairs.

They would have heard her clear her throat to signal to them that she was on her way, and they might have glimpsed her checking their two heads on two pillows, a red-brown mop in one room, a freckled arm thrown back – in the other a dark tangle of plaited hair, a careless red ribbon trailing from the covers. If Brigid and Francis had been able to read her thoughts, they might have learned that she wondered if this was the nearest she would come to having children of her own. They might have heard her, when the telephone rang, loud and shrill, run quickly down to the cloakroom to answer it.

Brigid and Francis saw and heard none of this, because they were tired that night and so relieved to have Rose with them that they slept the night through, children again, safe again, secure.

Chapter 3: Smoke

Brigid woke confused, feeling a difference in the house. On the chair by her bed sat a large box, coloured and shiny, like a Christmas present. Was it Christmas? It could not be – the warm light of summer was still filtering through the blinds. Rose. She remembered that Rose had come. Had Rose left her a present in the night? Brigid turned on her side, reached across, and pulled over the shiny box, smelling of newness. She could hardly open it, for the shaking of her hands and the beating of her heart. It was exactly like Christmas. Inside the box, her fingers found soft cloth. Sitting up, swinging out of bed, she lifted from folded tissue paper a fringed skirt, a waistcoat, a tin badge, a red neckerchief with a silver clasp, a hat with a band round it, little boots without feet and, best of all, a leather belt with a holster and a shiny toy revolver. Brigid wondered no more. It might not be Christmas, but this was a present and, where presents were concerned, she asked no questions.

She pulled all of it on over her pyjamas and, despite the chill under her feet, ran straight to Francis' room, right along the long corridor. Not even the cold following eyes of Blessed Oliver Plunkett, hanging like a reproach on the wall, could hold her back. She ran past him and pushed open Francis' door, spreading her arms with a flourish. Nothing happened. No one was there.

The only movement in the empty room came from the summer curtains, sucked in and out with a sigh. Through filmy light Brigid could see the Friday Tree, far away, spread out in its late green glory at the back of the plot. Yet, inside or out, there was no Francis. The cold of her feet spread through Brigid. Had he gone now too? She raced back past Blessed Oliver to the top of the stairs and there, looking down, she saw Francis standing quite still at the foot of the stairs, his head on one side as if he were listening for something. To her vexation, he did not seem to see her. With one hand on the newel post, he was looking without expression at the sitting-room door. When she called him he raised his eyes, yet, for a second, it was as if he did not know her, looking blankly as if she were a stranger. With some effort, she pulled out her new revolver from its stiff leather holster and, surprised by its heaviness, struggling to hold it in both hands, managed to point it at him.

"*Bang!*" she said, and was delighted to find that the gun made a bang of its own.

She watched his face break into a smile. He lifted his hands, and she saw he was holding a long tube, shining, with a glass window.

"Hello!" he said. "Do you like my new telescope? You look dangerous."

"*Bang!*" cried Brigid, again, the gun obligingly echoing, and was satisfied to see him crumple at the waist, clasping the newel post as he fell. His falling words, "You got me!" pleased her. Brigid blew away smoke – real smoke! – from the top of the pistol, just the way the cowboys did. Then she scrambled down the stairs, only to find that Francis had, yet again, disappeared. Put out, but no longer afraid, she paused just long enough to shoot into the air, and then she noticed that the sitting-room door was ajar. Low voices floated out.

Brigid stopped. Her heart grew loud. She knew those voices. She thought she knew those voices. Hardly daring to believe what she heard, Brigid once more blew the smoke, hard, from the top of her gun and pushed open the sitting-room door.

And there they were. Her parents, so suddenly gone, were just as suddenly back again. Her mother and father were sitting there, as if they had never gone away. Brigid found herself unable to speak. She found herself, also, angered, which she had not been when, all those days and days ago, they had disappeared. There her mother sat, quiet and composed, one hand out to her from the table, saying as though she had not gone off and left them: "Brigid. Your hair. Come here." Light caught the slender wedding band as her hand came towards Brigid, and danced on the bright white stones of her other ring.

Yet, to Brigid, distracted by the sudden shining, it seemed that her mother spoke without enthusiasm, her eyes all the time on Brigid's father. He was different, too. He looked strange.

Into Brigid's head from nowhere came a picture: a rainy winter Saturday when she had sat on the floor at his feet, his hand on her head. She had been held close between the rolled chair-arm and his knee. The radiogram sang quietly in the corner, and her father tapped out its rhythm on her hair. Outside it was cold, rain in grey needles beating against the window, but she was warm, watching mountains and caves in the fire. The music stopped. Her father's hand slid to her shoulder and, pressing her arm so that she turned to him, he stood her up and placed her between his knees. He covered one eye with his hand. "I can't see you, Brigid," he said, and when she looked, she could not see herself. There was no mirror in his uncovered eye. It was a stone, not an eye. She tried to pull away, but he held her. Then he covered the other eye, looked at her, the eye alive, her own frowning face reflected in the shining blackness in the centre. He said: "Now I can see my girlie." That night, she dreamed they had all, everyone in the house, turned to stone.

Now, today, mysteriously returned, he wore a large white bandage over one eye, and he did not extend his hand to her. Still angry, she told herself that the cowgirl suit must be to make up for leaving, and she said: "Daddy – Mama," but she did not go to them, and she did not thank them. Then, she said, "Where did you go?" and her mother looked down again at her hands before replying, "To London. Did you like your present?" and her father, at last, looked round, pointing his hand like a gun. "Bang, bang!" he said. "You're shot – you're dead."

Brigid thought: To London? Without us? Without me? But she did not say it. Instead, she said, "Thank you. I like it very much," but in her head she asked her questions, over and over, until a face appeared round the door and made her forget to be angry.

Francis, comically fearful, was peering out from under his hair. "Is she gone?" said his voice, low and hollow. "Somebody tell me when she's gone."

Brigid turned and shot him again. "*Bang, bang!* You're shot, you're dead!" she cried, looking, in spite of herself, to see if her father had heard her. He had not. Gazing out the window through the eye not covered, only his blind, bandaged face was turned towards her. Francis fell obligingly dead, but Brigid felt no elation. She no longer wanted to know why her parents had gone away. Her father had just told her.

And yet, though they had come back, everyone was quiet, and there was no rejoicing. Even Rose was quiet, not cold as when Uncle Conor came, simply saying very little. They all seemed to be living inside themselves. Brigid was not unhappy when they were told to get dressed, get their breakfast and go outside in the fresh air. In the hall, she stopped at the foot of the stairs and turned to her brother.

"Francis?"

He put his hands in the air. "Don't shoot me, ma'am. I'm real scared," he said, but Brigid did not respond.

"Francis. Don't they want to see us?" she said.

Francis sighed, dropped his hands and his head, suddenly deflated. "Brigid," he said, and then for a moment or two said nothing. He sighed, folded his arms, and looked at her, clear and straight, almost hard: "Do you know what, Brigid? Sometimes you disappoint me. He has been ill."

Brigid thought: he means Daddy, but he does not call him Daddy.

"He needs quiet," Francis said. "We're too noisy in the house. Don't you see that?"

"I saw the bandage."

"Exactly. The thing is, Brigid, we're a bit in the way here. Come on. Get ready and we'll go out to the garden. Do you know your hair looks as if a bird's been nesting in it?"

Brigid, confused, thinking of Ned and the rose thorns, did not know what to say. She pulled at her head, ineffectually. "It's always getting tangled," she said. "Nobody has time to fix it. I can't."

Francis did not reply. He seemed to be thinking about something else.

"Brigid?" he said.

She turned, halfway up the first stair.

"Don't say anything about yesterday. To anyone."

"Not to you?"

He had turned away. "Not to anyone, just for now."

In her room, Brigid looked at herself in the mirror. She was untidy. Mama had said nothing after that first abstracted remark. Mama had forgotten about her hair. Mama had forgotten about her. Brigid gave the plaits a good shake, took herself briskly past Blessed Oliver into the bathroom, still cold even on an August morning, and scrubbed and took short cuts, until she judged herself ready for her cowgirl suit, except that the hair still had to be replaited. Francis could not be asked to do this. She had to go to Isobel, knowing she would do it too tightly, and scold her all the while for failing to keep still. Brigid wished she could have gone to Rose, but Rose was in the silent room with her parents and Brigid decided that she had better just go and get breakfast with Isobel, and put up with her pulling at the hair.

By the time she got outside, she was cross and resentful.

Francis, with his new telescope, was crouched down in the garden, looking out towards the end of the plot. He did not seem to hear her come up behind him. "*Boo!*" she said, but he did not move.

"Boo yourself," he said, but he did not turn round. "You think I didn't hear you."

"Did you?" she asked, thumbs in her waistcoat, legs apart.

"No." He still did not turn round, so Brigid leaned on to his shoulder, trying to see what he was seeing.

"What is up there?" she said. "What are you looking at?"

He folded up the telescope, and turned to face her. His face was guarded. "Just birds," he said.

She clapped her hands. "Oh, let me see. Let me have a go."

"Sometime," he said. "Not in that gear. Did you ever see a marshal with a telescope . . . Marshal?"

That did it. Up she got, legs wide, thumbs so firmly in the waistcoat that they hurt.

Francis stood up against the sun, blotting it out. Then, as he shifted slightly, Brigid thought she saw something.

"Francis, is that smoke?" She could not be sure. Everything beyond a short distance had a haze round it, which Brigid quite liked unless, as now, she wanted to make something out. "Is it, Francis?" she said again.

He glanced round quickly, far too quickly, to Brigid's mind, to have looked at it properly, then immediately turned away.

"No," he said, training the telescope towards the house. "I don't think so. Or if it is, it's old smoke. Maybe a campfire. Maybe someone lit a fire to burn rubbish."

"A campfire!" Brigid, forgetting for a moment that she was a US Marshal, jumped up in excitement. "Francis," she said, "could it be whoever was there when we looked for Dicky?"

He did not respond. "Are we going to play, or not, Marshal?" he said. "Seems to me that could be Cherokee smoke . . ."

Immediately, as if a switch had been pulled, Brigid sprang into action and ran up the garden, close to the boundary of the plot.

"Yes!" she cried. "And I'll be the bad one. I've just ridden into town!"

"How can you be a bad one, with the marshal's badge?"

"I just am," answered Brigid. "I can be what I want."

Then she stopped. She had heard something across the fence. That voice, that whisper could only be Ned Silver.

"If you want to be a really bad one," it said, "just shout 'I'm the IRA'."

"I'm not lis . . ." she began. Then in spite of herself, she whispered back, "What? What's that?"

The whisper came again: "You want to be a bad one, these days, that's what to be. Go on. Try it."

"Brigid!" called Francis, from the end of the path. "Who are you going to be?"

And Brigid, without thinking, cried out, as loudly as she could: "*I'm the IRA!*"

Too late, she saw Francis' face change and move from side to side, and his mouth begin to frame the word 'no'.

Like a whirlwind from nowhere, up the garden steps, furious and white-faced, flew Isobel, flinging a large basket of washing to one side. "You tinker!" she cried. "You bold, brazen tinker!" Taking Brigid roughly by the arm, she spun her round: "How dare you say that? Don't you understand anything? God, if you were mine, I'd give you what for!"

Brigid had never seen Isobel so angry. She had never seen her violent. And her arm hurt.

"I'm sorry," she said, pulling away, shaking her head. "I'm sorry, Isobel." Isobel's face was lined and drawn, not like her face at all. "It was only a game – and it wasn't even me. It was Ned –"

She looked round for Ned, but he was nowhere. Instead, Francis was beside her. Gently removing the furious hold, he patted Isobel's arm. "It's all right, Bella," he said, quietly. "It was my fault. Brigid's just excited, and I made her worse without meaning to. It was, really, only a game. Brigid doesn't understand . . . what she said."

Isobel relaxed her grip, but her face did not soften.

"Bella," said Francis, "she's not very big. She really doesn't understand." He eased Brigid, too sore and frightened to protest, away from Isobel. His hand rested gently on the arm she had raised to Brigid, until she composed herself.

Yet, when finally Isobel did speak, her voice was strange. It was rougher and deeper yet, to Brigid's surprise, she could see something shining at the side of her eye. If it had been anyone else, Brigid would have said she was crying.

"Your mother wants you both inside," Isobel said. "Go on. There's a visitor come to call," and she turned round, cross and brisk again, to pick up the washing, strewn where she had thrown it over the hollyhocks.

Brigid saw that the blackcurrant bush was wearing her father's white shirt, and a small rose tree one of her own blue socks. That was good, that was fun, but when she turned to show Francis he drew her away, gently pulling her down the steps.

"Come on," he said. "Piccadilly Circus, this place, if you ask me," he added, under his breath.

"Oh, is there a circus? Is there, Francis?" Brigid trailed after him, pulling at him, but Francis did not reply. "Where is there a circus, Francis?" she tried again, but Francis said nothing more. He let go of her arm and Brigid, trotting to keep up, followed him as quickly as she could into the back yard, through the cool kitchen and, breathless, to the door of the sitting room, where another figure had joined their parents and Rose.

She came to a halt just behind Francis, stopped short at the door. She heard him say, "Uncle Conor" and she looked up, to see the tall figure of Cornelius Todd.

"Uncle Conor," she said, just as Francis had, politely, distantly.

"Well," said his deep voice, and his big hands caught her, held her up high above his head, shook her, brought her deep into his thick hair which, close up, smelled of spice. He swung her down on to her feet, then one hand brought her close in to stand by him. His other big hand, not a grizzly bear's today, more a lion's paw, reached out to Francis' head and bowed it towards him, ruffling the fringe till it stood out in spikes. "There's a big man," he said, "and a dangerous cowboy here."

Francis smoothed his hair with his hand.

Brigid, displeased without knowing why, heard herself say: "Cow*girl*, Uncle Conor."

"Cowgirl," he corrected himself, "my mistake," and he smiled again, this time with his teeth only, not his eyes. At the same time, he released his grip on her, and turned again to Francis. "Look what I have," he said, and from nowhere produced two bars of chocolate.

Brigid and Francis drew breath at the same moment. This chocolate could be bought only across the border.

"Cornelius," said their mother, in her warning voice, too low for comfort.

He looked up at her, with his eyebrow raised and his mouth in its half smile. He seemed apologetic, even regretful, yet the children knew he would not take back the gifts. "No rationing any more, is there, Grace? That war's over, at least. How will a bar of chocolate harm them?"

"It could," said Rose, even more quietly than her sister, "if it damages their teeth."

Cornelius Todd turned deliberately round to Rose. She was sitting a little out of the circle of the company, on a chair near the window. "Thank you, Matron," he said, one eyebrow higher than the other, but he did not smile.

Rose said nothing, turning instead to look out the window, her mouth set in its straight line. For one second, Brigid saw Rose almost old.

Silence hung in the air until her mother spoke. "You know, Cornelius," she said, "I think Rose will be matron of that hospital some day, and I'm certainly glad of her advice where my children are concerned. More tea?"

He did not seem to hear her. Brigid saw him look straight at Rose, but all Rose appeared to see was a trolleybus rolling past on the road.

"Tell us about the Commemoration in Down, Conor," said their father from his chair, as if none of them had said a word.

"Who spoke, you mean?" said Cornelius. Turning away from Rose, he pulled up the knees of his trouser-legs, and settled himself in the armchair. "Ah, you know, Maurice," he said, pleasantly, as if nothing had happened, "it was our friend – that character who . . ." and as if no one else were present in the room, began what seemed to Brigid a very long account of people talking in a field about someone who was dead.

Brigid could not imagine how it interested her father, in his weakened state, yet it clearly did. He nodded and leaned forward in his chair so that Brigid thought he might slide out of it altogether. He asked questions of Uncle Conor as he had not done of her, or of Francis. Back and forth, they repeated the same words and numbers over and over: Connolly, Collins, Pearse, Tans, Hunger, Strike, John Bull, Sixteen, Twenty-one, Treaty, Troubles.

Her father grew more animated with every minute. He finally left his chair, half standing as he said: "And the Captain, Conor? Did you hear about the bold Captain, and his so-called 'liberal policy towards the minority'? Did you read that? It was in the paper. Look." He slid back into the chair, and reached down beside him where, in his excitement, he had dropped the newspaper on the floor. "Here, yes. I have it. I can't make it out too well, but I can get the gist. Have you read it, Conor?"

"No need, Maurice," said Conor, his hand out to take the newspaper. "I know what it said. The good Captain said he was warning what he called the minority that they must not meet this liberal policy with what he described as ingratitude. The papers said it was a hot Twelfth this year, and they were not wrong. And, you know, I went over and heard that young clergyman – you remember I said I would? I heard him preach at his new church in the east of the city. I'm sure you'll be interested to learn that the Roman Catholic Church is not a Christian Church, and that the Pope is the Anti-Christ."

Their mother reached across and placed her hand on her husband's arm. "Maurice," she said. "The children," but he seemed not to hear, looking with his good eye only at Conor.

"Ah, that fellow's a firebrand," he said. "He'll burn himself out. I'm more concerned about the fifteen thousand Orangemen marching by the Longstone Road on the Twelfth. Their right! Their right! Holy cats o' cats!"

Uncle Conor, glancing at the children, turned to their mother. "All quiet now though, Grace, down that direction. There was no trouble in the end. It was a respectful remembrance of a brave man who died, all those years ago, for a principle."

"By starving himself? What was brave about that?"

To everyone's surprise, this voice belonged to Rose.

No one else spoke. Brigid tried to catch Francis' eye, in hope of escape, but Francis did not respond. His eyes were fixed upon their visitor.

"Does it still happen, Uncle Conor?" he said.

"Does what still happen, son?"

"Does it still happen in Ireland that people die because of politics, or get . . . you know, get killed?"

Conor looked at him straight in the eyes, as if Francis were an adult. "It still happens," he said.

Francis intent, a cub about to spring, seemed suddenly to hesitate.

"Go ahead, son," said Uncle Conor, and his voice was very quiet. "Say what's on your mind."

Francis stood up, ran his hand through his hair and said quickly, as if he could not stop the words: "Is there still an IRA, Uncle Conor?"

Brigid, no longer bored, felt herself stiffen, her eyes widen, and looked towards the door for Isobel. She was there, outside, Brigid knew. She had often seen her in the hall, quite still, listening. The clock on the mantel ticked for a long time before Uncle Conor stopped watching Francis. Brigid saw again his eyes grow cool, distant and appraising. She thought he would never answer.

Then, almost carelessly, he said: "Why do you ask that, Francis?"

Francis looked at the floor, then directly at Uncle Conor. "I thought the IRA was long ago. I thought it was over. I thought it was remembered in days like the one you were talking about, but just remembering, not happening any more."

More silence. More moments for the clock to mark.

Francis took a deep breath: "Then I read in the newspaper that the police found guns in London. Boxes of them. They said they were IRA guns. They were to blow up places, army barracks. It said police, Special Branch, were looking for IRA men in London, and at the ports. Liverpool. The paper said they could have come here."

The children's mother lifted the heavy silver teapot, holding it poised as if it were made of paper. "Cornelius," she said, "more tea?"

Uncle Conor looked at his hands, spread broadly in front of him. "The papers are full of stories, Francis," he said. "That's how papers are sold." He put his hands on his knees with a loud smack, and stood up. "I don't think I'll have any more tea, thank you, Grace. I must get on the road."

"Did you come up on the train this morning, Cornelius?" said their mother, rising as she spoke.

"Not this time. I got a lift, as it turned out. We came through the Mournes, through Eightmilebridge."

"I love the train," said their mother, turning all her attention on the children. "Maybe we'll do that some day. We'll go on the train, and you'll see the hedges and fields and houses all streaming past you in a whistle." She smiled, her warm smile, but there was in it a warning.

Francis, still watching Uncle Conor, turned with reluctance

and met her eyes. "*Faster than fairies*," he said, "*faster than witches.*"

"That's right," said his mother, and she reached out to stroke his head. "Good boy." She turned back to Conor. "Now, Cornelius, I'm going to send these two out again. It's a shame to have them inside this good day. Dear knows how many more we'll have before the summer's done."

"Ah, don't put them out," he said. "I'm away. I can hear the sound of a car, and it could be my transport." He smiled his crooked smile, and pulled them both close into his big arms. There was no softness in him today. Brigid, uncomfortable, remembered the grizzly bear. "And if your mother brings you over the border on the train, you can come and see me in my house, can't you?"

Even as they nodded "Yes", Brigid heard their mother say: "We'll see what happens, Cornelius," which both children knew meant 'No'.

With relief, and anxious to be outside, Brigid and Francis ran out again through the kitchen. Yet, even before they turned out of the back yard, they heard a car door open, and veered round the side of the house to see who was coming or going. They were in time to see Uncle Conor getting into a car, but they could not see who was driving it. Turning round as he swivelled in, Cornelius included Brigid and Francis in his friendly wave, a kindly lion again, the grizzly bear hidden away.

On the morning air their mother's voice carried through the window: "I don't know what to think when I see Cornelius Todd. He just appears, and then he disappears. Like the Cheshire cat, but less comfortable."

Then Rose's voice spoke, smaller, flatter, not Rose's voice at all: "And always when there is something going on," she said.

"You're right," they heard their mother say. "I'm sorry, Rose. I was forgetting. It must have been uncomfortable for you," and then the voices floated away.

Brigid and Francis looked at each other, but said nothing.

They walked back around the house.

At the foot of the steps, Brigid stopped and said up to Francis, already near the top: "Why do we call him 'Uncle' and 'Conor' when he is not our real uncle and the grown-ups call him that name I can't say?"

Francis said, reasonably: "That's why. You can't say Cornelius properly, and neither could I one time. Daddy calls him Conor, the Irish for it. And 'Uncle', well, people call their parents' friends that sometimes. That's about it."

"But we don't call Rose 'Aunt Rose' when we speak to her. Or Michael 'Uncle Michael' when we go to Tullybroughan."

"Because she is really our aunt," said Francis, shrugging his shoulders. "We don't need to. We know she's our aunt, and Michael's our uncle. Same with Laetitia in Lecale."

Brigid made a face. "I don't always like Laetitia," she said. "I'm not sure she likes me."

"Laetitia's all right," said Francis. "Don't annoy her, that's all."

"And there is an Uncle Laurence who is not really an uncle either?"

"Was, not is. Don't think too much about it all, Brigid. Here, take this."

Brigid, wondering what she would do if she did not have Francis to explain things to her, took the chocolate he handed her, and they sat, both thoughtful, on the grass.

"Francis," asked Brigid, as they peeled away the silver paper and broke off chunky squares. How good chocolate was! How smooth and velvety-warm in her mouth. "Why did you ask those questions about," she looked round, "that thing we aren't supposed to mention? You know," and she dropped her voice to a whisper, "IRA."

Francis took a square of chocolate, slowly inserting it between his teeth. "I wanted to know," he said.

Behind them, there was a sound in the plot. Turning, they saw Mr Doughty, his collar off, his face reddened with heat. He was coughing beneath his hand, quietly, to himself.

"Mr Doughty," they said together, getting to their feet.

"Would you like some chocolate, Mr Doughty?" asked Francis, moving towards the plot fence.

"Morning, children," he said, quite stiffly, then more kindly, "No, thank you. I'd spoil my dinner."

Brigid wondered if he had heard her shouting about the IRA or, worse, if he guessed – since he was a policeman – what they were not mentioning now. His hands were behind his back. Perhaps he had handcuffs. Brigid stiffened as he reached his hands forward towards her, and then she saw what they held seemed like two large bouquets. One was cabbage, the other rhubarb.

"Take those in to your mammy," he said, "like good children," and Brigid was ashamed to have thought badly of him.

They thanked him together; he saluted them with a hand to the side of his forehead and turned to walk back up the plot again, his slow tread measured and steady, like a farmer who walks behind his plough, not like a policeman at all.

Chapter 4: The Men

As the summer days shortened, and the nights began to draw in, the men came back. Each night, when it grew dark and Francis had gone past her on the landing, once she heard his light click off, Brigid would hear them. The voices floated upstairs to her, low and soft. She was not disturbed by them: she was even reassured. Brigid had decided that the men used the house for meetings, about important matters, after the family had gone to bed, and it seemed to her quite reasonable that once people were in bed, a house could be used for other purposes. The voices of the men kept her company as she slid into sleep.

Now that the men were back, it was no surprise to wake to the sound of the summer curtain being taken down from the front door. It had been brought out in the first days of summer, smelling stiffly of itself, green stripes and mothballs, and by the end of August its scent had softened, like the memory of cut grass. Brigid lay listening to her mother and Isobel as they worked.

She felt lazy and contented until she heard her mother say: "Shoes. I have to get shoes for them. School already."

"And the pair of them, this time," said Isobel. "I wonder how Miss Madam will like that."

"Oh, she'll like it well enough," said her mother. "I've already held her back a year: it's time she went. It's Francis I'm more concerned about. He's very young in some ways."

"He has an old head," said Isobel, "and he'll be twelve soon."

Then they moved from the hall, their voices fading under the stairs where they put the sun-curtain away.

To keep from thinking about school, or why Francis had an old head, Brigid began to think of the television she was allowed to watch with Francis. She closed her eyes, and conjured up the images she liked: a lion roaring or a man beating a gong to show the film would begin, and she heard again in her head the music that would surround them as they settled down by the fire. Then there would be more music, different, sweet or sad, magic girls in circles on black and white tiles, a man in dancing tails wonderfully spinning a feathered lady. Best of all was the one she saw at Christmas, where a great bell clanged, and a Christmas card appeared to the sound of sleighs, and a voice said they were now in Bedford Falls. Then bright stars in the sky told the story of a boy who saved his brother, and one star became an angel. He went down to the world to watch the boy become a man. He was George Bailey. There was an upstairs office like their father's, and the town was just like theirs. George wore a coat and hat like the ones her father wore, and when things were as bad for him as they could be, the angel showed him what would have happened if he had never been born. George Bailey learned that his life was good after all. Sometimes, listening at night to the comforting drone of the men, Brigid thought about George Bailey, and his wonderful life.

Now, weighed down with thoughts of school, Brigid found that not even George Bailey was any help. She turned over in bed. Everything good was coming to an end. Even Ned Silver, her tormentor, had left to go back to his school. She pulled the covers over her head, and burrowed down in the semi-darkness. Perhaps she could just stay there, not get up at all. Then, as if a light had been switched on, she remembered: school was all about learning to read. Her mother wanted her to be able to read before she started school, like Francis, and for some months had been urging her to do more than look at the pictures in her books and her comic, her *Robin*. It was simple. If she did not read, she would not have to go to school. If she could hide the fact that the shapes and patterns had begun more and more to speak to her, jumping into sense in her head, nothing would change.

The comics would be there today. She threw back the covers and jumped out of bed, pulled off her pyjamas and flung them into the tangle of bedclothes, pulled on the clothes she had abandoned the night before, and ran downstairs. There they were: on the sideboard, beside the newspaper and *The Eagle* lay her own *Robin*. Brigid watched them all through her breakfast, trying not to rush, and rushing all the more. She had almost slid down from her place, when her mother caught her firmly about the waist and pulled her to her.

"Now, reading, Miss," she said, "and no nonsense!" and holding Brigid near, she placed *Robin* in front of her. Brigid squirmed. Her mother turned her round. "Reading, Brigid."

"I like looking at the pictures, Mama," Brigid said, unhappily.

"Well, you'll like them better when you can read as well," said her mother.

Francis, across the table, wiggled his eyebrows up and down to make her laugh.

Her father said, "Maybe she should finish her breakfast," but he did not help her.

Her mother held fast. Brigid reached for one of her plaits, and put it in her mouth.

"And that hair," she heard her mother say. "I should cut it before school. We'll never manage with her and those plaits."

Isobel, listening in the kitchen, called out: "And think of what she might catch!"

Even Dicky squawked briefly in his cage, as if he, too, agreed. Brigid caught hold of both plaits. Clearly, the threat of school was very close.

"Do I have to go to school?" she asked. "If I learn to read here with you, can I not stay at home?"

Her mother turned her round to face her, and looked her in the eye.

"Brigid," she said, "I think you are well able to read. Can we just get on with it?"

Brigid met her eyes. Clearly, there was no way out. She turned back to her comic, looked at the pictures for help and, deep in her head, tried to make sense of the black shapes on the page.

"Break them up into bits. Come on. I've told you," said her mother, and she put her finger under the words.

Brigid looked. Black lines and circles. She broke them up into little bits. Nothing. She broke them further and began to say the sounds she knew. "*A*," she said. That was all right. The picture of a bird she knew. More sounds, slowly, slowly: "*R. R – R. R-o-b. Rob. In.*"

Everyone stopped. They were all looking at her.

"*A rob-in s-at . . .*"

Francis nodded encouragement, eyes alight, her father watched her with his good eye, Dicky put his head on one side, Isobel's head appeared at the door . . . but Brigid did not move. She knew they were all listening. She could hear their silence, she could see them out of the sides of her eyes, but she did not dare take her gaze away from the patterns which were suddenly starting to speak.

"*Bet . . .*"

"Yes, come on, good girl," said her mother, her voice low, and her arm firm about Brigid's waist.

"*Bet-ween h-is m-m-m . . .*"

She stopped. It was too hard. The shapes were starting to move away. She folded her arms. Isobel, shaking her head, disappeared from the door.

"Brigid," said her mother, "come on, like this, like Daddy, come on. Look!"

Brigid looked at her father, who had taken the paper in his

hand, looking over his teacup at her, the bandage gone, his good eye winking in encouragement. She took a deep breath.

"*M-m-mum-mummy a-nd . . .*"

Her father winked again.

"*D-a-dd-y!*"

She put down *Robin*, and her mother said: "That's a *good* girl," squeezing her once more before letting go.

They were all pleased with her. Even Dicky, in the spirit of celebration, clucked and rocked a little on his perch.

Isobel again put her face round the door from the kitchen, saying, "Well, it's not before time," and she withdrew her head, like a tortoise, it seemed to Brigid, just like a tortoise going back into its shell.

Brigid's head was spinning. She was stunned. She was singing in her head with the joy of it. The lines and circles had slid into place and stayed there. They had made sense. Now at night, she would be able to keep her light on like Francis, and the others would hear her click it off. And, maybe, because she had done it, she would not have to go to school. In this instant Brigid loved her whole family, and she wanted to share all her secrets. Still standing by her mother, still looking at the miracle of *Robin*, she said: "Do you know, Mama, that men come to this house every night, and sit here at this table, and talk about things, and I hear them upstairs?" She turned eagerly to her mother, and knew at once that she had made a mistake. Her mother's face had closed, and her father was frowning. Francis looked down.

Her mother put a hand on Brigid's forehead: "Don't tell me you're running a temperature," she said, "and school next week."

"But, Mama . . ." began Brigid, until Francis' face warned her to stop. She did stop, but it was not because of Francis. With a sickening that felt like a heavy weight, she heard the word "school". She was not saved. There was nothing to be done. There was not even a chance that her mother would understand about the men. Nobody would. "I'm not sick," she said. "I just had a strange dream last night."

She felt through her mother's body a wave of relaxation and relief. "Well, if that's all. Men coming to the house, indeed." She turned to her husband. "Killed with imagination. The wireless, maybe. Voices carrying on the air." She brushed her skirt, and moved Brigid slightly to one side. A little cool breeze seemed to have moved between them. "Time she was at school."

"But is she all right?" said her father, as if Brigid were not there.

"Well, her forehead's cool anyway." Her mother turned again to her, brisk, already rising from the table. Brigid's moment was over. "Go on now, you two, run up and get ready – or you'll have to start school in sandals, both of you."

Brigid's father spoke: "If I can get away in time, we'll meet and have tea later."

Her mother, the narrow arch of her eyebrows rising just a little, paused, hands on the table. She sat back into her chair, heavily. She looked for a moment at her hands, then at her husband, and said: "Are you going into the office today, Maurice?"

He said: "I think I will. A little later, for a time, anyway."

Both Francis and their mother looked at him for a moment, in silence, in a kind of concern.

He looked back with defiance, his good eye angry. "Am I to sit around the house all day? Am I to be a chronic invalid?" He gave the paper a sharp slap.

Dicky flapped in his cage, but no one spoke. Francis looked away, excused himself from the table, went to the cage and talked quietly to Dicky. Their father gathered up his glasses and, shaking his paper with another hard slap, as if there had been an argument, stared at it with his eye of stone. Brigid looked at the eye, and was afraid.

Apart from the low whisper of Francis to Dicky, and the squabbling of Dicky back to Francis, a harsh silence surrounded them.

"Maurice," said their mother, "I –"

39

"And you should get that fellow's hair cut, if you're in the mood to cut hair. He can't go to the College like a Shetland pony." He slapped the paper again, a snap like a boat's sail in the wind.

Their mother pressed her lips together. "Isobel?" she called. "Will you see to Brigid please, as soon as you're ready, and then could you come with me into town for an hour or two? I seem to have more to do today than I thought." She got up. Breakfast was at an end.

Brigid was trying to move away unnoticed when her father called her back, reaching out his arm and pulling her towards him. His voice was gentle again. "Here," he said, and handed her a piece of toast from his own plate. He offered her tea from his cup, and she looked at him over the rim as she drank it. He smiled with his good eye, the lines she liked forming in the corners. "We'll have some tea later, when everything's done."

Brigid whispered: "Do I have to get my hair cut, Daddy?"

He pulled one plait, gently, and into her ear his voice said: "No. You don't. I like your hair. You meet me later with your mama and your brother and I'll take you and your plaits for tea in the Abercorn – or the Bonne Bouche. Somewhere nice. Would you like that?"

Brigid nodded.

"Then it's a promise. Run now, do what your mama tells you."

Chapter 5: Miss Chalk

Brigid was happy. She had not escaped going to school, but she had a promise that she would meet her father for tea. She liked the thought that her mother would dress for town in her costume and her pearls. She looked forward to the walk to the bus stop where, looking back, she could see the tops of the seven trees. Their house would look down at them with friendly window eyes. She would see all the other proud houses falling away in a line, one side towards the park, the other side towards a low-roofed factory and quiet grey buildings leaning towards the cemetery. If they walked up to the bus stop, they would pass the thatched house where the shoemaker, in his leather apron, sat tapping behind a half-door. Across the road from him was a farm, where they could hear the lowing night and morning of the cows Brigid longed to ride, like a proper cowgirl, on their broad swaying backs, their sharp smell in her nostrils.

Today, they did not walk up to the bus stop, but down to the depot. It was a longer walk, which Brigid disliked: on the way, they would have to pass the Glen, where the houses sat so far back they could not be seen. Brigid feared the Glen. Isobel had told her a judge's daughter was murdered there. She said the papers called it "Murder in the Glen". "And," she said, leaning down to Brigid's face, "she was no bigger than you." When

Brigid told this to Francis, he shook his head. "Nope," he said. "She was much bigger and far older than you. And, it was another glen, very far away, where you will never be. Don't listen to stories like that."

Still, Brigid stayed afraid. The ghost of the judge's daughter might make the same mistake and, suddenly the same size as Brigid, a ghost child, appear in this glen. With ghosts, who could tell? She was glad to be safely beyond that green darkness, to be walking past the post office and the police station, square and solid, where the policemen grew their roses and parked their bicycles against the wall.

Just as they passed, Mr Steele came out, tipping his cap, harp and crown glinting. "Good morning, Mrs Arthur," he said. "Good morning, children," and, as he spoke, he threw his leg over his high bicycle.

Brigid was transfixed by the sight of this great leg directly in front of her. At its top, at his belt, was a black leather holster, and sitting up out of it, at the ready, the handle of a revolver. Brigid tugged her mother's hand and her mother squeezed it back, rather too hard for reassurance, and then shook her slightly as they waited to cross the road.

"I've told you," she said, "and I'm not going to tell you again. Pass no remarks."

"But, Mama, Mr Steele has a gun!"

Her mother did not answer. Instead she stopped in the street, turned, and looked down at Brigid.

"Brigid," she said, "did I or did I not tell you to change out of those shorts? I've a good mind to march you straight home."

"Oh, Mama," said Brigid, puzzled and displeased. How could she be in trouble for something she had not done? "You didn't tell me. Isobel got me ready. She said they were all right." She saw her mother's eyes travel upwards, beyond her.

"Did you, Isobel?" said their mother, but Isobel, now examining quite closely the brickwork on the barracks, did not respond.

42

As Brigid watched to see what might happen next, Francis suddenly reached behind and pulled at her sleeve. "Look," he said. "The new buses. See – there's one like a pirate."

Brigid swivelled round, and there they were. Beside the old, lazy trolleybuses, with their flat faces and straight horns attached to the wires above, there stood, reined in, the fierce new petrol models. They had angry faces, with a deep-set space at the side, as if they had only one eye apiece, a pirate's dark patch where the other should be.

"I don't want to go on one of those," said Brigid, immediately. "They look cross, and they don't hold on to anything."

"You won't be on one of those," said her mother, taking Brigid's hand as they crossed the last road to the depot. She was finished now with Isobel, whose face was red and closed. "Pick up your feet now, or you won't be on any of them."

They trotted in a linked chain to a trolleybus about to slide away, and Brigid was almost out of breath by the time her mother and Isobel lifted her on to the open platform. "Sit down, you spoiled monkey," Isobel said, in a voice too low for Brigid's mother to hear, but Brigid did not really mind. It was impossible to remain out of sorts on the bus. They sat on the long seats at the back, where they could see everyone and everything. Brigid was tucked between Isobel and Francis. He was close enough to reach out to the silver knob at the side of the first double seat. Brigid envied him that. Still, there was the conductor, with his glittering punching machine, like a little typewriter round his neck. He had black fingers, from the ink on the tickets. Standing over them, a dark shadow, he took the money their mother reached to him and, looking hard at Francis, punched two pink children's tickets. He said: "You're going to need full fare soon, sonny." Francis said nothing, but, in the window, Brigid saw on his face a small, pleased smile.

The bus rocked slowly down the road, past the park, the cemetery, and the hilly road leading right to the top of the mountain. Over a stone wall they saw the trees and golden stone of the convent. Far away, black-and-white penguin people walked in a line. They passed a narrow road leading upwards to black chimneys, lines of smoke above them darkening the sky.

Isobel nudged Brigid with a sharp elbow. "Your school's up there," she said, but Brigid saw only a street, bright, full of noise and children twisting and swinging on ropes round lamp-posts, row upon row of neat, busy shops, a great two-towered church and then the high, wide streets that meant they were down town.

To Brigid, town was not for summer days. There should be a purple sky above, and the bright promise of Christmas. The air should be patterned with wheeling birds, starlings calling to each other that it was coming towards evening. Down town there should not be blue sky, such vastness of wide singing blue, even above the ruined places that were blown up in the German Blitz. Isobel told them about that, about how she hid under the table in the time of the bombs. Even now, as they all got up and moved to the platform to get off the bus, Brigid could make out directly across the street, above the shining black of the cars, the last corner of a bombed house: an empty bedroom, the peeling of its tired paper, the cold remains of a fireplace. She pictured children there, getting ready for bed, and then that sound Isobel described, the low drone, the silence, the flash, and the explosion, and the world coming in . . .

"Wake up, Brigid," said her mother, taking her hand. "Francis, remind me to get fish."

Brigid, her mind on bombed-out houses, also remembered she hated the damp smell and chalky taste of fish, and her mood did not improve at the shoe shop. Brown shoes and black shoes with impossible laces, their very touch setting her teeth on edge, were pinched and poked, Brigid's feet still in them, and it was not just her mother doing this but also a stout lady in black. Brigid did not like her. She tried to concentrate when Francis pointed out the tin cylinders whirring along pulleys on the ceiling, carrying change to and from the great cash register where people paid, but it could not relieve her boredom and her sense that the day was slipping away.

Worst of all, the shoe lady suggested that the little girl might like to break in her new shoes by wearing them home, and then offered, to Brigid's despair, to dispose of her friendly summer sandals. "They're practically done, aren't they, madam?" she said, lifting them with disdain. Under her arms her black dress had white lines, like cracks in the wall. Brigid saw her taking the whole summer away, and closed her eyes. Then, to her surprise and relief, she heard: "Well, no, thank you," and then, "I think there's a little wear left in them yet, for playing about the garden, don't you, Brigid?" And Brigid, almost believing that playing about the garden was not over forever, could only nod her thanks.

Francis, his own lace-ups already in their box, nudged her elbow. "Tell you what," he said, "I'll watch TV with you when we get home."

Brigid said: "Will it be my film? With the angel? And George Bailey?"

"Well, maybe not," Francis said. "That's a Christmas film. *The Cisco Kid*, maybe? Or *The Range Rider*? Roy Rogers?"

"Trigger?" said Brigid.

"Yes," said Francis. "If it's Roy Rogers. I didn't look before we came out. I was too excited about the shoes." He nudged her again. "And the fish."

She nudged him back; he made a fish face.

When they were out on the street, Brigid watched a rag-and-bone man go by. His horse, leather patches over his eyes, looked tired and old. Brigid's heart contracted. She turned again to Francis: "You know in Cowboys and Indians? I don't like it when the horses get shot."

"You don't mind when the people get shot?"

"Only bad ones get shot, Francis."

"Maybe the horses are bad. Did you think of that?"

Brigid stopped walking, and he started to pull her along after him, laughing at her. Still, she held back. "Horses are not bad, Francis. You know that. And you told me they don't really get shot, any of them."

He nodded. "That's right. Everyone is just beyond the camera, all queuing up to collect their pay cheques."

"Even the horses?"

"Especially the horses – who works harder?" and he began to whistle.

"No whistling on the street, Francis," said their mother. "Now stand here while I talk to the pair of you."

"Daddy's office," cried Brigid, in surprise, pointing up to the high brown building before them. "I didn't know we were coming here. Can we go up? Can we go in the lift?"

"Don't interrupt," said her mother. "And don't point. I was about to say that I will go up and see if Daddy is ready. I know I'm ready for some tea, after that session. Then Isobel can take Francis to have his hair cut and I –"

"Have to get fish," said Francis, and no one told him he had interrupted.

"Yes, thank you, Francis," said their mother, tapping her forehead. "I would have forgotten – and I'll take Brigid on home with me."

"Mama!" said Brigid. First she was not to be in the lift, and now she was not to be in the barber's shop, and there was a rocking horse there. "Can I not go on the rocking horse?"

Her mother sighed, and passed a hand across her brow. "Brigid, sometimes you . . . Now listen, both of you. I'll go up in the lift – by myself, if you please – and see what way Daddy is for time. Isobel, will you stay here, please, with the children. We don't need a deputation."

Brigid breathed hard, but she said nothing, and in spite of herself listened as Francis whiled away the time with a story of the shoe lady, of the morning when, dreaming of Spanish leather, she had wakened and known without a shadow of a doubt that she must give her life to shoes, practising in any spare moments the only correct way to ascend and descend the high and precarious ladder.

"All this I learned," he said, "in a quiet moment when you

46

were deciding between the black and the brown." Brigid, light dawning, laughed and hit his elbow lightly with the side of her hand, but he caught it and, with a gentle shake, said: "You see, Brigid? When you laugh at it all, it's easier."

Their mother came through the glass door, but their father was not with her.

"Where's Daddy?" said both children at once.

"Daddy's . . ." She paused. Her face was tight. "Daddy's not feeling well, and I'm going to order a taxi and take him home."

"A taxi!" said Brigid. They did not take taxis.

Francis squeezed her arm, quite hard, and said: "What's the matter, Mama?"

She put her hand on his shoulder. "It's not very much, Francis. He just went out too soon, that's all, and now he has a bit of a headache."

"Tea will help him," said Brigid, her eyes on her mother's face. "Tea with us will make him better."

As if she had not spoken, she heard her mother say: "Isobel, take both of them to the barber's. I'm going to get my husband home," and then she said to the children: "We'll have tea with Daddy another day."

That was the end of it. She handed something from her purse to Isobel, then once again, without another word to them, disappeared through the glass door.

Brigid said: "He promised," but no one, not even Francis, was listening to her, and she trailed unhappily with Isobel's hard hand in hers down to the arcade where the barber had his shop. Not even the rocking horse, dappled and smooth and high, could cheer her. She shook her head when Francis offered to lift her up, and when Isobel said she could stand then as long as she wanted, she did not care. She sat down by the side of the horse, pushing its rocker back and forth. She did not care about anything. He had broken his promise.

Sitting on the ground, she tugged at one of her plaits, as he had done that morning and, as she did, she saw a shining something behind the rocking horse. Moving across on her hunkers, she picked up a pair of scissors, sharp, the kind the barbers used. She made a little cut on her finger just by touching the blade. A fine line of blood appeared, and it hurt just enough for her to feel that she had been wronged. She opened and closed the scissors: she wanted to cut something. And, then, on impulse, she pulled taut one of her plaits and cut it off. The deep, giving thickness of the hair as it suddenly sheared away, releasing itself into her hand, was a satisfying surprise and, hardly looking at the plait as she threw it with its neat blue ribbon across the floor, she pulled the other one tight, until it hurt. In a moment of inspiration, she cut it too, so close to her ear that she felt a sharp stinging pain in her lobe. Then, as she sat on the floor, with one blue-ribboned plait in her hand and the other abandoned under the rocking-horse, she felt suddenly flat. There was nothing else to cut. She was thinking seriously of slitting her shorts along the side when she heard above her a voice she knew.

"Hello! What's this: do-it-yourself?"

She looked up and up and was surprised to see Uncle Conor, looking, from her new low perspective, bigger and wider than ever.

"What have you been up to?" he said as he stretched out his hand to raise her. "That's a bit of a mess, isn't it?" His voice was unexpectedly gentle, and it made Brigid want to cry.

"Daddy was going to have tea with us," she said, "and then he didn't. I had nothing to do."

"Ah," he said, "so you found something. Well, maybe you'd better give me those scissors before you do damage, and we'll give them to whoever lost them – and maybe we'll try to get you tidied up before your mammy sees you. Or," and his voice changed, "perhaps you're here with Aunt Rose?"

Brigid thought, she is not your aunt, but all she said was: "Rose is gone," and then she heard Francis' voice, and looked round to see his eyes, oddly wide under the newly shortened fringe of hair, looking with anxiety first at her, then at Uncle Conor.

"Oh, Brigid," said Francis, reaching down and picking up one plait, like a little dead creature and, as he turned it over in his hand, Brigid felt a first pang of sorrow. Then, with the plait still in his hand, and his voice a little more guarded, he said: "Our Aunt Rose has gone back home, Uncle Conor. We're here with Isobel."

"And there she is," said Uncle Conor, looking over their heads at Isobel, gazing back at him with pink cheeks, eyes wide, smiling as Brigid rarely saw her do.

"I'm afraid we've had a little protest here," said Uncle Conor, and Brigid, seeing Isobel's face darken, stepped instinctively nearer to Uncle Conor. His eyes flicked rapidly from Isobel to Brigid and back again. He put one hand on Brigid's head, placed the other firmly on Isobel's forearm, and still looking at Isobel, said, "We can fix that, and no one need be annoyed."

Meeting his gaze, she somehow stopped looking cross, and to Brigid's surprise seemed almost pretty.

"Children," she said, "you can't watch them, can you?" and then she laughed, as if she was happy.

Conor said nothing but, raising his hand from Brigid's head, gestured to the barber. The barber instantly looked up, clicked his tongue, came quickly across to them, took the scissors from Conor's hand and looked down at Brigid.

"A rebel," he said. He had a face like wood, and smelled like Christmas trifle.

"Yes, indeed," said Conor, evenly, leading Brigid to the barber's chairs. "Desi will tidy you up, my little spitfire," he said, "while Sam does something with mine," and he ran his hand through his hair so that it stood up on end.

This took Brigid's attention, until the moment she noticed Isobel and Francis move towards the door, without her. Uncle Conor touched the top of her head.

"Don't worry," he said. "Isobel is going to go with Francis and get ice cream for us all. And do you know what? We're going to eat it on the street."

Brigid drew in her breath: "But Mama doesn't allow . . ."

"Mama isn't here," said Conor, lifting her with a swift movement of his arms into one seat, and settling back, his eyes closed, in the other. "Just tidy up this little renegade, Desi, before its parents die of shock. Temper the wind to the shorn lamb."

Desi said: "Come on, young man," which Brigid rather liked. Making clucking noises, Desi tied a white cloth round her and began to work on what was left of her hair. It was such a pleasant feeling, a melting buzzing along her neck, the glittering snip of the scissors, his hand gently pushing her head forward and back, forward and to the side, that Brigid almost fell asleep. In what seemed like a short time, she felt him pull away the white sheet. Without it, she was oddly cold, and put her hand up to her neck, to find nothing at all. In her nostrils was a scent, and she thought suddenly of her father.

"That's us," she heard Desi say to Cornelius, "and I've put plenty of Bay Rum on too. What'd he do, take the hedge clippers to it?"

Cornelius, opening his eyes, sat upright and laughed out loud. "My God, man, you've shorn her!"

"Her?" said Desi. "Well, you never told me. I thought that was a wee fellow, in his short trousers."

"Ah, Desi," said Conor, shaking his head, reaching in his pocket, and handing coins to the wooden-faced man, "there's no harm done."

Yet, as Desi walked away, shaking his head, saying, "I'd have sworn that was a wee fellow," Conor's face changed. His eyes narrowed as he turned to the barber who had cut his hair: "Desi's at it a bit early today, isn't he? You might want to watch that," and, with a quick movement of one hand, he snapped the cloth away from himself, and stepped down from the chair. He paid his bill, watching Brigid through half-closed eyes. Then he reached down and took her elbow.

"Come on, Tommy-Go-My," he said, giving the rocking horse a friendly pat as he walked her out of the shop, "and we'll get this ice cream."

Francis, standing patiently outside, handed her a cone, soft at the top where the ice cream had melted into the wafer. "I had to lick it a bit," he said, "so that it didn't – you know – run over the edges."

Isobel fell into step with Conor and the children trailed behind.

"Who is Tommy-Go-My?" asked Brigid, as she took the ice cream.

"Who said that to you?" he asked, but he did not smile. "Uncle Conor, I'll bet. It's Irish. *Tá mé go maith*. 'I am well.' He meant it as a joke, you looking like a boy."

"Oh," said Brigid, still puzzled. "Irish. Like Ireland, that he and Daddy talk about. Is that funny, Francis? I didn't think Ireland was supposed to be funny."

"I know what you mean," said Francis, with feeling. "Not much about Ireland is. But I suppose he means it to be funny. Your hair isn't, though," he added. "I should have minded you better. I don't know what'll happen when we get home."

They walked to the bus stop with their ice creams, and made their farewells to Uncle Conor. Isobel asked him if he would like to come to the house and have tea with them, but he said he could not: he had to see a man about a dog. He tipped the brim of his hat, said goodbye, and began to thread his way through the crowd. When Brigid looked out from the bus, he was swallowed up among them. Isobel seemed far away, not thinking of the children at all and Francis, too, was very quiet. Brigid asked him if Uncle Conor was going to buy a new dog, but he did not seem to hear, and she had to content herself with looking out at the grey church, and the houses, and the convent, and the shops, and the park, until they got off near home. She saw the blank eyes of the house from the bus stop, and felt its emptiness as soon as they entered it. No one was there.

Brigid was almost relieved that her parents were not yet home: it gave her a breathing space. She went into the sitting room and watched Francis put in the plug of the television. He switched it on then, and got up, just turning at the door to say,

"I'll be back in a moment, Brigid – just want to see to Dicky," and then he left her alone. She watched the picture grow large from a tiny point, and the grey spinning world fill the screen. Then a voice announced: "*The following is suitable for older children only*," and a play began, about a teacher named Miss Chalk. She was not kind to her pupils, and so she was turned into a large piece of chalk, shaped like a woman, thin and white. There were no eyes in her head, just emptiness. Her mouth was a rigid line, chalk teeth grinning. Miss Chalk was to be locked inside this body, forever. Brigid, unable to stop watching the terrible story, was transfixed. She could not speak. She could think only of the day her father showed her his blank and sightless eye, and the dream that followed it, where her family had been turned to stone.

Yet, she sat on. Her limbs would not take her from her father's chair, even when she heard voices outside, and the key of the front door was turned, even when she heard Francis run down the hall, and heard her mother's surprise: "Francis! What is the matter with you?"

Words tumbling from Francis carried through the air: "Brigid's had her hair cut. We met Uncle Conor. She didn't mean to cut it. It wasn't her fault." His voice trailed away. "Where were you? Where did you go?"

Brigid could not get up, could not stop watching the bleak white head on the screen. She could hear her mother's voice, but she could not go out to her. "At the hospital," her mother said. "Daddy's head was very sore, and we needed to check it because of, you know, the bother he had with his eyes. No, it's all right. He's all right. Just let him get upstairs and rest, and for heaven's sake let me through the door, like a good boy. What did you say Brigid had done? And where is she?"

Isobel called from the kitchen door: "Stuck in front of the television! I'll attend to her. Go you on and see to the invalid."

Brigid heard the word "invalid". She thought: that is what Daddy said he did not want to be, and now he is, and it is his eyes, he will be blind again, and he will look like that again, and we will be turned to stone. She waited for her mother to come, but she did not come. Brigid heard her voice and her father's voice, as they went slowly, heavily up the stairs, but only Francis came in, his face darkened with worry.

Isobel followed him, brisk and busy. She said: "Well, you chose a day and a half to throw your tantrum. Your poor daddy in the hospital and you giving everybody gip, cutting off your hair."

Brigid, miserable, could say nothing.

"Leave her alone, Bella," said Francis, sitting on the arm of the chair. "Brigid, what is this thing you're watching?" He picked up the *Radio Times*. "Oh, no," he said, and he moved across to the switch on the television. It clicked, and the picture began to disappear, slowly vanishing.

It made no difference to Brigid. To her, Miss Chalk's blind eyes and grimacing mouth were still on the screen long after it was blank and dully grey. "I didn't like it," she said, in a whisper. "She gets turned into chalk, with no eyes, and she can't get out."

Isobel straightened the furniture and moved Brigid out of her father's chair. "Well," she said. "I wouldn't be surprised if that happened to you, after the bother you've given this day."

Francis turned quickly round from the television. "Don't, Bella," he said, and his voice was sharp. "Leave her alone."

Isobel left her alone. The trouble was, everyone, even Francis, left her alone for the rest of the day, because of her father. Confusion and worry and hasty meals brought her too quickly to the time when it was decided that she needed to go to bed. Bed was the last thing Brigid needed. She knew for certain what would happen when she went to bed. That night, she did not hear the reassuring voices of the men. They were silent when Miss Chalk, with her rigid mouth and her sightless eyes, came down the chimney and stood, grinning, at the foot of Brigid's bed.

Chapter 6: George

Brigid could not tell anyone, even Francis, how frightened she was by Miss Chalk. She knew that if Francis had heard it announced that the programme was not suitable, he would not have let her watch it. If she told her parents, they would both be in trouble. It was obvious that Miss Chalk was her intimate, secret punishment, crouched inside the bedroom fireplace, waiting to come out at night, eyeless and grinning. It was the same fireplace, pale and tiled, which Brigid had watched with such hope on Christmas Eve, after she had seen her film about George Bailey. Now, as the evenings grew ever shorter and the nights colder, she watched the fireplace with dread, knowing Miss Chalk would wait in there until she was at the edge of sleep before sliding out to terrify her.

If she had feared going to school before Miss Chalk came to haunt her, it was worse afterwards. On the first Monday morning in September, serge and wool heavy on her limbs, she walked beside her mother up the small, hilly street near the mills, and stood in line in a great grey yard. Behind her were dark gates, a chain hanging loosely from them; all around her towered high brick walls, blackened and stained. Everything smelled of soot. Other girls stood in front and behind, some with mothers, some with bigger girls, one or two alone. No one spoke. Her feet wanted the smooth comfort of their sandals. Her legs wanted to run in the garden with Francis, or even with Ned Silver, but Ned was gone far away to school and Francis, too, was gone. Even now he would be standing in the yard of his new school, at the other side of the town. She would not see him until nearly nighttime. Everywhere she looked she saw only the scarred walls, topped with broken glass, and hazily, in the distance, a long row of windowless huts and wooden doors. Brigid saw a girl beside her make a puddle at her feet, and watched as she was brought to the huts, soaking and shamed. As her eyes followed, wondering uneasily if the same thing might not just happen to her any moment, she felt her mother's hand begin to loosen in hers and, hard though she tried to hold on, the hand eased away, and she was left empty.

Over her head other hands, bigger, not gentle, placed something about her neck. Brigid, startled, looked down. From her there hung, suspended on a green ribbon, a square pink card. She turned it round so that she could see it. Black letters spelled her own name, just as she had learned to write it with her mother: *Brigid Arthur*. Then her mother, reaching cooler, kinder hands to the back of Brigid's neck, adjusted the card so that it felt comfortable. She did not know why it was hung around her neck. She was a dog, with a collar. Then, a wide shadow covered her, and a large person said: "I'll take her now, Mrs Arthur," and, unbelievably, Brigid was handed over to the stranger and led away to join other children standing by the wall. Some of them were crying. Brigid, frozen, was unable to cry. All her effort was concentrated in the hope that something would happen to prevent her being left here. Incredulous, she watched her mother walk slowly away, as if she had forgotten something but could not remember what. She herself must be what had been forgotten. Then, Brigid saw her turn round at the gate and, heart leaping, made ready to run from the line. Instead, with one brief salute of her gloved hand, her mother, back straight, head high, walked away. Still, Brigid did not cry. Instead, she watched the empty place where she had last seen her, listening for the clicking of her heels on the pavement, until there was no more sound.

There was a sharp report. The large person clapped her hands, not loudly, but firmly, and said: "Infants! Over here."

They were the infants. Brigid had just time to take in this indignity before the large person began to move them, all the bewildered children, into a straggling line. Bigger girls, nearly women themselves, took them by the shoulders. Some were gentle, some pushed the children. Somehow, they were herded inside the dark building, instructed to hang up their coats on hooks, which a number could not reach, then taken into a square room with high windows and green walls. They were told to sit at wooden desks, set out in rows. The room smelled of pencils and paper, of dust that caught in the throat, and drains. It was at once too warm and too cold.

In the endless time that followed, Brigid learned that the large person was their teacher. She was "Miss". Some girls cried, but no one came. Then they were given small glass bottles of milk and paper straws and told to drink. The milk was warm and unpleasant, and the straws felt like candle wax. There were more puddles on the floor. All the children were lined up and brought to the huts outside, but Brigid held back and managed not to go in. They were herded back, and instructed to put their heads on their desks and go to sleep. Brigid could not sleep. It was daytime.

When they were allowed to sit up, the door opened and there entered a lady, immensely tall, in a long, bunched skirt. Perhaps she was a queen. Wooden beads dangled from her broad belt, and a vast hat like a white butterfly shadowed her face. Perhaps she came from long ago. Perhaps Brigid had wandered into a story, or was dreaming: all this might end any second.

Then Miss said: "Children, stand up, in silence."

The butterfly lady said she was the Principal. They were to call her "Sister". Sister said they were welcome to the school, and that, above all else, they must work hard and learn to be good, honest and useful girls. She told them to sit down, and then she went away.

All that morning, Brigid believed she would never be allowed to escape. She had been left there forever. Her parents must have found out about Miss Chalk, who was not suitable: this, on top of cutting her hair, her unwillingness to read, and the many transgressions of her life so far had proved too much. She had been sent away. Ned Silver had been sent away to a school where he had to stay except for holidays. Perhaps this was one of those schools, and they had not told her. Perhaps her father's illness meant children could be sent away. Perhaps Francis had been sent away too, and she would not see him in the evening, or ever again. This, more than anything else that was happening, brought Brigid close, but not quite, to the point of tears, but still she would not cry. It had not worked well for those already weeping in despair, and she had no wish for the kind of attention it appeared to bring. All she hoped was that her teacher was not like Miss Chalk. Maybe this was not the real teacher, but someone sent to prepare them, before Miss Chalk appeared.

Yet, the morning went on, and no Miss Chalk came. The large person stayed with them and, gradually the children learned to call her "Miss". She was not unkind. She called their names and they learned to answer. She handed out books and told them they must back them at home. Brigid didn't understand what that meant. Miss read a story. She led them out to the yard and told them to run about, and then she brought them back in again. Yet some still cried throughout the morning, even when Miss told them to put their heads down on their arms and close their eyes. The crying had still not stopped when a thin wailing began outside, growing terrible, like the sound of an animal in pain. Some girls started crying more loudly when they heard it, but Miss explained that that was the call to the mill workers to leave their machines and have their lunch, and that it meant the children could soon go home. Brigid was not sure she believed this, but a bell was rung through the school, and they were, at last, allowed to leave the airless room. As she reached up on her toes for her coat, Brigid saw that the corridor was policed by more of the people with butterfly hats. One had glasses that glinted sharply, another a soft face but a thin mouth, yet another had a face cut from stone. They were all extremely tall: on instinct Brigid resolved to stay away from all of them, especially the stone-faced one. That could be Sister Chalk. As soon as she was allowed to leave the line, she ran out of the building, determined to reach the gates and run away, with whoever came for her or, if there was no one, then by herself.

She did not reach the gates. Just outside the heavy door stood her mother. Brigid closed her eyes to make sure this was not a dream and, by a miracle, when she opened them, she was still there. She had come back for her. That was all that mattered. Relief made Brigid so weak that she did, finally, begin to cry, and she was not asked why, and she was grateful. Her mother's hand had never felt so warm, or so safe.

On the bus, Brigid did not even look out of the window, did not talk, was glad not to be asked a single question, glad to have her mother's hand pat hers now and again.

It was her father who opened the door to them. He reached down and ran his hand through her shorn hair. "Tommy-Go-My," he said, as Uncle Conor had done in the barber's shop. Now she knew it was meant to be funny, she also knew to laugh. "How was school, girlie?" he went on, adding, to Brigid's puzzlement, "Any slaps?"

Above her, Brigid felt her mother's hand on her shoulder. "Maurice," she said, and her voice held its low warning note. Her father seemed not to recognise it.

"Slaps," said Brigid, her own voice sounding to her as if it came from far away. "What are slaps?"

Her mother said: "Maurice. Please. Leave well alone."

But her father ran his hand again through her crop and said: "They slapped when I was at school. With a leather strap, too."

He laughed a short laugh. "It did me no harm." Then he shrugged his shoulders and turned away with his paper.

Brigid, watching his stooped back move slowly to the comfort of his chair, understood. Someone in that school might hit her.

All through the lunch she could hardly touch, all the time as the long strange day went on, she could not settle to the comfort of usual occupations. It was as if she had, indeed, left home, or home had left her, and she did not know how to find her way back. She longed to see Francis, yet it was late in the afternoon before he came in, and Brigid knew, by the heaviness of his tread in the hall, that his first day had been no better than hers.

When they sat down at five to their programmes, he said: "How was it? Are you all right?"

She said: "I'm afraid."

"Of school? It isn't as bad as it seems. It'll get better," and he laughed without smiling. "Or rather, you'll get used to it."

Brigid said: "It's Miss Chalk I'm afraid of, more than school."

Francis looked at her for a long time. "Because of what Bella said? She didn't mean it."

Brigid shook her head. "She comes in the night. Miss Chalk. She comes out of the chimney."

Francis was quiet. His face looked quite sad. "Brigid, if she comes again – and I hope she won't – you get me."

"What if I can't?"

"I'll stay up until you go to sleep. Call me. I'll come. I'll not let her get you."

Brigid felt the dark weight ease a little. She sat back in the sofa, and she was glad of his warmth near her. On the screen, the Cisco Kid rode away, his sombrero flat back in the wind.

"What are slaps?" she said, after a while.

Francis sighed. "You learn to avoid them. It's when you get something wrong, or don't do what they say. The teacher hits your hand."

"Daddy said, with a leather strap."

Francis shook his head. "No. Not in a girls' school. Anyway, don't give them the chance. Do what they tell you, and keep your head down. That's the best way through."

The Cisco Kid had ridden away with his sidekick Pancho, his sombrero even bigger and wilder in the wind. Soon it would be time to face her again.

"You call me, if you have any bother tonight," said Francis, which helped her through teatime, and the mystery of backing the books. She watched as her mother and Francis folded and wrapped them like presents, and she nearly did one by herself. When she climbed the stairs to bed, she was almost happy. That night Miss Chalk did not come, and Brigid slept till morning.

Francis was right. She did get used to it. Reading was no longer a game with her mother, but part of a new thing called homework. There was writing, which she liked, and there were numbers, which she did not. There were slaps: they happened to other people until one day, to her surprise, all the infants were lined up outside their room and slapped, one after the other. The long wooden rule stung like a wasp. Brigid did not know why they were slapped, and no one else in the wailing line of children did, either. Miss said what happened in school was to stay in school, that they were not to tell at home anything that went on within those four walls, and that if they did she would know. So, Brigid did not tell, though her hand hurt all day.

That night, Miss Chalk came back, her eyes dark holes, her white legs bent, creeping towards her, but she got only to the edge of the fireplace before Brigid called Francis, softly, urgently, and Francis came. He sat on the chair where Brigid had found the cowgirl suit on the day their parents came back. He stayed there till Miss Chalk went away, and Brigid fell into sleep, her last sight Francis in his dressing gown, reading by the light of his torch.

September meant school every morning. There seemed no possibility of escape. Brigid was slapped when the numbers on the board were not clear to her. She did not know how to explain that they were blurred, that she could not make them out. Her sums were wrong. Her father tried to help her, but he explained too quickly. He understood numbers. That was his job. He was a man who counted numbers. Foolishly, Brigid one day told Miss that, and saw that she laughed, saying something to another teacher who had come in with the long book of names. They looked at Brigid, curiously. Brigid waited all that morning to be slapped, but nothing happened. She saw there was no method to understand school, no means of knowing what would keep her safe and what would not. Increasingly, imprisoned at the wooden desk, she went into her own world, and thought of home, the back garden, Francis, Dicky, even Ned Silver. She thought herself back to the trees at the back of the plot, living again the summer days. She was careful not to go too far away, coming back in time to gather what was happening, and save herself a little longer.

September became October, and the new life settled round them. Brigid's father got slowly better, and began again to read from the paper as he used to do. Now, however, he read only the stories which worried him. He read that there was an outbreak of typhoid in Antrim, and their mother said they had no plans to go to Antrim. He said two men had been named as spies, and they had attended the University of Cambridge, and his wife must not think of Cambridge for Francis. Brigid's mother said she was not thinking quite that far ahead. He began to drive again, opening the garage doors in the morning as he used to, backing the car down the passage, and going off to the office. The trees shed most of their leaves, and all Brigid could make out when she looked out at the plot were branches like the ribs under her own cold skin.

One morning she woke suddenly. No one had called her. They had forgotten – had they forgotten? She jumped out of bed, pulled on her clothes any way she could, and ran downstairs out of breath. There, she found Francis sitting at the table in everyday clothes.

"Why are you dressed for school?" he said. "It's a holiday – didn't they tell you?"

"No," said Brigid. "I heard Miss say something about today, but I think she said . . ." Brigid searched about in her mind. All she found was: "Remember, children, what I told you about school tomorrow," but what that was she did not know.

"Well, there's no school for me," said Francis.

"Are you sure, Brigid?" said her mother, coming through the door with a teapot. "I was going to let you have a sleep."

"Maybe it's just the College," said their father. "I'll take Brigid on my way to the office," and he put on his new glasses, thick as the bottoms of milk bottles, and no one said anything more.

Even if she did have to go to school, Brigid was glad to be driven by her father. When she went to school with her mother or, more usually these days, with Isobel on the bus, it was different. It took a long time, and sometimes they had to stand, jostled by other people, bringing in from outside their own cold and damp. Some days, for no reason, her father would take her, settling her into the front seat, and on those days, gliding down the road in comfort, Brigid was sorry at how quickly the journey passed. Sometimes he would converse with her in the car but today he did not speak. He looked straight ahead at the road: she knew that he could not see her out of the sides of his eyes. Without his thick glasses, he was still blind as before. Only in the evening, when he was resting, sitting with no glasses in his chair, or in the morning, if he was coming from the bathroom, a towel over his shoulder, with his eyes creased as he tried to see her, did he really seem himself again.

Yet, quiet though he was today, and far away as his mind seemed to be, Brigid was surprised that he did not take her up the side street where the school was. Instead, as never before, he stopped the car at the junction of the main road and the hilly street, waited for her to climb out, then left her and, when she turned round to wave a final goodbye, he was gone. There was nothing where he had been. There was nobody on the street. It was all quiet, except for a dog barking somewhere far off and the sound, in one of the neat, narrow houses, of a baby fretting. Even the trees on the street looked lonely, sparse autumn leaves drifting like pennies towards her as she walked, listening to her own footsteps, up to the school gate.

At the entrance, she saw why there was no one. The high, black gates were wrapped round with their chain. The schoolyard, cold and bleak, was deserted. Brigid's heart began beating in her throat, in her ears. She did not know how to get home by herself. She had no money. She had never stood on a street by herself, and she did not know anyone here. It began to feel difficult to breathe, and the breaths that got through were ragged and scratchy. She started to run, this way, that, up the street, down, trying to get away from herself, from the fear and the painful beating. She said what she remembered of the only prayer she liked in school: "*Oh, Angel of God, My Guardian dear, to whom God's love commits me here,*" running again, saying it over, down the way she had come, towards the main road where her father had left her and, then, in an instant, she stopped. Her heart turned over. She saw, standing on the other side of the street, plain as could be, in his long tweed coat, her own father. Brigid did not hesitate. She held up her arms and threw herself towards the far side of the road.

Brigid did not see anything, not the woman opening her door, with hands to her face in horror, nor the great lorry trying to stop, screaming with effort as Brigid ran blindly across its path. Only as it managed to halt, an inch from her, did she finally see it, finally hear its screech, towering above her like a panting animal, a smell of burning rubber from its tyres, each one bigger than she was. She looked up, and up, as far as the sky. She saw a man's face flat, wild, almost grey, his eyes filled with terror, his eyes closing, opening, his head sinking down. He was leaning over his steering wheel, staring at her, as she stood, still and surprised, in the middle of the road.

When she moved, it was not of her doing. From the corner of her eye, she saw the tall figure in its long tweed coat standing above her. Sure that it was her father, she suddenly realised that it was not and she was flooded first with despair then, immediately, with joy, as she saw who it really was. She knew this face, this dark hair with its silver wings. She knew these kind eyes. When he said, "Whoa!" she knew his voice too. The man bending down to her with arms outstretched was George Bailey, George Bailey himself, straight from Bedford Falls. Brigid relaxed as he lifted her away from the lorry, spoke to the driver, carried her to the other side of the road, and set her lightly down. Brigid, far away now from his great height, looked up at him. His hands still on her shoulders, he bent to her level, easily, long, strong legs hunkered on his heels. His voice low and gentle, he asked: "Why did you do that?"

Brigid lifted her shoulders and let them fall. His hands rested on them, steadily, without weight. "My daddy went in his car," she said. "The school is closed. I thought my daddy had come back."

He said nothing. His face was quiet, listening, the lines round his eyes kindly, a man who liked to laugh. Yet, he was all stillness. He looked at her so long that she thought she might fall inside his eyes, deep blue, now grey, full of light, eyes like the sky or the sea. Since her father had gone away to have his eyes healed, since Francis had gone away every day to his school, Brigid had never felt so sure of anyone as she did of George Bailey. She reached out and took his hand.

He held her lightly, safely. He said: "Brigid."

She said: "You know my name."

He smiled a little, and the lines around his eyes deepened. "I know quite a bit," he said. "You live in the house near the lemonade factory, right at the edge of the town: the house with the plot and the trees behind."

Brigid nodded. She felt her heart slow down, the sadness ebbing away. She knew how he knew, because she had prayed for an angel and got George Bailey himself. No wings, no white. Her angel was George Bailey in a tweed coat. He stood up and reached out his other hand to her. Lying in the palm were two shiny chestnuts, polished like wood, one with a rough pale piece in the middle, the other a smooth deep chocolate that she could almost taste.

"Conkers," said Brigid. "Thank you!"

"I'll take you home now," he said.

She slid her hand once more into his, and stood with him in the sharp morning until the trolleybus, its bland face impassive, slid alongside them. Brigid and George sat at ease together on the long leather seats inside the door and, this time, Brigid was close enough to the forward-facing benches to hold, as Francis had done, the smooth knob at the edge of the first seat. The silver knob beneath her hand, and the warmth of George Bailey beside her took away all fear. She relaxed as they climbed the hill, watching the road dip down to where her house was. They passed the convent and the junctions for the roads to the mountain and the city, just as she had done with her family the day they had gone to buy shoes. All was the same – the park's green revolving gate, its sparse firs and poplars, the depot, the barracks – and Brigid felt content, at peace, as if she were with Francis. George Bailey did not speak, but to Brigid it was as though he had wrapped her in calm, so that she had no more worries. In her pocket, her hand turned over and over the silky chestnuts he had given her.

At the lemonade factory, they got off the bus, Brigid reaching her hand to him as if he were her father. He held her hand firmly as they crossed the wide road. She heard the cows in the farm's cowshed, contented now. She too was contented: she was safe. George Bailey had saved her.

As they reached the gate, he said: "Brigid, will you promise me never to run out on the road again, whoever you think you see?"

Brigid said: "Yes. I'm sorry."

He said: "Don't be sorry. Just don't do that again. Promise me."

Brigid nodded. "May I ask you something?"

George opened the wooden gates, and handed her in before him.

"Go ahead," he said.

"Are you really George Bailey?"

He smiled, and the kind lines deepened at his eyes. "George Bailey," he said, and he laughed, softly. "Yes. Okay, then. I'm George Bailey."

They were almost at the front steps.

"I knew it," said Brigid, as he walked with her before him up the steps at the side of the house, and rang the doorbell. He was standing with her, a little behind. She could feel his warmth, the protection of his whole body. She could hardly wait to show him to her mother. Perhaps they could keep him.

The door opened. She looked up at her mother's face, and saw that it was puzzled, surprised and afraid, all at once. "Brigid," she said. "What on earth . . . ?"

"It's all right, Mama," Brigid said, happily. "The school was closed. George Bailey brought me home."

Her mother looked hard at her, reaching out and drawing her into the house. She closed the door.

"Mama!" cried Brigid. "You shut the door on George Bailey!"

For the second time that morning, someone bent down in front of Brigid and looked deep into her. "Brigid," said her mother, "there was no one with you."

Brigid opened her mouth but, still holding her firmly by the hand, her mother opened the door.

"Look, Brigid," she said.

No one was there. Brigid twisted round to look up at her mother. "He must have gone when you closed the door. He was there, Mama. He brought me home. He's my angel. And look what he gave me!" She reached into her pocket for the chestnuts, but they were no longer there.

"Brigid," said her mother. "I'm going to get you to bed and call the doctor. I don't know where you've been, or what's happened to you, or how you got home, but I do know when I opened that door you were by yourself on the doorstep."

Brigid, baffled, consented to be led upstairs to her room, but she did not stay in bed. Once the door was closed, she slid down as quietly as she could to the floor, walked on careful tiptoe to the window, and looked out at the seven trees, shedding in slow spirals their last few leaves. There was the Friday Tree, its poor arms bare, and underneath, Brigid's hazy sight could just make out the same thin trail of smoke she and Francis had seen in the summer.

Chapter 7: Cannonball

If Brigid had thought she would be quizzed about George Bailey, she was wrong. As it happened, she did not think much more about anything that evening. Waiting in her room for the doctor, Brigid became slowly conscious of something surrounding her, something that was like a headache, yet not quite. She could not describe it to the doctor when he came. She heard him sigh and tell her mother that the child was suffering from strong imagination and mild shock. It was a good thing, he said, that she was able to find her way home, but she must learn not to talk to strangers. Then he snapped his bag shut, turned to her mother, and said: "When's the Boss in? I must have a yarn with him," and left the room without another word. For some time, she could hear his voice downstairs, low and comforting like the men in the night, but she could not hear what was being said, and it hurt her neck to crane.

Isobel brought up tea and toast, and said she should thank her stars she was alive, if only she knew, but Brigid found she did not want to eat, and as for the stars she was to thank, they could wait. The smell of toast, even of tea, made her – or the person who was wearing her pyjamas, the Not-Brigid who was somehow beside her – want to vomit. She could not speak of this. It was all outside her, all at a distance. Even when Francis came in, smelling of the open air, she could not tell him how it was with her. Sitting on the chair close beside her bed, he seemed a long way away, his voice nearly an echo. She began to describe what had happened, about George, yet he drifted, his edges shimmering, and she soon stopped trying.

The headache grew round her, as though the whole room had become a state of pain, and she was locked inside. The light from the window grew harsh, almost blinding, but she could not remember how to get up and pull the blinds. When the light darkened to purple, and shadows played like water on the wall, there was some relief. When the purple became grey, then nearly black, she was almost glad that even Francis had disappeared, and she was to be left a little while in peace.

It was when the room became fully dark, the pain at bay as long as she did not move, that she heard a key turn in the door. Her father's voice travelled through the stairwell, low and deep. A long time later, she heard the doctor leave, his old car rattling, spreading out in the air, then fading away. Brigid was only too willing to stay in bed as she had been told, and as she sank slowly into sleep her last thought was that nobody was interested in her morning with George, and that her father had not come up to see her.

That night she could not stay in her own sleep. Miss Chalk did not come, but others did. She heard the screaming of witches above the house, and voices spoke together, hoarse, high, singing and growling. They hurt her ears and her eyes like hot needles. Wires twisted in her head and her neck. The sheets on the bed grew wrinkled, damply writhing, an angry sea: she was a ship tossed about, and voices blew like the wind, lamenting and moaning. She tried to escape, and the floor came up to meet her. She was almost steadied by its cold, and the steel restraints of the pain: anything to be out of the terrible boiling bath her bed had become. Holding first on to the chair and then the door handle, Brigid inched her way from her bedroom. In her parents' room, she groped her way around the wall until she reached the side of their high bed. She could see her father's face, familiar again without his glasses, the curving arch of his nose. Her mother turned over with a sigh, her pale profile composed, even in sleep. Everything was still, except for a slight sound, a sliding, hissing sound. It was coming from the corner, the tallboy in the corner, but they did not hear. They did not waken, even when, to Brigid's silent horror, the sound took form: from the tallboy in the corner slithered an old woman, the witch whose scream she had heard in her nightmare, and she was making her bent way through the polished wood of the drawers as if they were water, tapping with her black stick as she slid towards Brigid who, inching backwards through the pain in her neck and her back and head, somehow managed to get to her own room, back to the drunken ship in the writhing sea. Too frightened to open her eyes, she kept them shut until, at last, she dropped into a black, troubled sleep, where German aeroplanes dropped bombs from the lightshade, and the bed was no longer a wrinkled sea but a burning building in which she, the last person alive, stood helpless as the world fell away.

When she woke, she was not in her room. She heard traffic, car horns and brakes. She was in her parents' room, at the front of the house. It was day, warm yellow light coming through the Holland blinds, all three pulled down to shade her eyes. Brigid could not look at the light. Everything hurt. Then, she saw Francis, sitting by the window with his cat's cradle of string, but there was too much pain to speak, and her eyes wanted to close, and the light had changed when she opened them again. The sounds were quieter, and it was no longer morning. It was an evening room, and she could see the tallboy, clear now: there was no witchwoman at the moment, but her mother was there, and the square man with his snapping bag who was the doctor. He had wakened her with cold metal on her chest, and now he lifted her up, gently, to put it on her back. He wanted her to breathe, and it hurt. He had to lift her; he told her she was a rag doll. She was very tired. He bent her neck over and over until it touched her chest, and she could not tell him how it hurt. Then he wrote on his pad, and put a wooden stick in her mouth until her throat came up to meet it. She could not breathe. Her throat closed over the stick, and she began to retch. Her mother, quiet, watching, suddenly reached forward and held her at her back. The doctor took the stick away, and her mother eased away her arm. Brigid fell back on the pillows, and all the pain of the night shot through her shoulders and her head.

"Well, Doctor?" her mother said, and her voice was a whisper.

"Not meningitis, anyway," he said, "or she'd squawk when I move her head. Not measles or mumps. Unspecified respiratory infection. Keep her in bed for a few days and don't let the other one catch it. Watch her neck. If you can't make it reach her chest, and if she complains about the light, call me at once."

He left. They both left, still talking low, voices fading on the stairs, and Brigid slid back into darkness.

When next she woke, she was not in her bed or theirs. All round her there were yellow flowers, and cool darkness, and the air smelled sharp, like the taste of medicine. She thought perhaps she had slept through the winter, like a squirrel or a bear, waking to sunshine and spring flowers, but when she reached out her hand to touch the flowers, they were just a curtain. Then she felt more. The aching of last night was stronger, deeper, and every movement, even lifting her hand to try to touch the flowers, sent pain all through her. Frightened, she lay still. The flowers parted. Tall people appeared. A man stood over her in a white coat. Round his neck hung a tube of rubber, and a circle of bright steel. Beside him was a person like a teacher or a nun, in blue with a white hard square behind her head, who moved towards Brigid. She lifted Brigid's wrist, not gently, and Brigid cried out.

"Gently, Sister," said the white-coated man and his voice, though low, was reproving. "The child is in some discomfort."

"Of course, Doctor," said the blue woman – *was* she a nun? – but her grip stayed hard.

Brigid thought for a second of Isobel, then the stone-faced

nuns in school, then she thought of nothing, because the doctor was pushing her head towards her chest and the pain was exquisite. It was a white light that screamed through her, and it said: "Mama!"

The blue woman said: "You can't see your mama yet," and the doctor, looking away from her with his medicine-smelling hands still on her burning head, said across her: "Lumbar puncture, Sister, straight away. With luck it may be viral."

They went through the curtains and disappeared. Perhaps, Brigid thought, this is another dream. There are so many. This may stop and I will be at home in my own bed. She kept her eyes closed to help this happen, but opened them suddenly as harsh light again intruded, the yellow flowers swishing away from her and two men in shorter white coats lifting her, not ungently, on to a trolley. The pain seared through her once again, and she could feel the hot wetness on her face.

"Poor lassie," said one of the men, and he stroked her arm, which made the tears worse.

Then, she was in a grey, cold room. One of the men put a white blanket on her, and turned her, slowly, on to her side.

She heard a soft padding behind her. "Hello, Brigid," said a voice, but Brigid hurt too much to answer. "I'm going to put a little pinprick in your back now," said the voice, "and it may hurt for a moment. Just hold still, like a good girl."

Brigid felt a cold that was different, and inhaled a sharp brightness, but she felt no new pain. The whole place, everywhere around her was already so full of it that there was no room for any more. When the voice said, "There, that wasn't too bad, was it?" Brigid did not even try to speak. Then there was silence, and someone, two someones, brought her back through the grey spaces to the room with the yellow flowers, and she was able to close her eyes again in semi-darkness.

When next she woke the doctor was standing above her. He had papers in his hands.

"Well, Brigid," he said. "You're a lucky little girl. You have what is called meningitis, but it is viral, and the pain will soon go. Meanwhile, look!"

A miracle happened. The doctor swept back the curtain, and above her stood her parents. She looked for Francis, but he was not there. "Where is Francis?" she said.

"Hello, Brigid," said her mother.

"Hello, girlie," said her father.

"Where is Francis?" asked Brigid again.

"He's at school," said her mother, "but he will come, now that we know it's not as serious as . . . it looked."

"Will you take me home?" asked Brigid. "I want to go home."

Her parents looked at each other.

"When the doctor lets you, we will," said her father.

Then Brigid closed her eyes, and when she opened them no one was there.

She drifted in and out of sleep in the yellow-flowered cocoon. Sometimes it was darker, sometimes lighter, but she did not leave it again until the day there came a young blue person, with a hat not stiff and square like the first one, but pleasantly rounded on soft curls.

"Come on, now, Missy," said the young person, "let's get you up," and very gently she slipped Brigid out of the bed and set her on her feet.

To Brigid, her legs seemed to belong to someone else. They were impossibly long and white, and her slippers were very far away. She swayed and buckled, but the blue person said: "Hold on to me. Once you can walk, you might even get home."

Brigid tried. She moved one foot and it bent, then the other, and it gave way. The wall tried to come over to her. There was bright spinning in her head. She tried again. She told her foot to move. She told the other one and, this time, they both listened. The pain came with her but she could walk, and after a time, past blank doors, past other blue-and-white people, studying her, watching her curiously, almost rudely, she found she was back again at the yellow flowers and she did not know if she was glad or sorry. The next day, she was propped up to eat, and she was hungry as she had not been before. That night, she slept without dreams.

The following morning, after the white coats and the blue dresses and the new normality of examinations and conversations that did not include her, Brigid saw at last the face she was looking for. Francis had come.

"Hello, you," he said. "Have you taken up residence?"

"Francis," she said. "Why haven't you come before? I've been here for . . . I don't know how long. You didn't come."

Francis laughed his quiet laugh, and shook his head. "Oh, foolish Brigitta," he said. "You have been here for over a week, and they wouldn't let me come, till they knew you couldn't pass it on. But," and he stood up, "I'm here now. It's Saturday. They're on their way up the stairs right now – and we're all going home."

The miracle continued. In clothes too heavy, on legs too light, Brigid finally left the yellow-flowered place and the people in blue and white who had no names and, though she still had pain outside her head and was very tired, when she lay back on her own cool bed, not wrinkled or hot any more, and watched on the wall opposite the window familiar shadows of the trees in the plot, she knew that this was bliss. Blissful too was the slowly dawning realisation that she did not now have to go to school. Perhaps she might never have to go to school again. There was a half-heard conversation that she thought was real, one night soon after she came home, drifting towards sleep. She thought she heard her parents outside her door, talking softly. She thought she could see tall shadows where the door angled to the wall, in the shaft of the landing light they left on for her since she had become afraid, and her father said, "Fifty children in that class, Grace. Fifty!" and her mother's voice said, with a sigh, "Private, then?" Brigid understood that: it meant not to be disturbed. Perhaps, after this, she need not be disturbed by school. She did not hear any more but a dim sound, like the men downstairs, and maybe it was the men downstairs, back after all. She drifted quite easily that night into a calm space, with no dreams, and a gentle sensation of floating.

Despite their doctor's advice, Francis came every day and sat with her. He even brought in his own wireless for her, and she listened in soft darkness, lit only by the glow from the wireless. Inside the green box, tiny people sang, played music, acted plays and read aloud. They became her friends. In those nights, Miss Chalk stayed away, the witch from the tallboy did not come back, the pain receded and she began to be happy again. She was given her father's wooden chessmen to play with, and as she lay back they climbed hills and danced with each other and hid in the eiderdown. The people inside the wireless got on with their busy lives. Sometimes they sang, of scarlet ribbons, or runaway trains, or her favourite, Davy Crockett, King of the Wild Frontier.

It was a time of quiet happiness, until Brigid grew restless, and nothing made her happy. When at last she was allowed to get up, she could not wait: she felt lighter and taller, but she was giddy, and her clothes were loose. Her legs did not quite work: downstairs seemed a long way away. That first day, she was glad to sit watching pictures in the fire, and at five o'clock, she climbed gratefully back up to bed.

Yet, next morning, with quiet but sudden certainty, she knew she was better. She sat up slowly, walked with care to the end of the bed, and looked out of the window. The Friday Tree had almost no leaves. From somewhere, faintly, there was the smell of smoke. It was time to be well again and, slowly, Brigid stayed downstairs for longer periods. She found she could support the weight of her head by herself, and sit in a chair. She could hold a book, without real pain.

Only then, as she sat occupying herself, did she notice that Isobel was not in the house. Brigid thought she heard her parents say she had gone for a holiday, but it was not summer. Still, she was more glad than sorry. Her mother did all the things Isobel had done, and did them with more care and more kindness. She even let her look at her own book of photographs, brown pictures where she herself was a child, then a girl, laughing with her friends.

The clock on the mantel ticked away the autumn days. When Francis came home he sat with her and at five o'clock they watched television, and all the while the year darkened down toward Hallowe'en, and every night the smell of woodsmoke rose in the air. Waiting for Francis to come home she watched caverns and mountains in the fire. Sometimes she fell asleep. Often she took down the books from her father's shelves to look at them, or to smell the old paper, or see what was in the pages – a photograph, or a postcard, in writing like stitching, or a square of newspaper, yellow, and soft, like cloth, too small to read. There was one book she liked, with photographs of a small boy in a sailor suit. He was David: he grew up, now he was a king, and he was Edward. In other books, other photographs, she discovered tribes in Africa, Russians in the snow, Italians in the sun, warriors in wooden ships. In her own world, far away from everyone, the days went past too quickly.

One morning, her mother woke her with the words she had almost forgotten. "Up you get, Brigid. School."

Brigid was stunned. She thought that was all finished. In a dream, she got out of bed, washed and dressed, but her clothes seemed shorter, and the heavy shoes pinched. Downstairs, the things she had left behind her forever were laid out for her: the leather schoolbag smelling of pencils and rubber and the prickly coat with the flat hood. She hated them all.

"Growing fast, girlie," said her father and she looked up at him.

Behind his thick black glasses, his face in the morning light looked thinner, whiter than she remembered. When he took off the glasses to clean them, she saw that his eyes had brown shadows beneath, and the kind creases, always at the edges when he smiled, were still there when he was not smiling. Without resentment, she saw that the concerns of the family were no longer directed towards her, but once more to her father. It was right it should be so. She was well again; he was not.

Looking about her in the frosty morning, seeing even Dicky in his cage huddled beneath his own wing, Brigid, in her warm home, felt cold – surrounded by her family, she felt alone. She did not need to ask whether her father would be taking her to school in the car. She saw that he would not, that she and her mother would brave the bus together. Something had gone from him. Brigid who, before her own brush with illness, would have asked why, or what, said nothing.

She went back to school, because there was no choice, liking it even less, saying even less about it at home. She did not see George at the school again, and she did not talk about him. Her mother took her on the bus and collected her in the afternoon, and there was still no Isobel. In the shortening days, her father did not leave her again at the end of the road. He did not take her to school at all, even in the wet, even in the cold. Most days, he stayed at home. Sometimes, in the evenings, as he listened to the wireless, and she asked him about her sums or her spellings, it seemed that he had not heard her. When those times happened, she climbed on his knee, and listened to his heart as he tapped pale fingers to his music.

Slowly, Brigid began to feel that school could be endured. She was surprised and pleased when, one bright morning towards the end of October, her teacher asked them to try to write a story. Brigid settled down, forgot where she was and wrote the story of David who became Edward, adding for interest a tribe who ate people and, in fact, ate everyone but him. Only when it was as good as she could make it did she show it to her teacher, and was very pleased when Miss took up her paper and showed it to another teacher, who had come in with books. Some of the children said the two teachers were sisters, but they did not look alike. Brigid's teacher was big, soft and round, whereas her sister, if she was her sister, was sharp and fox-faced. They both looked at Brigid's story, and Miss called her up to the desk, higher and more interesting than the children's desks, with drawers and shelves and hiding places in every wooden corner.

"Brigid, how did you know this word?" asked Miss, pointing to the page, while the foxy-faced sister looked sharply on.

Brigid felt her smile break open, because this was her new and favourite word. She had written: "*David was the only one the cannonball did not eat.*"

"I just knew it, Miss," she said.

The two women looked at each other, and they shared a smile, yet it was not a smile Brigid liked.

"Did you, indeed?" said Miss. "Sit down now."

That was all. There was no praise. When her back was turned, Brigid heard them laugh, and she was angry. She had written a good story, and they had laughed at her.

That night, Brigid's mother looked over her homework, hearing her reading and her numbers, and checking her spellings. "Brigid," she said, looking hard at her, her eyebrows drawn down, "are you worried about anything?"

Brigid looked at her. She thought of saying, I am worried about everything, but said instead: "No, Mama."

"Good girl," said her mother, and her eyebrows lifted, and she smiled. "They were a bit concerned in the school. Did you write something about murder?"

Brigid felt her anger return. They had gone behind her back. "I just wrote a story, Mama. A made-up story out of my head. That's all it was. I could show it to you, but they have it in school."

"I know," said her mother. "They telephoned me about it. The word is 'cannibal', Brigid, by the way. Cannonballs are large round bullets fired out of great guns called cannons."

Brigid said nothing. Her mother got up, smoothed her skirt, and went into the kitchen. Brigid heard tap water hissing into the kettle, the snap and the pop of the gas. In her mind she could see the blue leaping flame. Soon it would be hot-water bottles and bed. Brigid tried to find in herself the content she had known before she went back to school, the simplicity of days and nights with pictures, books and the wireless, but she could not recover it. They had all gone behind her back about the story, laughing at her, all of them. Perhaps no one could be trusted.

Across the table, ink on his fingers, thoughts almost audibly humming behind his eyes, Francis sat at his homework. He looked at her for a moment, and he smiled a little.

"Keep writing them, Brigid," he said. "Don't stop." Then he bent again to his books.

Brigid wanted to tell Francis how much she disliked school, and the people in it, but he looked so burdened, and there was so much ink on him, on his fingers and round his mouth, even on the collar of his grey shirt, that it did not seem fair. She said instead: "Francis, where is Isobel gone?"

He looked up. Shutters had come down on his face. He was no longer smiling. "Isobel's brother was taken ill," he said, after a moment. "She had to look after him."

"What brother?" asked Brigid. "I never heard Isobel say she had a brother."

"Well," said Francis, more like himself, "you don't always listen to what's going on, do you? She does have a brother. He was . . . away . . . and now he's back, and she has gone to take care of him."

"I thought she was supposed to take care of us," said Brigid, aggrieved, suddenly missing Isobel, after liking her so little when she was there.

"Well," said Francis, "not at the moment, when her brother needs her."

"Don't they have parents?"

"No," said Francis.

"What's his name?"

"I don't know."

"Where was he, anyway, turning up out of the blue?" She

liked that: out of the blue. She might use it again.

Francis' face closed over again. "England, I think."

"England!" said Brigid, surprised. "What for?"

"Brigid," said her mother from the door, "get on up to bed, and let Francis do his work. Go on, now, hop."

Brigid, obscurely unhappy, went up to bed. Yet, if she had been asked, she could not have said why.

That night Miss Chalk came back, grinning at her beside the bed, waiting for her. She did not speak to Brigid, but Brigid knew, without words, that Miss Chalk had not really gone away. She had been in England, and now she was back. Brigid screamed, and they all came, her parents as well as Francis. Miss Chalk was clever. She disappeared as soon as she heard the scream. Brigid had no proof, and all she could say was: "Bad dream." They settled her, and went back to bed.

Only Francis lingered at the door. "Call me if she comes back?" he said, and Brigid was able to let herself sleep.

The next morning, and every weekday morning after that, there was school. Francis could not be with her there. He never talked about his own school, but Brigid felt sure that he did not like it either. Why would he tell? She told no one how, in the days after she was called up over her story, the other girls began to mock the way she spoke and, at lunchtime, tore two buttons from her burberry and scraped her shoes against the brick until they were rough and ugly. She could not tell, when Miss had said they must never tell, or she would know. And she would know: Brigid was sure of that, now. So, every morning, she went to her prison, and stayed quiet, and offered no more stories.

Then, one day when the wind was whirling and the sky was cold as blue water, he came for her. He waited for her outside in his car, and it made her heart turn over. She forgot the jeering girls and the teachers who could not be trusted. She forgot the green schoolroom and the spiders and cockroaches in the outside lavatories. She forgot the bottles of warm curdled milk at break. She forgot that she must not run, and ran to him, utterly happy, and he bent down to her as George had done, and he said, from behind his glasses: "Mama's in town with Francis. You and I are going to my office, and I will show you the birds arriving for their winter holiday."

Brigid threw out her arms and wound them round his neck. School did not matter any more.

Chapter 8: A Sky Full of Starlings

On autumn afternoons down town, all the heavy buildings tried to touch their tops against the darkening sky. In the smoky twilight, large department stores showed the beginnings of their winter brightness. Brigid knew that her mother and Francis were probably buying fireworks for Hallowe'en, but she also realised that it would be a secret that she would not be supposed to know until the night itself, when they would wear their falsefaces and stand well back while their father lit the squibs: rockets and sparklers and Jumping Jacks and all the spinning colours of the Catherine wheels. She could see already the brightness, the rush and explosion of lights in the air above her and the ground about her, a smell like matches tickling her nose.

Best of all, she had her father to herself, from the time he opened the car door for her and put her into the front seat, through the excitement of the slow cranking lift which carried them slowly through the air to the other world of the office. The lift sat hidden behind the entrance to a shoe shop, a secret door suddenly appearing, with whirring and clanking, dark looping wheels and pulleys first, then the slow majestic descent of the travelling room. Crossed bars stood in front of it, open black diamonds. They had to be pushed back, and there was a strange moment of stepping in, over a space of black, yawning emptiness. Then slowly, and a little sickeningly, the lift lurched, wheezing and grinding, and pulled them up to the second floor.

Now there was the almost-office, a little square place with wooden panels and misted windows. Then another secret door in the panelling opened, and there was the high room, full of slanting white light, its bright curved window like the moon in the sky. Francis said it had once been the studio of an artist, but now it was the office. Tall men in suits, ladies in cardigans and tweed smiled down at her, and biscuits and orange juice appeared from nowhere, more magic. An old man, gently spoken, sat on a stool and wrote in beautiful numbers in a fat ledger, like the ones her father pored over at home, before he was ill.

A young lady sat Brigid in front of a big typewriter, huge and gleaming black, with all the letters crowded round like people in a theatre. The young lady helped her to type out her name on the heavy keys. Each time she pressed a letter, it jumped up, eager to see itself written on the page. The young lady said Brigid could write a letter to her teacher, if she liked. Brigid typed out her name several times, but she did not write a letter to her teacher. Instead, she asked the young lady what her name was. She said it was Maureen, and Brigid wrote: **dear Moren i like you thank you love from Brigid**. Then she wrote, on impulse, for no reason she could think of: **ned silver**.

She stared at the words. She had scarcely thought about Ned Silver since the end of the summer. She was still wondering at herself, her hands above the waiting keys, when Maureen appeared above her.

"Are you stuck?" she said, then "Oh!" and she clapped her hands in pleasure. "Thank you, Brigid! I don't get too many letters like that. May I keep it?" and she swiftly rolled and swished the paper out of the typewriter, and just as quickly rolled in another fresh white sheet. "Were you not going to write to your teacher?"

Brigid shook her head. "No, thank you," she said.

"But who's this?" said Maureen, pointing at the two words Brigid had written at the end of the page. "Who's Ned Silver?"

Brigid shook her head. She said: "Oh. Sorry. He's not anybody. He's just a boy we play with sometimes."

"Oh," said Maureen. "Well. Let's type it all out again. Will we?" Leaning over Brigid's head, not waiting for an answer, her fingers clicked and flew, and all the letters jumped to attention.

Dear Maureen,

I like you. Thank you.

Love from

Brigid

Underneath, she wrote: **Ned Silver.**

"You see?" said Maureen. "Capital letters for names – especially for your boyfriend!"

Brigid grew suddenly hot. She slipped down without help from the high stool.

"Thank you," she said, and in her head she spoke like her mother, "but he is not my boyfriend." She looked around, wanting to place distance between herself and this too rapid friend. "Please, where did my daddy go?"

Maureen had already turned away to answer an insistent telephone. Brigid, relieved, wandered across to the high window, and climbed on a chair below it. She was entranced by what she saw. There were always birds in the sky, but now, above and around her the sky was crowded with birds, wheeling and conversing, clear and cold as the evening air, higher and louder than the cars on the street far below, swooping in circles and semi-circles, darkening the deepening blue.

Then, close to, at her ear, she heard her father's voice. "Didn't I tell you?" he said. "The starlings come here for the winter, from far away up in the north of the world, because it's warmer here."

"Warmer!" said Brigid in astonishment. "Here?"

"For them, yes," said her father, "because they come from cold, cold places. Look, there's one coming across to speak to you," and his arm above her pointed to a ledge outside the window where a little bird hovered, ruffling feathers purple and green and blue, just spangled with creamy white.

A dark eye like a shining bead looked at her from a round, neat head. Then the bird spread its wings, pulled up its legs and swiftly, directly, launched itself into the air, gliding until it joined the calling, chattering crowd above.

Brigid was entranced. She was a starling, spinning and dipping and weaving in the evening sky. She drew in her breath. "A sky full of starlings," she said, almost to herself, as her father lifted her down from the chair, turning her head to look back at them through the enchanted space.

When they went outside, the noise of the starlings was louder, though less intense. Down on the street, she was once again part of the heavy earth, and it was as though her body felt too solid to move through the busy crowd. Her father's hand, warmly round hers, was all that kept her from floating away.

By the time he took her into his favourite store, she was back on the ground, back in this world with him, in yet another place of delights. This square shop, quiet and brown on the outside, was almost opposite the office. As they were turning into it, her father said: "Some men spend their time in a public house. This is my public house."

Brigid did not know what he meant by a public house, but she knew she was drawn by the smells and the colours in this bright house of books. She felt her heart turn over as they went in. In its quiet, she no longer heard the starlings. This was where books came from.

"Now," said her father, "a girl who has been sick deserves a nice book," and Brigid was flying again.

She inhaled the books. She picked them up. She felt them and smelt them, shiny pages, matt pages, brown wolves and green woodcutters, princesses with bronze tumbling hair, trees that talked and carpets that flew and in one, a young boy looking down into a cave where all the bright glittering jewels of the world were stored. Lost in the wonder of it, Brigid forgot where she was and, surprised to hear his voice, looked up to see her father above her, and to hear him say: "The shop is about to close now, Brídín. Have you decided?"

Brigid's heart thumped in her chest. How could she decide? She wanted them all. She picked them up, set them down, decided on this one, saw another, went back to the first, remembered a third. Her father did not hurry her. He waited, and watched, quiet and still. Finally, with a deep sigh, she held up a tall red book. Its name was *Children of Many Lands*, and in it she knew she could travel all over the world. "This one, please, Daddy," she said. He took it from her, pleased with her choice, and walked the length of the shop to the elderly bookseller. It seemed a long time to wait while the paper was folded and smoothed along the edges of the book, and the string tied. Brigid became impatient. She could spend that time looking at other books.

Unnoticed, she drifted back towards the aisles of books and, almost immediately, walked into a solid wall. It was a strange wall, giving way slightly, like a tree in a breeze. It was made of tweed and cloth, but it was much too big to be a person, so wide and broad and high. Brigid sensed life and movement, and realised, all in one second, that she had simply walked into a giant, reading a book. Only a little nervous, she looked up to see if there was a head to which she might apologise. The tweed and cloth covered a great distance before she found hands holding a large, dense book in dark brown. Even further up was the enormous head, intent, a huge head of a giant, reading, concentrating. Brigid had never seen anyone so big. She opened her mouth to apologise, and immediately realised the giant had not taken her under his notice, and that it would be safe, even prudent, to remove herself quickly. She backed away until she found herself, breathing hard, beside her father.

"Daddy," she said, slipping her hand in his, "I walked into a giant, but he didn't see me."

Her father, peacefully turning over more books while he and the shopkeeper conversed, looked down at her. "Well," he said, shaking her hand a little, "you're not too big yet, Brigid. You probably didn't do very much damage."

"But, Daddy," said Brigid, shaking his hand back, "it was a giant. There's a giant in this shop. Look!"

She raised their joined hands towards the back of the shop, forcing a half-turn on her father. He looked, stiffened, whistled beneath his breath, and put down the book he had been reading. He looked intently for a few seconds, then away, then back, almost in disbelief.

Brigid whispered: "Didn't I tell you? A giant."

"Yes, Brigid," said her father, slowly, his eyes still on the giant. "You did, indeed." Then, without ceremony, he took her hand firmly, caught up the parcel under his arm, bent his head, made a brisk farewell to the keeper of the shop, and the next thing Brigid knew they were outside on the pavement. Above them the starlings circled and called, as if nothing had happened.

"The shop's not closed yet, Daddy," said Brigid, a little surprised at their swift exit.

"Don't you want to have tea with me?" said her father. "Come on. Let's find your mama and your brother."

He led her across the road, across a lane into Fountain Street, climbing up stairs and more stairs to The Bonne Bouche. In that bright, warm room, kindly ladies in white aprons and caps served even children with china cups and saucers, placing sandwiches and cakes and hot scones on a dish that was three dishes in one, with lace paper beneath them. Outside the starlings wheeled and chittered in the evening air; inside, lamps wrapped them in soft light. This day was perfect. Her father had kept the promise made in the summer, and any moment her mother and Francis would join them. Brigid closed her eyes, and listened to the sound of the birds and the tinkle of spoons in cups and the low hum of voices at tables all around her.

When she opened them, she knew something was wrong. Her

father, napkin in hand, was on his feet, and he was looking straight at the door leading from the stairs. Brigid turned right round in her seat, almost taking with her the white tablecloth. At the top of the stairs, she saw her mother, in her heathery costume, small pearls at her neck. But something was wrong. Beside her, inside the circle of her arm, stood Francis, shaking and pale. Over one eye, he wore a thick white bandage. Francis, but not Francis – Brigid remembered her father in the summer. Quickly, she looked up at him. He had no bandage now, only the heavy glasses masked his eyes, but his hands were clenched and white, frozen on his napkin. Joy drained from the day.

Before they could speak, her mother moved quickly across to them, her hand under Francis' elbow. "I'm sorry, Maurice. I had no means of letting you know. Hello, Brigid," she said, absently, as Brigid, looking up, touched her sleeve. "Francis was hit by a brick as he was walking into town from school. We've had it stitched. He's all right. No," she said, as her husband's mouth opened to speak, "he *is* all right. Really. There's no damage to his eye."

Francis did not look all right. Everything in him seemed to be shaking, and his unbandaged eye had a look Brigid had never seen before.

Their father spoke, and his voice was tight, and high, like wire: "What are we doing here? Let's get him home," and he began to signal to the waitress.

His wife laid her hand on his sleeve, shaking her head: "Not quite yet, Maurice. He's had a shock. Hot sweet tea and something to eat will help him, and then we'll go. Besides," she said, and Brigid saw her mother incline towards her, "wasn't someone else promised tea with her daddy in town, a long time ago?"

Brigid was grateful, but even she, who had so longed for this treat, could not now enjoy it. "That's all right, Mama," she said, "we don't have to," but her mother, no longer looking at her, was suddenly sitting on the chair that had been Brigid's, her hands at her face.

"What are we to do?" she said. "What sort of a place is it where a child could have a brick thrown at him because of his uniform?"

"Easy," said her husband, looking behind him. "You don't know that was why."

"I do," came the low reply.

Both children turned towards their mother, and Brigid saw her, on an instant, fix her face into an expression she knew: interested, cheerful and distant. "Anyway, what sort of time did you two have?" she said.

"A fine time," said her father, catching the mood. "Brigid saw – what did you see, Brídín?"

Brigid took her attention away for a moment from Francis' stricken face. "A sky full of starlings," she said, instantly reliving that joy.

"That's right," said her father. "A sky full of starlings. And she has a new book, haven't you?"

Brigid nodded, and she began to take out the parcel from beneath her white napkin, but her mother put her hand on hers, and stilled her.

"I think we'll look at that together at home," she said.

"And then," said her father in a quiet, measured tone, "and then she walked right into a very large young reverend gentleman, no friend to those of the – shall we say – of the old faith."

There was silence.

"What?" said her mother, putting down the cup she had just, for the first time, raised. "Do you mean the person I think you mean? The man Cornelius Todd heard preach against . . . ?"

Brigid saw her father, the finger of one hand casually travelling to his lips, nod his head. "He was a giant," she said.

Her mother kept her eyes on her husband's face. "Is there something going on in the town? One of those . . . you know, those . . . meetings?"

"Not that I'm aware," he replied. "The man was standing

reading a book, and Brigid charged into him, didn't you, Brídín?" He turned again to Brigid, and his hands were spread open, inviting her to help him.

"No, Daddy," said Brigid, firmly, "I did not charge. I just walked into him by accident. And he was not a man. He was a giant. Do you know who he is?"

Her parents looked at each other. Brigid saw her mother shake her head, just perceptibly, and then her father said: "Just a man, Brigid. Just a big man – yes, all right, then, a giant – who came in to look at books in a bookshop, and didn't notice a little girl bumping into him. There was no harm done."

Brigid was not satisfied, and thought she might ask Francis about it later, if he was able to speak. He was still very pale. They left straight after tea, and walked to the sad car park, past the ruined house. Brigid saw again the corner room, cut away like a doll's house, its peeling wallpaper and the darker places where pictures had hung, and the empty grate where a fire had been. She looked away. In her dreams, she had been the child of that house.

When they reached home, Francis asked to go up to bed. On the stairs, he stumbled once, and their father made to move forward and catch him, but their mother, coming from the telephone, caught his arm and shook her head. "Leave him," she said. "Let the child be. I've sent for the doctor. He'll look at him."

Still, to Brigid, her father seemed restless, pacing the kitchen, until her mother led him out to the hall by the arm. "Maurice," she said, "please. It does no good to get excited, and you are really under my feet at the moment. Why don't you and Brigid go out for a walk, while I see to Francis? You'll see the car at the gate when the doctor comes, if you don't go far."

Brigid's father said nothing and, without looking at his wife, put Brigid's coat back on her, took her hand, and opened the door.

Superfluous, they set off together down the road. Neither was in the mood for a walk. Not far from the house, to the relief of both, they met Mr Doughty. Until now, Brigid had seen him only in the plot. How different he looked in his uniform, not exactly black, not quite green. His flat cap had a peak that hid the kindliness of his eyes. He looked much taller, not as tall as the giant in the bookshop but, because she could not see his eyes, he was forbidding. And like Mr Steele, he carried at his hip a great gun, in a holster. Brigid felt a slight shock. She had become used to the idea of Mr Steele carrying a gun, but she could not reconcile it with her picture of gentle Mr Doughty. She did remember, from the meeting with Mr Steele, that she must not mention the gun. Still, she could not avoid looking at it, on a level with her eyes, as her father and the policeman stopped in greeting. They spoke of the kindness of the weather, and a surprising result in a match they had both watched on television the previous Saturday. Mr Doughty inquired after Mrs Arthur. He said Brigid was growing taller by the day, and asked after her brother.

"He was hit on the head, Mr Doughty," said Brigid and, immediately, just as her mother had done when she stared at Mr Steele and his gun, her father squeezed her hand very tightly.

"How's that, Mr Arthur?" said Mr Doughty, with concern.

"Oh," said her father, and his hand on hers tightened even more. "Schoolboys, you know, Mr Doughty. Horseplay."

"Oh, indeed," said Mr Doughty, shaking his head. "Boys are holy terrors for horseplay."

Amazed, Brigid looked up at her father, who did not respond. Why did he not tell what happened to Francis? Wasn't it something he should tell a policeman? She could make no sense of it.

Then, just as her father was touching his hat, ready to walk on, Mr Doughty said: "All the same, Mr Arthur. Schoolboys and horseplay apart, we need all to be careful these days, nearer home."

"Indeed," said Brigid's father, carefully.

Mr Doughty cleared his throat, and looked over Brigid's head, to the plot, and the mountain beyond. "Those IRA fellows in England haven't been caught yet, planting their packages. It's said they were on the Liverpool boat in the summer. Could be anywhere now." He paused again, took out a large white handkerchief from under his tunic, and blew his nose. For a moment he looked like the Mr Doughty Brigid knew from the plot. Then, just as suddenly, he was the policeman again. "Could be here among us."

"Aye, indeed, Mr Doughty," said her father, lifting his hat a little from his head. "Well, good evening to you, now. I must get this girl of mine home."

Mr Doughty looked down at Brigid, and she saw her old friend. His face softened.

"Good night to you, Miss Brigid," he said. "I haven't seen you out in the garden now a while. Too cold to play, is it?" and he ruffled her hair. The action sent the gun swinging heavily towards her, almost into her face and, just as she stiffened, Mr Doughty took back his hand, and the menacing blackness pulled away.

They turned back to the house. "There's the doctor's car," said her father. "Come on, Brigid. Pick up your feet."

"Daddy," she said, "why did you not tell Mr Doughty what really happened to Francis?"

He did not reply for a moment and then he said: "Brigid, I was going to tell you this later, but I'll do it now. Say nothing to anyone about Francis."

"But why, Daddy?"

He sighed, stopped, and hunkered down to face her on her own level. For an instant, she thought of George Bailey. "Brigid," said her father, and his eyes were not smiling. "Listen. I'm only going to say this once. In this place, we keep our business to ourselves. Can you remember that?"

Brigid, not understanding, nodded her head. She had thought she might tell Mr Doughty, the next time she saw him in the plot, until that moment when the gun came close to her, swinging near her face like a live thing. Now, after that, and because her father asked her, she would never tell Mr Doughty, or anybody, what really happened to Francis.

Chapter 9: Children of Other Lands

Now it was Francis who had to stay in bed. When Brigid went in to see him, he was not even reading. Beside him the wireless sat oddly silent and this, more than anything, made Brigid feel uneasy. Without him the house felt too still, though Francis himself was all stillness. What was missing was his light, his peaceful acceptance of whatever came his way. Francis in bed, Francis not reading or listening to the wireless, Francis looking listlessly from of his window at the seven trees, was wrong.

As much to cheer herself as him, Brigid brought him her new book, invited him to run his hand over its cover of red cloth, rough yet warm to the touch, showed him the colours and sounds of the pictures inside, easing herself onto the bed until she sat beside him. The hospital had put on a white bandage, far too much like the bandage their father had worn when he came home from London. When their own doctor had come, he had shaken his head. He had redone it, so that now there was a small bandage; all around it, his skin was purple and blue.

"Some of the words are too hard for me, Francis," Brigid said. "Will you help me?"

Francis turned his head as if he had been a long way away. At first, he did not speak, then he said: "I can't read at the moment, Brigid. Tell me what you think they are. I'll tell you if I know."

Now, she was afraid. Francis not reading could be an accident: Francis not wanting to read, or worse, not knowing the answer, was too much like the latest bad dream, where she came home from school, by herself, and the door was opened by someone who was nearly Mama, but not, and inside were people who were Not-Isobel and Not-Francis, and Not-Daddy, and she could tell no one because in this town they must keep their business to themselves. Perhaps this was real, and the Not-people were taking over. Perhaps the happy life was the dream? No. No to that. There was Francis. There would always be Francis, even if he lived to be a hundred, and when he was a hundred, he would wait for her to be a hundred too.

"Well," she said, opening at one of the pictures, "one shows a boy with his finger in a wall. He has a blue coat on and a cap, and fair hair. He looks cold. Why is his finger in the wall?"

Francis smiled a little. "Ah. This I can do. He is the Little Dutch Boy. If the water comes through the wall, the dyke, all of his country, a flat country, will be flooded and everyone will drown. He doesn't have time to tell anyone, so he puts his finger in the hole he's found and stays there till someone comes."

"He saves the country?"

"Yes," said Francis, "he saves the country."

Brigid looked at the cold little boy, all alone by his wall. "Would you do that, Francis, to save a country?"

"I don't know, said Francis. "I've never thought about it. If I had to, I suppose I might."

"I think you would, Francis," said Brigid. "But I know *I* wouldn't."

She laughed, and Francis almost joined her.

"Do you know who else wouldn't?" she said.

The corners of his mouth turned up in something like his old smile. "Tell me," he said.

"Ned!" cried Brigid. "Ned Silver wouldn't."

Francis laughed, at last. "I think you're right," he said but, as he spoke, he drew in his breath and his hand went up to his head.

Brigid, concerned, looked at the bruises beneath his fingers. They were like a map of a country.

"Francis, what did happen to your head?"

Francis turned away; she felt him shift in the bed. "I don't really know. There's a street that runs between the road below your school and a road that's near my school. Like the bar in the capital H?"

Brigid nodded her head.

"Well, there are quite a few of those streets round there. They're like the rungs in a ladder. Do you know what I mean?"

Brigid nodded again.

"Those are short cuts for me when I'm going to the College. I get off the bus, and go across one of them – Agnes Street, usually, or sometimes over Dover Street."

Brigid laughed. "Over Dover!" she said.

This time, he did not laugh. "Yes," he said. "That's it. Well, that's where I was going when something hit me on the head. They said in the hospital it was a brick or a big stone. I don't even go that way, usually, after school. I was coming to meet you all." Now, he laughed a little, but he did not smile. "Trust me to get it wrong," he said.

"Yes, but who did that?" Brigid asked. "Why? Who would want to hit you with a big stone?"

"I don't know," said Francis, his voice flat. "That's the thing. They say it could have been children."

"But, why?" said Brigid, and she felt the bed springs twang. "Who? Why?"

Francis turned in the bed, and looked away. "Brigid, would you please not bounce? Maybe because I was wearing a uniform that says I am a Catholic, and I went across a street where somebody didn't like that. Someone, they think a Protestant boy, hit me because of that."

"I don't understand. I know Catholic from school. But what is prodoson? What does that mean?"

"Brigid," he said, and his voice sounded very tired now, "I

don't have the energy to explain it to you now. We are Catholic. You know that. But not everyone in the world is. Some are Protestant. Some are Jews. Some are Muslims. There are many, many different religions in the world. There's a good word for you, if you want one. Religion."

"I hear that one in school," said Brigid, "but I don't really know what it means."

"It comes from Latin, *religare*, to join together. I only learned the meaning myself last week. Then I learned it a different way today." He started to laugh, and then stopped, as if it hurt. "Sometime I might tell you why that seems a good joke to me right now." He smiled, but his eyes did not smile. He looked away again and the skin round his eyes was blue. "The thing is, they are all meant to be roads to God and heaven."

"I don't understand, Francis," said Brigid, and she meant it. She had no idea what he was talking about.

"Well, don't worry about it," he said. "Your book. What's it called?"

She held it out to him.

"*Children of Other Lands*," he read, then he let it fall back behind the folds of the eiderdown. "That's it," he said. "Maybe just think about that. We're all children of other lands, to somebody. That's it."

Still, Brigid did not understand but, seeing that he had closed his eyes, that his hands had slipped from the book, she picked it up gently, slipped off the bed and backed from the room as quietly as she could. She wondered what he meant. How could they be children of other lands, if this was their land? And, now, who was there to ask? She looked up at Blessed Oliver as she went past, but there was no hope there.

The house sat silent. Her mother was in the cloakroom on the telephone, her voice indistinct. Brigid walked past on tiptoe, then swiftly through the kitchen, out into the yard with its comforting stack of coal and wood. She reached up, closed, with some effort, the high latch on the back door, and ran up to the garden.

Without Francis, everything felt too big. The garden seemed asleep, and all the trees had lost their leaves. Even the Friday Tree stood empty. Through its bare ribs, she saw a vast and lowering grey sky. Beyond the fence, the ground in the plot looked hard, dark and brown, unrelieved by anything green or soft. Everything seemed tired, as Francis was tired and, though it was Saturday, neither Mr Doughty nor Mr Steele seemed to have any work to do in the plot. All Brigid could hear was silence. Somewhere, there was a distant smell of smoke. She sniffed it, and a memory shifted inside her. Had there not been a day in summer when they had gone up to the Friday Tree and known someone had been there? She tried to remember. Had they not seen the remains of a little fire then, or did she make that up? She shaded her brow against the steely sun, and half-closed her eyes to see far away. Maybe there was a wisp of smoke beneath the Friday Tree, maybe not. Francis would know, if she could ask him. She looked up to his room, hoping she might see him at the window in his old way, looking beyond the trees, following a bird with his telescope, listening to sounds that only he could hear. There was no one. The window was a blank, sightless eye. Brigid, looking up, shivered quickly. What if Francis did not get better?

A voice sounded far away, a man's voice, calling a child. Brigid, cold and suddenly lonely, in the damp air, went back inside. She could be in trouble for going out without a coat, but she did not care. Then again, as her parents were so concerned about Francis, she might escape notice. For a moment, she almost wished Isobel was still there. She did not like her, but she knew her. That was her mother she could see inside, apron round her, working at the sink. That was her mother pushing back the hair from her forehead as she moved to the stove. It was not right. Isobel should be there. Then, she heard the front door open, and close, and sped unchecked through the kitchen: her father must be home from the office.

On Saturdays he worked only until lunchtime. He did not see

her as he took off his hat and his heavy coat, but she heard the rustle of paper and saw a brown-paper parcel in his hand – a new book for Francis, probably. He did not know that Francis did not want to read. From the kitchen door, she watched his long legs go up the stairs, steadily, firmly. In the kitchen she smelled shepherd's pie. There would be plenty of the burnt, brown, crispy furrows across the potato. She saw the sauce bottle; she saw Francis in the summer, reading French from the label. *Absolument pure.*

"Were you outside without a coat?" said her mother.

"I'm sorry," said Brigid absently, watching for her father.

"You suit your sorrow. Don't blame me when you get pneumonia," said her mother, but she did not stop working between sink and stove.

Brigid looked at her back, moving from board to saucepan, peeling and slicing, the fragrance of apples and cinnamon floating above. Apple crumble.

Brigid was not going to get pneumonia. She was better, and she was not going to be sick again, even to get away from school. Too much time got lost with sickness. All she wanted was for everyone to be well, and stay well, and life to be the way it used to be.

She watched the stairwell, and presently saw her father come carefully down the last few steps, his hand on the newel post as if to steady himself.

In her head she said: Don't have bad eyes again. See me. See me, and make everything right.

As if in answer, he looked up from the ground where he had carefully placed his last step, saw her, and put his hand on her head, the long fingers covering most of her scalp.

"How's my girlie?" he said as they went into the kitchen. "And how's the new book?"

"It's very good, Daddy," said Brigid, because she did not have the heart to tell him it was too hard for her. "It's my nicest book," she said, which was not untrue because it was certainly the most colourful.

He smiled, all the creases round his eyes appearing in their kind lines. "Good girl. Your brother has a new book too. I got him a Maurice Walsh," he said above Brigid's head to her mother, who was leaning to take out the pie. "He'll like that."

The smell of lamb and potato and apple drifted through the room.

Her mother nodded. "He will," she said, but her voice was sad. Francis had clearly not told their father he did not want to read, and nobody else was going to do it. Nobody wanted him upset, too.

The next morning brought a change: she was to go with her father to Mass. Brigid had never before been considered suitable for Mass but, with Francis out of action, she found herself in her father's car, travelling the school route, down to the monastery, with its great spires. It was different from school days: everywhere was quiet, like the day she met George Bailey. There were so few cars. No children played on the lamp-posts, and in the parks all the swings were looped back with chains. The whole town seemed to be holding its breath.

In the vast lofty space of the monastery, her nostrils filled with scented smoke, and singing voices floated across pictures of Heaven. Perhaps they were angels? It was very beautiful, and very strange, and Brigid did not do very well. The elastic of her hat hurt. She took it off. A lady behind her tapped her on the shoulder. "Ladies wear hats," she whispered, and her breath smelled of sour fruit. "Brigid," said her father, in a cold whisper she had not heard him use before, and she put her hat back on. Then, everything went on too long. The priest talked and talked, and Brigid could not understand him, though she gathered his news was not good. It was easier not to listen. If Francis had been there, she might have followed what was happening, but her father seemed to think she knew what to do. It irked him to find her watching him twirl his hat as the priest spoke, and her fascination at the practised flick with which he pulled up his trouser leg before he knelt down seemed to irritate him further.

He told her to be still and Brigid, several times rebuked, hardly dared move. She tried to pass the time by counting the number of pink hats and blue hats on the ladies' heads, but their edges softened and merged the further away they got. Then, she could not understand why only ladies and girls wore hats, and why she had to wear this tight elastic strap under her chin to keep her own hat on, while the men and boys did not. And, where was the priest? She could see a green shape moving very far away, she could hear bells and smell scented smoke, but where was the priest when he was not in the high stone well, shaking his arm and warning them?

Brigid pulled her father's sleeve. She had to know. "Daddy," she said, "are we meant to be able to see the priest?"

He took her arm in a firm grip and, leaning in to her said, crossly: "Brigid, I won't tell you again. Behave yourself. I'm surprised at you."

Brigid was silent then, but she thought: I'm not coming here again if I can help it. Maybe they were not meant to be able to see the priest, just believe in him, like God.

She took her father's hand when it finally came to an end – all the standing and sitting and kneeling, and the prayers in words she did not understand. She had never been so glad to see daylight as she was when they approached the great door that stood open at the back of the monastery.

Outside, she drank in the cold air like water. She stood quietly in the shadow of her father's coat while a tall, wide, wild-haired man swung towards them in a long black frock, like a nun without the butterfly hat. That must be the priest, out of his colours. He showed no interest in Brigid but, as she was all too conscious of having behaved badly, she did not question this. The wild-haired man talked to her father over her head as if she were not there.

"How's the young man? Been in the wars, I hear?" he said.

"Oh, he'll live," said her father.

"A bad business, all the same," said the priest.

"Yes," said her father, "but, still, it could have been worse."

"Times are dangerous still, no matter what anybody says," said the priest, just like Mr Doughty, just like Mr Steele.

Why did everybody have to keep saying that?

They shook their heads, then shook hands.

"We can only pray," said the priest. "Prayer moves mountains."

That was a new and interesting thought but, before she had time to consider it, to Brigid's surprise, the priest put out his hand, a wide hand bigger than her father's, and placed it hard on the top of her head. It hurt in her head and her neck, but she did not say. She would not remember the time when her head hurt.

"We'll not make a Redemptorist out of this one. Still, I'm sure she's a good girl, and a big help to her mammy."

Her father pulled her close to him: "She's the best girl," he said, and Brigid knew she was forgiven.

Smiling her goodbyes to the priest, suddenly her friend, she caught out of the side of her eye a glimpse of a shape she knew. It was just a shape, and too far away for her to be sure, but it was so like Isobel that, in spite of herself, Brigid felt a pang. Then the figure turned round, and she was sure. Under that pink hat was Isobel's face. She was standing beside a young man, and their heads were together.

"Daddy!" she said. "Look! There's Isobel. She must be back from her holidays. Can we drive her home?"

To her surprise, he did not look round. "You must be mistaken, Brigid," he said. "How could that be Isobel? And, in any case, I had an idea we might go somewhere – and it's not in the direction of home."

"Oh, where, Daddy?" asked Brigid, all thought of Isobel falling from her head. Perhaps it was unkind of her not to want to go home, but it was sad and lonely there at the moment, and Brigid did not want to be sad, or lonely. She much preferred to go somewhere and be happy.

"Well, for a start, after that long morning, I thought you might like an ice cream."

Brigid closed her eyes. "Oh, Daddy," she said and, already tasting in her mind the bliss of that cold delicious shock, she jumped up and down at the side of the car until he opened the door. She climbed in, pulling off the hat with grim pleasure, and tossed it into the back seat.

And, to her joy, her father kept his word. They did not turn for home, but swung towards town, past all the little shops, quiet for Sunday, and her father parked in the bombed-out car park. Brigid was too happy to think of the sad child's bedroom. If she did not look at it, it was not there. He walked her into the Continental Café, the only place in all the town that was open, and he bought her a large cone, the answer to her prayers. They sat in a red booth, and he drank coffee, its dark burnt smell carrying over the ice cream. She ran her tongue round the creamy loveliness, watching him. She saw him happy, drinking a very little cup of coffee and, for a small contented time, they sat quietly together.

Then, Brigid said: "Daddy, where is Dover Street?"

He inclined his head a little to the side: "Just up there, a little way up the road. We passed it on the way down. Why do you ask?" He looked at her, but his face held no expression she could read.

"Just the name," she said, carefully. "I just like the name."

"I doubt your brother does," he replied.

"Oh, no," Brigid heard herself say, too late to stop it, "he does."

"How do you know that?" said her father, in surprise.

She could smell his coffee-breath, and her ice cream was melting.

"He told me," she said.

"Did he?"

"Yes," said Brigid. "And he said we are all children of other lands, but I don't know what he meant."

Her father looked away, then down at his hands. "I think I know what he meant."

102

Brigid's hopes rose. "Well, Daddy, will you tell . . ."

Then she stopped. The door had opened, the mist of the warmth inside dispersing to show two figures. One was the housekeeper from next door and, at her side, reluctant, truculent, dark hair tumbling, breathing hard as if he had been running, stood Ned Silver. If her father was surprised, he did not show it. He rose to his feet, and invited them to join them.

Ned slid in beside her, and, to her surprise, Brigid heard her father say: "This is a coincidence! Mrs Mulvey, with your permission, I'd like to take your young charge with us on a little outing I'm planning for my daughter. It would be nice for her to have company, when her brother's not well. Would you allow him to go with us?"

Mrs Mulvey lifted a hand to her brow. "Mr Arthur," she said, "at this moment, I'd give him away with a packet of cornflakes. He has come home from school a little . . . shall we say, a little early. His father, I'm sure you know, is not at home, and I am finding this young man . . ."

Here, Ned turned and looked straight at her, and Brigid could not help noticing how blue his eyes were, deep like the sea, and cold as ice.

Mrs Mulvey checked herself. "He needs interesting things to do until he goes back to . . . back to school."

Ned snorted. It was a new noise to Brigid, and she resolved to try it as soon as she could.

"Perfect," said her father. "Then we can have a proper trip to the country, and Mrs Mulvey can have a rest. How will that do for a surprise, Brídín?"

Before she could respond, he rose and went to the counter, holding up his hand to get the attention of the waitress.

Mrs Mulvey took her handbag, said, "No, Mr Arthur, please, let me," and propelled herself towards the counter to stand beside him.

Brigid, suddenly unprotected, was almost too taken aback to speak. She swallowed, and tried to think what was not right about this, but she could not. Her mind was a muddle. She rather wanted to go home, now that she had had her ice cream, but she also wanted the surprise of . . . a surprise.

Then, Ned dug his sharp elbow in her ribs. "Mulvey took me to the monastery," he said, and he snorted again. It really was an impressive noise.

"Me, too," said Brigid. "Don't poke me."

"Yes, but you're a Catholic. I'm not. There'll be hell to pay when my father finds out. I wasn't poking you. "

"Ned, you're not allowed to say –"

"Oh, shut up, Brigid. I want to tell you something."

"What?"

"In the car."

"What about? Tell me?"

"For a start, about your Isobel."

"I thought I saw her at the monastery!"

"I know," said Ned. "You did. Me too. But that's not all."

"What, Ned, what?"

"In the car," said Ned and, smiling in such a way that for a moment his eyes looked warm, and soft, he took the ice cream Brigid's father handed him.

Chapter 10: Isle Lecale

Still uneasy, Brigid found herself in the back of the car with Ned Silver, heading out of town past the gasworks, through the markets, all shut down for Sunday. The town might be asleep, but she was not, and Ned Silver was to tell her something she wanted to hear. Yet, to her annoyance, as soon as Ned felt the motion of the car, he lay back and closed his eyes.

"Ned," she said, elbowing him as he folded, catlike, into the seat, "what were you going to tell me?"

Ned shifted, languidly. He opened his eyes. They were navy blue now, telling her nothing. He said: "Did I say I was going to tell you something?" He closed his eyes again, and a slow smile curved upwards from his mouth. "I wonder what it was."

Exasperated, Brigid snorted. It was a good snort, for a first effort – but it was a mistake.

"Brigid!" said her father. "Behave yourself, or I'll turn the car and there'll be no visit to Granda."

"Are we going to see Granda?" said Brigid, surprised.

"Haven't I just said so?" replied her father, and drove on in silence.

Brigid sat back beside Ned, conscious in spite of her annoyance of his sleepy warmth. Dark buildings streamed past her, shuttered windows and empty streets. She watched the town turn into scattered houses, barren roads. Above her waved a few forlorn leaves on cold trees, and she remembered with longing the delicate dancing green of summer mornings. Then the close, tight-packed houses cleared away and there, spread out before her, rising and falling in little hills, was the countryside.

"I've never been in an aeroplane," her father said suddenly, "and I don't intend to be, but I have heard the county of Down, if you see it from the air, looks like a basket of eggs. I can't say."

"Yes, it does," said Ned, unexpectedly. "I have."

"And me," added Brigid, not to be left out.

"Liar," said Ned, and turned his shoulder away from her.

"What did your mama tell you about drumlins, Brigid? Do you remember?" said her father, as if Ned had not spoken.

"Ice," said Brigid. "It left . . . a basket of eggs."

"Fool," muttered Ned, from the far side of the seat. "I did this in school. The ice age left them behind – sheets of ice across the land." He yawned and, turning a little towards Brigid, opened his eyes. "Thousands of years ago. When it melted, there were drumlin hills. In France too. Even in America."

"Well done, Ned," said Brigid's father. "That's a powerful school they sent you to, isn't it?"

Ned, eyes closed again, folded his arms and lay back in silence. Brigid looked at her father's eyes in the mirror and saw his admiration for Ned's knowledge. She felt, as Ned had said, a fool, yet still she was entranced by the light through the autumn branches, bright moments like happy thoughts in the time before school. She loved to see the trees marching up the hill on the road outside the town of Tonaghneave. Her father said it meant "the field of saints", though why the saints were in a field she could not fathom, unless the saints were the people she saw in the trees, old and gnarled, young and dancing, many legs and arms in joyous movement. Sometimes one or two stood whispering together, and others waved branchy arms at them, or changed shape, playing with them, just as they came close enough to see their faces, suddenly shifting or else just standing like a tree, just standing as if that was all they did. The warm car purring, the leather seat soft and giving as a pillow, Ned's breathing slowing beside her, Brigid let time and place subside.

It was with surprise that she found herself suddenly in the town of Downpatrick, unable at first to know why she was in the back of her father's car, or why Ned Silver lolled sleeping beside her. His hands lay loosely clasped in his lap, and one skinned kneecap swung towards her. His legs were longer since the summer. He had long fingers, too, slender and delicate and, somehow, that was perplexing. Then Ned's knee jerked as the car swung past the old gaol, and hit Brigid's own knee. It was hard, and it hurt. She wished she had a pin, or a sharp pencil.

"Nearly there," said her father, and his voice came as a shock in the humming silence. "If anyone's awake, we're in Isle Lecale."

Ned opened his eyes, and shot upright as if he had never been asleep.

"But it's not an island, is it, Mr Arthur?"

"Hello, again, Ned. I thought you two were out for the count."

Ned's face, eager and alive, closed up again. "I'm sorry, sir," he said, as though he were at school.

"There's no need to be," said Brigid's father. "It's a good point you make. Once it was an island, surrounded by water, and it was called Isle Lecale. It's an old place and our family is part of it. My father courted my mother here."

At this, Ned's face shut down again, and he was once more dark and watchful. He sank back on the seat and stared out of the window.

Brigid's father looked backward in the driving mirror. "You'll see the place we lived in, Ned. It stands at the edge of the world."

Ned said nothing, but Brigid saw him look up, and meet the eyes of her father in the mirror. In a burning, jealous moment, she felt she had no part in the outing and she hated Ned Silver.

She also hated her father for bringing him. She longed for Francis, but he was far away. She was on her own here.

They made their way through Downpatrick's hills and steep slopes, out into country again and, in the reflection of the glass she so sullenly watched, the car itself was curved and rounded like a drumlin. In spite of herself, she felt first quiet, then almost content as they turned away from Downpatrick, down into the hedges and stubble fields, past the shining stillness of the lough. They drove through a large port, smelling of fish, little boats in the harbour touching then separating, birds wheeling and crying their secret messages above in the mackerel sky. The car cruised through little coastal towns, empty now of the sounds of summer people and, as they passed beneath the trees of Port St Anne, Brigid and Ned, forgetting their quarrels, turned to each other and held their noses, united in disgust at the odour of seaweed. Brigid's father laughed, and she forgot the seaweed. She could not remember the last time she had heard him laugh.

They pulled up in front of a dark, stone-clad house. The engine stopped, and Brigid's mind filled with the silence of the sea. Gradually, she began to hear the off-key clinking of two masts hob-bobbing below in the waters. Beyond, she saw little islands, the drowned drumlins, and above them lonely seabirds, calling back as they flew towards a far-off windmill on a hill.

The children slid out of the car, and Ned slammed the door shut, watching with satisfaction its effect on the startled birds. Brigid, not to be outdone, climbed boldly up the high sloping sidewall of the steps, balancing like a tightrope walker, as she had often seen Francis do. It piqued her that her father, knocking the heavy iron on the recessed door, did not notice that she had managed this by herself, and Ned said nothing, moving from one foot to the other, staring out to the wide sea, and the vast open sky, scudding away from them. Brigid's father rang the bell a second time. Nothing happened. He rang it again and, then, slowly they heard bolts being undone.

A tall woman like a gatekeeper blocked the doorway. Behind

in the hall, a grandfather clock sang one calm chime.

Then Brigid's father reached to his head to raise his hat, a curious, graceful movement which meant the hat did not leave his head, yet rose, as if in a light wind and then resettled, all in a second. "Tish," he said.

"Maurice," said the woman, without expression, and Brigid wished herself far away. "You've brought the children," she said, and looked at Brigid without warmth. She stepped aside, one sharp eyebrow raised as she saw Ned. "Or, no," she said. "You haven't. Who's this?"

She stared at Ned, and Brigid wanted to stand in front of him.

"Our neighbour," said Brigid's father, taking his hat from his head and moving towards the door. "Aren't you going to let us in, Tish? This is Ned Silver. Ned, let me introduce you to my sister, Miss Laetitia Arthur."

Ned, suddenly gracious, extended his hand: "How do you do, Miss Arthur?" he said, in a voice Brigid had never heard him use. She was impressed.

Laetitia looked at him. "Where's my Frankie?" she said. "Where's my boy?"

Brigid's father did not reply for a moment, his mouth a sudden pale line. Then he said: "He got a bit of a knock. Horseplay near the school. Boys."

That half-truth. Brigid, silently ashamed, met Ned's eyes out of sight of the adults. Lies, said Ned's eyes, and the half-lift of his lip said: What do you expect?

Now Brigid moved closer to Ned and her father, hanging back slightly. Perhaps Laetitia would go away. They stepped into the hall, dark-panelled, its chequered pattern of tiles cold as the air outside, and Brigid looked up at Laetitia, standing above her, as in judgment. Her hair was like a greying bush, wild and tame at the same time, and had a streak of dark running through it at one side. She was a backwards badger, she said, sometimes, when she was in good humour.

"Well, Biddy," she said, "you're no beauty, anyway." She

laughed, as if she had made a joke. "You take after your mother. They should have left your hair long. Who did you say this is?"

She had turned from Brigid and now stood appraising Ned. Brigid kept close to her father as he introduced Ned all over again. Laetitia said she liked him because, she said, she did prefer boys to girls, who were sneaky and hard to teach and she ought to know for she had taught enough of them, and you could give her a boy any day over a sleekit girl, sly and lazy, and where was her Frankie, her own boy, and it all had to be explained again, to be slid over again. Laetitia said they should have let her know they were coming, because she was going out to Mass and she would be back later, but they weren't to count on her if they had somewhere else to be. Brigid did not relax until her sharp perfume swept past her, and she heard the front door close, and felt the silence that said she was gone.

"Bloody hell. What was that?" said Ned, under his breath.

Brigid, glad of the advantage, said, "Tell you later. You've to tell me stuff first," though how she was to explain Laetitia she did not know.

At least, while Laetitia was out, she could go into the back room and hope to find her grandfather. Her father led them into the room and there, at last, she saw the long figure of her grandfather unfold from a chair, tall, a gleam of a fob in his waistcoat. Her heart began to be happy again as he reached down to shake her hand. He was gentle, and very quiet today. He looked for a moment at Ned. Then, he reached into the pocket of his waistcoat and lifted out a silver watch, detaching the chain from his waistcoat and its buttonhole. He handed the watch to Ned. Brigid was not pleased: on other visits, Francis had been given this, but she never had. Why should Ned?

Brigid's grandfather sat down again and watched Ned turn over the watch. Brigid, aggrieved, really wished her grandfather would stop looking at Ned, and give her something to play with, but he did not. He sat, watching, and then he said: "Do you know, Maurice, I was thinking the other day about Parnell."

Brigid's father shifted in his chair. It creaked, and he sighed. "A few weeks ago, that was, Pop," he said. "Ivy Day is the sixth of October. According to Mr Joyce, anyway." He turned to the children, perched together on a narrow wooden settle, Ned absorbed, Brigid truculent. "There's something new for you two. Ivy Day is the name for the anniversary of the death of Parnell."

Ned and Brigid, bemused, looked at each other.

"Do you know what that means?" Brigid asked Ned, under her breath.

He shrugged. "Of course," he said. "Everybody does. But it's ancient history."

"Like the drumlins?"

Ned slid his eyes across to her, and then back to her grandfather's watch. "Round the same time," he said, looking hard at the watch.

"Yes, well, when you get to my age, a few weeks here and there hardly matters," Brigid's grandfather was saying. "Do you know, children," he said, and now he turned to them, "I stood on the platform with Parnell?"

More of this Parnell. What was it, and why did it matter, all of a sudden? Nobody had said anything about it before. Brigid, confused, shook her head, but Ned sat up. Maybe he did know something: after all, there was the drumlin business. In any case, interested or not, she was going to have to hear whatever it was, because her grandfather had settled back, placed the tips of his fingers together, crossed one leg over the other, and that meant he was going to tell them whatever was on his mind.

"It must have been 1881," he said.

"Told you," whispered Ned. "Ice age."

"Or was it '81? I can't have been much more than your age." He leaned forward. "Maybe not even as old as this young man!"

Ned sat up, so suddenly that Brigid almost went right off the settle. She wished they would give them a chair each. Then, as if he had heard her, her grandfather reached out and took her onto his knee. In his pocket he sometimes had sweets for her, she knew, and she slipped her hand into it as she settled down and, sure enough, there was one. She slid it out and, as if by magic, all her rage dispersed. She gave no sweet to Ned. She was comfortable in the crook of her grandfather's arm, enjoying the sound of the paper she was unwrapping, the smooth sharp colours sliding and crunching between her teeth, and the smell of his tobacco and soap, and the look on Ned's face when he lifted his eyes and saw that she had a sweet and he did not. Brigid's eyes sent him a message: he's my granda, not yours, so there.

Ned's eyes sent back: so what?

Brigid felt less triumphant, and her grandfather was still talking. "You know," he said, "I did not realise the importance of that day. My father – your great-grandfather, Brigid – was the secretary to the Land League and he believed in the right of the farmer to the land where he wrought."

Brigid felt her mind glaze, but she tried to follow. It would be over more quickly if she tried, like school.

"So he built a platform for Parnell outside his baker's shop. Did you know he was a baker, as well as a farmer?"

Brigid shook her head, thinking: I don't care. She found it even harder to pay attention to this story.

"Well, Parnell came, and addressed the people at a big meeting of the Land League and I stood beside him, beside my father. I can hear the roars of the people. I can hear them clapping Parnell and my poor father."

Brigid, giving up, drifted, and noted that Ned seemed interested. Good, she thought: you like this story, you can have it.

"Why was your father poor, Mr Arthur?" said Ned. "Did he lose his money?"

"Oh, son, he lost more than his money. When the sca – when things went wrong for Parnell, the people turned against my father because he had supported him, and we had to leave our farm and that town."

Brigid, drifting back, heard her grandfather say that they had to leave the farm. The farm her mother grew up on was a happy place. She said: "It would have been nicer for you to stay on your farm."

Her grandfather, with a short laugh, replied: "Girlie, there may be happiness in a family, or there may not, but there is nothing nice about a farm. It is hard, unremitting and thankless work."

"Mr Arthur, sir," said Ned, so polite and so interested that Brigid thought she was hearing things, "how did things go wrong for Mr Parnell?"

Her grandfather set Brigid down on the ground, but he did not answer. Then he drew something from his wallet. "Look, now. Here's his Land League Card. I doubt you will ever see one of these again."

"Pop. Do you think they're ready for that?" said her father, and Brigid saw the animation die in her grandfather's eyes.

Sadly, the grandfather put away the faded card, and Brigid felt sorry. It had got more interesting. It was suddenly a story, and now she wanted to know what happened next, and to look at the pictures and the writing on the card.

Ned seemed disappointed, too. He shifted in the seat. "Mr Arthur," he said, "may I visit your bathroom?" and with a glance at Brigid that said, you're on your own, he went off up the stairs, two at a time.

Brigid's heart dropped. She wished she had Francis here. Ned was mean to leave her, when the only interesting story had been stopped. She slid, unnoticed, out of the room, thinking to find Ned. In the hall, as if far away, she could hear the voices of the two men, their brown voices going over another time . . . "Land League . . . Parnell . . . even today . . ." No help there: they were still in the past. Then, suddenly, she heard the words change. "That wild night. January . . ."

This was different. This might be another story. Brigid began to listen again and, as she did, she heard the front door open and close. Laetitia was back. Brigid, safely in the shadows, could see her, slowly taking off her coat, and it was clear that she was listening too and then Brigid saw her walk boldly into the room without announcing herself. She slipped back in herself, then, lingering near the door.

"The storm," Laetitia said, as if she had been there all along. "All those people lost. He tried to save a woman. They told us that. But he was lost."

Brigid was interested now. Was this the story no one would tell her? The almost-uncle who was lost? He was lost trying to save someone, but from what? And how was he lost? She decided to risk asking. "How was he lost, Laetitia?"

"I just said. On the *Princess Victoria*, of course, trying to save someone," said Laetitia.

But Brigid still did not know how, because no one ever answered her question.

A chair scraped: her father was on his feet. That was enough talk, she heard him say, his voice rising: there was no point going over it all again, nothing would bring him back, or anyone for that matter, and if they were to be home that night, they'd better get on.

Brigid said: "Aren't we going down to see the house at the edge of the world?"

"Not today," said her father, and his voice told Brigid there was no room for discussion.

So, there was no trip to the edge of the world after all, and still no story about the *Princess Victoria*. No one did what they said they would do and, as well, there was no tea. It did not make sense: they talked and talked about things in the ice age, but people got lost and could not be found, and she had no one at all to discuss it with her, now that Francis was ill. She stopped: what if Francis were lost? Would they not find him either? And where had Ned Silver got to?

"Where's Ned?" she said aloud. She did not see him, but she felt his eyes, somewhere, looking at her. Turning, she saw him crouched at the turn of the stairs, looking down from the landing, like a small ghost. Brigid wondered how long he had been there. For no reason, watching him, she felt cold, and seeing that his eyes were not on her after all, but past her, she realised he was looking straight at Laetitia, and that he had heard what she said about the *Princess Victoria*, and she remembered: his mother. His mother was lost too.

"Did you find the bathroom, Ned?" said her grandfather, suddenly behind her.

Ned met the old man's eyes, and nodded. He uncurled, slowly, and seemed to tumble down the stairs, as if his legs were not quite steady.

"Do you know," said Brigid's grandfather, looking straight at Ned, "I think there would be time to run down quickly and see the house, if the children would like it, before the evening draws in." He reached out his hand to Ned, and Ned took it, trustingly, like a small child. "Come on," he said, "till we see what we shall see."

Outside, in the blessed light, Brigid turned to Ned: "Where did you get to?"

"Tell you later," said Ned.

"You haven't told me anything, Ned," said Brigid and dug him hard with her nails.

He dug her back, hard, far harder than she had him. "And I won't, now," he said, "but I could. If I wanted."

"I'm not telling you anything, either, then," Brigid replied. "And I could, too. If I wanted, which I don't."

The car slid away from the dark house, and the October sun dappled over the faces of the silent children.

Chapter 11: The Point

They drove out of Port St Anne, away from the narrow dark house, down towards the sea. Still, the children did not speak. Brigid's father opened the window: the salty air, the sharp bite of the wind and the sound of one lone seagull hit Brigid like a slap.

In the mirror, she met her father's eyes.

"Brigid, try to be less sullen," he said. "This is for your benefit."

Brigid opened her mouth, then closed it again. She wanted to blame Ned, but could not think how. And there was no fight in him now. She felt a little sorry for him, small and curled into the corner of the car. There was nothing to fight with.

She said: "Sorry, Daddy."

He was no longer listening. He had turned off the road into a narrow lane, and driven in a circle so that they pointed again towards the little town of Port St Anne. The car stopped, he opened the window, and the cold salt of the sea floated in.

"Look outside to your right," he said, "and you will see the house."

The children looked. Far away, across a headland of grass and sheep, they saw a small chimney with no smoke, a sad and lonely little house right at the side of a cliff. Seabirds hovered about it and, in a cove below, water boiled and bubbled in frothy foam.

Brigid drew a sharp breath. "Granda!" she said. "It *is* the edge of the world!"

Ned, white-faced, pressed his forehead to the window, and said nothing.

"Right," said Brigid's father. "Home, I think."

"But . . . Daddy? Aren't we going to get out?"

"Brigid, for the love of . . ."

"Too cold today," said her grandfather, "and too near the edge of dark. The next day you come, maybe we'll go out to the farm on the Point. But you can see the lighthouse. Look now, it's over there. You can just make it out!"

Brigid, disappointed, looked across the grey sea and saw a tall shape like the pillar of a gate, standing lonely on a rock. She shivered. She did not want to go there, now. She wanted to go home. In the silence, she heard her father turn the key. The engine rattled and started, throbbing as though impatient for them to be gone.

"Maurice," said her grandfather, "is something the matter? You're out of sorts."

Her father, already easing the car across the gravel, gave his head a slight shake. "I have a slight headache, Pop. That's all."

There was a silence.

"Still?" said his father. "Still, that headache? Shouldn't you see about it?"

There was no reply. In a stiff silence, they drove back to the house. All the while, Brigid's grandfather told the children the story of the house at the edge of the world.

The farm, he said, where he had come to court Brigid's grandmother was tucked away at the end of a narrow lane, a loanen. In summer, it was thick with brambles and red flowers of fuchsia, and if they came at the right time they might eat the sweet blackberries. For a second, Brigid tasted the blackcurrants from the summer garden at home. Ned did not appear to be listening, but Brigid did not care. It was her family, her story. When you walked down the loanen, said her grandfather, fields fell away on either side, silent, golden. Far away would be the sound of men working, distant shouts, no word distinct. Nearby, the quiet would be complete, not silence, but stillness, one bird singing, the sea breathing itself in and out, and they would taste salt in their nostrils as they walked through the cart-ruts, dried on the ground between the high hedges. Then they would see it, tucked away in a hollow.

It would come and go, he said, through the brambles, till they would round a small bend, and they would look across the gate and the pillar into the field, and then they would walk down to the edge of the world, to the Churn Rock they had just seen, boiling and bubbling, and they would hear the sound of the great sea crashing against the rocks below the lighthouse, winking far away. They would make their way over the field, between the grooves where the tractor had made its cuts, and then they would see the water swirling and splashing below, a high crescent of salt spray dashing the inside of the little inlet below the house. He said smugglers came past in the old days. Ned turned towards him for a moment, but only a moment, and the grandfather said he knew a sheltered place for a picnic, big rocks behind them, the calm sea away from the Churn Rock, smooth but white-capped, and they would look out as far as the Isle of Man.

Brigid settled into the back of the car, and she felt she had been, after all, to the house on the Point. Ned, silent again, seemed to be watching the sky go by through the hedge, over the horizon. Brigid turned her head. Behind them, the lighthouse had begun to blink in the gathering gloom and she could no longer see the little house.

"Granda," she said, "why is no one there now?"

"Oh, families die out, Brigid," he said, and then there was no sound but the engine of the car.

In the cooling evening, lonely seabirds calling, the car drew up once again outside the stone house. Brigid's father turned off the engine, pulled on the brake, and then the silence was, for a moment, complete.

118

Her grandfather reached for the door handle, and opened it to the air. "Frost," he said. "I can feel it in my bones."

"I can feel it in mine," said his son.

Brigid, who could not feel it in her bones, had a more pressing concern. "Granda," she said, "will you come and see us? See Francis?"

"I will," he said. "Very soon." He looked across at his son, sitting silent at the wheel. "I have business anyway to see to in the city, and one of these mornings I'll be on your doorstep." He paused again, still looking at his son. "I'll tell you what: I'll come next week at Samhain. Would you like that?"

"Yes," said Brigid, "but what is sow-an?"

It was too late. A light came on in the hall, and her grandfather, unfolding stiffly from the car, stood up straight.

"I'm done," he said. "I'm an old done man."

Ned, pulling at the door handle, made to get out of the car.

"You children don't need to come in," said Brigid's father, with some irritation. "We should get on the road."

His father looked at him in mild surprise. "They might need to pay a visit before the journey."

Ned spoke up. "May I visit the bathroom, sir?"

"Oh," said Brigid's father. "Yes. I didn't think. Of course, I suppose so."

"And Brigid had probably better, too, hadn't she?" said Ned.

"I think so," said the grandfather, eyeing Brigid as he reached in a deep pocket for his latchkey.

"But I don't want . . ." Brigid began.

"You do," said Ned and, most unexpectedly, took her hand and squeezed it hard. He whispered in her ear, so close that his lips tickled her: "I'm going to show you something."

He held on to her, not comfortably, but tightly, as they climbed out of the car and followed her grandfather's slow step. Once through the door, Ned steered her straight upstairs, and along a dim corridor.

"Ned," said Brigid, pulling back on his arm, "that was the

bathroom there. You've passed it!"

"Oh, bugger the bathroom," said Ned.

"Ned!" said Brigid, shocked, though secretly she was impressed, and stored it up.

"In here," said Ned, and he pushed her into one of the rooms.

"Ned, this is one of the bedrooms. We're not meant to . . ."

"Oh, shut up, Brigid."

Another forbidden phrase was squirrelled away. "Do you want to see something or not?"

Brigid was torn. She knew they should not be here. She wished she were out in the car with her father. She did not know whose room this was, and looked nervously behind her. It had a silver-backed hairbrush on the dressing table, and hanging on the wardrobe was a coat of fine wool. Over its shoulder hung a silver fox, its eyes glittering at her. Her mother had one of those in her wardrobe, but it was dark brown, soft and sad, and its eyes did not glitter. Only one person she knew had a silver, glittering fox: Laetitia. They were in Laetitia's room.

She could hear her grandfather's voice downstairs, coming through the hall: "Are you children nearly ready? Maurice wants to get on the road."

"Ned," she began again. "How did you . . . ? Why did you . . . ?"

"For God's sake, Brigid, don't you want to know things? This place is full of . . . Here. Pull open that cupboard."

It was a narrow cupboard, part of the dressing table.

"Go on," said Ned. "She keeps secret things in there."

Still, Brigid did not move.

"Maybe things for Christmas," he said. "Presents, maybe?"

That was too much. She pulled open the door: it gave with a soft pop, like a sigh. Then, suddenly, horribly, something sprang at her, dark and formless, and she inhaled a musty staleness so pungent that she put out her hands to push it back in again, yet she could not and, as she pushed, another thing, white, snapped viciously in her face. She tumbled backwards, one hand to her face, the other pushing away the enveloping cloud of dusty cloth.

On the ground, sitting, she tried to fight her way free, and found that the thing had collapsed on her. It was cloth, lots of cloth, and the white was a shirt collar, stiff and yellowing, and there was a dark square of something. These empty objects lay harmless, dead, in her lap. Now, she saw the dark cloth was almost green, the white tinged with yellow, and the things were just a man's jacket, a black shirt front, and a round collar. Brigid, her breathing coming more slowly, realised they were only old clothes.

She turned to Ned. He was watching her, smiling, and Brigid, in an instant, knew what he had done.

"You came in here that other time, when you went up to the bathroom. You knew what was in here. You did this on purpose."

"Go to the top of the class," he said. "Nice surprise?"

"But . . . why? Why did you do this to me, Ned?"

He did not move, and his smile stayed in place. "You're such good value, Brigid. You fall for anything."

"You're a horrible boy, Ned Silver," said Brigid, and she started to roll up the clothes, trying to push them back into the narrow space. It was not easy, and Ned did not help. He moved in an easy, leisurely way, like a young cat, prowling round the room, feeling the material of the curtains, picking up books, turning over the mirror, drawing out a hair from a hairbrush. Brigid grew hot, ashamed to be there, to be there with Ned.

"Brigid!" she heard. "Ned! Come on!" It was her grandfather's voice again.

Outside, the engine was revving. Her father must be growing impatient. She badly wanted to leave, but she could not, how could she, until the clothes were put away – and something was blocking them. Frustrated, and anxious now in case someone came to find them, she rolled and pushed, yet still something blocked her. She reached round the bundle, skinning her fingers as she pushed against the side of the cupboard. There was something in the jacket pocket.

Skinning her knuckles further, she reached in: her fingers

closed round a shiny pouch, slippery as a raincoat, and pulling it out, she felt it open. It held a packet of brown tobacco, musty, like damp leaves: tucked into the back of the pouch was a small piece of paper, with writing on it. The writing was very small, and blurred in places, but the signature was large, and Brigid read: *My-ra.*

"Myra," she said, aloud, but it made no sense, as a word or a name.

As she worked with one hand to squash the bundle of cloth into the cupboard, the box was suddenly snatched from the other and, angered and surprised, she saw Ned pull the paper from the box and stand, white-faced, staring at it.

"God," he said. "God."

"Ned," she said, "that has to go back. It has all to go back."

Ned said nothing, and at that moment Laetitia entered, a pale furious storm.

"You sneak, Brigid Arthur," she said, and her voice was a hiss. "You sly little . . ." She raised her hand to strike her, and Brigid, lifting her arm to protect herself, remembered Isobel, furious in the garden. She looked in despair for Ned, catching sight of him just behind the door. Then she saw him slide round it, and ease out into the corridor.

As Laetitia's hand fell on her upraised arm, she heard the lavatory flush, and Ned's voice saying: "I don't know, Mr Arthur. She was waiting out here while I went to the lavatory. I don't know where she is now."

So then there was her grandfather, standing at the doorway. He did not come in.

"Laetitia," he said. "Leave that child, now."

Laetitia, suddenly limp, took her hand away, and left the room. Brigid could hear her crying as she rattled down the stairs.

"I'm sorry, Granda," said Brigid, and she could not hold up her head. "I am really sorry."

Her grandfather lifted up her chin. "There's no harm done," he said. "It's time we cleared out some of those things anyway.

What good are they, now?" He took Brigid's hand, and led her gently down the stairs and out the door, past the silent woman standing in silence beside the car.

Her father's profile was like stone, his eyes looking straight ahead as she got in, and she knew, without a word being said, that Laetitia had told him what had happened.

Her grandfather said: "Go easy, Maurice. It was just curiosity. You were a child once yourself, and no angel." Then, turning to Brigid, he said to her: "I'll see you soon, girlie, and your brother too," and he reached into the car and placed his hand on her shoulder. "Don't mind Laetitia," he said, very quietly. "She takes it hard, still," but he did not say what she took hard, or why.

At the other side of the car, noiselessly, unnoticed, Ned Silver let himself in, and then they were driving away. Brigid watched her grandfather standing with his hands up, as if he were waving down an aeroplane from the sky. He grew smaller as the car gathered speed and Brigid still did not know what he meant, and her father had not said a word, and she was deeply ashamed.

Shocked still, baffled, and angry at Ned, she waited for him to speak. To her surprise, he was quiet, almost docile. His face was pale, turned away from her. She thought: someone must have found him out. Yet, no one had chided Ned that she had heard. Her father, his silent face in the mirror showing his disappointment in her, made no difference in his manner to Ned.

Brigid was cold, and could smell in her nostrils still the mustiness and neglect of the clothes in the cupboard. She did not know whose they were. Smelling the tobacco still on her fingers, she wondered why a piece of paper with writing on it was tucked into a packet of tobacco, or why Ned wanted it, and why he started to pray to God. She did not know why everyone was upset except Granda, and there was clearly no one she could ask. She concluded that Isobel had been right: she was just bad, and Ned was as bad – perhaps even worse – and they deserved all they got. Only, Ned got nothing. She looked at him again, and she was instantly sorry. Something had happened to him. His eyes were closed, and from under them she could see tears running down his face.

"Ned," she said, but there was no answer.

It began to rain, and the swishing of the water beneath the wheels ended the outing. Their drive was silent, the wet road sliding along below the wheels. The tree people were not to be seen; the drumlins crouched, hidden, under misted blankets. After a long, uncomfortable time, with no word spoken, they turned into their driveway, and saw a figure silhouetted in the door.

There would come a time in her life when Brigid would know what it was to stand at a door, waiting for someone who had gone away, but that time was not yet. On the October night in 1955 when she sat behind her father in his car, drawing up to the house that was her home, all she saw in the silhouette at the lighted door was trouble. She knew in that moment that her father had not told her mother he was taking her away for the day. Looking across at Ned, she knew, too, that there was no help there. In the silence after the shutting off of the engine, he sat motionless, then pulled at the silver handle on the inside of the door.

"Thank you, Mr Arthur," he said. "You were very kind to take me with you," and then, halfway out of the car, he turned to Brigid, whispering something so low, so indistinctly that she could make out only two words.

She hissed back at him, secrecy now instinctive: "Isobel's brother *what*?"

He was gone. The door closed with a bang, and she was left, with her father, to face her mother. As she climbed the steps, slowly, she was prepared, following the scene with Laetitia, for anything, except what happened. Her mother, dark against the door, began to cry when she saw them, saying over and over: "Thank God."

Brigid saw her father hang his head, and watched the lines at the side of his face deepen.

"I'm sorry, Grace," he said. "I should have let you know. I . . . I didn't think."

Her mother stood crying in the doorway, and Brigid, feeling the cold, did not know how to go into her own house, until Francis appeared, took her hand, and said to his mother: "Brigid's getting cold." Then they were inside, and in the kitchen, and their parents went into the sitting room where she heard only the rise and fall of their voices, soft, loud, deep, high, until the sobbing stopped, and silence washed back.

"Daddy didn't tell her," Brigid said.

Francis shook his head. "No. About half an hour ago, Mrs Mulvey was putting out the milk bottles, and she saw Mama at our door and she said to her, 'Waiting for the travellers?' so Mama knew then he'd gone somewhere with you and Ned."

"But not where?" said Brigid.

"Not where," said Francis, and the silence of the night folded round the children until they grew tired, and went to bed. The closed door of the sitting room did not open, and no one said goodnight to them, except themselves.

Yet, next morning, it was as if none of it had happened. For a few seconds after she wakened, Brigid thought it had all been a strange and disturbing dream. Then, stretching out, she saw on her forearm a blue mark turning green, and she remembered. It had all happened. Yet, she could not talk about it, even to Francis, and part of her wanted to forget it all. Ned, the cause of it, was gone. When she came downstairs, the front door was open, and she heard her mother talking. Was it to herself? Brigid put her head, cautiously, round the front door, and was relieved to see that there was another person talking, unseen, from the other side of the garden fence. It was Mrs Mulvey. She knew the voice.

As she listened, Brigid heard Mrs Mulvey tell her mother that the little clip had been packed off to another school: "And let's hope he lasts a bit longer there," she said, "though I doubt it, the light-fingered monkey."

Ned's fingers had not seemed light to Brigid. Nonetheless, she was glad he had gone. Adventures with Ned came at a price.

Chapter 12: Samhain

It was good to have Granda come to stay, except that he brought Ireland with him, and far too much time was spent discussing the news. True, there was some excitement over a princess, and whether the Queen should let the princess marry her group captain, but Brigid did not care what the Prime Minister had said about partition, or know what it meant, even if everyone else did. Even Francis did.

"What was he asked, Granda?" he said. "The Prime Minister. What exactly?"

"He was asked," said his grandfather, adjusting his glasses and holding the paper away, "to comment on the possibility of settling the partition question, and he replied – I'm quoting this now – 'Ah, that is a matter for Irishmen. It's your show'."

"Is that all he said?" asked Francis.

"Let me see. My old eyes aren't as good as they were."

Brigid felt very bored, until her grandfather reached across to her and touched her arm: "Brigid, do you remember the word I told you in Irish for Hallowe'en?"

Francis, forgetting Ireland for a moment, caught her eye, and wrinkled his nose. He said: "Oink."

Brigid opened her eyes wide.

"Oink," said Francis again.

"Is it pig?"

"Close enough," he said. "*Samhain*: sow-an," and he touched his grandson's elbow, but Brigid remained confused about the pig, and how it got in there.

"Come for a walk with me to the post office," said her grandfather. "And don't mind that brother of yours."

Still, Brigid wondered about the pig. She wondered about it until they were some way down the road. "Granda?" she said. "Sow? Is that not for pig?"

He gave a little laugh, tipping his hat to Ned's housekeeper who walked past with her shopping bag. "Did you see the villain off to his school, ma'am?"

"Oh, I did, Mr Arthur," she said. "And villain he is!" She shook her head as she went on past.

"Granda," said Brigid. "Please. The sow."

"*Samhain*. Brigid. The night of Hallowe'en in Gaelic, the old Irish language, is *Oíche Shamhna*. Can you say that?"

"*Sow-an*," said Brigid, slowly. "*Ee-ha howna*. Where did the sow go?"

"It turned into 'how'," said her grandfather, and now they both laughed.

Brigid tried it a few more times, and found it pleased her.

They walked on, past the cemetery, and her grandfather crossed himself. Brigid thought of Mass.

"Is howna a Catholic word, Granda?"

He stopped. He was not laughing any more. "A what?" he said. "Brigid, what do you mean?"

"Francis says we're Catholic, but other people are other things. Do we have our own words? Catholic words?"

"Brigid," said her grandfather, and he shook her hand in his when he said it. "Ah, Brigid. What age are you now?"

"Five, Granda. Nearly five and a half."

"God above," he said. "Five years old, to be asking that."

"Nearly five and a half."

He nodded, shook her hand in his once more, and said nothing.

"Granda?" said Brigid.

"Yes, Brigid," he replied. "I'm coming to your question," but he walked on, and still said nothing.

Brigid opened her mouth to ask about howna again but, as she did, he spoke.

"Brigid," he said. "Listen carefully to what I have to say. The language belongs to us all. It's not anyone's property."

"But what does the howna mean, Granda?"

"As I told you, *Oíche Shamhna* means 'The Night of Hallowe'en', the eve of All Hallows, the night before the feast of all the saints. It's the night when the souls of the dead are free to visit their old homes."

Brigid drew breath, sharply. She could see the whiteness of it in the air, like a ghost. She said: "Ghosts, Granda?" and she held his hand more tightly.

"Ah, not ghosts, Brigid. One time, long ago, I heard an old man say: 'How would I be afraid with the souls of my own dead as thick as bees around me?' And how would he, or anybody? They're our own families and friends, who have gone on the journey we've all to take some day. We cannot see the spirits of our dead, but on this night they come back to be with us, and they are gentle and good, as they were in life. If we pay attention, we know they're there."

They turned to go into the post office. Brigid was not at all sure she liked the idea of the return of the dead, however friendly. Besides, there was a large queue in the post office, and she did not want to stand still in the crowded space. Yet, her grandfather did not seem to mind. He reached deep in his overcoat pocket for his money, standing with Brigid's hand in his behind the other people, some straight, some bent. Their coats brought in the cold from outside, and some of them shrugged their shoulders and rubbed their hands as they came in. "Skin fairies," said a man. "Hardy day," another.

Now her breath was not white, but steamy, and wet. Brigid moved from foot to foot, and wished the queue forward.

"Granda," she said, when a long time had passed. "Why are we standing?"

"I've some money to collect. And, I'm going to post a letter to Laetitia. She didn't behave very well the day you came to call, but she's a good girl at heart."

Brigid felt him sigh. "What is it, Granda?" she said. "Are you sad because she's a good girl at heart?"

"No, no," he said. "I'm always glad when I see that, though I don't see it often enough. No, I was wondering, so close to Samhain, how I lived to be so old, when young people lie across there in the cemetery."

Brigid followed his eyes. Through the misted window of the small post office, no bigger than a little house, she could make out the jagged stone wall of the cemetery. A long line of crosses faced towards them: they were the priests' graves. Were they saints? Brigid did not care for that stern, unbending line, staring at her as she stood in the post office. And now, she thought with alarm, all these saints under the crosses might be getting ready to visit tonight.

Just in time, the queue took a large step forward. The window moved behind her, and suddenly there was another window, small, with a grid. She saw a hand, long fingers flittering through a sea of papers and brown books and sets of stamps, then reaching for a big, shining stamper and stamping them with a thumping click, rolling it back and forth, flipping the book shut, then handing rustling papers under the grid. Her grandfather took the papers from the hands – where was the head? – and then, all at once, they were released from the steamy press to the blessed cold outside and turned, at last, away from the graves and the headless hands.

They passed the Glen and Brigid, remembering the judge's murdered daughter, tried to quicken the pace, but her grandfather was not a man to move quickly. It was a relief to see the smoke spiralling from their own chimney, up into the chilly sky. How warm the house looked! Brigid began to want to be inside. Then, from the corner of her eye, she saw that Francis was in the garage. Her heart leaped. He was not sitting in the house, listless and tired. He was out in the garage! She let go her grandfather's hand without a word, left him to go up the steps by himself, ran up the hilly passage and straight into Francis, busily rolling a spare tyre from the pile at the back of the garage. He looked up. He did not seem surprised to see her.

"Good," he said, as if she had been there all along. "You can help me. Take the small ones."

Brigid clapped her hands, and jumped. "Francis! Are we going to build the tyres?"

They had not done this since the summer.

"Yes, but don't jump. Roll them. Tyre houses, what do you think? A well, and – will we do a tunnel?"

Brigid, still jumping, nodded her agreement. She knew what to do. They rolled them, heavy and black, smelling of rubber and old petrol, out onto the square between the passageway and the house. Behind the kitchen windows she could hear the sounds of cooking, a clink of saucepans and the running of water, and the slow drifting smells of carrots and onions, sweet and sharp. Brigid stood and sniffed, and Francis, not stopping, said: "Come on, Bisto Kid, roll!"

It had been a long time since they had spent a morning rolling and crawling and calling and climbing. No one told them to be quiet; no one said they were making too much noise. Francis put Brigid in the well, and she followed him through a cavern to safety. A high stack was a tower; toppled, it was an escape tunnel, and Brigid followed Francis – he was now a group captain, she was a princess – scraping and crawling through the tyres, emerging dirty and breathless.

They were about to start a castle for the princess when they were called in for dinner, and Brigid gave her hands the scantest of washes before sitting down to the fragrance of carrots and onions and lamb. Francis took every vegetable he could find out of his food and set it on the side of his plate. No one said anything, no one minded that he did that, not even Brigid, because Francis was almost himself again.

Then the adults started again about the paper and the news, and Brigid grew restless. Once they started, Ireland would be the next thing. She signalled to Francis, nudging him with her knee beneath the table, but he ignored her. He was listening.

Their father said: "There's to be parole again for Christmas."

"Really?" said their grandfather.

"Apparently," and the paper got another slap, in the motion Brigid had come to dislike. "Yes, here it is. '*The Minister of Home Affairs in the Six Counties, Mr G.B. Newe, is to follow this year again the practice of allowing certain prisoners parole to spend Christmas with their families. Last year more than forty men in Crumlin Road Prison were allowed out on giving their word to return at the time fixed after Christmas.*'"

Francis said: "Don't they get out any other time?"

His father looked at Francis over his glasses. "Well, it seems they do," he said. "It says here that last Christmas '*not one man had broken his word*' and '*since then parole has been extended to include a summer break and liberty for family and business reasons*'." He stopped, looking away from his son to his father, and the two men exchanged glances.

"Well," said the grandfather, "that's humane."

"Yes," came the reply, "if it's right that they are there in the first place."

"Easy," said his grandfather, swivelling his eyes to the children and back. "No politics before . . ."

Brigid, impatient, tugged at the sleeve of her brother's jersey. "Francis," she whispered, "the tyres!" but he shook her off. He did it gently, but he still shook her off. Dicky clucked, and turned his back. You, too, thought Brigid and, affronted, got up without excusing herself and wandered over to the window. She wanted to be outside, playing, and she wanted Francis to hear her think it, and come with her – but Francis was as bad as the rest of them.

"I've seen them," he was saying, "over the wall from the College."

"Have you, son?" said his grandfather, in some surprise.

Francis nodded. "They always seem cold," he said.

His grandfather looked at him for a moment, then across at his own son. "Are they as close as that, Maurice?" he said.

"Close enough. The prison's next door to the College."

"Yes, but I didn't realise the boys would be able to see in," said the grandfather, turning back to Francis. "And they look cold?"

"Yes," said Francis. "They shiver. I think it's their exercise time when I see them. They look up at the sky. There's one man who always looks down at a book. He doesn't seem to mind as much." He paused. "I'm glad they're going to get home."

Brigid, edging beside him, moved from one foot to the other. "Francis," she said.

"I am, too," said the grandfather.

"Francis," said Brigid.

"Whatever they may have done," said the grandfather, looking at his son as though he too were a child, "I'm glad they get the chance to see their families at Christmas."

"Oh, please," said Brigid, tugging at Francis' sleeve, unable to wait any longer.

"Francis, please."

"What is it, Brigid?" said Francis, and he even sounded like an adult. "I'll be with you in a minute. Hold on."

"I . . . Nothing, Francis," said Brigid, and he turned back to the two men.

"I've . . . I've seen someone else, too," said Francis, his voice shaking a little, as if he were nervous. "I've seen Uncle Conor. With the man who reads. He talks to him, in the yard. Is he, do you think, is he visiting?"

"Cornelius Todd?" said his grandfather, in surprise. He turned to his son: "Maurice? Is young Todd still rebelly? I thought he . . ."

Brigid did not hear what her grandfather thought about Cornelius Todd, or her father's reply. Bored and impatient, she left the room and walked straight to the kitchen. Her mother was standing at the stove. She wore a loose blouse, long and navy-spotted, which Brigid did not like. It did not suit her. It widened her. She was leaning backward, holding her spine, stretching.

"Mama," said Brigid.

"What is it, Brigid?" said her mother, turning round. Her face was pale. Shadows showed beneath her eyes.

"I have nothing to do, Mama. Francis won't play with me. He just wants to sit and talk to Granda and Daddy about prisoners and Uncle Conor."

Her mother stood up straight. "Prisoners and . . . ? Tell Francis I want him. I've better things for both of you to do. Hop, now, go on!"

Brigid hopped. At the table, the long and tiresome conversation was still dragging on. "Nationalist," she heard, and "good family" and "interned" and "decent people" and "broke his mother's heart", before she delivered the message to Francis. She saw his frustration as he excused himself and got up, but he came and, before long, she had what she wanted. Together with Francis, she was standing wrapping threepenny bits in greaseproof paper to put inside apple tarts, and no one talked about prisons or Ireland or Uncle Conor.

"Wrap them up well, Francis," said his mother. "We don't want to choke anybody."

"Some people have rings in theirs," said Brigid. "Isobel said."

"We have threepenny bits," said her mother, "and that'll do us. You, Miss, get me over that basin."

Brigid, wondering if she could ask about Isobel, reached under the sink and brought out a white circular basin. She put it on the table and watched as Francis followed his mother's instructions, half-filling it with water from a jug. Then their mother placed two apples in it and set it on the floor.

"Now, down on your knees, hands behind your backs, take turns, and try to get the apple out with your teeth."

They splashed and snuffled until the tiles round the floor were awash, and their mother, the blue spotted smock splashed, put her hands on her hips, and laughed out loud as they had not heard her do in a long time.

Quickly, skilfully, she took one of the apples, dried it on a linen cloth, scooped out the core, and knotted a length of twine. Then she hung it from a hook in the ceiling. Still damp, but excited and happy, the children ducked and bobbed round the moving apple, hands firmly behind their backs, until Francis caught it and with the nearest thing to a snarl that they had ever heard from him, took a huge, crunching bite out of the apple.

"Well," said their mother. "Thank goodness."

"But me, Mama!" cried Brigid, and dived at the swinging half-eaten apple. She felt Francis steady the string and then the apple was in her mouth, and she was satisfied.

Finally, they sat down, their mother rubbing their heads with a rough towel, the tyres forgotten.

As the evening settled into night, Brigid's excitement grew. It was Hallowe'en.

Their mother looked out the window. "A lantern," she said. "We'll hollow out turnips," and she placed two turnips, heavy, woody-smelling, in front of them, and handed Francis a knife. She took another knife, started Brigid's off for her, then handed her a fairly robust and ancient spoon. "Do what you can with that," she said, "and Francis will help you if you get stuck."

They began to scrape, Francis much quicker than Brigid. At last the turnips were hollowed and Francis set to work on his, cutting out the face. An eye appeared, two eyes, a grinning mouth, while Brigid had only the beginning of one hideous eye-socket gouged out in hers. She asked her mother to help her, but there was no reply. Her mother was standing at the window. Brigid looked up.

"Francis," their mother said. "Did you put away the tyres

when you finished your game?"

Francis stood up. "Oh, I'm sorry," he said. "I forgot. I'll do it now."

Their mother shook her head. "No," she said. "No need. I'm afraid they're gone."

"Gone!" said Brigid and Francis together.

All animation suddenly lost, her face white, their mother said: "Gone, yes. Excuse me, children. I'm going inside to sit down for a little bit," and though Francis watched her as she walked out the door and passed into the sitting room to join the men, he said nothing. Then he walked, slowly, to the back door, Brigid at his heels.

Outside, together, they stood staring at the empty space where the tyres had been. There was nothing: the wells and tunnels, the tower and the beginnings of the castle had all disappeared.

"They've gone, all right," said Francis, shaking his head in disbelief, "but I don't know where, or how."

Behind them, unheard, their father and grandfather had joined them.

"I'll phone the barracks," their father began, but their grandfather stopped him with a hand on his shoulder.

"There's no point, Maurice. It's Hallowe'en. Youngsters will have taken them for bonfires. What puzzles me is how they did it without us noticing."

They filed slowly back into the house, their father's shoulders tense at the loss of his spare tyres, collected over years from forgotten cars, and kept there, just in case. Brigid, who rarely gave the tyres a thought unless Francis suggested a game, felt oddly bereft. She walked back into the kitchen, and sat down to the cold, ugly turnip she had been gouging. Francis was already there. He worked for a few moments in silence, then he reached across to Brigid and took over, cutting into the rough vegetable flesh. Brigid was glad. It was too hard and sore for her hands.

"There!" said Francis, after some minutes, and held up Brigid's grim turnip, where a large and woody piece had just come away in his hands to reveal a gaping mouth. "That's it, now." He looked around. "It's dark. I'm going to put candles in them."

"Francis!" said Brigid. "Are we allowed? Shouldn't we ask? Where did Mama go, anyway?"

Francis' face closed. "She's lying down. She's tired . . . I think. Anyway, what age am I?" he said, quite cross.

"Eleven," said Brigid, then: "No, nearly twelve."

"That's right," he said. "I'm allowed – you're not. You sit there."

Brigid sat. Francis went to the cupboard, found two half-used candles and a box of matches and, with care, placed the candles in the heart of the orange-fleshed heads. Then he struck a match, and Brigid heard its hiss, and smelt its sulphury burning in her nostrils. She was not sure that Francis was allowed, but for a second his face too was fearsome – he was a lurid ghost, and Brigid caught her breath and decided not to question his authority. The kitchen became gloomy, the evening outside a dark blue-black, and the smell of smoke surrounded them. From the sitting room they heard Big Ben strike, and a sonorous voice announced the news.

"I hate the news," said Brigid. "And I hate the newspaper."

Francis, putting the match to the white waxen candles in the middle of the turnips, did not reply. The match hissed and sputtered, and suddenly the turnip was a leering, fearsome mask, eyeless sockets staring, toothless lips grinning. Brigid stood up, pushing away from the table.

"Careful!" cried Francis. "You'll tip it over."

Brigid, backing away, could not take her eyes away from the horrible thing they had made. And at that moment, just when she thought she could never again be so afraid, there came a loud rap at the back door. She froze. Francis instantly stepped beside her, putting his arm round her, and she felt the tension all through him.

"Stay here," he said, "I'll look," and, stealthily, moved to the back door.

Brigid, ignoring his instruction, stayed right beside him, gripping his sleeve, and she felt both her heart and his pounding in her ears. The door rapped again, and this time it was loud, peremptory. Francis, stiffening, opened a narrow crack. Brigid felt his shock with her own as the door was suddenly and sharply pushed inwards and, together, the children fell back in fear.

Outside the door stood a figure in black, bent, glittering like a frost sprite. It began to unstraighten, and Brigid thought of Miss Chalk. Then Francis, his breathing uneven, managed to reach up to the light switch, and the figure was suddenly smoothly bathed in light. Something, and it was not relief, washed over Brigid as the terrible figure straightened, to become Isobel, Isobel smoothing her hair, Isobel dressed up for Hallowe'en in a shawl and a scarf and hard, shining, steel-rimmed glasses. The children together breathed out hard. Francis did not move, but Brigid edged back into the kitchen.

"Bella!" cried Francis. "You scared us!"

"Did I?" said Isobel, and the glasses glittered an extra bit by themselves. "Maybe it's the glasses. I borrowed those," she said. She took them off. Now she looked more like Isobel. "Are you going to let me in?"

Francis said. "I'm sorry, Bella. I was just so . . . We didn't expect to see you . . . tonight."

"No," said Isobel, "I'm sure you didn't, or Miss Prim over there, either. I heard I was needed. So here I am, like the Bad Fairy."

Brigid started. That was exactly what she was like.

"Did I give you a fright?" she said, seeing Brigid look up.

"Yes," said Brigid, hating her.

"Good," said Isobel. "That's what Hallowe'en is for. And, by the way, Francis, did you read that *Our Boys* I sent you when you got that wallop with the stone? Did you read 'Kitty the Hare'?"

Brigid looked at Francis in surprise. She had not known that

Isobel sent Francis anything when he was hit. That meant Isobel knew what had happened to Francis. Yet, how?

Francis nodded and widened his eyes: "It *was* frightening," he said.

Isobel laughed to herself. "I thought that would shake you. Take your mind off yourself. *Now* do you still not believe in ghosts?"

Francis frowned a little, and signalled sideways to Brigid, but Isobel only lifted her eyelids, gazed coolly across at Brigid and slanted them away again.

"She doesn't heed you," said Isobel. "She doesn't even listen, half the time."

Brigid was stung. "I do so heed him. I do so listen. And I do understand about ghosts, only," she paused, then lifted her head and stood up, wishing herself tall as Isobel, "they're not ghosts. They're our friends and our family and on this one night they can visit their homes. They are good to us."

Isobel raised her eyebrows above insolent, staring eyes: "Well, Mouse woke up!" she said. "Where did you learn all that? At a keyhole?"

Brigid set her mouth in a straight line. She did not say 'Like you,' but she thought it. "From my granda," she said, and picked a piece of warm crust from one of the apple tarts her mother had made. She was not missing Isobel any more.

Yet, something in her was almost relieved she was back. She was here, so Mama would not have to be tired with all the housework and have to take rests. If she was here, she could make the tea, and call them when it was time to go outside and watch Daddy light the fireworks. Indeed, Isobel did all of that, that night, and she brought tea to their mother, who was still lying down. She was there when hats and coats and the scratchy papier-mâché falsefaces had to be put on and, though Brigid hated the feel of the masks, her skin going cold and her teeth shuddering, she wore hers because they had been specially got the day Francis had his accident. It was Isobel, not their mother, who stood with them and their grandfather that night, while their father stepped forward to light the fireworks.

"'*Light blue touch paper*'," he read, "'*and retire to a safe distance*.'" He stretched out his arm to make sure the children were nowhere near, and his hand looked very long, and very white.

Brigid watched in a daze, entranced by the spirals of colour springing from the Catherine wheels, the Jumping Jacks like live things hopping round the square in front of the garage, the glorious rockets shooting green and red and yellow as they sped into space. All the while the children held sparklers, candyfloss of light, silver and gold, dropping them just before they burnt down to a sad metal needle in the hand. In the distance, there was a smell, like burning eggs. "Our tyres," Francis said just once, and no one said anything. Above them, the sky was alive with colours, soaring and whistling through the sky. Brigid thought: perhaps they are the souls of the dead trying to find their way home. But she was not troubled. Her family was close by, and the spirits, if they visited that night, were gentle.

Chapter 13: On Broadway

They whizzed above her, tiny spaceships, zinging along their lines with lightning intent. Brigid could not take her eyes from them, little steel canisters in the air. She would not move.

Isobel said: "Right," and pulled her arm until she came into the queue for Santa Claus.

"Look at them!" cried Brigid, craning back.

Isobel, still pulling, did not reply, but Francis, a little ahead, heard her. He took his own eyes away from the flying canisters, and turned around: "You've seen them before. They're for sending change and receipts to different parts of the store."

"I still think they're magic," Brigid said.

Francis shrugged his shoulders. "Who knows," he said. "Maybe they are."

This much Brigid knew: she and Francis were here, in Robbs' Store to travel in a spaceship and visit Santa Claus. How this could happen in a shop Brigid did not question: magic could happen anywhere. Still, looking up at Isobel, and her mouth's unpromising set, Brigid felt faith waver. The queue was long, and hot: before long, she tired of the slow shuffling. She wanted to meet Santa Claus, now. So, when it was suddenly their turn to step into the spaceship, and they zoomed upwards, she was quite taken by surprise. Here was magic, spinning them through space

140

to Santa's house. Brigid's heart filled with little fluttering birds. It was almost like being sick: in fact, she thought she would be sick if it went on any longer. It would have to stop before she . . . and then it did, just as suddenly as it had begun as, with a shuddering jolt, the spaceship wall opened to show a shining winter kingdom, glittering with bright points of light. And there he wonderfully was, in his warm red fur-tipped coat, and his white, kind, snowy face. His eyes, deep and soft, looked into her as he reached down, and she did not feel sick any more. He put his hand on her head and it was like her grandfather's, long and cool. Then, he handed her a pink parcel, and he gave Francis a blue one. He put an arm round each of them, drawing them into the warm circle of his arms. For a second Brigid was back with her father, as his eye turned to stone. She felt herself go stiff and cold, until she came back to the winter landscape, to the kindly face of Santa Claus, and he was saying: "What would you like me to bring you for Christmas?"

Brigid took his hand in both of hers, and placed her trust in him. "Please," she said, "may I have a theatre?"

Francis, in Santa's other arm, looked quickly towards her, the fading scar beside his eye beating like a pulse: he seemed surprised, but Santa Claus could not be. It was true that in the letter she had written with painstaking care, and which Francis had kindly posted up the chimney for her, she had asked for a doll, but really, until Santa Claus asked her, she did not know that she had changed her mind.

Yet, Francis seemed troubled. "I didn't know that was what you wanted, Brigid," he said.

"I didn't either," said Brigid. "I just thought of it now," which was true, and it seemed to her an inspired choice. This way, she could see the stories come alive, without the labour of writing them down.

"Hm," said Isobel, to no one. "Trust her. Anything to give trouble."

They had left Santa Claus's grotto by another door, and now

they were on ordinary echoing stairs, green-walled back stairs, and the magic was gone. Brigid, put out, could not think how she had given trouble by answering a question, but she shrugged her shoulders as she had seen Francis do, and was surprised to find that as she did so, her irritation fell away.

Isobel even let them open their presents: Francis had a set of Travel Draughts, Brigid Travel Ludo. There were bigger games like these at home, with stronger boards and bigger pieces: but these were special because Santa had sent them early.

Brigid was content to turn out into the evening, Christmas in the very air of the frosty street, carols in the distant darkening sky. It would not have surprised her to find a host of angels in the gloaming space above her, like the starlings she saw the day Francis was hit; and just as she thought it, Francis touched her elbow.

"See that red light up there?"

She followed his eyes. Sure enough, up above a red light made a trail across the sky.

"That could be him," he said.

"Isn't he in there, where we were, with the other children?"

"No," Francis said. "We were the last. Look behind you."

Brigid looked, and she saw that the doors of the store were closed. So he could be up there in the sky. She stretched her neck to see, then stopped. Sometimes, it was still painful.

"Does that hurt?" asked Francis. "You shouldn't do it if it does."

"Only sometimes," said Brigid, "if I turn it too far."

"Don't then," said Isobel, not unkindly, taking her hand. "And watch where you're going."

There was too much to see to watch where she was going. She stayed craned up towards the sky, until finally, crossly, Isobel tugged her back.

"Brigid," she said, "in the name of God would you –" and then she stopped, and her voice changed. "Why, hello," she said, quite softly, and Brigid, looked up and saw Uncle Conor, that crooked tooth gleaming.

"Well, well," he said and, dropping down to squat before Brigid, he put an arm round her, and drew her to him.

She could not pull away; she did not lean towards him.

"Christmas shopping?" he said, one finger on the pink parcel, loosely rewrapped.

"We've been to see Santa Claus, Uncle Conor," said Francis, but he did not sound happy any more.

"Indeed?" said Uncle Conor. "And am I allowed to know what you asked for?"

Brigid looked at Francis, and both looked at Isobel.

"Oh, you can tell Mr Todd," said Isobel, in her suddenly girlish voice. Her face was as pink as Brigid's parcel.

"I asked for a theatre," said Brigid. "I changed my mind from before."

Uncle Conor whistled. "Oh?" he said, and his eyebrows went up. "Is that not a bit risky, so close to Christmas?"

Brigid did not understand him.

Francis stepped closer, filling the space next to her. "Well, we know it's up to Santa Claus to decide what we are given," he said, very slowly, looking straight at Uncle Conor. "We know he decides."

Brigid, who knew nothing of the kind, opened her mouth to protest, but Francis' elbow pressed hers, and she understood. "We know that," she said.

"Well," said Uncle Conor, unfolding himself to his great height, "you can never tell what Santa Claus will decide," and he tipped his hand in salute. "I would see you all home," he said, "but I have to see a man about a dog." He turned to Isobel. "I'll leave them in your good hands, Bella," he said.

Brigid and Francis, taken aback, exchanged glances and, before anyone stopped her, Brigid said: "Uncle Conor, however did you know that? Nobody calls her that but Francis."

He looked down at her, one eyebrow far above the other. "Why . . . I must have heard Francis say it, then. My apologies, Miss, to you, and to your brother and – most of all," here he turned again to Isobel, "to you, Isobel."

To Brigid's surprise, Isobel's smile widened, and her cheeks turned a deeper pink, but she said nothing at all.

With a final, dismissive wave, Uncle Conor turned away, and was quickly swallowed in the evening crowd. The children said their puzzled goodbyes to his back, and followed Isobel's newly jaunty step through the cold streets to their own bus, scarcely stopping until they sank down, with one sigh, on the dark, hard leather bench. The bus pulled away, the glass of the windows misting beside them.

Brigid, puzzling over something, breathed warm circles on the glass. "Is Uncle Conor getting a dog?" she said, but Francis did not answer, and Isobel did not seem to hear. Her face was soft, her eyes far away. Brigid let it go: she would find out some time if he got the dog. Tired, she leaned towards Francis, watching the evening darken on the hill as they climbed past Broadway, and was almost asleep when her comfortable pillow suddenly jerked itself upright.

"There's Uncle Conor!" cried Francis.

"Where?" said Isobel, and she twisted in her seat. Brigid, rudely awakened, opened her eyes, pressed with Isobel against the window, and saw that Francis was right. Walking purposefully up Broadway was Uncle Conor, just as he had said, but he was not alone.

"And, Francis, look – Rose!" said Brigid, for Rose was walking with him. Uncle Conor had his hand under her elbow, the way her father took her mother's arm as they crossed the road. "Rose is with him," she said, tugging at her brother. "Francis, Rose is with him!" but Francis, staring out, said nothing, and Isobel, silent, seemed suddenly heavy against her. Brigid rapped the window, calling "Rose!", and Isobel did not stop her, but neither Rose nor Uncle Conor heard her. His hair stood up, brown, springy as heather. Rose's face wore a smile, her small teeth wide and white, and her eyes were bright. Then, Francis knocked the window, quite sharply. Still, nothing

144

happened. No one turned towards them. The bus moved on, slowly, inexorably and the figures of Rose and Cornelius Todd, close together, like dancers just taking the floor, grew smaller and more distant until they were just a speck in the dimming light. With one instinct, the children turned for explanation to Isobel: but Isobel said nothing. Her face was not pink any more, but white. She was white as Miss Chalk. The children looked at each other, and kept quiet.

Francis shifted his seat, closer to Brigid, and the bus moved down the hill towards home. When they were at the depot, he nudged Brigid. "Look," he said. "The buses have had a hard day. Probably nod off in a minute."

Brigid looked, and laughed, and agreed. Trolleybuses had a sleepy air even in the mornings, but now, in the winter evening, even the fierce petrol buses had a mellow look as if, though vigilant still behind their black eyepatches, they had dropped off standing up, like horses in a field.

"And, look!" said Francis. "There's the boy who lights the lamps."

Brigid looked out and saw a thin boy at the top of the tall lamp-post outside their house. When they got off the bus and crossed the road he was standing by it, on the pavement looking up. Francis stopped beside him, and Brigid stopped too.

"Excuse me," Francis said. "Can I ask you, do you climb up all of them?"

"No, not all of them," said the boy pleasantly. "Only when I have to check the pilot light."

"The pilot light?" said Francis.

Isobel stood holding the open gate, but Francis did not move, and Brigid stood her ground.

"If it goes out," said the boy, "in a high wind, say, I have to get up and relight it. But I'm only checking today. It was wavering, that's all."

"I'd love to be you," said Francis. "I'm Francis." They shook hands. "This is Brigid, my sister and . . ." he turned to introduce

Isobel, but she had turned her back.

"I'm Bobby," said the boy, and he laughed. "You wouldn't love to be me when there's a storm."

"You climb up there in storms?" Brigid was impressed.

"Oh yes," said the boy, hunkering down beside her. "I climbed up every lamp-post between here and the Ormeau Road the night the *Princess Victoria* went down."

"Our sort of uncle was lost on that," said Brigid.

"Was he?" said the lamplighter. "What's a 'sort of uncle'?"

"And no one has gone to –" began Brigid, but Isobel's voice cut across.

"Brigid! Francis! Come on! Now!" Isobel was taking no more.

Francis and Brigid said goodbye, hurriedly, shamefacedly to the young lamplighter.

"She's getting worse since she came back," said Brigid to Francis, beneath her breath, but Isobel heard her.

"Who's 'she'? The cat's mother?" she said. "And it's *your* mother I came back for, not you, Miss."

Brigid said nothing, because at least Isobel no longer slept in the house, which was something.

When they got inside, their mother was standing in the sitting room, her arms full of colours, and rustling silver strings. A little strand of silver dangled from one wave of her hair. Brigid thought she looked beautiful. The newly lit fire was leaping in the grate, its flames still white, not yet mellowed to its orange and red, and she was hanging a string of lights on a fir tree which was neatly standing in a wooden bucket.

Turning to them, she said: "Ah, the wanderers have returned! What's strange in the town? Did you see anybody on your travels?"

Isobel said nothing, and went straight into the kitchen.

Their mother paused, looking after her. "Has something upset Isobel?" she said. "Was anyone bold?" and to Brigid's irritation, she looked over Brigid's head at Francis.

Brigid opened her mouth to speak, but Francis pressed her back, warningly. "I think Isobel is just tired, Mama. The town was busy."

"Well, that would do it," agreed his mother, nodding her head. "But I don't want her upset. She's needed here. Come on, you two, now, and get something to eat. Daddy will be in any minute . . ."

A key turned in the front door, and a voice called "Hello?" from the hall.

"There he is – and nothing ready," said their mother, running her hands through her hair. "Go on, children, into the kitchen and get some tea, at least, with Isobel."

"Francis," said Brigid, as she followed him out the door, "why do you keep nudging me and telling me to be quiet?"

"Say nothing," he said.

"About what?"

"About anything."

Brigid sighed: it was the summer and the plot all over again.

Chapter 14: Truce

Brigid woke, knowing it was Christmas Eve. Even in the warmth of her bed she could see expectation in her own frosty breath. The sunlight, pale, almost white, was trying to drift through the yellow of the blind. She made the chilly hop from bed to window, and snapped the blind, sharply, sending it speeding to a quivering, abrupt halt. There it was: the winter sun, pale as the moon through the empty branches of the Friday Tree. Spreading coldly from it, the plot lay bare, brown furrows almost grey. For no reason, Brigid remembered, with a suddenness that was almost painful, the summer sun on her head, birds soaring above, bees busily circling nearby. She shook her head. Then she shook it again: her hair had grown long enough to make a curtain round her face in the morning and, until someone clipped it back, Brigid looked out from the safety of a dark, soft screen.

"Hold on, Veronica Lake," said her mother, catching her as she went into the kitchen. "Come here and see who's arrived."

Brigid pushed back her hair, and looked, and her heart lifted. "Rose!" she cried, then with an immediate tightening in her stomach looked to see who else might be there. No one. No one stood behind her. No Uncle Conor. Not even Isobel. Perhaps Isobel had gone for her own Christmas somewhere. Brigid could only hope.

148

"Yes," said her mother. "Rose arrived out of the blue last night, and she's going to help us finish the tree before she has to go home, aren't you, Rose?"

"I am," said Rose, "and before I go, I may put something under that tree, too."

Brigid caught her breath.

"But not," said Rose, "unless I see porridge eaten this morning."

Brigid felt her happiness deflate. "Will Francis have to, too?"

Francis, rubbing his eyes, covered a yawn as he walked through the door: "Do what?" he said, then: "Morning."

"Eat porridge," said Brigid. "I have to."

"All right," said Francis, and ran his hand through his own hair.

"Good morning to you," said his mother. "What time did you stop rooting around last night?"

Francis let his hand drop. "Did I keep people up? I'm sorry. I was . . . looking for something."

"They're like two longhorns under that hair," said Rose. "It's a wonder they can see at all. Good morning, Francis."

With a glance at one another, the sisters left the children at the table, and left the kitchen. They did not say where they were going or what they were going to do.

Brigid was sure that what occupied them was to do with Christmas – smells and spices and rustlings that could only come to good. She tried to eat the porridge. She did not relish it, but she persevered. Something extra might go under the tree if she did.

"Francis," said Brigid, swallowing, "am I still not allowed to say we saw Rose and Uncle Conor yesterday?"

Francis, moving his spoon round and round the bowl, thought for some moments, then looked up. "Yes," he said. "If Rose wants to tell us, she will. If she doesn't, it's not our business."

"Do you think it was about the dog?"

"Dog?"

"The dog. Uncle Conor said he had to see a man about a dog."

Francis reached for the milk, and poured it in a slow spiral round his bowl. "I wish I could like porridge," he said. "I don't know what it was about, Brigid. It's not our business. I told you. Can you finish that?"

"I hate it," said Brigid.

He shrugged. "Better try. It's not bad, really."

Brigid sighed, and swallowed three more spoonfuls, the graininess catching in her throat.

"Well done," said Francis. "Now, here's something for you to do. I'm supposed to finish doing the tree, and you can give me advice and encouragement. Come on," and he was up and away from the table, her bowl and his rinsed and left to drain before Brigid was properly out of her chair.

The sitting room was filled with a bright smell: sharp, like a forest. Brigid could not touch the lights: if one bulb got damaged, Francis said, the whole thing would go. All she could do was gaze in wonder at the string of lights as they came out from their box with a slow clinking, like little china cups. They were coloured bells, the size of Brigid's palm, pale blue and green and red and yellow. Here was Cinderella in rags on one, there was the plump Fairy Godmother bibbidi-bobbing in her blue cape, there was the star-shining ball gown, and, best of all for Brigid, was the bright green bell with the pumpkin-coach and the mouse-horses.

It took forever until the lights were in place, and Francis said: "Now, Brigid. Your turn," and held out his hand.

One by one she picked out the decorations: she handed him the baker boy who had come from a threepenny lucky bag, the tiny basket full of bright coloured balls, the home-sewn Santa Claus, soft as a cushion, glass baubles of emerald and ruby, delicate, ready to shatter in a grip too tight, and the glittering tinsel, catching every colour it came near. Last of all, Brigid handed Francis the angel in her paper gown. He pushed the back

150

of their father's armchair against the wall, steadied it, climbed up to stand on the arm, wobbled a little, righted himself, reached up, and placed the little angel at the top of the tree. Then he leapt down from the chair, knees bent. "Call me Errol Flynn!" he said, landing like a cat.

"Why?" said Brigid, but he did not explain.

He stood back, moved forward and made some adjustments: a loop of tinsel, a coloured ball too near the edge of the branch, Santa Claus in danger of plummeting through the fir branches. Finally, he said, "That should do", pushed the chair back to its place, went to the window, pulled the heavy curtains and quickly, surprisingly, shut out the morning. Bending, he unfurled the twisted trailing flex, pushed the plug into the wall socket, and flicked the switch. Sharply, Brigid drew in breath. They were in their own fairy tale. For an endless moment, they stood together in stillness. Then Francis switched off again.

"Oh, Francis," said Brigid, "don't put it away."

"I'm not," he said. "Don't worry. Wait till it's dark, and we'll put them on, and it'll be magic all the time till Santa Claus comes."

Brigid sighed. "All right," she said. "Maybe you'd better do the curtains, too, before they catch us."

"Good thinking," said Francis, and swished aside the curtain.

In that moment, two things happened. The doorbell rang and, just as she heard her mother say from the top of the stairs, "Somebody see who that is, will you?", Brigid's eyes were filled with a terrible image at the window: a face squashed, a red, raw tongue plastered against the glass. She heard a low, groaning sound, and was just about to dive behind her father's chair when Francis said: "Oh, boy. The gang's all here." He rapped the window, hard, against the flattened face. It sprang back, startled, and Brigid saw who it was.

"Francis," she cried, "that was Ned Silver!"

"Was," he said, drawing back the rest of the curtain sharply, "and is. And – don't ask me why – he's with Uncle Conor. Remember what I told you. Not a word about yesterday unless someone mentions it first. Maybe not even then."

Brigid, her head full of lights and colours, could not think at first what had happened yesterday: it was already a long time ago. Still, she nodded, then shook her head. "Not a word," she said. Then it came back: "Uncle Conor?" she said. "But, why, *why* is he with Ned?"

"I don't know, any more than you," said Francis, exasperated. "But stay put, stay quiet and we may just find out."

Out in the hall there was a commotion, sounds of surprise and greeting: men's voices as Brigid's father arrived home early from the office, surprised and pleased to see his friend – softer, higher voices as Rose and her sister brought in the unexpected visitors. There was another surprise, less pleasant: Isobel's voice was among them. She had not gone yet, after all.

It looked for a mad moment as if everybody was about to spill into the sitting room on top of Brigid and Francis, until a voice, taking charge, put a stop to that. "Isobel," called their mother, skilfully guiding Ned Silver into the sitting room to the children. "Would you mind putting down the groceries and checking that oven for me? Then, would you set two more places in the dining-room? You children can stay in here for the moment, and," she said, with a glance that in one sweep included, encouraged and warned, "I am trusting you" – she looked for a moment at Ned – "all of you, to behave. This is a big occasion."

Well, of course it is, thought Brigid: it's Christmas Eve, and something's being baked in the kitchen, and up in the North Pole Santa must be getting ready . . .

For better or worse, the three children were left together.

No one said anything, until Ned, looking at Brigid, put out his tongue. "Got you at the window," he said. "Again."

"I knew it was you," said Brigid, and Ned snorted.

"Ha," he said.

"I did," said Brigid, "because it was so ugly."

"Stop it, the two of you," Francis cut across, sharply. "Just stop, will you?"

Ned and Brigid looked at each other from under their eyelashes, but said nothing.

Ned wandered over to the tree. "Nice," he said. "You do this, Francis?"

"Yes," said Francis, without any of his earlier enthusiasm. "I always do it."

"Nice," said Ned again, and he pushed one of the Cinderella bells, idly. It made a tiny noise, the tinsel shimmered, and the tree trembled, as though it still stood in the forest, shaking off frost and snow. Ned was still, then, for a moment, and his face was quiet.

Despite herself, Brigid felt sorry for fighting with him. "Is your tree up, Ned?" she said.

Ned turned away from the tree. "No," he said. "My father doesn't any more . . . and, anyway, he isn't there."

"Who is there?" asked Francis, and his voice had lost its irritation.

"Probably nobody." said Ned, and he turned his back on both of them. He looked out the window, as if something were going on.

Brigid looked, but there was nothing to see.

"Mulvey goes to her own family at Christmas," said Ned.

"But then, where do you go?" asked Brigid, and prayed every prayer she knew that he would not say he was going to be with them.

He smiled, in an instant his unpleasant self again.

He raised one eyebrow, and Brigid thought: now he's copying Uncle Conor.

"Don't you know?" he asked.

"Of course I do," said Brigid, immediately.

"Good," said Ned. "Then I don't have the bother of telling you."

"Well, I don't know," said Francis. "So you can tell me. Where are you going, Ned, and why doesn't your father ever come home? We never see him."

Ned, to Brigid's annoyance, turned immediately to Francis and said, quite simply: "He can't. His work in Egypt is too important . . . to do with the government," and he paused, lifting up his chin, letting the information sink in. "It takes him away a lot. He keeps the house pretty much for me, for holidays. I think he was going to sell it when . . . one time. Then he didn't. Mulvey says it was because of me." He tossed his head, and his hair shone like a chestnut in the light of the fire. "I don't think he would keep it if it weren't for me."

Francis' voice was quiet. "I'm sure he'd rather be here with you, now, at Christmas."

Ned's ears, turned away from Brigid, grew first pink, then red.

Brigid thought: he's going to tell a lie.

"He does," said Ned. "He does want to be here with me. He's just busy, that's all, all the time, and Mulvey can't always be there. That's why I was going to stay at school over Christmas."

"At school!" cried Brigid. She could think of nothing worse.

"It would have been fun," shot back Ned, his ears redder even than before, his eyes bright in the firelight. "I wanted to. I was looking forward to it. I was going to get in all the places we're not allowed. Really good ones, secret places." He breathed in, his mouth a pale straight line. "Secret as the plot," he said, and he shot them both a glance that was a warning, just short of a threat.

There was silence. Brigid listened to her own breathing, while Francis sat down on the arm of the chair.

"So, Ned," he said, his voice still quiet, "where will you be spending Christmas?"

Ned looked straight at him. His eyes were calm now, a clear dark blue. "With your Aunt Rose. She asked me when Mr Todd told her I had to stay in school."

Francis sat still.

Brigid puzzled, said: "But how did he know?"

Ned pushed the Cinderella bell again, harder: "Don't you

know already?" he said. "I thought you said you did."

"How, Ned?" said Francis, and his voice was very steady, but not so quiet.

Ned shrugged. "Because he came to see me, that's how."

"At your school?" said Brigid and Francis together.

"But isn't that in England?" added Francis. "He went to see you in England?"

Ned, though he opened his mouth to reply, closed it again as the door opened, and Rose herself put her head round its edge.

"My goodness," she said, "it's quiet in here. What's going on? Are you colloguing?"

Francis stood up. "No, Rose. Ned was telling us he's going to spend Christmas with you," he said, his voice now quite flat.

"Yes," said Rose, her smile a little apologetic. "I was going to tell you about that, but everyone arriving together, and I –"

"Children," called their mother's voice. "Come in here to the dining room, will you, please?"

Rose reached across to the tree to straighten the bell Ned had disturbed and, as she did so, Brigid glimpsed, nestled at her throat, peeping out from underneath the collar of her blouse, something shining, bright as a star.

"On you go," said Rose, giving Brigid a gentle push. "I was sent to get you."

Francis and Brigid looked at each other.

"Go on," said Rose, with her wide, warm smile. "All will be revealed!"

Ned at their heels, Rose behind, Brigid and Francis did as they were told.

"It is good news, all the same, Cornelius," their mother was saying. "When did you last read such a hopeful headline? What a Christmas present for the world!"

Standing at the door of the dining room, Brigid felt her spirits sink. Not the world again. Not the news. The next thing, it would be Ireland.

"All it means, Grace," said their father, "and I think this is

155

Conor's point, is that they have stopped their fighting for the moment. Look at it. Yes, the headline says: '*Guns are silent in Bethlehem*,' and yes, that's good. But read on: '*Israel and Jordan laid aside their guns today and opened the border to hundreds of Christmas pilgrims*.' It doesn't say they have settled their differences."

"It's a truce, Grace," said Cornelius. "Maurice is right. All it is, is a temporary gesture of goodwill – like the business of letting prisoners out of the gaol here for Christmas, a cheap . . ."

Here it comes, Brigid thought. Here comes Ireland; but instead, to her relief, he saw the children, and stopped. He got to his feet, pulling out Rose's chair for her. She sat down, her wide dress spreading its flowers and its perfume round her. He seated himself beside her and, as she smiled at him, the bright shining at her neck caught the light, flamed like fire, then settled white against her skin. The children took their places at the table.

"Well," said their father, "are we all met? Children, there is some news!"

The children sat down, looking from one to another, apprehensive.

"We know Ned is going to spend Christmas at the farm with Rose," Brigid said.

"Well, yes," said Uncle Conor. "That is part of it. I'm driving your Aunt Rose down today, and Ned's going, too. I don't think school would be the best place at Christmas, do you?"

Brigid looked at her parents. Her father was smiling, her mother not. She seemed preoccupied, absently twisting on her left hand the thin gold wedding band. Probably, Brigid thought, Isobel had forgotten to get something she needs. As if to confirm this, Isobel came in, unsmiling, unfriendly, with a pot of tea.

"But how . . . ?" started Brigid.

Cornelius looked at Rose, who nodded and gestured with her hand. "You go on," she said.

"Well, look," said Cornelius, "that's not the news we were going to tell you, but that can wait a moment or two more. Ned:

well, something your Aunt Rose said a few months ago made me aware that I knew of Ned's . . . family, some time ago. And, I happened to be in England a little while back, and I tracked down this young man and found he was going to be spending his holidays at school. Then your Aunt Rose," and he stopped and smiled at her again, "said she and her brother would be happy to have Ned as their guest. So, we . . . well, Rose, really, obtained the necessary permission from his father and the school, and here he is, and he's going to have a very nice Christmas with your aunt and your uncle."

Brigid was silent. She could not bear to think of Ned having Christmas with anyone in her family. She wished he had stayed in school for Christmas. She could not see why he did not just go to Egypt. It could not be much further away than England, and he would be with his own family, not hers.

Francis, who had been listening quietly, said: "What was the news you were going to tell us, Uncle Conor?"

"Ah yes," he said, "our news." He drew his napkin from his lap, dabbed at his mouth, and replaced the napkin beside his plate. "The news is," and here, to their surprise, he reached over and took Rose's hand, "that your Aunt Rose has agreed to be my wife and, just as soon as we have told your Uncle Michael – because, you know," and he laughed, and Rose laughed too, "I must inform the man of the house, if not quite ask his permission, we will make it formal."

Rose looked down, and the shining something swung forward. Brigid saw that it was a ring, like her mother's engagement ring, of glittering white stones, hanging on a chain round her neck. Brigid looked at her mother, whose eyes were still cast down. She was not smiling.

Her father, heartier than she had seen him since the summer, said: "Now, isn't that good news, children?"

Ned glanced sideways at Brigid, and raised his eyebrow. He *is* copying Uncle Conor, Brigid thought, and she was put out, though precisely why she could not have said. Yet, the feeling that her day had been stolen persisted as the visitors stayed, and stayed, so that Isobel had to stay on too, and Brigid could see her mother's face grow pinched and tired. Yet, Rose, who always noticed everything, seemed not to notice this. She spent her time gazing at Uncle Conor, and he smiled and kept smiling until the crooked tooth Brigid had come to dislike seemed to have developed a life of its own.

Eventually, after a very long lunch, the visitors set off in Rose's little car. Francis and their father saw them off at the gate, but Brigid did not go with them. She did not want to have to look at Ned Silver sitting gloating in the back. It pleased her to think that Uncle Conor would have to fold himself up to fit into the front seat. She hoped he would be uncomfortable. She was not sorry they were gone, yet the quiet of the house washing back to her was now empty, drained of the morning's promise. They had taken that with them.

Chapter 15: Under the Tree

The visitors had stayed so long that the day had grown dark. She could see her father, after watching them off from the gate, remain standing there, lost in his own thoughts. She heard her mother go upstairs, calling to Isobel that she would be down in ten minutes. Francis was nowhere to be seen.

Brigid, obscurely disconsolate, set out to find him. Out through the kitchen, warm with currants and spices and steam, to the back yard: no Francis, but she could see where he had been. His Stanley knife, a glint beneath the gap at the bottom of the coalhouse door, first caught her eye. She pushed the door back and looked around it: beside the knife, flattened, pushed well back against the wall furthest from the coalstack, was a large newspaper parcel. She drew it out slowly and, trying not to get black coal dust on her hands, opened it up carefully without touching its contents. Inside lay the remains of a cardboard box. It had arrived, full of fragrant oranges, the day before. Brigid had seen it. On it now there were pencil drawings, arches and balconies, sweeping swathes like cloth, like curtains. He had done that: Francis had done it. He had cut out a huge square. He had folded it back so that it looked like . . . Brigid stopped. She knew what it looked like. She knew what he was doing. He was making her a theatre, because she had asked Santa Claus for one.

159

Brigid felt her heart expand within her and, for no reason at all, her eyes filled with tears. She swallowed hard, wrapped the parcel back up, replaced it just where he had hidden it and pulled the door closed. She crept quietly back into the house, hoping that no one had seen her.

She had just finished washing her hands at the sink when she saw Isobel through the kitchen door. She was standing at the door of the cloakroom, crossly pulling on her coat, tying a headscarf under her chin. She was breathing hard, and talking to herself: "One more wouldn't have killed them, as far as the bus."

Still unseen, as Isobel reached into the darkness of the cloakroom for her bag, Brigid slid into the hall and then into the sitting room. From next door she could hear Dicky clucking in complaint. "Quiet, you," she heard Isobel say. "You're another one." Standing behind the door, Brigid looked at the Christmas tree, as yet unlit, and tried to recapture the happiness she and Francis had felt, before Ned Silver and Cornelius and Rose – yes, Rose too – had broken their peace. Then she remembered: Francis was making her a theatre. She looked again at the tree: the tinsel catching the firelight; the coloured baubles gently turning in the draught from the door, the Cinderella bells heavy and still, the angel in her paper frock gazing at nothing from the top of the tree. A hopeful thought came to Brigid: Rose had said she would leave something if the porridge were eaten. It had been eaten.

Her eyes travelled downward. She bent her knees and crouched by the tree. There was something, right at the back, tucked away almost out of sight. It was oddly shaped, with points in strange places, like a sailing ship, and it was loosely wrapped in brown paper with string, and a label. Brigid burrowed down, and above her felt the branches of the tree shiver. She shivered, too, because the parcel's label showed her name. Beside it, another parcel, square, heavy-looking, was inscribed "*Francis*". She did not touch them: she wanted to touch them, but she did not. Yet, she could see, in clear, sharp print, a label saying, "*With love from Rose,*" and beneath, in black, bold letters, there leapt the words: "*And Uncle Conor.*" Brigid sat back on her heels. He was going to be her uncle, really. She shook her head. She did not want him to become her real uncle. For a moment, Brigid felt dislike, almost hatred for Rose, for letting this happen.

Then, from nowhere, a sibilance like a winter wind sounded in her ear: "You got your way."

Startled, Brigid looked up. Above her stood Isobel. Oh, where was Francis?

"You got your way," she said again, "you monkey." Brigid stayed silent. "Telling him what you said to that Santa in the shop. You had a lot to do, telling him."

Brigid, stunned, still said nothing. Did Isobel mean Francis?

"Well," said Isobel, "you'll get what you wanted, much good may it do you. Look!" And catching Brigid roughly by the shoulder, she pulled towards her Rose's parcel and, surprisingly easily, eased away the string, so that Brigid could not help seeing what was inside.

As she looked the world and everything in it went away, and she sat in the silence of joy. In its nest of paper sat a perfect little theatre: its pale wooden frame simple and fine; its backdrop a blue sky and silver clouds, green rounded bushes and branchy trees; delicate dowels holding magnets to attach the little figures; small boy; small girl; prince and princess; witch and fairy; a baron and an old king. There was a dragon with fiery tongue; there was a horse, proudly plumed, and on him sat an armoured knight. Everything she needed to make stories come to life sat below her, waiting for her.

"There," said Isobel again, breaking the spell. Brigid could smell her breath, like onions. "Now are you satisfied, you selfish little –"

Brigid pulled away, scrambled to her feet, and ran from the room to the foot of the stairs. "Francis!" she called. "Francis!" She could hear the tears in her voice.

"He went outside," called her mother from upstairs. "Don't bring the house down!"

Behind her, Brigid heard the front door slam.

"Is Isobel away?" called her mother again. There was a sound of running water, as if from the bathroom. "I didn't get a chance to . . . Brigid, go after her, there's a good girl, but don't go past the gate!"

Brigid had no intention of going after Isobel, even as far as the gate. She ran into the kitchen, calling "Francis!" Dicky, hearing Francis' name, squawked as Brigid passed him, dancing from one clawed foot to the other. She ran out the back door into the yard, past the work on the theatre Francis was making – oh, what would happen when he found out? Up the garden steps she ran and looked about but there was no sign of Francis. She stopped, listening to the drumbeat of her heart. If Santa Claus was on his way to bring her a theatre, and Rose had already given her the one under the tree, and Francis was making her one in the back yard, where would she put them all? There was no answer but her own heartbeat, as she ran back down to the yard.

She heard a car door open and close. She ran into the passage. Was somebody else coming, or going? She was in time to see her father and Isobel getting into his car. And then, to her surprise and relief, Francis came out of the garage with something in his hand.

"Francis!" she said. "I was looking for you!"

"Well," he said, "you've found me," and whatever he held in his hand he slipped into his pocket.

With sinking heart, Brigid was suddenly certain it was something to do with making the theatre. Their father kept tools and sharp things in the garage, and Francis must have gone in to get one of them. Now was the moment to tell him. And then she realised he was speaking to her.

"Brigid, are you not listening? I said: give Daddy and Isobel a wave."

Brigid waved. "But where are they going?"

"He's driving her home, to save her getting the bus."

"Oh, no, stop them, Francis! Mama wants to see Isobel."

So then Francis raced down the passage, and Brigid saw the car stop. Francis disappeared into the house, and a few minutes later came once again into view, their mother by his side. She reached in through the car window, handed a package to Isobel and, finally, the car started again, and reversed out. Francis stood with his mother at the gate as the car drew away, and the engine sound grew loud, faint, then disappeared.

Brigid did not join them. There was too much coming and going, and she still had not told Francis about the theatre.

Disconsolate, she went back inside, past Dicky still wanting company. "Hello, Dicky," she said, and she saw him dance at the sound of her voice, but she did not stop.

In the sitting room, the tree stood still and quiet. Underneath, Rose's parcels sat, Brigid's one innocently wrapped again as if they had never been disturbed. Isobel must have replaced the paper.

She heard her mother and Francis come back in to the house, and then Francis put his head round the door. "Where did you get to?" he said. "I thought you were looking for me . . . That's funny."

"What?" asked Brigid, looking guiltily at the parcels.

"Did you move the Santa from the middle of the tree?"

"No," said Brigid. She thought back. She had not touched the tree. Ned had, and Isobel had, but she had not.

"Oh. It's probably further down underneath." He shrugged. "It'll turn up. Anyway, I've – I've – things to do. But I'll put the television on for you now, if you like, because," and he smiled widely, "I know there's something on you'll want to see. And – it's time to light the tree!"

Brigid clapped her hands.

"You can watch television by the fire. All right?"

Brigid nodded. That was all right.

"Was that what you wanted me for?"

Brigid nodded again. It was not a lie, because really, secretly, she did want to sit down now and watch something on television.

"And then, in a little while, I'll come in and watch with you. Okay?"

"Okay, Francis," said Brigid, and sheer happiness overtook her as he pressed the switch, and the Christmas tree came alive, the lights deep, like jewels, mirrored, shining back through the window.

"Look! It might even snow. It's nearly Christmas, Brigid!"

"I know," said Brigid, and she hugged her knees to herself. "I know."

The television warmed up, and the picture began to come clear. Francis got up to go, and Brigid felt sudden compunction. Should she tell him? "Francis . . ." she said. "Stay a minute? I want to . . . Rose . . . Iso . . ."

"Later," Francis, halfway out the door. "Watch this, and I'll be back very soon," and then he was gone.

Brigid slid down to the floor, easing her back against the arm of her father's chair, and wished with a pang that he were with her now, sitting in it, his hand on her head. He would know what to do about telling Francis, or not telling Francis . . . or, would he? She remembered he was taking Isobel somewhere, but she dismissed that. No Isobel, not now. But Francis . . . Francis . . . what to do? Brigid leaned back, the hiss and leap of the fire at her side, behind her the lights of the glowing tree, all around her voices from the television, in front of her the pictures on the . . .

Suddenly she stopped still. Someone she knew well was in front of her on the screen. He was standing on a bridge, a great curved metal bridge, and it was snowing hard on his eyes and his hair and his tweed coat, and he was telling another man he wanted to live again. His mouth was bleeding, but he did not care. He saw that it was bleeding, but he was happy. He took out from a pocket at his belt some little flower petals. He cried: "Zuzu's petals!" Then he ran through the town, calling "Merry

164

Christmas", and he burst through the door into his own house and his children were there, and his wife came in, and she ran up the stairs to him, and they all came down the stairs together in a great laughing rush to stand below their Christmas tree. Brigid's heart filled. It was George Bailey, in the film she remembered. It was her own George Bailey, who had brought her home the day her father left her alone at the school. All the people in the town stood gathered about him now and gave him money to make up for money somebody had lost, and he did not have to go to prison, and they sang Christmas carols, all standing in George's sitting room.

Brigid stood up. She would bring Francis back and, with George Bailey behind her, she would tell him about Rose, and the parcel Isobel had opened. She would do it now. Moments took her through the kitchen, and out to the yard, out to where she found him, his Stanley knife glinting in his hand, working head down in the cold, in his winter coat and his school cap. "Francis," she said, and then she stopped. Francis, cutting into the cardboard, turned round and saw her. He stood up in front of the cardboard, pushed it with his foot into the coalhouse behind him, and said: "What is it?" but Brigid could not do it. She could not tell him about the theatre.

"George," was all she said, "George Bailey."

"Didn't I tell you there was something good on?" he said, and steered her in front of him into the house. "Let's see him," he said.

Brigid pulled him by the hand, through the house, fast as the wind, until they stood in front of the television.

They were too late. George Bailey had gone. Now on the screen there was a woman dressed like a fish, singing "Climb Up the Wall," and their father stood in front of it. He had taken off his hat but his coat was still on, and all the cold air from outside seemed to have come into the room with him. Brigid thought: his coat is like George's coat. Unlike George, he was far from happy.

"What is this tripe?" he asked. "On the very eve of

Christmas!" and he leaned over and turned the switch, and the picture diminished and disappeared. Suddenly there was no sound but the crackle of the fire.

"He was there, Francis," Brigid said, as quietly as she could. "I wanted to show him to you."

"It's all right, Brigid," said Francis, and he squeezed the hand still placed in his. "I know he was."

Her father called their mother and she came, slowly, her hand on the small of her back, wearing again the dotted smock Brigid did not like. "What is it, Maurice?" she said, her voice tired. "I've still things to do for tomorrow," and she inclined her head toward the children.

"Is it not time this lassie was in bed? The stuff they're showing on Christmas Eve is not fit for children."

"I'm not tired at all," said Brigid. "I want to stay up. Please!"

Her mother sighed. "Well," she said, and she looked at Brigid thoughtfully, "I need to get everybody something to eat before I do anything. I'll tell you what. If Brigid is still awake, she can go with you two to Midnight Mass."

"Midnight Mass?" said Brigid. "Stay up till midnight? Can I?"

"If you can stay awake," said her mother.

"Yes, you can," said her father, and Brigid immediately began to feel tired.

She was determined, however, to stay awake. After teatime she went in and sat down again in her favourite place, watching the fire and turning now and again to look at the tree. Her eyes began to feel smoky, and once or twice her head dropped heavily on her chest, but she would not sleep. Never in her life had she stayed up until midnight and, even if it meant going to Mass, she was going to stay awake. She simply closed her eyes, now and again, and once she heard her mother say, "I don't know what I was thinking about. She's not fit to . . ." and her father said, "You may be right," and then Brigid felt herself drift and suddenly she was in the monastery or, rather, she was above it, travelling in the sky. She was wearing her pyjamas and her slippers, not her Sunday clothes, but it did not seem to matter. Below her the monastery looked up, graceful and slender against the dark blue Christmas sky. Light flooded from it, and from inside floated angel voices, and the lights of Bethlehem were far away, and she thought of her own house, under the Black Mountain, under the trees. The singing was softer now, and the lights very dim; there was a smell like perfume, like her mother's faint scent, and Brigid felt herself soften and drift, gently, peacefully, until to her surprise she started awake, hearing a small sound. She found that she was in her own bed, in her own room, that beside her on the chair was a little pile of presents, and on the end of the bed her school stocking, which she had hopefully hung up early on the morning of Christmas Eve, was filled to the brim with bright things.

Half awake, she saw something, like the tail of a robe, disappearing through the door and her first thought was that it must be Santa Claus. Then, she saw that the tail of the robe was blue, but there was no time to wonder.

She knelt up on the eiderdown, going to the pile on the chair, then to the stocking, not knowing where to begin. There was a book, with a picture on the front of the Sleeping Beauty, and all around her were Puss in Boots, and Jack looking down from the top of the beanstalk, and Aladdin with his wonderful lamp. It said *Four . . . Nursery Stories*, with a long word in the middle. She tried again. She put the sounds together. The long word was 'favo-our-ite'. *Four Favourite Nursery Stories*.

There was a little sewing set, like her mother's, with tiny reels of thread and red quilting on the inside of the box. There was a card game: *Happy Families*. And there was a doll. He had brought her the doll. Indeed, she was exquisite, brown eyes and hair so pale it was almost silver, delicate eyebrows permanently raised. Brigid smelled her newness, and watched her close her eyes full of secrets. Her mouth looked as though it might be about to smile, or might not, and her dress was dark, and ruched, and soft. She wore white buckled shoes and socks. She was not a doll: she was a princess.

Yet, placing her back in her box, Brigid was puzzled. She had told Santa Claus about her change of mind, and he had still brought her the doll. She was glad he had not, after all, brought her a theatre. Still, she did not understand. She had told him.

Brigid slid out of bed, lifted the doll in her box and padded in to Francis. He was sitting on his bed, turning over and over a shiny camera, with a round shell-shaped glass on its top, raising it to his eyes, working at the dials on the back, reading the instructions, examining every angle of the camera. Books and an orange and an apple lay beside him on the bed.

"Happy Christmas," he said, pointing his camera at her. It flashed, and Brigid saw a kaleidoscope of colours.

"Francis," she said. "Look. He brought me the doll."

He looked from behind his camera: "Ah!" he said. "That's a French doll. *Une poupée*. Happy Christmas to you, *poupée*," he said to the doll, reaching over and taking her hard little hand. "*Joyeux Noël*."

"How did you know to say that to her?" Brigid asked, impressed. "How do you know she is a French doll?"

"Look at the box in your hand," Francis said.

Brigid looked, but it made no sense.

"See?" said Francis. "See that word there? '*Poupée*." French for doll."

"Then she needs a proper French name. I don't know any. Do you?"

Francis thought. "Marianne," he said. "That's as French as they get."

"Marianne. All right. Santa Claus does get around, doesn't he, Francis?"

"He does, yes. He's some traveller."

"But, Francis . . ." Brigid struggled to frame her question. "Did you . . . did you get what you asked him for?"

He did not look up. "I got this camera. It's excellent. It's got a flash. Look!" and he held up the small box of leather and plastic and glass. "Do you want to hold it?" He held it out.

She placed Marianne on his bed and reached out to take it but, still, he had not answered her question. He held his hands over hers and, distracted, she was surprised by the camera's heaviness.

"That's what you asked for?" said Brigid. Francis seemed not to hear. "But, Francis, when we saw Santa, I asked . . ."

"Tell you what," said Francis, and he took her hand. "Race you downstairs."

They tumbled downstairs together. Through the railings of the banister, they could see their mother bending down, switching on the Cinderella lights. She was wearing her blue dressing gown. That was another thing Brigid meant to ask about.

"Francis," she said, at the foot of the stairs. He paused, holding the newel post.

"There is *really* Santa Claus, isn't there?"

Francis did not hesitate: "Of course," he said. "Come on. I've something a bit special to show you later."

She held his arm, and felt his excitement running through it. She would tell him, quickly, before he saw what was in the parcel.

"What?" he said. "What is it?"

"Oh, Francis . . ." She still could not tell him about the theatre . . . but the dressing gown . . . ? "I . . . just . . . I saw blue, not red, blue like Mama's dressing gown going out the door, just when I woke up and found the presents."

Francis nudged her across the doorway to the sitting room. "Daft Brigid. Mama would have been checking to make sure we hadn't wakened. Do you think she would let us see him, or he would let us see him? And don't you want to know what I'm going to show you?"

"He might," said Brigid. "And, yes, I do . . . but Francis . . ."

"Then come on," he said, and took her arm into the room.

Now it was, finally, too late.

"Well, children!" said their mother. "Happy Christmas! Did he come?"

Brigid held out her doll in its box, and Francis his camera. Sitting down, lines under her eyes darker than the blue of her dressing gown, she seemed pleased. Francis stroked her arm.

"Shall I take a photograph, Mama?" he said, and pointed the new camera.

"Oh, please, Francis," she said, and she pushed it gently away, "have mercy. But, come here, both of you. What are these under the tree? Look. I see your names!"

Brigid looked at Francis, and watched him as he dropped to his knees and began to open his parcel. Brigid watched him untie the string, fold back the paper.

"Ah!" cried Francis, as he put aside the wrapping. "Meccano! Excellent!" and his eyes, as he turned to Brigid, were bright and dancing. "Go on," he said, nudging her elbow. "Open yours. And then . . . you know what I told you. There is something else . . ."

Brigid, her heart contracting, began to undo the string and, once again, she saw emerge the little theatre in its shining morning colour. "Oh," she said, and she did not look up. A long moment passed, and then she had to look up.

Francis, his face closed, sat perfectly still on his heels. "Well, now," he said. "That's . . . something you really wanted."

"Francis, I . . ."

"You are two lucky children!" said her mother, as if Brigid had not spoken. "Rose has spoiled the pair of you, hasn't she, Maurice?" She turned to her husband who, already dressed in his Sunday suit, had come into the room unnoticed.

"Yes," he said, his eyes showing the kindly lines of his smile, "and I'd say that Conor Todd had a hand in it, too."

"Oh, I don't know about that," said his wife, smoothing and folding the wrapping paper against her knees. "I think it was really Rose. Now, look at that clock! Time to get dressed." Slowly, holding her back, she straightened. "Francis," she said, "could you take . . . ?" She looked around, puzzled, her hands full of the folded paper.

Francis was no longer in the room.

No one but Brigid had seen him go. Looking down at the present she had asked for, she felt suddenly hot and ashamed. "I'll get him," she said, and ran out through the hall to the kitchen, to the back door.

She lifted the latch and stepped out into the back yard, the sharp wind taking her breath. For a moment, she stopped, her eyes travelling up beyond the back yard, beyond the house and the plot to the trees. She could just see their tops, poor skeletons touched by frost for Christmas, and beyond them the dark mountain, hung with late stars. Her eyes travelled downwards: cold points like diamonds glistened on the roof of the coalhouse, and on the bolt of the door which was hanging a little ajar. Brigid, with the remains of hope, picked her way across the frozen ground, and pulled the door open. There was no one there: she had known there would be no one there. There was nothing to be seen but coal, and logs. The cardboard theatre, with its careful balconies and marked doors, its brave square opening, was gone, as if it had never been, and there was no Francis.

In the corner of the yard, the frosted bin sat forlorn, its lid a little askew. Brigid, sadness and shame running through her like fire, did not need to look further. She saw the corner of an abandoned box jutting out from the top of the bin, its edges squared away as if it had been cut with a knife.

Chapter 16: The Princess Victoria

Christmas could not last forever. One morning she woke up, and knew it was over. Her theatre stood on a stool in the corner, Marianne in front of it, disdainful. Her book and her games sat bright and inviting by her bed, and the wintry world outside spoke still of Christmas, but the music of wonder had ceased.

Brigid got up and followed the sound of voices downstairs. She saw at once what was different: the tree was gone. A great empty space showed too much light from the window; a trail of sharp pine needles led to the door.

Her mother sat propped on the arm of a chair, one hand on her chest. She was wearing the polka-dot smock again. "Ah, Brigid," she said. "The very one. Have you seen the Santa Claus? You know it, the one I sewed."

Brigid shook her head, but her mother still seemed to be waiting. "Oh, well," she said, after a moment, sounding suddenly tired. "I daresay it'll turn up. It just would be nice to get it all tidied and away. But, Brigid?"

Brigid, wary, turned at the door.

"After you get dressed – I'm sure that's where you're going now – have a good think about where that Santa might be. And have a good look, too."

Outside the wind was gathering, and the sky sat low. In the

warmth of the house, Brigid felt a chill: everything was flat. She really did not know where the Santa had gone, but she understood that she was under suspicion, after the hoking. Even now, it came back. Even here, sitting on the stairs at home, she was once more in Laetitia's bedroom, breathing that smell as the door came suddenly away. Once again the choking mustiness, once again the nightmare musty mouldering, springing at her, and that yellowing boomerang thing she fought with and tried to stuff back. She could not shake the memory away.

The back door opened and shut: another chill swept through the hall. Then, Francis came out of the kitchen, smelling of pine needles.

"What's the matter with you?" he said.

"I just remembered something horrible," she said.

Francis swung round the newel post and sat down beside her. He leaned his back against the wall. "What?" he said.

"I don't want to tell you."

Francis moved to get up. "All right," he said. "You don't have to."

Brigid caught his ankle. "No. No. Don't go. I do. I do want to tell you."

"Tell me, then," said Francis.

"Just don't be cross."

Francis waited.

"When we went with Daddy – me and Ned, not you – you had your head thing, remember?"

Francis passed his hand over the fading scar. He nodded.

"That time, I . . . I went hoking in Granda's. But it wasn't me really – it was Ned Silver's fault. He made me."

Francis said nothing.

"He did make me. He's a horrible boy. And nobody said a word to him about it, and he pretended it was all me. It wasn't fair."

"You went hoking," said Francis, with a shrug. "Everybody knows that. Is that all?"

"It's not really. There was this horrible thing. It jumped at me, green and dark and smelly, and a roundy thing that was yellowy-white, and a slimy pouch coming open and a paper with writing . . . and I could smell it and Laetitia came in and she shouted, and she hit me on the arm . . . I just remembered it and it was worse. It was worse than when it happened, Francis."

"Laetitia hit you?" he said, and his face changed.

"Just once. Granda stopped her. Daddy said nothing all the way home. I thought I had forgotten, Francis. I thought it was gone."

He dropped his eyes, silent and still, close beside her on stairs. "Come on," he said, getting to his feet. He reached his hand down to her. "Let's go and sit for a moment in my room."

Brigid followed him down the corridor, Blessed Oliver especially severe as she passed below. Francis swung her up and perched her on the edge of his high bed. He left her there and sat on the window ledge, shadowing the window's wintry light. Behind him the branches of the Friday Tree spread out, cold and forlorn.

Francis looked down at his shoes, and then straight at Brigid. "Listen to me," he said. "What you did wasn't good."

Brigid's head hung down.

"Look up," he said. "Look up, Brigid." She looked up, swallowing. Francis was the only one who had never been cross with her. "It's not the end of the world, but you have got to think about things more. You didn't mean to do any harm, but you can't . . . you don't go hoking in other people's things. Do you get that?"

Brigid nodded, vigorously, several times. She opened her mouth to speak.

Francis held up his hand, square, palm towards her. "Don't say anything," he said. "I haven't finished."

She said nothing.

"Those things you found in Granda's belonged to our Uncle Laurence, who was lost. Remember?"

Brigid nodded again. Perhaps they had gone and found him. "On the *Princess Victoria*?"

"Yes. He died on the *Princess Victoria*."

Brigid drew in her breath. "He died? I thought he was lost?"

Francis paused. "Listen. Laetitia was very upset about Laurence."

"I know," said Brigid, with feeling. "I'm the one she hit. But I don't really see why. He was only a sort of uncle, wasn't he?"

"No, well, that's it, you see. He wasn't exactly her brother, but he was like a brother, because Granda Arthur took care of him after his own parents died – and he spent so much time in the house, he became like one of the family."

So that was why he was only a sort of uncle. Brigid began to see.

"And, three years ago," Francis continued, "just around this time of the year – well, a bit later, end of January, he died, and nobody has ever felt able to get rid of his things. They can't. It's too hard. How do you think they felt, Daddy or Granda, or Laetitia, to find you going through them?"

Brigid, unable to help herself, began to sniffle. "It was Ned Silver's fault. He made me."

Francis handed her his handkerchief, but he did not soften. "Stop that," he said, "and listen."

Brigid swallowed, and stopped.

"For a start, nobody makes you do anything. You chose to go hoking. Remember that."

Brigid breathed hard, but said nothing. She knew Ned Silver had made her.

"Next. Those were his clothes you found. They were the clothes he was wearing when he died. The white thing was his collar, a stiff collar. Daddy has some a bit like it."

"It jumped," said Brigid, still stung. "Collars don't jump."

"They don't if you leave them be. Anyway, Laurence died when the *Princess Victoria* went down in a storm coming from Scotland. It was just a few miles from the shore, at the Copeland

175

Islands, nearly home, but it was a terrible storm, and it hit all round the coast of here and Scotland and England, and lots of people died. The boy who lights the lamps outside?"

"Bobby? Bobby we said hello to one day?"

"Bobby, yes. You remember Bobby told us about that night? When every lamp he lit was put out, and he had to climb up in the storm and light them all again?"

She nodded: "He said it went down." She had not forgotten Bobby: the storm raging, the boy clinging to the pole. Now, finally, she knew what it meant to be lost, and she knew where the *Princess Victoria* had gone, and why Laurence was lost. It went down to the bottom of the sea, and to be lost was to be dead. "Francis," she said. "I'm sorry, Francis. I am, really. Don't be cross."

"I'm not cross," he said, in surprise. "I've nothing to be cross about. I'm only telling you, so you understand. Anyway, just don't hoke. Okay?"

"Okay," said Brigid, and then Francis got up, and the light came flooding into the room, and she scrambled down. As she landed on the floor, she said: "Francis, did anybody else we know die?"

"On the *Princess Victoria*? Well, Ned's mother, for one."

Brigid was silent.

"And now you know why Ned gets away with things we never will, and why nobody ever gets cross with him."

Brigid felt a hot wave of jealousy: Ned was probably still enjoying Christmas on her family's farm. Their tree might even still be up. Then she checked herself: he had no mother, and his father was always away.

"Is that why his father is always away?" she said. "In Egypt?"

"I suppose so. But, he has a big job – there's a lot about Egypt in the news, and he has something to do with the government."

The government, like Ireland, meant the end of interest for Brigid. She said she would be good, and when he replied that it would help if she meant it, said that she did mean it, and then she left his room.

It seemed to Brigid that Blessed Oliver looked down almost kindly as she walked beneath him. She was fairly penitent: perhaps that had impressed Blessed Oliver.

Nonetheless, for the rest of that day, in the flatness of winter without Christmas, she continued to wonder about the *Princess Victoria*: how it came to be lost, what happened to all the people, what happened to her almost-uncle whose death made Granda and Daddy and Laetitia so sad. Yet, with the feeling of one who has had a narrow escape, she thought it best not to raise the subject again.

January settled in, and life picked up again. Isobel came most days as before, but she no longer stayed overnight. Too late for Christmas, proper snow came, and the world for a time sparkled and shone. Then the weather worsened. Every day the newspaper told of gales hitting the coast, ships struggling in distress. Slates like sharp knives flew from roofs, walls tumbled in the fury of the wind. Dustbins fell helpless on their sides, trees blew across the roads, travel was discouraged. There were fuel shortages. Sometimes, miraculously, there was no school.

By the middle of the month, it was even worse. At breakfast one Sunday, their father picked up the newspaper, then set it down and, abruptly, stood up and left the room. The children heard him call their mother.

Francis picked up the paper. "'*The air was filled with SOS messages from all around the British coast,*'" he read. "'*For the first time in living memory, the island on which the Copeland lighthouse stands was completely submerged.*'"

The Copeland Islands. That was where Francis said the *Princess Victoria* went down. The children, looking at one another in silence, stayed sitting still until their father came back in, alone, and sat down.

Almost immediately, he got up again. "I think I'll take a drive down to see my father."

His wife, coming slowly into the room, stopped in the doorway. "You're not serious, Maurice. In that weather?"

He stood up, patting his pocket, tightening his tie. "Oh, talk sense," he said. "Didn't we make it out to Mass this morning?"

"Yes, just about, but . . ."

"But nothing. I've been waiting for the weather to settle since Christmas. I want to go down and see my family, and I can wait no longer. They need a visit round this time. You know that as well as I do."

"Well, I . . . Isobel isn't here today. I thought I'd rest . . ."

"Rest, then," said her husband, buttoning his jacket. "The children will come with me, and you'll have plenty of time to rest," and before their mother could protest he had shooed the children out to get hats and gloves and warm coats, and they, surprised and delighted, were in the car before they knew it, rolling in the sharp wind through the drumlins and the bare whipping trees, down to where the sea sent up high spray, and they could taste the salt in the air.

Their good humour lasted until they went through the door their grandfather, unsurprised and clearly pleased, opened to them. Yet, from the kitchen, its door almost closed, there was no sound. They looked at each other, sure that Laetitia was in there, and equally sure she was not going to come out to greet them. Their grandfather, without a word, closed the door to the kitchen and, taking Brigid's hand and Francis' shoulder, led them across the hall to the tall long-case clock.

"Did you ever see how I wind it up?" he said.

Brigid and Francis stood beside him as he inserted the key, like a letter Z, into two holes on the clock's white face. They stood watching the great weights move up the inside, the sun and moon inching round the dial, and the pendulum ticking away undisturbed as if its insides were not being moved around. High above them, on the top of the clock, a brown wooden eagle stood poised for flight. Then the clock struck, clear and bell-like, eleven times, and though it echoed around the hall and the whole house, it could not erase the bitter silence from the kitchen.

Brigid's father, slapping his pocket, said, "Right. I've had enough of this," and he opened the kitchen door. A warm rush of cooking, like meat, or onions, filled the air. The door closed behind him, but the voices were clear.

"What are the histrionics about now?"

"He didn't read out the name. I gave him the name for the prayers, and he didn't read it out."

"He probably did. You were probably asleep. Probably snoring." His tone, dismissive, was familiar to Brigid. For a second, she thought of Ned Silver.

"I was not asleep, though I could have been, up since the crack of dawn, cooking and . . . Ah, what do you care? It's all right for you, taking it easy."

"Yes. I take it very easy," Brigid heard her father say. "That's why I drove down here in a winter gale. Well, if the priest didn't read out Laurence's name, or if he did, would it bring him back? We all lost him. Not just you."

The door opened, and the smell of cooking wafted out once more. Laetitia swept into the hall, then stopped as she saw Brigid and Francis. Ignoring them, she stood, her face white.

"Make some tea, Tish, will you?" said Brigid's grandfather, and he calmly replaced the key on top of the clock.

In silence, uncertain, Brigid looked up at her father, emerging from the kitchen.

"Make tea. That's all I ever hear," Laetitia said, her eyes on Brigid. "You back to go hoking where you've no business?" It was her only greeting. She turned to Francis, her face for an instant softening, then again to Brigid, and there was little liking there.

Silent, taken aback, the children watched her turn away and, once more, the kitchen door closed.

"I'm not having any more of this nonsense," said their father. He rapped on the door, then pushed it until it stood open.

Their Aunt Laetitia stood there, unconcerned by the bubbling and steaming of the pots on the stove. She was looking from the window at the grey and sullen sky. One hand held a lighted cigarette, the other sat on her hip, the peppery tweed of her slim skirt skimming her body, one leg elegantly pointed, like a dancer's. The grey-and-dark striped hair showed starkly clear, as she turned round, walked towards them, then closed the door of the kitchen in their faces.

Brigid's grandfather joined his son. Together, they stood looking at the door.

"Pop," said the children's father, "what started it this time?"

The grandfather sighed. "What starts it any time?" he said. "I could say it's the time of the year, and the weather. I could say it's reading about the Copeland Island lighthouse." He sighed again, heavily. "I could say that the young priest did forget to read out Laurie's name in the list of the anniversaries."

"She said that . . . but I don't see . . . it's not the anniversary yet," said his son, puzzled.

"No, but Laetitia got it into her head that . . . the weather lately . . . she . . . and, oh, I don't know. I could say it was any number of things, but really what it is, is . . . her."

Brigid said: "Are we going to stay, Daddy? It's hot in our coats."

Her father looked down, as if he had forgotten her. "Coats," he said, absently. "Yes, take them off," and he took off his own, and hung it by the mirror. He did not bother to hang it by its loop. "Ah, Pop," he said, still standing in the hall, running his hand through his hair, "can you and she not agree, even at this hard time of the year?"

"I think it's because it is this hard time of the year," the grandfather said quietly and, taking Brigid by the hand, he led her into the sitting room and sat her on his knee.

Francis did not follow them. Brigid heard him go into the kitchen and close the door behind him.

"Granda," said Brigid, "I'm sorry for hoking the last day I was here."

"It's all right, girlie. You're only a child."

Brigid said: "I won't do it again. But . . ."

"But what?"

"But . . . I would like you to tell me about my sort of uncle who was lost."

She heard her father's exasperated sigh. He got up, turned his back, and crossed to the window, looking out at the angry sea.

Brigid knew she had taken advantage, and was almost remorseful. Her father would not have told her if she had asked him. Yet, she wanted to know.

Her grandfather sat back and brought her with him. "Laurie. Ah, Laurie. He was like one of my own – a big, gentle boy. I did my best for him, after his parents died. I knew them well, the parents: the father was a far-out connection of my own. They had often been here, and the child with them. He would have played with my two, outside there, the way you would with your brother. Maurice, now, he was older, but Laurie and Tish, they were very close: you never saw one without the other – like you and Francis, or young Silver."

Brigid, struggling, fought back a strong urge to correct him about Ned Silver, but she managed to stay quiet.

"Then, an aeroplane crash: that's what killed them. An aeroplane, on the way to Lourdes. The mother, she was very religious – the father, well, he did his best, like most of us. But it was terrible – and Laurie, you see, he was away at school. He had it in his head that he must become a priest: maybe he thought it would please his mother, I don't know. He was a nice lad, but he wasn't the easiest to deal with when he got a notion in his head and, God help him, he got a terrible shock when they died. He did go on to Maynooth, and he was ordained, but he found it tough enough. Maybe because of what happened, maybe not. Anyway, he was always able to treat this house as his home, and us as his family. Wasn't he, Maurice?"

Brigid's father nodded his head, but said nothing.

"Do you remember, earlier it was to be medicine – nothing would do him but he'd be a doctor? He wanted to do something useful, do you see, Brigid? He wanted to do something for other people. Anyway, a priest is what he became."

"Laetitia stayed close to him?" Brigid asked, intrigued by this new picture, of a Laetitia who ran about and played, a Laetitia who cared about somebody.

Her grandfather paused before he answered. Her father looked across, watching them both.

"She thought there was no one like him," said her grandfather, at last.

"What did he think about her?" asked Brigid. "Uncle Laurie?"

Her father was still watching, but she could not read his face.

"Well, he was good with her. They got on well. I think he brought out the best in her. No one's been able to do that, since he . . . since he left us. And she's never been the same since, so you need to make allowances."

Brigid heard her father make a sound that was almost like a snort.

"Francis can make her laugh," said Brigid, leaning back against his waistcoat – she felt something missing from it, but she could not think what it was.

"Well, yes, that's true. Francis can. Anyway, two – no, three, dear God, three years ago, he went across to make a retreat, outside Edinburgh. That's in Scotland, girlie, just over the water. He was to be there for a week, but for whatever reason he decided to come back early. We never could understand why he set out that bad morning. But he did, and it was a bad day, and a bad night after. I spoke to a man who survived. I met him at a memorial for the ones who died. He saw Laurie."

Brigid's father turned from the window. "Why go over this, Pop," he said. "It won't bring him back."

"Because the child asked me," said her grandfather, more sharply than she had ever heard him speak. "The man saw poor Laurie," he continued, as if his son had not spoken. "The ship was lying over to starboard. Do you know what that means?" Brigid shook her head. "It means to the right." He held up his right hand, the fingers long and fine, like Francis' hands, like her father's. "The ship was full of water. There were cars on it, and the doors were buckled by a huge wave. A vast wall of water, the man told me. All the people who could climbed up the deck. Oh, this man, he said it was like climbing a sheer mountainside. They were trying to climb to the port side – the left side. The man who survived told me he saw a young clergyman holding on, talking to a woman, distressed, because she had lost someone."

"Who?"

"He didn't know." Her grandfather shook his head. "Who knows? A child, maybe? A husband? A parent? The man I spoke to said he could hear her lamenting, and this young clergyman, this man told me, he kept trying to get her to go on the lifeboat. There was a boat for the women and children, but she wouldn't go, and he wouldn't leave her, talking to her, all in the waves and the wind, and then finally he did get her to go, and he put her on, the man said . . . and then the whole ship cowped."

"Cowped, Granda?"

"Turned turtle. Turned over. Went upside down in the water."

"Did she get away, in the boat for the women and the children?"

"The boat got away at first, but another big wave came along and threw them upside down, beneath the ship as she was going under the sea. They were all lost. All the women and children."

"And our almost-uncle was lost, too." Brigid understood now, and she was not sorry that she had asked.

"Yes, he was lost, with other souls too."

Brigid thought: Ned's mother.

"We heard in the afternoon that the ship had sunk, but we didn't know he was on it until the next day. That was a Sunday. It was Wednesday before they found the body. From Sunday to Wednesday we prayed that by some miracle he would be safe, but there was no miracle for Laurie, or for us."

She was leaning against her grandfather's face, and felt it wet. She was sorry, but there was one more thing she needed to know.

"Granda, how did the man know it was Laurence he saw?"

"The length of him, the length of him laid out like that," was all he said.

They heard the kitchen door open and close again, and Francis looked through the door. "She's better now," he said. "I'll just stay with her for a bit," and he went back towards the kitchen.

Brigid's father, unsmiling, spoke for the first time: "She might give you your dinner yet, Pop. Francis has smoothed it over."

"She does her best, in her own way," said his father, and reached his hand to his waistcoat. "What time of the day is it, anyway? Oh, my blessed watch. I forgot. I can't find it anywhere, this last while."

"Past midday. It'll turn up," said his son. "It's time we were on the road anyway, if you think you're all right."

"Oh, I am. And it will turn up, I'm sure," said his father. "I just can't think where I . . . I'm getting old, Maurice . . . an old man."

Her father put his hand on the old man's shoulder. "Not you, Pop," he said. "You'll see us all out."

Brigid took this to mean they were going home, and went to collect her coat. Through the half-open door of the kitchen she saw to her surprise her aunt sitting at the table, a wreath of smoke about her head. Beside her sat Francis. They were sitting, quietly, companionably, chatting. To Brigid's surprise her aunt looked lively, and, if not pretty like Rose, at least warm, approachable. Brigid, puzzled, went back in to the others, pulling on her coat.

Her grandfather said: "Well, somebody's ready for the road," and the two men laughed, the first time that morning, and their father called Francis to come on.

It was a quiet journey, the children tacitly agreeing to let their father have his time to himself, and the wind and the weather stayed kind long enough to let them reach home without incident. Yet, in the car, an image stayed with Brigid. It was not of her father, or her grandfather, or Laetitia, or even Laurence whom she had never known. Brigid imagined Ned, hearing at six years old that his mother was never coming back, and she was truly sorry.

Back at home, their father locking the car in the garage, Brigid walked down the passage with her brother.

"Did you know Ned's mother, Francis?" she said.

He shook his head. "No," he said. "They just moved here before Mrs Silver was lost. Mrs Silver's family owned all this land – you know, the plot and everything – but they had never lived here. I think her family came from somewhere quite near Granda. I think he knew Mrs Silver, or her family, anyway – I mean her family before she was married. I remember that house next door was empty for a while, and then we heard the Silvers were going to live in it themselves. Was it something to do with Ned? I can't remember. I used to see his mother from time to time, but I never saw his father."

"I've never seen him," said Brigid. "I've never seen anybody but Mrs Mulvey."

"Did you know she was famous? Mrs Silver, I mean, not Mrs Mulvey."

"Famous? Famous for what?"

"She was a singer. I was brought to see her in the Opera House. *The Mikado*, I think."

"Was she good?"

"I don't remember which one she was. She was away a lot, I remember that. She had been in Scotland, I think, singing in something. That's why she was on the *Princess Victoria*. It was in the paper: '*Myra Silver among Dead on Princess Victoria*'. It was shocking. Everybody talked about it – and then, Ned had nowhere really to go but next door, and that's why he is off at school, and only here some holidays, and that is why – though you weren't pleased – everybody else was glad that Rose took Ned home for Christmas. Brigid, are you listening?"

Brigid, puzzled, was trying to remember something. "I am

listening. Did you say she was called 'Myra'?"

"Myra Silver, yes."

Brigid concentrated. "Francis, I've seen that name."

"Where?"

Brigid bit her lip. "When I was hoking that time, in Granda's. There was a pouch of tobacco in among the things, and they all crumbled, and there was a piece of paper folded up in the box, and there was writing on it. The writing was hard for me to read, but I could read it in the end. It said: M – Y – R – A. Isn't that Myra?"

Francis looked thoughtful. "It is. But why . . ." He stopped. "Brigid. What happened to it? Did you put it back? Did you tell anyone about it?"

"I'm sorry, Francis. I couldn't put it back."

"Why not? Don't tell me you kept it."

"No. No, I didn't. I wouldn't. Ned took it. He kept it."

Francis was silent. "Are you sure?" he said. "Are you really sure?"

"Yes. He took it."

"You are telling me the truth, Brigid? Ned Silver saw that paper in Granda's house, and took it?"

"I am telling you the truth, Francis."

Francis drew in a breath. He tapped her shoulder, absently, as if he had something else on his mind. They were at the door, and they could hear their father's step behind them, and she knew she was taking a chance, but Brigid had one more question.

"Francis," she said urgently. "There is something else I need to know, then I promise I won't ask about the *Princess Victoria* any more."

Francis looked warily behind them. "Make it quick, then."

"The man who saw Uncle Laurie? The man who talked to Granda? How did he know it was him?"

"Oh," said Francis. "The clothes, I think. And then, I suppose, Granda had to identify him."

The clothes! The clothes leaping out at her that day, horribly alive – yes, that made sense, but what to identify meant, she could not ask, not because of her promise, but because their father caught up with them, and shooed them into the house.

Chapter 17: Imbolc

February began, just as cold, blustery and disappointing as January had been. At the breakfast table, trying to eat her porridge, Brigid watched grey rain drive slantingly against the window. She tried to invent ways to avoid school, but could think of nothing that had not yet been attempted. Her mother, though tired and moving slowly, was not to be fooled. It was clear from her father's face, scanning the newspaper, that he would not be taken in either.

"My God," he suddenly said, and slapped the paper down.

Brigid and Francis looked up in surprise.

"Maurice," said his wife. "Please. The children."

"Have you seen this?" he said, waving the newspaper at her.

"No one has had the opportunity," she replied, reaching for the teapot, "except you."

"Well, you'll have the opportunity now," he said, flicking the paper with a snap. "Listen to this, all of you. There is a call from Stormont to ban an Irish text book for schoolchildren – *for schoolchildren* – because the children are seen to carry the Irish flag, which contravenes the Flags and Emblems Act." He began to read from the newspaper: "'*Editorial: Three Boys and a Dog. We suppose we should feel relieved that the boy with the toy gun has not also been singled out for criticism. Who knows whether the gun was meant for Ireland – or Israel? It was the flag upon which most interest was directed at Stormont. Since the Flags Act may not be capable of dealing with children's lesson books containing pictures of the Tricolour, another Banner Bill may now have to be introduced. Soon we may know whether the boys holding Irish flags in school primers are to be disqualified, as if they held offices of profit under the Crown.'"*

There was silence.

Brigid said: "I don't understand what that means, Daddy."

A key turned in the door, and Isobel came in, wet and out of breath. Her coat was streaked with dark dampness, and she smelled of rain: "I'm sorry, Mrs Arthur. This rain! I'll take her down now."

"No, I'll take her in the car, and Francis too," said Brigid's father. "You stay here, Isobel – you're wet through."

"Maurice," said his wife. "Please. In the car – no politics in front of the children."

"Ah, holy cats," he said. "Maybe it's time they knew the state we're in." He laughed. "The State we're in! Where the police are empowered *by law* to remove any emblem other than the Union Jack! Dear God. What a place to try to bring up children!" He began to laugh again.

"Maurice," said their mother, frowning, "you're not yourself. I don't think you should go out today at all." She got to her feet, quite like her old self, before she grew round and slow. "Isobel," she said, an edge to her voice, "I'm sorry to ask you, but you'll have to go out again. Borrow my raincoat and take Brigid to school. Francis, get your coat on too. You'll both be late at this rate."

Brigid was sure her father would protest, but he did nothing. He sat back in his chair, head on his chest, arms folded. To her bewilderment, she found herself facing out into the rain with Isobel and Francis.

It was a strange day even at school. Brigid's teacher, for whatever reason, did not come in, and all the infants were dispersed to other classes. Brigid found herself in a large warm room, full of the biggest girls she had ever seen.

At the top sat a nun she had never seen: round yet wide, head on one side, she was like a plump, black-eyed bird. "Ah," she said. "You're the child who writes the stories?"

Brigid nodded, uncertainly.

"Good," said the round nun. "I asked them to send you up to me," and she sat Brigid down near the front. She gave her paper, pencils and crayons, and told her to write or draw as she pleased.

Brigid, still wary, waited for a moment – then slowly she began to draw a boy who was Francis, and a girl who was herself, the seven trees, and under the Friday Tree she drew a wigwam, with smoke. She became absorbed, and did not notice the time passing, did not hear the voices of the nun or the girls. Once, when she looked up, she saw they were sewing, their bright needles flashing in and out of folds of cloth.

By twelve o'clock Brigid, used to the half-day granted only to the infants, was tired and more than ready for home, but Sister was telling the big girls what they were going to do next. It was something special, she said, and then, most unexpectedly, called Brigid to stand beside her. "Watch, now," she said. Brigid watched. Sister took from her desk a sheaf of green reeds, and began to fold and plait, rapidly bending and sliding and twisting the pliable greenery until, by a miracle, she had woven a cross. "Now, girls," she said, "that's a Saint Brigid's cross, and I want you all to reach inside your desks and take out the reeds I have placed there, and do as I have done. I'll come round and see how you do."

After a puzzled silence, the big girls began to do it, some with dexterity, others with slow frustration.

Sister took Brigid by the hand and walked her about the room. Brigid watched with fascination as the nun lifted up the girls' work, her hands guiding theirs, her fingers flying in and out, swift as knitting needles, plaiting and weaving the green stems until a cross of rushes appeared on each desk.

When she went back up to her desk, Sister let Brigid try one with her, her hands, cool and dry, over Brigid's. As they worked, Sister said: "So you are the child who likes to try new words?"

Brigid thought of her cannonball story, and all her wariness returned. "Not any more," she said, quickly adding "Sister."

The nun went on guiding Brigid's fingers through the plait of rushes. "Well," she said finally, "I think you should keep at it. I hear you have a great store of general knowledge. When you are a bigger girl and come up here to my class, I'll want you to write a great deal, and I'll want to see all the words you know."

As Brigid turned to look at her, she found the face no longer watchful, the eyes kinder than she had thought.

"Meanwhile, when you write stories, if you want to, you can show them to me. St Brigid herself was a writer. Did you know?"

Brigid shook her head.

Sister looked out the window. "The other infants are going home now," she said, "and so must you." She stood up, her roundness made rounder by the full pleats of her skirt. She motioned with her finger to a tall girl with a fiery pony-tail: "Take Brigid Arthur downstairs to the other infants. And come straight back." She turned to Brigid as if she were an adult and, cocking her head to one side, as she had when Brigid saw her first, she said, "That girl would forget her own head if it wasn't attached, but she'll mind you going down. On you go now, and don't forget what I told you. Oh, and Brigid?"

Brigid turned round.

"I liked the cannonball," the nun said.

It was a long time before Francis came home that day. He was in the middle of school examinations, and when he did come in, he went straight up to his room, and Isobel brought him something to eat. He had to study: no one was to disturb him, and the house was to be kept quiet. Brigid, with no homework and no television, found the silence exhausting, and nothing, books or puzzles, caught her interest. She went from room to room, restless, ending up in the sitting room, where her mother sat sewing a small something, white and fine. Seeing Brigid, she put it down.

"Stop prowling," she said, "and come here." She reached out her hand, pulling Brigid gently to stand beside her. "Brigid," she said, "would you like a little brother or sister?"

Brigid thought. "I have a brother. Perhaps a sister. Are we getting one?"

"We may be," said her mother. "God may send us a new baby."

Brigid clapped her hands. "A baby? When?"

"Oh, in the longer day. Now, I want you to do something for me, like a good girl."

Brigid did not reply: she was not sure if they were really getting a baby. 'In the longer day', like 'we'll see' and 'perhaps after the holidays' often meant 'never': it might be unwise to count on it.

"Brigid, are you listening? Go up and tell Francis to come down and take a break: you can watch some television with him."

Brigid did not need to be asked twice. She ran upstairs as fast as she could. Somewhere, low, she heard a throbbing beat, and when she opened the door of his room, it grew louder.

"Francis, is your wireless on?"

Francis, his head bent over his work, looked up: "Yes."

"Can you turn it up?"

"No," said Francis. "It's not supposed to be on."

Brigid stood by the radio: softly, it danced and pulsed, joyous and energetic. "Who is that singing?" she said.

"Buddy Holly," he said, wearily. "How was today?"

Brigid could see his eyes were tired and strained, but she climbed on the bed anyway.

"It was St Brigid's day," she said. "I learned that."

"Oh, did you?" he said. "So, what happens on St Brigid's day?"

"Crosses. The big girls upstairs in school make them. I helped make one today, Francis, nearly all by myself." She flushed: that was not really true.

"Did you?" said Francis. "By yourself? That *was* something. She's the patron saint of cattle. Bet you didn't know that. Spring begins today. That's why people make Brigid's crosses from grassy things, like reeds and rushes. That was what you . . . helped to make today."

"I did do some of it."

"I don't doubt that," said Francis. "Anyway, it is a holy time."

Brigid felt even more ashamed. "I'm not very holy," she said.

"No, you're not," Francis agreed. "But, you don't have to be. You might like the original Brigid better. The fire goddess."

"Fire goddess!" said Brigid, starting. This was better. "Is that the one with stories?"

"Yes, that too. In the old days they needed fire to cook and to keep warm. Brigit – with a 't' – was very powerful, and the feast to keep her happy was called Imbolc."

Imbolc. Imbolc. Rolling around her tongue and inside her head, like the fire he described. What a word. "But, fire?" she said. "We aren't meant to go near fire."

"No," he said, "not real fire. The fire is inside, in the head, not a fire that burns you. It's a fire that makes you want to make things. In the old stories, she was the goddess of wisdom, the goddess of poets, of writers, protecting them, helping them make their songs and their stories. In Britain she was Britannia – in Scotland, St Bride. Some people think the name means 'Fiery Arrow' and some 'High One'. Here in Ireland they say she was Mary's friend."

"What, Mary the Mother of God? How do you know all this, Francis?" Brigid asked, shaking her head.

He laughed. "I read. Apparently too much, and not the right things, but that's another story."

"Another story? Now?"

"No," he said, firmly. "Go. Begone. Go and think what you can do with your name."

"How?"

"That's up to you. You could write something, maybe. Now, I'm tired, Brigid, and I'm supposed to be working, and I want to stop, and I can't, yet. Go. I mean it."

Francis stopped talking, and Brigid, disappointed to be dismissed, climbed down from the bed, telling him quickly as he walked her to the door that she had met a nun who turned out to be kind, and wanted her to write more stories.

"Well, didn't I just tell you to? Now, Brigid, please . . ."

Brigid stopped. "Francis! Look!" She pointed to the window. Dim though her vision was, she could make out a shape that could only be Isobel coming down the bare winter plot, stepping on the hard ridges of the frosted soil. Under her arm she carried what looked like a roll of cloth, but Brigid could not see what it was. "Look, Francis! Turn round and look! Why is Isobel in the plot? What is she doing?"

Francis turned, too slowly for Brigid's satisfaction. "I don't see anyone."

Brigid crossed quickly to the window, pulling Francis by the arm. "Look! She . . ."

There was no one there. The trees stood bare and lonely at the back of the plot, and there was no one to be seen. "She was there, Francis. She was. I saw her."

"Brigid," said Francis, "you *are* killed with imagination. You know Isobel isn't even here this afternoon. Now, I give up. And I am starving. Please go and do something useful somewhere else, or let me go downstairs."

"Oh, yes, I was to tell you to do that. Come downstairs. And we can watch television, if we like."

"Well, thanks for telling me," Francis said. He got up and pushed her firmly out before him, closing the door after them.

Brigid let him go ahead, and slowly followed him, Imbolc in her head. It paused for a second, then bounced to her lips and struck off from her tongue and her teeth. What a lovely word.

Francis called her for television, and she joined him, but her heart was not in it. She was certain that it was Isobel she had seen in the plot. She was certain, too, that there was no point in mentioning it to anyone, when even Francis thought it was her imagination. Instead, she named the princess in her theatre Brigit the Fire Goddess, and set her to defeat Isobel the Wicked, Enemy of Imbolc.

Chapter 18: Naming the Fields

The days remained cold and bright, but the sun and wind eased and, slowly, light began to return. Brigid's mother grew larger and slower; her father seemed to drift more and more into his own thoughts. Even Francis grew up and away from her, more in his room with his music than downstairs with her. There were few visits from her grandfather, none from Rose. Brigid did not see Ned Silver, away at his new school, and Uncle Conor kept away from their house. Had it not been for her theatre and the new adventures of Brigit the Fire Goddess and George Bailey – who got on surprisingly well – Brigid would have thought herself in February a very lonely child.

March was brighter still, but cold breezes cut sharply at the bus stop on school mornings. Brigid lived for Saturdays and any possible holiday. Everything was grey as the ashy thumbprint the priest gave their foreheads on the first day of Lent. All through the long weeks that followed, any sweets they were given had to be saved in a jar, to be eaten on St Patrick's Day, a brief respite, but the effect of eating so many at one time made Brigid feel rather more ill than happy, and the remaining weeks of Lent seemed gloomier still.

Yet, one day in late March, Brigid looked from the window and saw that, under the broom bush between their garden and the plot, small daffodils had begun to push through, and frail yellow primroses to appear beneath the hedge. That was the beginning of hope. Very slowly, the weather grew a little warmer, and the rain softer. One morning, she felt sure she could make out on the Friday Tree a thin tracery of leaves, palest green, the brown of the bark still showing through. The tree swayed, but did not struggle to keep upright as it had through the storms of winter. Now, finally in their spring attire, light and delicate, the seven trees at the back of the plot seemed almost ready for the dance, for the summer to come.

At last, the day before Easter arrived, and with it came Rose, the bright shining ring sparkling, not on her neck, but on her left hand. True to her promise of the summer, as soon as lunch was over she put the children in her car, and they found themselves to their delight on the way to the farm at Tullybroughan. Brigid did not have time to consider that her parents were not coming with them, her mother too tired and the smock so big, and her father tired too, differently, in the sad weariness growing on him since the autumn. There was no time to be anxious: the prospect of time on the farm was too delightful to be missed. Besides, Rose said she had a surprise for them when they got there, but, despite much questioning, Brigid could not find out what it was.

The journey took a while, but everything on the way down was a source of excitement, even the Burnhouse where glue was made, though the car windows had to be shut tight to keep out the smell. The towns grew strange and different: more walls, more arches, bridges, drumlins again, then the leafy road of the old city where, as they climbed a steep hill, the children saw two cathedrals up ahead, one square and solid, the other tall and slender, with twin spires. One of them was tolling its bells just beside the hospital where Rose worked: she brought them in and showed them the plaque on the wall to the railway disaster, and made them tea from the great pot she kept in her office. Rose's tea was like no other, dark and strong and sweet. Brigid enjoyed it but, despite herself, she knew she was fidgeting. At last, at long

last, they left, piled into the little car, and set off down the steep
hill, past the twin spires stretching towards the sky, past the
shambling marketplace, out along the broad road, past the old
graveyard where all their mother's family lay buried, right back
to the first one who was French. Brigid, half-listening, heard
"war of religion" and paid no more attention: it sounded too
much like the news.

They turned into the lane, and Rose stopped the story. The
lane, always longer than Brigid thought any lane could possibly
be, was narrow and twisted, with ferns, feathered fingers in the
ditch, and primroses in pale clumps. Behind them, waving in
greeting, danced bluebells: delicate and frail, they managed to
live out in the lane, all through the rain and the cold of night,
and they survived. The year before, when the children picked
them, they died in a day, but there were more, hundreds more,
and now this year they had all come back.

All of a sudden, round a corner, down a hill, there was
Tullybroughan. As if they had seen the sea, both children
exclaimed at the sight of the haggard, the white-washed barn, and
then the house itself, tucked away behind it in its own little shelter.
Smoke rose from the chimney and, suddenly, for a second, Brigid
remembered the other little house, at the edge of the world in
Lecale, where there was no more smoke. Then, just as quickly, she
forgot. This house was living, and she could smell bread baking.

They turned in at the white posts of the gate, and Brigid
clutched Francis as she saw that their Uncle Michael had set up
the swing in the chestnut tree. It seemed that he had been trying
it out, too: it was swinging lightly as if someone had just jumped
off. Then they saw Michael's long hooked nose and narrow face
as, brown and wiry, he lifted a milk churn on to the back of a
lorry. He stopped what he was doing at the sound of the car,
waved at the children, and called to Rose, "Take her on round!"
They had arrived.

Out of the side of her eye, Brigid thought she glimpsed
another figure, but was not sure. Then a voice called, "Hero!

198

Bruno!" and round the corner of the lorry came two collie dogs, winding themselves in a U-shape, bending low in greeting to a small thin figure. Brigid drew in her breath. The figure was Ned Silver. The children looked at each other, climbed out of the car, and steadied themselves on the clean-swept ground.

"Now, you two," said Rose, closing the car door, "I told you I had a surprise. Here's your friend Ned to keep you company for Easter!"

She seemed not to notice their silence, ushering them inside, seating them at the table. She made tea that was strong and good as the tea in the hospital, and she gave them each a boiled egg, in a delph eggcup, blue and white, and there was wheaten bread she had made herself that morning. It was all they could have hoped. Yet, Brigid could hardly swallow. Ned Silver was here, in yet another of their family places, sitting with his feet under the table as if he belonged. Rose was telling them that there would be extra special eggs the next morning, for Easter, and Brigid, who had scarcely touched anything sweet for six long weeks, thought longingly of the end of their fast. Then Ned's covert look at Rose under his lashes, as if he had the right to love her, renewed her fury. Suddenly the food tasted of nothing, and she pushed it away.

"Are you sick, Brigid?" asked Rose. "You're not eating."

"She's in a Lenten frame of mind," said Francis, buttering a warm, nutty farl of bread, and placing it on her plate.

The fragrance of the oaten cake, and the warm melting butter, drifted across to Brigid, and hunger began to return.

"Material things mean nothing to Brigid. She's a walking saint," Francis said and, in spite of herself, Brigid had to relent.

So, Ned was here. Brigit the Fire Goddess and walking saint would consider the matter. Brigid herself took another slice of bread.

Then, when they had eaten to Rose's satisfaction, and helped to clear away their dishes, they were told they could go outside, but they were not to get in Michael's way if they saw the tractor.

Ready to stretch legs too long confined, the children stood up, excused themselves, and made it quietly as far as the half wall in front of the door.

"Fairy House," said Francis, very low, in Brigid's ear. No one could have heard it, but Ned Silver looked narrowly at them as if he had, and made for the Big Field. Francis said, "Right," then broke into a loping run, out across the narrow lane, and overtook Ned, followed by Brigid who, in a swerve and a scramble, managed to avoid an offended chicken, pecking its way with careful dignity across the yard. Francis cleared the gate into the Big Field with ease, Ned with effort, but Brigid, following them, struggled. Francis, to her surprise and disappointment, seemed to have forgotten her. He had already begun to sprint across the field as if he were by himself.

"Help me, Ned," she said.

Ned reached out his hand but, instead of pulling her over, he suddenly pushed her, so that she landed on her back in the grass.

Brigid, breathless and angry, shouted, "Ned, you pig!" and Francis, hearing this, stopped, turned, sighed and ran back.

Ned, well over the gate, passed him without a word, running as if the field were his own. Brigid was speechless with fury.

Francis, looking grimly after Ned's departing back, said nothing. He lifted Brigid with ease, and placed her on the other side of the gate. "Take my hand," he said. "You'll have to keep up, if we're to get to the Fairy House before him," and he began to run, followed hard by Brigid. They ran to the top of the field, where the Fairy House sat, and when they reached the place, a cluster of thorn trees, they stopped and, hearts beating in time, caught their breath.

They looked about them. There was no Ned. All around was simply silence, but for the grass of the field and its birds, its insects and, somewhere, the sound of water.

"Made it," said Francis. "He doesn't know about this. Come on. Race you!" and he began to scour the ground.

At the Fairy House, Brigid knew, there was something that

could not be found anywhere else: fairy pipes. She was the first to find one and, proudly, she held it up.

"Francis!" she called.

Francis stopped searching and stood up straight. "Ha! The first! Well done."

"Not quite," said a voice. From behind the thorns, Ned came out. "I got one first," he said, "if you mean these little acorns."

"They're fairy pipes," said Brigid, scornfully. "The gentry left them for us. For *us*. You have no right." She tried to snatch the little pipe from Ned.

He held it over her head, just out of reach. "No?" he said. "I'm just collecting acorns, as Rose showed me how to do."

"They are fairy pipes!" cried Brigid. Rose knows that, she thought, and how did he dare to call her by her name?

Ned laughed. "To little girls they may be fairy pipes, but, in fact, they are just acorns. Francis?" he said, his eyebrow raised. "What do you think?"

Francis, his face flushed and closed, looked hard at Ned. "I think you needn't have spoiled the Fairy House for Brigid, especially when you're a guest here," and he stood closer to Brigid, taking her hand.

"Superstition," said Ned. "My father says you Catholics," and he paused, turning over in his hand the shining little pipe, "are riddled with superstition."

Francis said nothing, but Brigid felt his hand grow tight and still on hers. Then he turned round, and drew her with him. "Come on, Brigid," he said. "Let's go back to the house."

Brigid and Francis walked back down the field in silence. Ned did not accompany them. Brigid could not understand why Francis had not simply told Ned that he was wrong, and that these were the fairy pipes left behind by the gentry, the Good People, since he knew it as well as she did. He saw they had left a fairy pipe for her. And she did not know what superstition was, or why Ned's father had said Catholics were riddled with it, or what it meant to be riddled. Looking carefully at her brother's flushed face, she saw it was not the time to ask.

Back at the gate, Brigid once more found herself trying several times to gain a foothold. In frustration, she pushed Francis. Then, she was sorry, because his face as he turned it to her looked so surprised.

"Don't take it out on me," he said.

The day felt spoiled.

Then, as if the sun had come out from behind clouds, Francis smiled. "I know!" he said. "We'll go round all the fields, and we'll do the names. Would you like that?"

"Oh Francis!" cried Brigid. "Just us?"

"Just us," he said, and he took her hand again. "Let's see how much you remember from last time with Mama. Okay?"

"Okay!" said Brigid, and they made across the yard straight into the Limekiln Field, at the bottom of the hill before the house. He told her the lime was for spreading on crops, like the potatoes just planted on St Patrick's Day, and to make whitewash for the house. They ran on to the field where the undertakers used to keep their black horses. There were none now: Brigid and Francis were the horses, galloping across the meadow, nodding to each other their imagined black plumes, whinnying as they flew across the field. Their canter took them into the Bog, with the trembling grass where the men cut turf, and on again to the Whinny Brae where wild pansies and primroses grew, Francis pausing to look at the spring well. He explained how water was pumped up there, and pumped through again for the farm horses, Nelly and Charlie. Francis liked being with the horses; Brigid did not. Nelly, blind in one eye, was gentle, but Charlie had bitten her once, and she had not gone near the horses again. Francis told her to forget about all that and look at the clear water bubbling out of the ground, and the forget-me-nots, and the rabbits scuttering away at their approach. He led her across the Near Hill and then the Middle Hill, on to the Back Hill and its hazelnut tree with only one nut, and then to the Field Above the Road, with its hedge of wild cherries, then to the field that was taken by neighbours for strawberries, and the field that had once belonged to an old man, his abandoned house still on it – and Brigid thought again of the little house by the sea – then on to the huge field, the Towns Meadow, where in the summer they had heard bees humming in the grass. And now, their circle almost complete, the sun no longer high in the sky, they arrived at the Field Above the House and the Field Behind the Garden. Brigid, who had climbed and run without fatigue, felt suddenly tired as they came to the haggard, behind the house, where hay was kept, and Charlie himself sometimes went round and round to turn the churn and make butter. Remembering his teeth, Brigid was glad he was not there. Now, they were in a little garden, long overgrown: no one had time to tend it any more. Then it was the front orchard and the back orchard. Bramley apples grew there, Francis said, and Beauty of Bath and Lord Derby. One tree was the Buttermilk tree, and the green and white apples in autumn from that were oval, not round. Blackcurrant bushes grew through the apple trees, and over across the lane, beside a gate into the Big Field where they had begun, they could see the crab-apple tree: it gave apples for Rose's jelly. Now, the apple trees were just coming into bloom, their light, delicate scent wafting towards them as they came back to the house.

Brigid's annoyance had dispersed on the air. "I'm sorry, Francis," she said. "I shouldn't have pushed you. It was Ned I was angry at."

Francis pulled a piece of grass and began to chew it. "I know that," he said.

"And Ned didn't see any of this, did he?" said Brigid. "He only knows the Fairy House."

"That's all," said Francis, and then he stopped. Shading his eyes with his hands, he looked across to the Fairy House.

Even Brigid, with her dim vision, could see, sitting there, a small solitary figure. "Ha," she said. "Serve him right. He's on his own."

Francis stood still, chewing. "He is on his own," he echoed

and, to Brigid's surprise, he said, "Stay here," ran again to the gate, vaulted over it, ran up to the Fairy House, and ran down it again with Ned Silver by his side. Ned arrived first at the gate, which Brigid could not understand, because Francis was taller and faster than Ned, and could easily have beaten him. Yet Ned won the race, if it was a race, and stood by the gate with his hands on his knees and a grin on his face.

Francis let him go through the door before him, and held Brigid back so that she had to do the same. "We shouldn't forget," said Francis.

"Forget what," said Brigid. "He was horrible."

"That he is on his own," said Francis, "and that he is our guest, too. Come on. We have to."

Rose came through the back doorway with a round brown teapot in her hand.

"Ah, timing! A minute earlier and you could have emptied these tea-leaves for me."

From the heavy kettle simmering on the range, Rose poured water into the teapot, extra drops hissing and scudding across the black stove. "Come, come on," she said, and motioned them to the table, where their hungry eyes took in sweet ham and lettuce and little tomatoes and bright green scallions on plates. On the dresser, big and dark against the white wall, there sat a fragrant apple pie, brown and crimped at the edges, the scent of cinnamon and clove floating unbidden into Brigid's mouth. She sighed, content.

"Where did you go, today?" Rose asked, when they were seated. "Brigid?"

Brigid, avoiding Ned's sidelong glance, looked at her plate. "Round the fields. We said their names."

Rose said: "Look up when you speak, Brigid. Good work. I'm glad you remember the names of the fields, for when that's lost, all your family has worked for is forgotten. And what did you make of that, Ned?" she added, turning to the silent boy. "You're not usually so quiet." She stopped, put down the plate she was offering, and looked from one child to the other. "There was no quarrel, I hope?"

Brigid, eyes cast down again, said nothing. Even Francis was silent.

Ned opened his mouth, and Brigid thought: now he will tell, the clashbag, and we will all be in trouble, but all Ned said was: "I stayed at the Fairy House. I like it there."

Brigid looked up. He had behaved.

Rose nodded. "You wouldn't be the first child to like it there," and Ned met her smile.

For a second Brigid thought: how different his eyes are when he is not scowling. Then she dismissed the thought.

"Besides," Ned, said, accepting from Rose the plate she offered him, "they're not my family's fields."

Rose said nothing, then, but Brigid saw that she looked at him for several moments, then at Francis, quietly lost in his own thoughts. Brigid flicked her eyes down to her own plate and kept them there. No one spoke for a while, until all the good lunch was eaten, ending with the glory of the apple tart, which left Brigid sighing with satisfaction. She was truly sorry when Rose signalled that the meal was over.

"Come, children," she said. "Michael will soon be in, and he'll be tired after his day. Help me clear away, now, and give him the place to himself. You've had a busy afternoon, running round. Tomorrow will be a holiday for us all, and you must have a good rest."

It was almost April, yet the evening was drawing in to darkness, the warmth from the range making Brigid's eyes sleepy and hot, pictures beginning to dance. She was not sorry when Rose brought her to the room where Brigid's mother had slept when she and Rose were children. Later, she heard Francis climb the narrow brown stairs with Ned, their feet on the wood like horses' hooves, up to the room they would share beneath the eaves; and she remembered running over the fields with Francis, and she began to slide away into dreams. The last thing she heard was a car coming into the yard, its lights sweeping above the curtains in an arc that was just outside sleep. A dog barked, far away. She felt, but did not see, Rose get up to answer the door, and then she was deep in sleep, where fairies danced in the Big Field, coney rabbits slept quiet in their burrows down in the Whinny Brae, and she and Francis were plumed horses, flying across the grass.

Chapter 19: The Easter House

On the morning of Easter Sunday, Brigid woke to the sound of her uncle's steady tread, then the hurtling of feet: Francis and Ned were up. First there was to be breakfast, then Mass.

Brigid and Francis started to get ready: Ned did not.

"Aren't you coming?" said Brigid, rubbing her mouth with her sleeve.

"Ned goes to his own church," said Rose, lifting Brigid's hand away and scrubbing her face with something quite rough. "Go all three of you and clean your teeth. Quickly now. Do you not hear the bells?"

"His own church? By himself?" asked Brigid, getting up. She felt a prickle of envy, though for which of these two freedoms she did not know. "Is he allowed to go by himself?"

"Not by himself," said a voice at the door, and the light of the April morning was momentarily obscured by the tall form of Cornelius Todd. "Happy Easter," he said and he leaned across and kissed Rose on her cheek.

Brigid, embarrassed, looked at Francis, but he kept his eyes on a spot above the door.

Cornelius turned to the children. "Ned'll go with me, won't you, Master Silver?"

Ned looked up, not at all displeased. "I don't always go, but . . ."

"You'll go today," said Michael's voice from the door. He wore his Sunday suit, double-breasted, and his hair shone wetly, as if he were a seal. "Good morning, Cornelius," he said, and his voice was not over-friendly. "Come, children. It's time we weren't here."

Michael stepped outside. They could hear him start the engine, a black, square sound. Rose went to collect her missal and her gloves, and she handed Brigid the hat she disliked, with the elastic that cut her chin. In the hall, pulling it on, Brigid said, as quietly as she could: "Is Ned really not Catholic like us?"

"No," said Francis. "Why should he be?"

"But Uncle Conor? Is he not?"

"No," said Francis, without surprise. "Did you think he was?"

Brigid had not thought about it until that moment, and it had never occurred to her that people she knew went to different churches. Unless, she thought, as she climbed into the back seat of Michael's car, there just was not room for everybody in one.

Slowly and carefully Michael drove Rose, Brigid and Francis down the hill, along the broad road past the slanting gravestones, and into the quiet white church. He led Francis to one side where the men sat; Brigid took Rose to sit on the other with the women. They could have sat together: there were plenty of seats. Brigid, baffled, gave up trying to comprehend, and settled for the dreaming doze of Mass, remembering only to kneel and stand when Rose did, and to keep her eyes open when she drifted away. The first thing that interested her, beyond the morning light dancing on the walls, was when they walked up afterwards to the hilly cemetery and stood at their family grave. Brigid could see nothing but smooth grey stone.

Francis took out from his trouser pocket a small piece of chalk, and said: "Okay, Michael?"

Michael nodded. Francis rubbed the chalk over the smooth slate and, as if by magic, Brigid saw the name 'Francis', and then her uncle's name, 'Durrant' and the numbers, '1715'.

"What does it mean, Michael?" said Brigid.

"It's the death date of the first of us, two hundred and . . . forty, yes . . . forty, years ago."

"Two hundred and forty?" cried Brigid. It was an unimaginable number of years.

"Yes," he said, as if it were nothing at all. "Say your prayers for the happy repose of all their souls. I'd like to get back home for the dinner." He paused. "But maybe you're not hungry?"

"Oh, no," said Brigid, "or yes, I mean, I am!" and she scrambled away in haste down the steep hill, holding on to the slabs as she went, no longer interested in the names or the numbers of the long dead, or anything now but her lunch.

Yet, at first, despite her hunger, Brigid found it hard to concentrate on the food before her. Uncle Conor looked at Rose all the time, as if he owned her, and Michael looked at Uncle Conor as if he did not care for him. Rose looked at neither, concentrating on the children and the serving and clearing of food. Ned and Francis addressed themselves with joy to all she had put before them and, gradually, the smells and the tastes of Rose's preparation worked on Brigid, too, and she relished every mouthful. At the end of the meal, she was once more content.

Michael, who had stopped looking at Cornelius, turned to Brigid. "Well," he said, "you were hungry after all. I hope you've left a little room for –"

"Michael!" said Rose, and Michael stopped.

"I think I'll stretch my legs," he said, "if anyone wants to come for a walk." Then he was on his feet, a signal that the meal was over.

Cornelius stood up, and Rose began to collect the dishes.

Through the window waved tiny pink blossoms from the orchard: Brigid wanted to be outside. She stood up.

"Now," Michael said, "who'll walk down the lane with me?"

"Go you on with the children," said Rose. "I'll clear up here. Cornelius?"

Brigid saw her uncle stiffen where he stood, yet he said nothing.

Cornelius looked at Michael, then back to Rose. "Well, no, I think I'll go into the town. I have a man to see about a dog."

Still, thought Brigid, still that man and the dog. Rose stopped clearing. Michael stopped still. On the wall, the clock ticked through silence.

"Into the town, here?" Rose said. "Do you mean up to the city?"

There was a brief silence.

"Just the town here," he said, but he did not look at her, then added, reaching for his overcoat: "I've a number of things to do."

"Just as you wish," said Rose, her voice devoid of emotion. He got up and left, and she did not see him to the door, or wave him away in his car. Instead she turned to her brother. "I may run over later next door to Jack Polly's and use his telephone. I'd like to know how things are in the city."

Home was in the city. "Is Mama coming here tonight?" asked Brigid. "And Daddy?"

Rose tied on an apron. "I told you, Brigid. Your mama is resting at home for a day or two. And you," she covered the remains of the apple pie, and looked towards the door, "are going for a good walk that nice day with Michael, while I prepare . . ."

Francis, who had been silently listening said, quietly: "A surprise."

"That's right," said Rose. "Now, go, while the day is good."

Michael, standing, looked over at Rose, and went to the door. His eyes, deep in his head, looked almost navy blue, dark as the clothes he wore, and his long nose when he lifted it had a slight curve. His mouth, too, was long and straight, even when he smiled or laughed, and his laugh carried the sound of his pipe tobacco. "Did I say to you, Rose," he said, "that I had a dream last night?" He reached for his coat, and lifted the latch on the door.

"Please don't tell me," said Rose, brushing down the table.

He was clean and scrubbed in his dark suit yet, despite the scent of soap and the whiteness of his shirt and handkerchief, Michael carried with him the air of the farm – of grass, and earth, and faintly, a scent like the dogs who followed him when he was outside, coming to meet him now as he came through the door. They bowed their narrow heads, black and white, sleekly padding from their house by the gate.

"Good enough," said Michael. "Tell Jack Polly I'll be over later to call. Maybe I'll tell him my dream," and he ushered the children before him through the door.

Now in the lane there hung the scent of early blossom, drifting from the orchard behind the house and, setting out to climb the long hill, Michael pointed out the ferns and the primroses showing new and damp; the pale fragile flowers played in the light wind, peeping and swaying as the walkers picked their way down the uneven track. Up the hill they went, growing warm, then down, cooler again. The farm was all hills, rising and falling in its own cluster of drumlins. Looking back, it seemed to Brigid the farm lay in hiding behind the hill of the Limekiln Field, with its low grey house where they were not allowed.

Something hooted, and Brigid stood behind Michael. "What was that?" she asked.

Michael said: "Oh, there's an old lady lives in there. She doesn't like visitors."

"In the Limekiln house?" said Brigid. "But . . ."

Ned said: "Could that noise not be a bird?"

But Michael did not reply. He quickened his step, and walked on.

"It could be an owl," said Francis.

"Do you think there's lime still in there?" Ned asked, but Michael was still not answering. "Could we see it?"

"Well, I think there is," said Francis, "but you can't see it. We're not allowed there because the lime is in a deep pit."

"It burns without fire," said Ned, gleefully. "They use it in prisons, when they hang people. I know! The little old lady is the ghost of a –"

"Stop that," said Michael, finally turning round. "I think you may be right about the bird. I think it's an owl. I was mistaken about the little old lady. She's long gone."

"Will the dogs know not to go into the pit, Michael?" asked Brigid.

He turned round on the road. "Dogs have more sense," he said, and they continued on their walk, out beyond the lane on to the road and beyond. Michael was a steady walker, and it seemed to Brigid that he might just keep going. Her feet began to drag, and she was greatly relieved, after what seemed like a long time, to find that he had looped them round, and that they were somehow back at the entrance to their own lane.

"Michael," said Brigid, as the farm came back into view, "do you want to tell us about your dream?" She took his hand, to encourage him.

He laughed his smoky laugh. "Not if Rose says no. Rose thinks I dream straight, and she could be right."

Brigid was about to ask him what he meant, when he suddenly lifted her up in his arms and said: "Look across the fields. See the trees at the side of the house? See? The horse chestnuts are putting out their candelabra for you."

It was true. The trees in blossom were hung with creamy light, like the Easter candles in church.

Brigid stayed high up in Michael's arms as they rounded the last corner, and together they saw Rose come out with a covered pot. She motioned to Michael. He swung Brigid down, bent to go through the door, and came out a few moments later with a shovel of coal.

"Mind now," he said. "We want no catastrophes." He took the pot over to the side of the haggard, to a little hollow before a big branchy tree, where Rose had made a ring of stones. The fire was laid in this and the pot, which was filled with water, put on it.

Rose told the children to sit on stools Michael had carried out to them. "This is our Easter House," she said. "We always did this, with your grandparents, and your mama, and Michael."

"And James, God rest him," Michael added.

The pot was beginning to bubble.

"You have another brother?" asked Brigid. Where were they coming from, all these brothers?

Rose shook her head. "He was our uncle. He's dead now. He lived a while in New York."

"Why?" asked Brigid.

"A farm can't keep all that many people," said Michael. "Some have to go out foreign."

Ned said: "Did you ever go out foreign, Mr Durrant?"

Michael said: "I had no call to go anywhere. The wireless and the newspaper will tell me all I need to know. Why would I want to go running about the world?"

"What happened to your uncle?" said Ned.

"He came home from America, very sick, and he died," said Rose. "We don't need to go into that now."

Michael, ignoring his sister, said: "The night he died, I was sent on my bicycle for the doctor. I cycled and then I walked the bicycle up the hill – just the way we did today – and as I walked my uncle James walked up the hill beside me."

Brigid could not understand. "How, Michael? How did he walk if he was sick?"

Michael looked at her in surprise. "He didn't. It was his spirit walked beside me. I went on and got the doctor and, when I came home with him, sure enough James had died that time."

Brigid, not entirely comfortably, thought back to Hallowe'en, and wished again that the dead would stay where they were put, and not go round annoying people. Yet, nobody else was troubled.

Rose certainly was not, lifting perfect brown eggs into the blue-and-white eggcups. "Don't heed him," she said. "He dreams straight. You know that."

"Rose, did you go over to Jack Polly and telephone to the city?" said Michael, unperturbed.

"Not yet," said Rose. "I will after this."

"Did you put onion skins in the pot, by the way?" asked Michael.

"No need. Those need nothing but fresh air and the hot water."

"Grandma always put them in," said Michael, and he knocked his pipe against the stone beside him. "I'll telephone, if you like, when I go over later to see Jack."

"Well, maybe you would, when you're over there, and I'll stay with the children," said Rose. "Eat up now, you three, eat your Easter eggs."

Brigid, warm in the shade of the haggard and the sheltering trees, saw why she had been told to leave some room: she wished she had. The house sat low and content, and the dogs snoozed in a patch of light. High up, the rooks were calling that it was time to make a nest, and the apple trees, tinged with pale pink, sat like young girls in spring dresses. Tea, and eggs and wheaten bread left the children sleepily content, yet when, from somewhere on her person, Rose produced little sugar eggs, pink and white, they found even more room. Michael lit his pipe, and lay back against the tree, and one of the dogs curled in beside his feet. Everything grew still, and time stopped.

A voice above them broke the peace. Between them and the sun came a cold shadow. The shadow moved, the heat came back, and Cornelius Todd stood above them. Brigid thought: he always stands in our light. Yet, he was smiling, his glinting crooked tooth showing at the side of his mouth. His hands were behind his back, and then they swung round, holding three boxes: two were pirate ships, in jewelled paper, and one was a basket of card, painted with primroses and violets. He handed them to the children, and they saw with delight that each one held a chocolate egg.

Michael got up, buttoning his waistcoat. He did not seem

pleased. Neither did Rose, her face pink, a little flushed. Michael said nothing, but Rose, unsmiling, spoke: "That's too much sweet stuff, Cornelius. They've been eating all day. It was good of you, but really, they . . ."

"It's from . . . Grace sent them. I saw her."

Here was silence. The Easter House and its glowing embers seemed to fade, and the air grew cold. Brigid felt a shiver run through her.

"My sister? You went to the city?" said Rose.

Cornelius looked at the children. Michael, his pipe between his teeth, walked towards the house.

"Go and play, children," said Rose.

No one argued.

Rose and Cornelius stood silently looking at each other.

"Bags first on the swing," said Ned.

"No, you don't," cried Brigid, and she scrambled to her feet – but Francis was ahead of her.

"On you go," said Michael. "I'm going to bring in the cows. Don't fall off."

"The cows! Can I come?" asked Francis at once, and when Michael nodded he swung into step with him.

Brigid was left with Ned, already on the swing.

"Push," he said. "I'll give you a turn in a minute."

Brigid, angry and frustrated, pushed.

"If you want a turn, you'd better push harder," said Ned.

She pushed until her arms hurt, then she stopped.

"What's wrong with you?" said Ned.

"You push," she said, and folded her arms.

"Oh, Brigid," said Ned, sliding off the seat. "I do love it when you're bossy. Get on the swing."

She pulled the swing to a halt, and hitched herself into the seat. Ned immediately sent her flying into the air with a mighty push, nearly unseating her, and the swing spun in the air.

As she swung drunkenly back towards him, she heard him say: "I know what's happening."

She swung away. "What?" she said, flying higher and higher out over the wall. "Don't spin me," but each time she came back, Ned pushed harder. "What is it you know?" she asked, breathless, the world reeling.

"It's simple," said Ned. "Your mother's having a . . ."

Brigid swung away and did not hear the rest.

She did not see Rose walk towards the swing until she was almost upon them. Rose put out a hand, gradually slowing the swing, and the crazy hills and spinning trees came quietly back into order. Brigid sat, out of breath, her head still running in circles. Far away by the dying Easter House, Uncle Conor stood alone, one foot kicking at the ring of stones.

"Down from there," said Rose, her voice sharp. "That was too high. There could have been an accident, and then what would I have told your mother? Come inside."

There was no point in telling her it was Ned's fault. She did not sound like Rose, and her face was white, and Brigid did not think she would listen if she did tell her.

"Ned, you pig," said Brigid. "What's my mother having?"

As if she had not spoken Ned stood still, his eyes on Rose, stooping as she bent below the lintel. He said nothing, his eyes swivelling to Cornelius, still standing by the dying embers of the Easter House.

The air had cooled: the day was ending. Brigid, irrationally disappointed in something, trailed with Ned into the house.

From somewhere came the sound of the cows coming home: she could see Francis with Michael, back in his working clothes. Their shoulders were touching, their heads together, over by the byre, and Brigid wished she had gone with them rather than stayed with Ned. They would probably go on and visit kind Jack Polly in the next farm, and she would be left out.

"Ned," she said again, "what is my mother having?"

Ned, looking away from Cornelius, seemed not to understand the question at first. Then he shrugged. "How do I know? A rest, probably – a good rest from you," and he slid away before

Brigid could reach him.

She sat alone at the window, wondering how it was that all the good had gone out of their Easter day.

Brigid was glad to get to bed that night. She curled beneath the eiderdown, waiting for Rose. Drifting towards sleep she thought, or dreamed, that she heard Rose's voice: "Because you lied. You lied. I cannot trust you to tell me the truth." She dreamed she heard Uncle Conor: "I didn't lie. I changed my plans – and I brought you news of your sister," and Rose's reply: "You did. There are places in the world where they kill the bringer of bad news. Did you know?" Brigid, falling towards sleep, thought she heard Uncle Conor's engine starting, widening out into the night, leaving the air empty but for the sound, distant but distinct, of a woman's weeping.

Chapter 20: Dreaming Straight

That night, Brigid dreamed that she wakened in the yard and the house was a ruin. It stood blackened and eyeless, the orchard in bloom but overgrown, choked with nettles and docken leaves. No hens pecked across the yard, no dogs lay in the sunshine, no cattle brayed from the byre, and from the chimney there rose no smoke. In her dream the farm was silent, and everyone was gone. The only noise she heard was the ragged cawing of rooks, circling the orchard, the chestnut tree and all the unheeded blossom. In her dream she knew she was alone, her parents gone from her, her grandfather, Rose and Michael. Worst of all, in her dream, Francis was gone. She would never see him again. Brigid came out of sleep as she had gone in, to the sound of weeping, and found that it was now herself, the pillow wet when she woke.

She threw back the covers, got out and pulled open the door and, suddenly, in the ticking quiet of the morning, everything became itself again. In the kitchen, Francis stood by the window watching Michael outside, and Rose, stretched on her tiptoes, was lifting down a suitcase from a high shelf. So: they were to go back home. That was all right. Brigid suddenly longed for the smell of her own house, for the faded red of the carpet on the stairs, the light through the blinds in the morning; the black and white tiles of the hall; Dicky complaining in his cage; Isobel

218

truculent by the sink; Daddy reading the news; Mama, thoughtful in the kitchen; the Friday Tree, steady as a sentinel at the back of the plot.

With an effort, she brought herself back to Tullybroughan. The front door was open. Standing there, just sheltered from the soft drizzle, she could see where their Easter House had been, the ring of blackened stones cold, stained and dampened by a fall of rain in the night. A blackbird sang in the hedge. Michael, outside the door, was hefting a milk churn to be taken to the road, the hens were clucking and a proud cockerel crew. Michael straightened. The rooster, picking his way across the stones, crew again.

"Good morning, lazybones," Michael said. "I thought you were going to stay in bed all day."

Brigid looked down at her pyjamas. She shook her head, tumbling its untidy hair all about her face. "No," she said. "I'm getting up, now. Why does she do that?"

"Why does who do what?"

"That hen." Brigid indicated the rooster. "The big one. Why does she make that noise?"

"That's a rooster," he said. "That's no hen. 'A whistling woman and a crowing hen, good for neither beasts nor men'," and without further comment he began to move on to his work.

"Michael," called Brigid, and he turned to look at her. She hesitated. She did not know quite what she wanted to ask.

"What is it?" he said. "Do you want to go with me on the tractor?"

She pointed to her pyjamas, and shook her head again. "Michael," she began once more, "could this farm ever be empty, ever be a ruin?"

Michael reached down to the place where the wall met the yard, and pulled out green leaves. "There's some good mint for you," he said. "That's near as good for you as toothpaste."

"Could it?" asked Brigid, again. The leaves did smell of toothpaste.

Michael straightened, looked up at the greying sky, raised his hand to the mizzling rain, and said: "That rain's on for the day. No. Not while I'm alive, it couldn't."

Brigid was not quite satisfied by this answer. "Michael," she said, "when you dream straight, do you know it?"

He said, steadily, no laughter about him: "When you dream straight, you know it." He resumed his measured walk towards the haggard, calling back over his shoulder: "Still, you're safer telling no one. People aren't that happy with straight dreams, or the ones who dream them." He moved on, leaning forward with a straight back, feet turned slightly out as if, already, he were behind his plough.

Soon after breakfast, Michael stood once more in the yard, checked that the boot was closed and pushed shut the doors of Rose's car. "Safe home," he called, and stood with one arm raised as the tyres crunched on the gravel. From the hilly lane, turning to wave, Brigid watched the farm go away from her with a rush of regret, the dream of the night before suddenly reality, and the firm certainties of her life elusive as shadow. White and clean as the house stood behind the apple-blossom, wiry and strong as Michael looked at the gate, she had seen the farm old and empty, broken and neglected, and no one could promise her it would not be so. Easter eggs, Easter House, dogs and tractors and the rooster's crow could all disappear, like the life in the house of her other grandparents, lonely and empty by the water's edge. And, mild though the morning was, Brigid felt cold.

The journey home was faster than the journey down, hedges filling with a fresh green, rooks building high, hidden birds sending one to the other their songs of the summer to come. The children were quiet: Francis thoughtful, Ned sleepy, his sharp shoulder turned from Brigid, no sound but the steady thrumming of the car's engine. Yet, when they began to see the signs for home, Brigid felt gladness return.

As they stopped outside the house, and the engine died away, Rose turned round in the car. "Now Ned, hop in to Mrs Mulvey,

220

like a good boy, and I'll see you soon." She smiled her wide smile. "Won't I?"

To Brigid's surprise, Ned, uncurling, leaned forward and placed his straight arms as near as he could round Rose's neck, and kissed her cheek. Why everyone was going round kissing Rose, all of a sudden, was a mystery to Brigid, especially as Rose seemed to have no objection. She put her hand up to pat his cheek and Brigid saw, to her surprise, that she wore no sparkling ring. She forgot about it again, almost immediately, as Ned climbed over her to get out on the safe side of the car, scraping her knee with his sandal and digging his elbow into her ribs.

"Pig, Ned," she spat, and he stood on her foot.

Ned turned as he got out of the car and suddenly, to her surprise and disgust, kissed her too, loudly and wetly. She drew her hand across her mouth. "You love it," he said into her ear, then, "I'm going to see Davy Crockett, and you're not, so there," but before Brigid, red-faced, could register any protest, he had turned away. "Bye, Francis," he said, sliding out of the car. Then he suddenly said: "Can I write to you from school?" and he caught Francis' shoulder.

Francis said: "Yes, Ned, why not?" just as if Ned were not a horrible boy who was going to see Davy Crockett when they were not.

Rose was nearly as bad. "That's a good idea," she said. "But Ned, wasn't there something you wanted to talk to Francis about *today*? Maybe Francis might bring your case up to your room for you?"

Brigid saw Ned Silver pause before nodding his head, and she saw Francis turn in surprise to Rose. He had rarely been in Ned Silver's house, and he was obviously puzzled about why Rose wanted him to go now; but he said nothing, got out of the car with Ned, and went off into the next-door house with him.

Brigid, angry and once more excluded, made to follow the boys out of the car, but Rose did not move to go with her.

Instead, she tapped her hand on the front seat, and said: "Hop in here a minute, Brigid."

Brigid scrambled over the armrest and slid into the seat beside Rose.

"Rose," she said, sure of at least some sympathy, "Ned says he's going to see Davy Crockett. Ned's going to see him and we're not. It isn't fair. He gets everything." She put her hands to her eyes, knuckling the fists, conscious that a wrong had been done. She was put out when Rose lifted her hands away, quite firmly, almost impatiently.

"Brigid," said Rose. "Stop your nonsense and listen. I don't know anything about this Davy Crockett business. Stop it now. Listen. Mama is not at home at the moment, and I don't need any fuss from you. No, don't say anything till I'm finished. She's resting."

"Not in the house?" asked Brigid, puzzled.

"She's in hospital for a few days," said Rose. "She hasn't been well, but she's getting better, and she will soon be home."

"But why?" asked Brigid. "She wasn't sick when we went down to the farm."

Rose paused, drew a deep breath, and swallowed. Brigid saw her neck, without ornament, move up and down.

"Brigid," she said, "I want you to concentrate, and be a very big girl. God was sending a baby to Mama. You knew that, didn't you?"

Brigid, suddenly clear, clapped her hands. Davy Crockett, King of the Wild Frontier, faded away. "And that's why she's tired? We have a baby?"

"Brigid, listen, please, and don't interrupt," said Rose, and Brigid could hear that her voice was weary. "The baby . . . stayed with God. She was not ready to come here, and God kept her with him."

A stone dropped in Brigid's heart. "She? We had a sister, and she didn't come?"

Rose looked away, then back. She twisted with one hand the

222

finger where her ring should have been, as if she thought it were still there. "She couldn't come, Brigid. She wasn't big enough or strong enough for the journey, and so, God kept her. And, now, your mama needs a rest, because she tried to help her come, to carry her through. Can you try to understand? She's tired, and sad that your sister had to stay with God. You must be a very big help to her now."

Brigid sat, cold and disappointed, and deeply afraid. If her mother could not help a little baby get here, how would Brigid herself be safe? How would Francis?

Rose sat silent, as though waiting for a response.

"Did she look like me? Did Mama say?" Brigid asked.

"No, she didn't," said Rose, "but I am sure she looked like you, and like Francis, too."

"But more like me," persisted Brigid, "because she was a girl."

Rose said nothing.

"Will I ever see my sister? Will Francis?"

Rose paused, then pulled down the handle that opened the car door. "One day, Brigid," she said, "when we go home to God, we'll all be together."

Rose stood up. Brigid, dissatisfied, saw that the conversation was at an end. She got out of the car, and turned again to Rose. Rose's face was white and tired, and Brigid was quite sorry to trouble her, yet she had to ask another question. Something else was puzzling her.

"Rose," she said, "where did Uncle Conor go? He wasn't there this morning, and I thought I heard his car leave in the night."

Rose lifted out the suitcase and pulled down the door of the boot. Her nose had become very sharp, pinched round the edge. "He had business to attend to," she said.

The man about the dog again, probably: not that anyone would explain what that was about.

Still. She was home again. Running up the steps, Brigid

longed for small things, like Dicky scolding in his cage. When Isobel opened the door, Brigid found herself almost pleased to see her. Yet, as Rose stepped into the hall, she saw that Isobel looked for someone else behind her.

"All by your lone?" said Isobel.

Rose's answer, floating back to Brigid as she ran into the kitchen, seemed cold, even harsh: "Were you expecting someone, Isobel?" and, for a second, Brigid was back in her almost-sleep of the night before, hearing Rose's voice, sharp, accusing. Then, seeing at the table not only her father but also her grandfather, Brigid felt the world of the farm fall away into memory, and the night's dark dream faded back into the shadows.

They were reading to each other from the paper; it was as if Brigid had never been away.

"'*Orange Band to march on Longstone Road*'," her father read. "Ah, Brigid. Good girlie. Come in, and get something to eat."

"It's bad surely," said her grandfather. "They've no call to go that route again. It's asking for trouble. Come over here, Brigid, and sit on my knee. Are you pleased to see your granda up again?"

Brigid, climbing up, nodded. Absently, her father reached over and stroked her hair.

"They are asking for trouble," he said to her grandfather. "They'll get it, too, according to Conor Todd yesterday."

"Yes," said her grandfather, settling Brigid against his chest. "That young man tends to be close to . . . whatever's going on, does he not? Rather too close, you might say."

"What young man is that?" asked Rose, coming through the door.

"Young Todd," said Brigid's grandfather. "Your fiancé, I believe."

"Would you call Mr Todd young?" asked Rose, smoothing her skirt as she sat down. Her lips were pressed together. She said nothing more, and the men resumed their talk of marches and lodges and rights and wrongs.

Rose sat only long enough to take tea, and no one pressed her to stay.

Brigid, comfortably lodged on her grandfather's knee, heard Rose say that she wanted to go and see her sister in the hospital.

"Can I come?" said Brigid, sliding from her perch.

"You can come later, with me and your daddy and your brother," said her grandfather.

"Is that a good idea?" asked her father, over her head.

"Yes," said her grandfather and Rose together, and Rose added: "I'll tell her you're coming."

Brigid moved to stand beside her father, taking his hand. "I'm dying to see Mama, Daddy," she said.

He looked at her over his glasses: "You hardly look dying to me, Brigid," he said. His eyes travelled past her, out to the garden. Brigid followed his gaze. "What's going on out there? Are those boys fighting?" He stood up, threw down his napkin, and striding to the window, rapped it sharply. "Stop that," he called. "Francis, get in here at once!"

Brigid saw Ned Silver, his face red, his collar torn, standing belligerently at the foot of the garden steps, and Francis, equally flushed and dishevelled, pulling his own shirt back into shape as he disappeared through the back-yard door. When she looked again to the bottom of the steps, Brigid saw that Ned was gone.

Chapter 21: Wild Frontiers

The door opened. Francis came in, breathing hard, his hair standing away from his head, the collar of his shirt half torn away. In his cage, Dicky squawked, hopping in joy or agitation from one foot to the other. Francis turned quickly to Dicky, reached out one finger and stroked the bird's curling claws through the bars of the cage. Then he withdrew his hand, and stood with his arms folded, looking at the floor.

"Francis," said his father, "what in the name of all that's holy did you think you were doing?"

Francis walked to the table and reached in his pocket. He took out a small red object, and Brigid, open-mouthed, saw that it was the lost Santa Claus from the Christmas tree.

Francis placed it on the table, without a word.

"Well," said his father, "that's a pity, but I don't think it warranted that dogfight, Francis."

Francis, chest still rising and falling, reached again into his pocket, but he did not take his eyes off his father's face. He placed on the table before him his grandfather's watch.

There was silence.

"My God," said his father. "My God. The little thief."

Brigid's grandfather placed his hand on his son's arm.

"Steady, Maurice," he said. "I gave that to the child to play with when he visited us in Lecale. I daresay he forgot to return it."

Brigid's father said nothing, but his face had not lost its look of disgust.

"Francis," he said, "I'm sorry to have been angry with you. I see why you fought with young Silver. I would have done the same."

"I didn't fight with him about the watch, Daddy," said Francis, "or about the Santa. He gave those back. He wanted to give them back. He was sorry about taking them. It was all right. Everything was all right. And then . . ."

"What, then?"

Francis twisted his hands, as if in despair.

"Francis. Speak up," said his father. "Why did you hit a boy younger than you?"

Francis' head grew red, but he looked his father in the eye. "He said things, and I . . . I hit him."

The words, the fact of what he had done, seemed to cause almost as much surprise to Francis as to everyone else.

"What things?" said his father, and his voice was quiet.

"I don't want to say," said Francis, and he lifted up his chin. "I dealt with it. He won't say them again."

"You will say," said his father. "You'll tell me, now."

Francis opened his mouth, then closed it. "Granda mightn't like it," he said.

"Let me decide that," said his grandfather and, for the first time, Brigid noticed not only how much alike her father's and grandfather's voices sounded, but also how their faces seemed the same, and how the young face of Francis, his high cheekbones and his straight mouth, had become a mirror image of both of them.

Francis breathed in, then out. "He has a picture of his mother in his room. I was just going out the door and I saw it, and I thought she looked lovely, but I didn't say anything, in case it upset him. And then we came back here and I said did he want to go up the garden and have a game and he said he did. And it was still all right, I thought, except he kept starting to say something and then stopping, and then all of a sudden he asked me why I was looking at his mother's picture, and I just said I thought she looked lovely. Then he said what did I mean by that, and I said I meant she looked lovely. She did. And then he said we were all the same. And I said what did *he* mean by that. And he said . . . he said that our Uncle Laurence ran after his mother, and that . . ."

"Go on," said his grandfather, a warning hand on his son's clenched fist.

"Brigid, leave the room," said her father, but Brigid did not move, and no one made her go.

"And that we should all be ashamed of him, and ourselves. He said you could expect nothing more of Catholics and their priests. That's when I hit him. I didn't even know I was going to. I never hit anybody before. It just happened. I . . . I sort of wish I had just talked to him."

Silence filled the room. Not even Dicky made a sound. From the corner of her eye, Brigid saw Isobel hovering on the other side of the door, listening. She did not think anyone else saw her, until her grandfather called out, "Isobel?" and she came in, busily dusting the door with the corner of her apron.

Her grandfather looked at his son, who seemed to be stricken dumb.

"Yes, Mr Arthur?" said Isobel, as though she had heard nothing, and Brigid thought again: I don't like Isobel.

"If you're not too busy," said her grandfather, and his eye rested on the corner of the apron, idly bundled in Isobel's hand, "would you go next door and ask if young Ned could come in here for a moment?"

Isobel's eyes gleamed, and Brigid thought: she's enjoying this.

"I will, Mr Arthur," she said, earnestly, and went out.

Brigid heard her open the front door.

Several minutes passed in silence, until Isobel reappeared,

Ned Silver in tow. He was still wearing his torn shirt, and a blue shadow was beginning to show on his cheek. His hand rubbed at dried blood by his nose. Otherwise, he was still and silent as Francis himself. Neither boy looked at the other.

Isobel took up a position by the door, until Brigid's father said, "You must have things to do, Isobel," and when, slowly polishing the doorknob, she left, he said, "Brigid, shut the door, please," which Brigid gladly did.

"Ned," said Brigid's grandfather, "do you remember me?"

Ned nodded. "Yes, sir."

"Will you tell me why you and my grandson fought? No one will be angry. Just tell me, please."

"I don't want to, sir," said Ned, "if you don't mind."

"Well, I mind!" said Brigid's father, and he brought his hand down, hard, on the table. "Tell us, and be quick about it."

Brigid saw that Ned had begun to shake, and she felt a little sorry for him. Then she remembered Davy Crockett, and the feeling vanished.

Francis looked sorry for him now, all his truculence suddenly gone. "Daddy, please," he said. "I said I was sorry I . . ."

"Quiet," said his father. "You've had your say."

"No," said his grandfather, lifting his hand and placing it again over his son's. "You stay quiet this time, Maurice," he said, and his voice was stronger than Brigid had ever heard it. "I'll do the talking."

There was silence. Outside, in the garden, a dove called; a train rattled by in the distance. In his cage, Dicky clucked.

"Ned," said Brigid's grandfather, "listen to me. Long ago, before you were born or thought of, we were all acquainted with your mother, God rest her. Her family lived quite near ours. She was a lovely young girl, and we sometimes had the privilege of hearing her sing. She had a beautiful voice, and it was properly trained."

Ned said nothing.

"She sang in the choir in our church, and she sang with the operatic society. You know that?"

229

Ned nodded. His eyes were full of darkness. He looked as if he might cry.

"Laurence Carey, God rest his soul, not my son but dear as my own, sang in the same choir as your mother. And he sang once or twice in the operatic society. Did you know that?"

Ned shook his head.

"Well, he did. And they were quite good friends, until he went away to study for the priesthood and she got married to your father and then, you understand, they could not be quite such good friends. Do you follow?"

Ned's lips said, "Yes, sir," but no sound came.

"Later, for reasons which are none of my business, or any one's business, your mother was unhappy, and all I know is that she asked Laurence for advice. I know . . . I knew him. I know he would have remembered their friendship. But I also know he was faithful to his work and his calling: and his calling required him to give aid to the suffering. I believe they both died on the day he was trying to do just that. Just that, Ned."

Now, Ned opened his mouth.

"And," said Brigid's grandfather, raising his hand to prevent interruption, "I know you know she asked him for help, because you . . . borrowed the piece of paper which was in Laurence's effects. Isn't that right?"

Ned hung his head, and nodded. He had flushed a dull red.

"Have you got it? The paper?"

Ned, reddening even more, shook his head: "I'm sorry, Mr Arthur. I tore it up."

"Well," said the old man. He sighed, and tapped his foot on the ground. "Well. No matter. It may have been for the best." He looked up again, and the skin round his eyes was damp. "Do you remember what it said?"

Ned looked at the floor. His voice was very low. "It said: '*Laurie. I've tried. Please help me. Stranraer. Sat. P. Vic. Myra.*'"

Brigid remembered the piece of paper that Ned had taken away. She remembered the word 'Myra', in its bold black hand.

230

"And that is why he set out on that Saturday to come home on the *Princess Victoria*, earlier than he needed to, in order to answer a call for help. He did his best. If he could have, I believe he would have saved your mother. It is what I would have expected from him, and what I would expect from myself, or my son, or from Francis, or from little Brigid there, if the situation were the same, or from you, Ned. But, because Laurence was a clergyman, a dedicated servant of God, he tried to do more, and he lost his life. That I would never have wanted, or expected, of him or anyone, Catholic, or Protestant, or any of the world's religions you care to name."

Ned's head was sunk on his chest, his knees bent as if they would buckle.

"Come over here," said Brigid's grandfather, and Ned, head down, went to him, like a much smaller child than he was.

Brigid saw her grandfather put his hand on Ned's head, and, reaching in his fob pocket, take out his watch. He looked at the time, unhooked the round silver moon from his buttonhole, and then handed it, shining, to Ned.

Ned looked up, the dark bruise vivid in his white face.

"I lent this to you once to play with. Do you remember?"

Ned said: "Sir, I . . ."

"Take it now and play with it, if you like, till it's time for us to go the hospital. Then you can bring it back."

Ned looked up. His eyes showed blue again, clear as the sky. "Thank you, Mr Arthur," he said, and he moved backwards.

"Ned Silver," said Brigid's father, and his eyes were hard, "you're a lucky boy it wasn't me you had to deal with. Never let me hear of you saying anything about my family, or our Church, or for that matter anybody's Church, ever again."

Ned, whose eyes had darkened again momentarily, flinched a little. "I'm sorry, sir," he said.

"And to Francis?"

Ned breathed in, and turned to Francis. "I'm sorry, Francis," he said.

"I am too, Ned," said Francis, and he held out his hand.

Ned took it quickly, and then he ran out of the room.

"You can say goodbye to your watch," said Brigid's father, and he ran his hand through his hair. "Bigoted little brat."

"We'll see," said her grandfather. He spread his long hands out on the table, and looked at them for a long time.

After that strange morning Brigid found herself torn between relief at being the onlooker rather than the miscreant and jealousy at Ned's good fortune in getting away with it and being allowed to play with the watch. She struggled with even more jealousy that he was going to see Davy Crockett, and she was glad to get out of the room, and leave her father and grandfather in their companionable silence. Francis was sent upstairs to change, and Brigid, in the confusion of solitude, wandered out to the garden. She expected, though she did not wish, to encounter Isobel. Yet, Isobel was nowhere to be seen. Brigid, standing in the garden, was surprised to see her emerge from the corner where she and Francis had once, in the summer, climbed over the fence into the plot. Isobel looked equally taken aback, and not at all pleased.

"What are you doing here?" said Isobel, sharply. "Spying on me?"

"No," said Brigid, with indignation. "I was just . . ."

"Brigid!" called her father's voice from the back door. "What are you doing out there? Come on, get in the car. We're going across to see your mama."

Brigid, turning to go down the steps, thought she glimpsed from the corner of her eye another figure, like a man, just moving out of sight on the other side of the fence. There was no time to look. It must be Mr Doughty, or Mr Steele. She ran down the steps, ready to get in the car. Yet, as she climbed in, it occurred to her that the person was not dressed to work in the plot, as Mr Doughty and Mr Steele would be. She thought she had glimpsed a tweed coat and, for a moment, with a bright stab of memory, she remembered George Bailey, whom she had not seen since the day he was her angel.

Her father drove. His grey hat nodded to her grandfather's black hat, their faces hidden beneath the brims, then both hats turned to face forward. Easter Monday: there was very little traffic on the road. It was quiet, and the sun shone even on the streets down town.

Francis, looking out, said suddenly, "I love it when it's quiet like this."

Their grandfather's hat turned so that they could see half his face. "It's not always a good sign," he said.

Their father's hat nodded.

"You remember that?" said their grandfather, and their father's hat nodded again.

"Too well. And if the Orangemen get their way and march again on the Longstone Road . . ."

"Which they will. It's shaping up to be hot round the border towns. I've always said, it could all happen again."

"What could all happen again?" asked Brigid.

No one answered. Brigid nudged Francis in the ribs. He had started this and now took no part. He went on looking out the window, as if nothing interested him more than the writing on the advertisement hoardings and then, quite suddenly, he turned and caught Brigid's arm: "Look!" he cried. "Look, Brigid! It's Davy Crockett!"

Brigid craned past his arm and saw a scene from a dream. There, before her eyes, was Davy Crockett, hand to his raccoon hat, musket in hand, diving into a car outside Robbs' store, and behind him was a crowd of children, shouting his name and waving papers and their own, smaller hairy-tailed hats.

"Holy cats," said Brigid's father. "What the . . . ?"

"Drive, Maurice," said his father. "It's some kind of publicity business for a picture they're showing. I saw something about it in the paper. Don't get caught up in that."

Brigid and Francis, holding on to each other, were entranced.

"Francis," said Brigid, "is it really him?"

233

"It looks very like him," said Francis. "I think it is him! But why's he running away? Look, Brigid, look. It's him, it is him!"

Brigid had not seen Francis so excited since the day Dicky flew into the plot. She looked, but all she saw was a car door shutting.

"Daddy, please," Francis cried. "Please stop the car!"

"I'll stop the car for no actor," said his father, sharply. "I'm surprised at you, Francis, and your poor mother in the hospital. If it were Brigid, I could understand."

Francis, his face reddening, slackened his hold on Brigid, and sank back in the seat.

Brigid thought: Stop for me, then. I want to get out. I want to see Davy Crockett. But she glimpsed the stony profile in the mirror, and stayed silent, her breath matching that of Francis, fast and beating in the back of the car.

Slowly, irrevocably, the car pulled away. Brigid and Francis stared hopelessly from the window at the other car, Davy Crockett's car, and the noisy, jostling posse behind it. Brigid, longing with all her heart to be part of that joyous crowd, suddenly saw among them a familiar figure. As Davy's car slid around a corner, Brigid was sure that the loudest shouter and the foremost pursuer was Ned Silver, Ned Silver himself.

"Oh," she said to Francis. "Oh, Francis. It must have been him. It must have been Davy Crockett. Ned Silver said he was going to see him, but I didn't know it was the real one," and she leaned back against Francis' shoulder because, for once, he had nothing to say that could comfort her, and she cried silently, inside her head, until they arrived at the hospital. Leaning against his shoulder, it seemed to her that Francis was crying inside his head too.

The hospital was an old building, full of crannies: a warren, her father called it. They went up winding stairs, and more stairs, smelling of darkness, and then they were brought into a little room, a cosy room with a fire in the grate. Outside it was spring, but in this big old building, the fire warmed the chill of the hospital. To Brigid's joy, there was Mama, her hair lying flat and straight on her head, her eyes tired, but still Mama, and that look was gone from her, that look of being in another world. Brigid was glad: she'd had enough of that. She ran towards her, until checked by her father.

"You'll hurt your mama, doing that," he said.

"Oh, let her come on," said her mother, and she reached out her other arm to Francis, who allowed himself to be circled into her with Brigid, into her lavender smell and her warm safety.

Their father and grandfather sat together formally, on two chairs, their hats on their knees, as if they were waiting for a train, until the children emerged, all in a tangle, and Brigid slid onto her grandfather's knee, and Francis stayed by his mother, holding her hand.

Beside their mother was a tray of food, barely touched. "Can you not eat yet, Grace?" asked their father.

"Not too hungry yet," said their mother, then lifted her fingers as she had often done at home. "I know who might help me, though," and she motioned them over, and divided out her dinner, which Brigid and Francis obligingly ate.

"I thought Rose would have been here," said their father, after watching the children for a moment.

"She was, briefly," said their mother, "but she didn't stay."

"Why?" asked their father, and his brow was furrowed. "She left specifically to see you."

"Well," said his wife, and Brigid, one eye on the spoon in the custard, one eye on her parents, saw that her mother glanced at her before replying, "she had a visitor here herself. Unless Cornelius Todd happened to be on this side of the town just to see me, which I doubt."

"He might have been," said her husband, and Brigid saw her grandfather turn in surprise.

"Yes," said the children's mother, plucking idly at the cotton coverlet, "and there might be a blue moon in the sky, too."

Brigid glanced out the window. She saw the prison, and

beyond it the College, Francis' school. They were like twin buildings: both tall, grim-eyed, brick-built buildings, blocking out the sky. Between them there was a patch of blue: but there was no blue moon. Her eye drifted down to the street below the hospital and there she saw, unmistakably, even to her limited sight, the tall broad form of Uncle Conor. He was alone. He was not with Rose. Brigid sensed Francis beside her, and knew that he, too, had seen this. His eyes met hers and, without a word, they stayed quiet.

"What are you two at, over there?" said their mother.

"Looking over at the College, Mama," said Francis, with a warning glance at Brigid, who did not need to be told to say nothing.

She could see her mother was tired. She had blue shadows under her eyes, like the bruise on Ned Silver's face, and when a nurse, a small neat lady like Rose, came in with tea, they followed their father's signal and got up, and hugged their mother again, and let themselves be shepherded out.

"When will Mama come home?" asked Brigid.

"When she's well," said her father, and nothing more.

He still seemed preoccupied as they went out of the hospital, and at the corner of the road he stalled the car.

The dance of the hats began again.

"Did you stall the car, there?" said their grandfather's hat.

"You saw that I did," came from the other one, and then there was silence.

He started the car up again.

At the main road another car, big, black and sleek, stopped suddenly, and Brigid and Francis shot forward as their father slammed the brakes. The car died again. "Holy cats!" said their father.

"Maurice, what are you doing?" said their grandfather, and Brigid heard fear in his voice.

"I didn't see him," said their father.

"Then get those eyes checked," said the grandfather, his face fully visible in profile below the black hat, his voice strong as it had been when he spoke to Ned Silver, "before you take these children in the car again."

They drove home in a silence heavy as an argument. At the house, the adults got out first, and still no one spoke. Her grandfather opened the back door of the car, and put out his hand to Brigid.

"Granda," she said, as he handed her out, "were they bad, the things that happened that could happen again?"

He said nothing for a moment, and then he said: "They were."

"And could they happen again? Really?"

"Brigid," said her father from the gate, and his voice was impatient, "are you going to stand out there the whole evening?"

"I hope and I pray that they will not, girlie," said her grandfather, and he placed his hand on her shoulder.

Brigid, her hand on the car door handle, silver and straight against the shining grey panel, stood her ground.

"Granda," she said, and her voice sounded desperate even to herself, "do you dream straight?"

Her grandfather took her hand in his. "I don't know what you mean, girlie," he said. "Come on. Let's go in." He guided her gently through the gate, and she heard him say again to his son: "Get you those eyes checked, for the love of God."

Before her father could reply, a small figure slid suddenly through the hedge and, to Brigid's astonishment, she saw Ned Silver place something round and gleaming into her grandfather's hand, and just as swiftly she saw him disappear through the hedge, as though he had never been there.

Chapter 22: Brigid of the Flowers

The day after they saw Davy Crockett down town, Francis knocked on the door of Brigid's room. "Want to hear the latest?" he said, putting his head round the door. On his face was a slight smile.

"Latest what?" said Brigid, puzzled.

Francis flapped out the newspaper as she had seen their father do. "'*Crush for Crockett*'," he read. "'*Davy's Dash from Stampeding Children*'."

Brigid sat up. "So it was really him?" Her disappointment returned.

"Listen," said Francis. "It's good." He cleared his throat, flapped the paper as their father did, and began to read: "'*Traffic was brought to a standstill, women fainted and children were parted from their mothers yesterday afternoon as over four thousand children milled round the premises of Messrs. Robbs, Castle Place, some of them for over two hours, for the arrival of Fess Parker, star of the Walt Disney film, Davy Crockett, King of the Wild Frontier. As they pushed and scuffled for a better position, the children kept chanting 'We want Davy'. Before Davy arrived, however, glass in a front door of the store was smashed and police had a difficult time keeping the highly excited children under control. Fess Parker, complete with Davy*

Crockett hat and gun, was smuggled into the store through a side door nearly thirty minutes later as children stampeded the store. The programme planned by the senior management was that Davy should stand behind a trading post erected in the store and shake hands with the children as they filed in one door and out the other. But the children were restless after waiting so long and, brushing aside all barriers, they clambered over furniture to get a closer look at Davy who, in vain, put up his hands and tried to talk to the children. In a final effort to restore order, Davy jumped on to a table and tried to quieten the shouting youngsters, but they surged on. 'I'd better leave,' said Davy, and off he went.'"

"And they ran after him?" said Brigid.

"I think that's what we saw," said Francis, with a laugh. "Isn't it great? Here's another bit. A news reporter interviewed Fess Parker afterwards in the Grand Central Hotel, and he said he was very sorry he had to leave – '"*but it was for the safety of the kids. I didn't want any more casualties,*" he said.'"

"What are cas-ul-aties?" said Brigid.

"In a war, the casualties are the ones who get killed."

Brigid thought for a moment. "Did he think coming here was like being in a war?"

"Well," said Francis, "he seems to have. Wait till you hear what he said next – I love this," and he laughed as he read: "'*We had a pretty rough battle at the Alamo, but I'd say there were more casualties at Robbs' this afternoon.*'" Francis put down the paper. "Isn't it great?" he said, his eyes dancing.

Brigid was still puzzled. "He thought we were like the people he was fighting in a battle?"

"Not us, silly," said Francis. "The ones who stampeded."

"That sort of means us. Ned Silver was there. I saw him."

"Was he?" asked Francis, and his face grew serious. "Are you sure? But he was here with us . . ."

"I saw him. I did see him, at the front of the crowd chasing Davy Crockett."

Francis laughed then, but his smile had gone. "Ned," he said. "Always in there. Sure as there's trouble." He put down the paper. "I suppose . . . I don't know . . . he would have had time to get a bus and be down town the same time as us . . . but would he have been allowed?" He seemed to be speaking to himself.

"Ned Silver is allowed to do anything he wants," said Brigid. "Anything at all."

Francis, his brow furrowed, nodded. "He gets away with things, all right," he said, "but I wouldn't be him." He folded up the paper. "I'd better take this back down. Anyway, Brigid, I wouldn't worry too much about not seeing Davy Crockett. It was an actor playing him. He's in this new film about him. I'm sure the real Davy Crockett wouldn't have run away from a crowd of children."

"No," said Brigid, loyally. "The real Davy wouldn't have. He killed him a bear when he was only three."

"He did not," said Francis. "He *kilt* him a *bar*. You have to get these things right," he said, and then he was gone.

Brigid followed him downstairs. She was still put out. When Ned said he was going to see Davy Crockett, she had thought he was being brought to the picture house, something rare enough to be remarkable in itself. It had not occurred to her that he might be going to see Davy Crockett himself, and it had never struck her that he might be going to do such a thing alone. Meanwhile, whatever Francis said, she had missed the nearest thing to an adventure. She might think up as many stories as she liked, but she would never meet Davy Crockett now.

Her disappointment, however, was short-lived. April brought longer, brighter days, and her mother came home from hospital. Brigid's first, sharp disappointment about the baby was brief. She had never known the baby, had hardly taken in that she was expected, and had not yet learned to feign emotion. What she wanted was her mother at home, and life as it had always been. She welcomed every return to normality, glad even to hear her father read out the news, telling his wife what was going on in the world as if she had caused it, getting excited about who should speak for the people in Mid-Ulster, or why the government was cutting the children's allowance. "In England," he declared, "they have two shillings for third and following children. And we are to make do with one shilling and sixpence! Because Stormont doesn't want to extend encouragement to people to have large families! Holy cats!"

"I don't think we need worry, Maurice," came the quiet reply.

Brigid, watching the blue lines on her mother's thin hands, and the brown shadows beneath her eyes, felt a sadness she did not understand.

And then, though the days lengthened further and the leaves on the trees grew bolder, the Friday Tree waving to her its early summer bloom, time slowed. Even Brigid's birthday, due in the middle of May, seemed to have stopped its steady approach. She could not understand why the days had extra hours and minutes, each longer than the one before, and began to believe she would never get to her birthday. She longed to be six, yet was sorry to leave five behind. It had been such an achievement to reach five that it seemed unkind just to abandon it, yet every lengthening day, every creamy blossom on the rowan or burst of pale yellow on the broom, the flowers that would become blackcurrants, every sound of the proud blackbird and his tired brown wife planning their day, and the cackling magpies swaggering up the garden, told her it was time to move into another summer. She wanted to get into short socks, but Isobel, whose business Brigid considered it was not, said, "Ne'er cast a clout till May be out", and Brigid thought she would be in woollen socks forever. One morning, however, when the birthday was very near, Brigid asked again, and heard Isobel say the thing about clouts yet again. Just as she was about to pull on the grey woollens, her mother, frail still, but less tired, more like herself, called from the landing as she went past: "That refers to the May flower, Isobel, the hawthorn, not the month. And it's well out. Put her in short socks, please." Brigid felt a surge of happiness, and when she heard her mother say, "It'll be time for sandals soon too," she believed at last the summer days might come again.

There was something else going on, as the summer came in. Though nothing had been said to Brigid, she gathered on this first day of short socks that new schools were being considered. Coming along the hall in anticipation of breakfast, she heard her mother's voice.

"I boarded," she heard her say. "I came to like it all right in the end."

Boarding meant going away to school, like Ned Silver. Brigid did not want that.

Then she heard her father: "I don't want him sent away," and Brigid, understanding, with relief, that she was not to be sent away, quickly realised with a cold jolt that it was Francis they were discussing. She stopped in the hall, still and silent, hardly breathing, listening as she had seen Isobel do.

"But that blow," she heard her mother say. "Those streets across to the College. If he should be hurt again . . ."

She heard her father flap the paper, the signal that discussion was at an end.

"Well, anyway," her mother said, "we'll try to get Brigid changed – yes, Maurice, we will – even if she should have to pluck daisies and play with plasticine. She's not even six, yet. There's lots of time and, for heaven's sake, can't I bring her on myself at home?"

Brigid, wondering still if she ever would be six, felt her heart lift at the thought that she might be able to escape from her school. With a spring to her step, she announced her presence, and settled to her breakfast with new hope.

In fact, it was not so very bad any more in school. Now that she was reading well, and writing, and had learned to keep her stories to herself, she managed quite well. It was important to know the group games, to avoid being singled out. Skipping was essential. She learned to join the end of a line, poised on one foot, and not to miss her turn. Then, to the sound of a chant of a lady on a hillside, wanting quantities of gold and silver, she learned to jump through the semi-circle of rope without becoming tangled. If it caught in her legs it stung like a wasp, and on rainy days it smelled like wet washing, but Brigid mastered the rope, and got through playtime most days without much incident. Some days, hard voices closed about her, girls with folded arms lined up in twos and threes at the gate, at the door of the outside toilets, even in the classroom if the teacher stepped outside for more than a moment. Brigid learned to saw her natural voice to a harsh edge and to use this voice when the gang came after her to pull buttons off her coat or hold her down in mud. Approaching six, she knew that the most important thing in school was to keep her head down. She learned the things that would protect her, and protect her family from knowing what it was like. Her mother was still frail, and her father was far away these days, there but not there, always thinking, sitting with his head in his hands, holding the paper at different angles as though things would change if he looked at them another way. And, in the glorious month of her birthday, it began to seem that she might escape to a school where children plucked daisies and played with plasticine.

Every morning in May, a statue was carried to the front of the schoolyard, and flowers were placed in front of it. The statue was to remind them that Mary was the Mother of God, and that the month of May was hers. At first, Brigid thought that the statue itself was Mary the Mother of God, but it was quickly made clear that this was not so. She liked only one of the hymns, of flowers from woodlands and hillside: it made her think of Tullybroughan and the farm, and she decided that she, too, would bring flowers of the fairest. She would bring flowers of the fairest and blossoms the rarest, to Mary, the loveliest flower of the May, and perhaps then Mary would ask her son who was God to give her a new school, and keep Francis from being sent away, and make her mother strong, and help her father see the paper properly.

On the morning of her birthday, therefore, before anyone was up, Brigid managed to take scissors and a little string from the kitchen. She turned the lock and undid the latch of the back door without difficulty, and it struck her that this was because she was now six. She was able, with some effort, to cut a little of the pale broom with its slender stalk; and buttercups and daisies were easy. She picked white bells from the hedge, and long-stemmed daisies and yellow buttercups from the grass. She was tying this bundle when she had a sudden thought, and picked a bright flower, golden as the sun, and then another, and soon she had made a fitting bouquet for the May altar. It was fortunate that, the weather was still considered cold enough for a coat: it meant she was able to conceal her flowers fairly well. Her mother told her to behave in school, because when she got home, she would find surprises; and Brigid did not point out that in school there was no choice but to behave.

By happy chance she did not have to go with Isobel: her father drove her, and he was very quiet, not noticing the flowers tucked inside the coat, not noticing anything but the road ahead. Brigid wondered why he did not mention her birthday. She stood at the gate and waved to him, puzzled at his forgetting, then turned in to place her offering with those of the others.

As she stood back to admire them, she heard a thin voice, tall above her. "What do you think you are doing?" asked the voice, narrow and cutting, like wire. Even before she looked, Brigid knew it was the nun with steel-rimmed glasses, the nun she had thought on her first day might be Sister Chalk. Brigid felt the chill sweep of her habit past her head, and saw Sister Chalk's handless wide sleeves joined at her wrist.

"Sister," she said, standing up, eyes down, as she had learned, "I'm making an offering for . . ." she searched frantically for the right description, "for Our Lady, Queen of the . . . loveliest flower of the . . . fairest."

The nun grew even taller: even the sunlight of the spring morning failed to make its way round her sharp pointing headdress. "An offering?" she said, her voice like ice. "Of weeds?" She took one hand out of the sleeve, and her long fingers flicked Brigid's bouquet with disdain. "Hedge weeds, daisies, buttercups and – what are these – dandelions?" The bright yellow flowers were plucked out and torn. "How dare you," said the nun, and her voice was deathly quiet. "How dare you insult Our Lady with your weeds!" In a moment she had reached out and caught Brigid's wrist, produced from deep inside her sleeve a thick ruler, raised it high against the sun and brought it down hard, three times, on Brigid's hand. Then she turned and swept away, her rosary beads clicking against the bunched skirt and her thin stick body.

Brigid, shocked, could not move, could not hear, could not see. Gradually she heard the laughing, the jeering. The gang was forming: "*Dandelions! Dandelions! You'll wet the bed! You'll wet the bed!*" The chant gathered momentum, turning in seconds to "*She wet the bed,*" and the mockery grew louder, until Brigid thought she must run, run away, run anywhere, and she thought she would burst, burst everything when, somewhere in the chaos, she heard a quiet voice.

Commanding silence, there stood above her another nun. Brigid stiffened, then saw that it was the kind round sister who had shown her how to make Brigid's crosses. The nun dismissed the crowd of girls, then looked down at Brigid for a few moments before she spoke. Her arms, like the arms of Sister Chalk, were buried in her wide sleeves, and Brigid watched them carefully.

"You brought flowers for the altar, Brigid." It was not a question.

Brigid nodded, then added, "Yes, Sister," but did not look up to meet her eye.

The nun withdrew her hands from her folded sleeves, and Brigid stepped back. Yet the hand now extended towards her held not a ruler but a handkerchief, big like a man's, but sewn with small neat stitches. She handed it to Brigid. "Dry your eyes," she said, "like a good child. Blow your nose. There's no call for all that drama."

Brigid reached out her hand and took the handkerchief. "Thank you, Sister," she said.

The nun did not move, or speak. Then she put her head on one side, and she was once more like a mother bird, her dark round bird eyes small and bright, and she said: "I remember reading somewhere that the dandelion is the flower of Brigid." Then she reached behind her, lifted a large hand bell and, leaving Brigid with the big handkerchief in her hand, walked about the yard ringing the bell, until the girls scrambled and squeezed into lines.

To Brigid, joining her own line, the nun had performed a kind of magic. Brigit the Fire Goddess, Brigid the Saint and Brigid of the Flowers were all now one with Brigid Arthur and the girls were just girls again, small girls and big in straight lines on a May morning, singing their hymns to Mary. Brigid saw that the kind Sister had retrieved some of her golden dandelions and placed them, with her daisies and her buttercups, and her pale spiky broom, close by Mary and her silent blue folds. Brigid lifted her head. She was Brigid of the Flowers.

Throughout the remainder of that day, however, she moved very carefully. She did not want to attract any more attention. At the end of school, she stood at the gate, waiting for Isobel, who was never on time. The day was blue and the breeze light, and for a moment she remembered the other cold blue day when she had stood alone until George Bailey brought her home. She turned her eyes to the end of the road where she had run to him, thinking he was her father and, out of the corner of her eye, softened by distance, she thought for a moment that she saw him again. It almost seemed that George Bailey, her own George, was standing at the other side of the main road, near the park. It was too far for her to see clearly, but it was, for that second, so like him, as she remembered him, the day he brought her home. That day, so strange at the time, now seemed a lost and lovely place. In the deep pocket of her raincoat, she still had the two chestnuts he had given her, their rough and smooth sensations sliding and rolling beneath her anxious fingers. She had thought they were lost: when she found them, through a hole in the lining of her coat, she had shown them to no one, not even Francis. They were her secret with George Bailey, and now, today, she put her hands round them for comfort, as if she had really found George again. Her eyes closed, lost in her thoughts, she did not hear the engine of her father's car, but when she opened her eyes, there he stood before her, his hand outstretched.

"Daddy!" she cried, in joy. "I thought it would be Isobel. I'm so glad it's you. Daddy, I thought I saw . . ."

He spoke across her. "I telephoned home and told your mama I would bring you. I left the office early." He never left the office early, even on Christmas Eve, and she could scarcely remember a time when he had collected her after school.

"For me, Daddy?" said Brigid.

"For you, Brigid," he said, and Brigid was content.

She climbed into the car; her father told her to pull in her arms, and then he closed the door. They drove away from the school and turned on to the main road. At the corner, she saw some of the gang looking at the car and she could see she would pay for this pleasure, but that was for tomorrow, not today. The railings by the park where she thought she had glimpsed George were blank again; there was no George there. Yet, beside her father in the big grey car, Brigid stopped missing George Bailey. The day was soft and bright; she was with her father; she was going home to surprises. Beside them a young girl in a blazer and a summer dress cycled on the inside lane, the light breeze catching her hair.

"Tell me," said her father, "does somebody have a birthday, today? Let me see. Who is it?"

Brigid saw that the corners of his eyes were crinkled; he looked like Francis, young and playful.

"You know fine well it's me, Daddy," she said, and gave his arm a little nudge with hers.

In that moment she heard two things. The first was her father saying, "Brigid, don't . . ." Then she heard a mighty thump, and the car stopped heavily in the middle of the road. The girl in her bright dress sat awkwardly on the kerb, all the pretty flowers of her skirt stained with brown and red. Brigid heard her father's breathing, sharp, gasping: "What did she . . . What was she . . . turning there . . . ?"

Then he was out of the car, picking the girl up, settling her. Her knee appeared to be cut, and he bound it with his handkerchief. The girl got up and, with only a slight limp, wheeled her bicycle across the road, and walked into the neat garden of one of the houses. He waited until she turned her key in the door, and lifted his hand in farewell. She waved at him, a bright and friendly wave, as if he were her father, too. Then he got in the car again, starting up the engine.

"Turning there, in front of me," he said. "She's lucky she wasn't killed."

"Is she all right, Daddy?" Brigid heard her own voice, small and afraid. She should not have nudged him.

"She is, no thanks to herself. The knee is cut, but it's not bad. She lives there, she says, in one of those houses. She wouldn't let me go across with her to explain."

"Daddy," said Brigid, looking straight ahead, "I'm sorry I pushed your arm."

He said: "It wasn't your fault, Brigid. I didn't see her. I'm not paying attention these days. I should have gone across with her."

"But, thank you for collecting me, Daddy," Brigid said, to feel better.

He did not reply, and she knew he was gone again, into that distant place where he could not be found.

Back at the house, Brigid's heart was heavy. The journey home had begun so well. She felt she herself had gone far away, that everything was happening at a distance. Even the voices, her mother asking her father what was wrong, sounded distant, a little muffled. Yet, from behind her glass wall, she knew a great effort had been made, and that she must be pleased.

In the sitting room, on the table, there sat a box wrapped up in white paper, and in it, in cardboard compartments, there were more people for her theatre: a woodcutter, and a wolf, and a small girl in a red hood with a basket. She knew this story. The box itself had trees, and a thatched house, and scenes of woods and the inside of a house. She heard her voice say that it was lovely. In a parcel of brown paper there was a new book, and on its cover was a picture of a lion, a witch and a wardrobe. She heard herself thank her parents. Her grandfather arrived as a surprise for her birthday: she felt herself being lifted up, and heard herself saying she was very glad he was there. There was a cake her mother had made while Brigid was at school, with six lighted candles, and there were tomato sandwiches and rock cakes. She blew out all six candles at one go, ate the sandwiches and the cake, and everyone seemed pleased, even Isobel, and when her grandfather told her to go upstairs and see what she would find, Brigid obediently went.

Brigid climbed to her room, wondering still why she could feel nothing. Then she saw on her bed a little hat with a tail, like the one Davy Crockett had worn. At the door behind her stood her grandfather. Brigid had not heard him come up.

"That's for the day we didn't stop, Brigid, when your cowboy friend was in the town," he said.

Inside her, Brigid felt something, hard like a rock, shift slightly. She lifted her arms to him and he swung her up. "Granda," she said, but she could not begin to explain, and instead she felt tears go down her face.

"Who's my girl?" he said, and Brigid, leaning against him, saw far outside at the top of the plot, that the Friday Tree was dressed for her birthday in delicate green, its feathery breezy leaves catching the light, and she imagined she could hear its whispers. Then she stiffened. Under it, again, there was a soft spiral of smoke, as if someone was there.

"What is it, Brigid," said her grandfather. "Are you all right?"

Before Brigid could reply, she saw over his shoulder that Francis had come into the room.

"Francis!" she cried, and she drew her hand across her nose and mouth. "I didn't hear you!"

"I am too subtle," said Francis. "Happy Birthday."

"You'll need long trousers soon," said her grandfather, turning round with her in his arm, so that her head spun a little.

"I want long trousers soon," said Francis.

"Haven't you something to show this birthday girl?"

Francis' eyes crinkled and danced as he nodded. "I do," he said. Then he slid to his knees, right beside the theatre.

Brigid tried to scramble down from her grandfather's arm, but he held her fast. "I have new people for it, Francis," she said.

Francis held out his hand, but did not move. "Wait," he said. He reached behind the theatre, and though his head and face remained in view, Brigid could see from his expression that he was working at something on the other side of the theatre.

Her grandfather, still holding her in his arm, walked over to the window and drew the curtain, shutting out the light. Brigid's mouth opened in surprise as, finding herself eased to the floor, she saw her theatre light up, magical and mysterious, like a house on the mountain at night.

Enchanted, she took her new people, arranged and rearranged them over and over: closed the curtains, opened them, walked away, came back and, after a time, saw that she was by herself, Granda and Francis no longer in the room. She had not seen them go. Brigid, alone, was finally happy on her birthday.

Chapter 23: A Whistling Woman

After the accident with the cyclist, the car sat unused in the garage. Now, her father took the bus in the morning, and left her off at the school. To Brigid, though she missed the comfort of the car, this was companionable and pleasant, and she did not have to have Isobel. She had heard her mother use a new word of Isobel: she was unreliable. Whatever this meant, it reflected Brigid's own unease about her.

One Saturday morning towards the end of June, there came an unexpected knock at the front door. A dark shadow showed through the leaded lights and, for an instant, Brigid thought of Uncle Conor, but it was not Uncle Conor. On the doorstep stood Brigid's friend, Mr Doughty. Though his great holster hung by his side, he was not especially alarming: not nearly as much as Mr Steele. Yet, he did not seem quite as mild and friendly as when he was in the plot. He was different in little things, like the shining ring that appeared in his hair when he took off his cap to come in. He never had that in the plot. The hall seemed smaller as he stepped inside: he looked too big for it and, glancing at him in the mirror so that he would not see her looking, Brigid saw for the first time that one side of his face seemed to go down more than the other, as if one side was the kind man in the garden, and the other the stern man with the gun.

251

Mr Doughty bowed his head to step into the sitting room, and, with an air of apology, sat down. Even sitting towards the edge of the seat, he filled the chair, and his legs stretched almost to the fireplace. Brigid waited with Mr Doughty while her mother went to make tea. There was no Isobel today. She was being unreliable. He asked Brigid how she was, and how her brother was; he said she was going to be tall like her mother; he was kind, but he was clearly uncomfortable. When Mrs Arthur came into the room, fragile still, with a tray in her hands, he stood up at once to take it from her.

"I am sorry, Mrs Arthur," he said. "I wouldn't disturb you at such an hour, and on a Saturday morning, if it were not necessary." He paused, and twisted his cap in his hands. "I was wondering," he said, after a moment, "if your husband might be at home this morning. I have a little matter I need to talk to him about, if it is convenient."

Brigid thought for a moment of the smoke under the Friday Tree. She wished Francis were there: but Francis, of course, had school on Saturday morning.

"He was about to go down to his office, Mr Doughty," said Brigid's mother in some surprise, "but I am sure he will see you. Brigid," she said, gently turning her away from the gun and the holster, "go up and ask Daddy to come down to see Mr Doughty."

Brigid took her eyes away with some reluctance.

"And Brigid?"

Brigid stopped, one hand on the door handle.

"Don't run."

Brigid nodded, and ran upstairs.

Her father was standing in the bathroom, his face white with foam. In one hand he held the shining curve of his razor, sweeping it up and down the length of a leather strap.

"Daddy," said Brigid, running into the bathroom, "can you please . . ."

"Brigid," he said, and raised his hand away from her. "Be

252

careful. This is sharp. Were you not told not to run in the house? Go on, you should be outside playing that good day."

Brigid, on a reflex, was about to turn round and do just that, when she remembered why she had come upstairs. "But Daddy," she said, "I have to get you. Mr Doughty is downstairs. He has his cap and his gun."

Her father stopped moving the razor, and stood perfectly still. He turned and looked in the mirror and then, slowly, carefully, he towelled away the white cream, and Brigid could see a dark shadow on his face. "I'll have to put on my collar," he said, reaching for the stiff crescent of cloth. Then, quite suddenly, he seemed to fold in the middle, and Brigid saw him sink into a kind of crooked sitting, on the edge of the bath. The collar fell unheeded to the floor.

Brigid let it fall. She put out her hand and caught her father's arm. It felt thin and bony in a way she did not remember. "Daddy?" she said. "Daddy?"

He passed a hand across his forehead, then removed it and placed it on hers, still on his arm, and patted her twice. "It's all right, Brídín," he said. "I just moved too quickly."

Brigid saw a frown cross his face, a swift shot like pain, and she remembered when her head had caused her so much pain in the autumn. "Does your head hurt, Daddy?"

He looked up at her from his awkward seat on the edge of the bath, and touched his hand to his forehead again. "It does," he said. "But it often does when I wake. It goes away. It's nothing. Anno Domini, probably."

Brigid was puzzled. "Who is that, Daddy?"

He smiled a little, and the creases at the sides of his eyes deepened. On impulse, Brigid reached out her arm, placed her hand on his face, and gently stroked it. He reached his own hand again to his face, and kept it there, over hers, for a moment.

"Wee soft hand," he said. "*A Bhrídín dhílís*. Anno Domini just means your daddy is getting old."

Just as Brigid felt the cold of fear run all through her, he stood up, quite steadily, reached down with one hand on the wash basin and, retrieving the collar, placed it round his neck, swiftly and accurately, pushing in a stud, right at the back.

For a second, Brigid remembered the round collar that had sprung at her in the house at Lecale, but she blinked that memory away.

Then her father eased on his jacket, patted the pocket, ran his hand over his hair, and said: "Mr Doughty, then." He sighed. "All right. Let's go."

He took her hand as they went downstairs. The weakness of the minutes before seemed like a dream: he was strong now, himself again. She felt almost happy as she prepared to go in with him to see what Mr Doughty had come to say. Yet, at the door of the sitting room, he released her hand. "Off you go, now," he said, patting her shoulder. "Go up into the garden and play, like a good girl." Then he closed the door, and Brigid was left alone in the hall.

Making her way to the garden, she did not know what to do with herself, so suddenly excluded from everything that was happening. Idly, she picked berries from the blackcurrant bushes. Some were green and bitter, but others were turning a promising red-purple. Brigid, with Francis, had been sent to collect them the summer before, and she thought she might put some in her pocket and be useful without being told. They were hard to pull away, and she soon gave it up, wandering without purpose to the fence at the edge of the plot. She trailed her hand along the tops of the bushes, and took a covert glance over to the Silvers' garden, for she would have been glad just then to see even Ned Silver, though she knew he must still be away at whatever school he was trying now. There was no one there but Mrs Mulvey, sweeping the passageway. Brigid waved at her, but Mrs Mulvey did not see her, or pause in her work. After only a few minutes, the sound of her stiff brush on concrete stopped, a door opened and closed, and there was nothing then to hear but the silence of the garden, and the calling of the birds above.

Brigid climbed a little way up the fence. She had never been in the plot without Francis, and she had no intention of going in now. Stretched on tiptoe, she leaned against the concrete post: she might climb up a little more, but she would not go in, though she thought she could get over quite easily; she would just put both legs over to the other side, to see how far it was to jump down. And then, to her own surprise, she was in the plot, and it was easy. Brigid looked back quickly to the house, but it gave away nothing. In any case, her parents were inside with Mr Doughty. They would not be looking for her.

All round her feet young things gathered, green shoots and bright flowers. There was the waving blue of the plants Mr Doughty would dig later on from the ground: potatoes would be on the end of them, smelling of earth. Feathery green tops had little carrots hiding beneath: he would pull those too from the ground, and give them to her to take in. It was like last summer, but with a delicious sense of freedom, Brigid realised it was even better, for she had not asked anyone to help her. She was here by herself, big enough to climb in by herself, and she moved easily through the tall grasses, picking one and chewing it as she had seen Francis do. It was sweet, and it felt very daring and free to be doing it. She looked up at the Friday Tree and wondered if she might make her way by herself to it. She drew a deep breath, and took a step. That was when the first nettles stung her and, though she reached for a docken leaf and rubbed hard, the stings remained painful. Brigid rubbed until the leaf came away in green streaks on her fingers, backing towards the fence as she did so: she no longer wanted to make her way to the Friday Tree by herself. Her leg was coming up in ugly raised welts, and it was all she could do not to cry. She had managed to get as far as the overhanging trees between the Silvers' house and her own, just at the fence, when she heard a sound. It was a low whistle, like a bird's call, but it was not a bird's call. It was more like the whistle Francis had used for Dicky when he was lost in the plot. Someone was in the plot and was whistling.

Brigid pulled back into the shadow of the trees, and then she saw something strange. It was a coat, quite like the one George Bailey had worn, very like the one she had thought she saw outside school on her birthday. It was not George who was wearing it. Someone was whistling, but not to Dicky, and not to her. She flattened herself into the bushes. The whistle came again, and now she saw a head, sleek and dark like the head of a seal, emerge from the blue and green of the potato bushes, halfway up the plot. It was too far for her to see features, but she knew it was not the shape of George, and somehow she also knew to stay still and remain quiet. Another whistle came, from further away and, this time, she saw that a person was standing at the edge of the plot, almost too far for Brigid to see. She stopped. It was not too far to see, after all. That outline. She knew who it was. Standing at the edge of the plot, whistling with two fingers to her mouth, was the unmistakable shape of Isobel, unreliable Isobel. Brigid thought of her mother, frail and thin, struggling with the tray for Mr Doughty. She enjoyed a new, brief rush of anger at Isobel for being in the plot and whistling instead of helping her mother in the house. In the same moment, she wondered why Isobel was standing whistling at a man with a head like a seal, crouching in the potato plants.

It was scarcely possible to draw back any further into the bushes. Brigid did her best, and held her breath as the seal-man slid quite close to her, through the plants, crushing the delicate fronds of the little carrots, and she hoped the nettles would sting him for that. If they did, he did not stop, and he slid on towards the top of the plot, where Isobel, from the opposite direction, was making her stealthy way. Now and again one, or the other, disappeared: then, at the very foot of the Friday Tree, Brigid, screwing her eyes half-shut, could just make out the shape of their two forms, standing close together. It seemed to her that Isobel handed something to the seal-man, and then he slid back into the bushes and Isobel, glancing from left to right, retraced her steps, and disappeared from Brigid's view. She had her chance then to climb back over the fence, and wish with all her heart that Francis would come back so that she could tell him what she had seen.

As she dropped to the path from the fence, she heard the sound of the gate, one long creaking note, and her father's tread on the passage. His steps were heavy. Brigid ran down the steps and through the back yard, reaching up easily for the latch of the back door. In the cool kitchen there was such a waiting, so much silence and anxiety that she almost turned and ran out again, but she could see the outside world shining in through the length of the kitchen and the hall. Mr Doughty must have gone. She heard the clanging scrape of the gate: then, her father stood tall in the open doorway, and the sun shone round his darkness. Beside him, another light shadow crossed the doorway: Francis was home from school. Brigid heard his voice, asking what was happening; she did not hear her father's reply, but she saw him put his hand on Francis' shoulder. Then she saw him shake his head, go into the sitting room, and close the door. Whatever had happened, he was no longer going out to the office.

"Francis," called Brigid. "I have to tell . . ."

"Oh, Brigid," said Francis, "please, can it wait a minute?" and he went upstairs, and his tread was as heavy as their father's had been. She heard him shut his door.

Something was happening, and no one would tell Brigid what it was. Stopping at the sitting-room door, she heard the low voice of her father, the softer voice of her mother, but the sounds were muffled. Guiltily, she listened for a moment, thinking of Isobel. All she heard was one word: "Sue." What was Sue? Was that a person? Brigid was prepared to wait no longer. She ran up the stairs as she had been forbidden to do, down the corridor, under Blessed Oliver, and straight into Francis' room.

Looking up, he did not even tell her that she should have knocked. He sat on his bed, his fingers stained with ink, his tie loosened at the neck. He looked tired, and Brigid knew she should not trouble him, but she had to know what was happening.

"Francis," she said, "do you know what's wrong?"

He sighed and nodded his head, patting the bed beside him so that she could climb up.

"Do you remember a day when you were with Daddy and there was a bump in the car?"

Brigid said: "Yes. My birthday. A girl on a bicycle. Daddy said she shouldn't have tried to turn in front of him."

"Yes. Well. The girl's family has pressed charges. That means she says it was Daddy's fault. They're going to sue. He may have to go to court."

Sue. That is what that meant. Brigid felt fear rise, not hidden now, but full and beating with black wings. She knew it was her fault that he had hit the girl. She had jogged his arm.

"Francis. What will happen? Will he go to jail?"

"No," said Francis, "No. He won't go to jail, but he could lose his licence to drive, or he could be fined, or both." He nudged his elbow against hers. "He won't go to jail."

"That's what Mr Doughty came to tell him?" said Brigid, trying to take it in.

Francis bit his lip, and nodded his head. "It was, yes."

Brigid felt the enormity of what she had done. Daddy not able to drive would be Daddy sad, his wings clipped, and she had caused it. She put her hands over her own eyes.

Francis nudged her again. "Don't, Brigid," he said. "That won't help."

Brigid shook her head. "I did it, Francis. It was my fault."

"What was your fault?" His voice was patient, but very tired.

"I bumped his elbow. I made him drive into her."

Francis reached away, and pulled her hands down. "Turn round," he said, "and look at me. You didn't cause it."

She shook her head. "I did. I nudged him."

He took both her hands. "You didn't cause it. It wasn't a sensible thing to do, but that isn't why it happened. He didn't see her. He didn't see her, because his eyes are bad again. Do you remember the way they were before he came back with the bandages?"

Brigid remembered when he covered his eye and the other one could not see. She said: "His eyes were open but he couldn't see me."

Francis nodded, still looking straight at her. "It's that way again. That's why it happened. A Brigid nudge wouldn't do it. You can believe me." He looked straight at her, his eyes full of light, and Brigid knew he could see her, right through her. "Do you believe me?" he said.

"It's because he can't see out of part of his eyes?" she said.

"Yes," said Francis. "He has to have his eyes tested again."

"He gets headaches," said Brigid, "when he wakes up."

"Does he?" said Francis. "I didn't know that."

"Yes," she said, "but then they go. He told me this morning."

Francis looked thoughtful. "Poor Daddy," he said. Then he sighed, as their father had done. "Do you think you could let me change out of these clothes and go downstairs and get myself something to eat?" He steered her to the door. "Go."

Once again, Brigid found herself outside a closed door. In the same instant, she realised that she had not told him about the plot and seeing Isobel give something to the man with a head like a seal. Just as she turned round to knock on the door and tell Francis she heard, to her surprise, the voice of Isobel herself. "I'm sorry to be so late, Mrs Arthur," she heard her call from the kitchen. "I couldn't get a bus from town." Brigid, her hand raised to knock, let it fall. She knew now what unreliable meant. It meant telling lies.

Chapter 24: The Churn Rock

The following Monday was Brigid's last school day before the summer. On that morning, both parents went with her on the bus as far as the school. Her father was going to have his eyes tested, and her mother was going with him. They walked with her to the gate. Her mother told her to be a good girl, and her father told her not to get any slaps, and then he stroked her head with his hand.

"Will you come back for me after school?" Brigid said, touching her hand to his.

"Grace?" he said, turning to her mother.

There was a hesitation. Please, said Brigid in her head, please come.

"If there's time," said her mother. "If not, Isobel will come," and Brigid felt her father's hand slip from hers. She watched as they went away from her down the little street. Walking in step, they made an elegant pair, tall, complete and self-contained. Her father held his hand under her mother's elbow as if it were she, not he, whose sight was in question. At the bottom of the street they turned, as one, and lifted their hands to her in a wave. Brigid, waving back, just stopped herself from running after them. Instead, she watched them disappear, then turned into the yard on the last clang of the bell, and joined the end of the line. All day, she hoped they would come back for her, but it was Isobel, unreliable Isobel, who stood at the school gate that afternoon.

"Isobel," said Brigid, when she saw her, unable to hide her disappointment.

Isobel said nothing. She simply started walking, with Brigid by her side, down the street towards the bus stop.

It was not until they had been on the bus for some time, and the hill began to descend towards home, that Isobel finally turned to Brigid and spoke: "You'd better behave today. None of your nonsense."

Brigid, by now indifferent, knew better than to give Isobel an argument. She stayed silent as Isobel herself. They approached the park and the depot, and then the stop, opposite her home. Behind the house the trees waved, soft and dreamlike in the quiet afternoon. Despite herself, despite Isobel's surly, silent antagonism, Brigid felt a surge of happiness.

"Did you hear what I said back there?" said Isobel, as she took her arm to cross the road.

"Yes, Isobel," said Brigid, without expression.

"Because it's serious, you know," said Isobel.

In spite of her resolve, Brigid could not help herself. "What is serious, Isobel?"

She saw the gleam of satisfaction in Isobel's eyes as she turned to her: "Your father has to have another operation to his eyes." She waited for Brigid's response, but Brigid could only stare.

"In London?" she said.

"Here. Immediately," said Isobel, her triumph visible. "He had to go straight to the hospital after he had his eyes checked. The specialist insisted. And they're keeping him in, and they're going to operate first thing tomorrow."

Brigid could not speak. Above her, she could still see the trees in the plot, but their leaves no longer waved in greeting. Now, they were agitated, shivering in distress.

"So, you behave yourself," said Isobel, as she turned the key in the door.

"Is my mama here?" asked Brigid, in the silent hall.

"Of course not," said Isobel. "Put your school bag in the cloakroom. Don't leave it at your heels for someone else to pick up."

"Is Francis here?" asked Brigid.

"Use your head," said Isobel. "Isn't the College beside the hospital? Where would he be but with his parents?"

But, Brigid thought, I'm left here with you, and she could not hide her distress.

For a moment, Isobel's features seemed to soften. "Your Aunt Rose is on her way," she said. "Your mama telephoned her from the hospital, and as soon as she finishes her work she'll drive up here."

Brigid, unusually grateful to Isobel, tried her best to behave. She changed her clothes, came downstairs, picked at the bread and took a little of the soup Isobel warmed for her on the stove, then took herself, as instructed, out to the garden, with no purpose at all but to pass time.

She had no desire, now, to go over into the plot, or to think any more about who had been there or what Isobel was doing. She no longer cared. She hardly glanced over the fence: yet, when she did, she could not help noticing that there was something unusual there. Someone was in the plot: not George, not Isobel, not the man with a head like a seal. It was one of the policemen, and he was dressed in uniform. Brigid half-closed her eyes to try to make out who it was, but she could not. Both policemen were tall and of similar build: it could be either Mr Steele or Mr Doughty.

"It's Steele," said a voice beside her. "Old Steely," and from behind the bushes at the edge of the fence, she saw the head of Ned Silver, clamped to a pair of binoculars.

Brigid was not surprised: she was beyond surprise where he was concerned. "Ned," she said. "You must get your holidays before we do. I thought you were in England or somewhere."

Ned Silver laughed. "I know how to get holidays when I want," he said.

Brigid saw. "Were you sent home?"

Ned shrugged. "I got myself sent home. Like these?" He held up the shining binoculars.

"They're like the ones Uncle Conor had last summer," she said.

"Go to the top of the class. They *are* the ones Uncle Conor had last summer."

Brigid, about to speak, bit her lip to stop herself.

"What?" said Ned. "What did you say?"

"I didn't say anything," said Brigid.

"Yes, you did. First you said: 'He's not your uncle,' and then you said, 'How did you get those, Ned Silver?'" and he copied her voice with cruel accuracy.

Brigid bit her lip again, and this time it hurt. It was exactly what she had wanted to say.

"Well," she said, "how did you?"

"Ha," said Ned. "Made you ask. I got them," he said, and his insolent eyes held hers as he spoke, "from Uncle Conor. He lent them to me."

"Why? When?" For no reason that she could name, Brigid felt jealous.

"Oh," said Ned, raising the binoculars again to his eyes, "the day he took me to see Davy Crockett."

There was nothing to say after that. Brigid stood in stunned silence, and Ned, enjoying himself, dropped the binoculars from his eyes and let the leather strap spin. "He did intend – I mean I did consider asking him – to take you and Francis, too, or maybe it was just Francis. I forget."

Brigid really wanted to hit him: she felt her hands curling into furious fists.

"But then he had that spat with Rose – do you remember?" he paused, and smiled, without warmth, "and I suppose he didn't like to call to your house when Rose was there. So, he just took me, and then he went and did some things he had to do, and he came back for me, and brought me on up here, and he lent me these . . . for a while." He raised the binoculars once more. "Yes, it's Steely, all right."

"He probably forgot to take them with him," said Brigid, in her coldest voice. "More likely. He probably wanted to get away from you. And, anyway, we didn't want to go and see Davy Crockett, and we couldn't have, because we had other things to do. But we did see him anyway, from our car. He didn't seem that good. He was only an actor. And I saw you, Ned Silver, screaming your head off. And Francis said you were on your own in town."

"Did he?" said Ned, through the binoculars, to no one. "Well, scaring Davy Crockett out of Robbs was some fun, tell him." He suddenly dropped the binoculars, laughing, his whole face transformed by merriment. "You should've seen it. That man ran for his life! We scared the . . ." He stopped laughing, and looked across at her, his eyes again cool. "Anyway, Uncle Conor knows I can take care of myself – not like some people. It would have been different if he'd had you to look after. But you weren't with us, were you?"

Just as Brigid, all resolves forgotten, opened her mouth to tackle him, two voices called: Mrs Mulvey from Ned's house, Isobel from Brigid's. Ned, binoculars in his hands, began to sing in her face, about Davy Crockett and the mountain top in Tennessee. Blazing with anger and renewed disappointment, Brigid ran down the garden, Ned keeping pace on his side of the fence, singing away about greenest states and the land of the free.

"Brigid!" Isobel's voice was loud. "Where are you? Your Aunt Rose is here."

Ned had got to killing him a bear. It was too much.

"It's *kilt* him a *bar*, Ned," she said, her eyes straight ahead. "Get it right." She turned at the top of the steps to see Ned Silver's insolent face turned towards hers, singing Davy's name as if Brigid didn't know he was King of the Wild Frontier.

Then both children disappeared down their steps like rabbits into separate burrows.

That afternoon and evening passed slowly. Rose explained that it was a good thing that her father was going to hospital, so that they could see to his eyes, try to take away his headaches, and make him well again.

"I've seen these things in the hospital," Rose said. "He's in good hands, and I'll stay with you till your mama gets back."

Brigid, safe with Rose, felt reassured, especially since Isobel was not in charge any more: she retreated into the background where, in Brigid's view, she ought to stay.

Then when, late in the evening, her mother and Francis came home, Brigid was so well schooled by Rose that she did not tire them with questions. Instead, she went to bed without protest, because Rose told her that the next day, all being well, she had a plan to do something special.

True to her word, Rose came in next morning before Brigid was properly awake. She pinched Brigid's toe beneath the bedclothes, and shook it. "All right, Miss," she said. "Up you get – or I'll have to visit your granda without you."

Brigid was out of bed, in and out of the bathroom, and dressed in record time – in a way that satisfied her if no one else – and, after Rose had made some adjustments to the outfit, she was pronounced ready to go, just as soon as breakfast was over. Through it all, her mother sat still, leaving Brigid entirely to Rose.

"Are you sure this is all right, Grace?" said Rose. "You don't want me to come over with you?"

Brigid's mother shook her head. "No. It's the first day of their holidays. Take them out for the day. It'll be a while before he comes round. I don't want them waiting and wondering."

"But, company, Grace. Maybe Francis . . .?"

Francis had just come in through the door.

"No. Take Francis, too. Yes, you, Francis," she said, as his face expressed surprise. "I'd like you to go with Rose and Brigid. You had a long day yesterday, and I want you to get out in the air."

"I'll stay with you, Mama," said Francis.

"Francis," said his mother, and her eyes, though tired, brooked no argument, "Did you not hear me? I want you to go with Rose and Brigid."

Brigid thought: I want you to, as well.

Francis met his mother's eyes, held them for a moment, then dropped his own. "If you say so, Mama," he said, but he did not look happy.

Rose got to her feet. "That's settled then. We'll go. I'll contact you, Grace. Isn't there a telephone box near the Arthurs'?"

"Just beside," said Francis. "I'll show you."

In the car, as they settled themselves Brigid noticed two things. Rose, always slender, was now very thin, nearly as thin as their mother. The bones round her neck and shoulders formed ridges and hollows beneath the skin. The second thing was that when Francis got into the front seat, the set of his head was very still, as if he were waiting, or displeased.

Just as Rose was about to turn the key in the ignition, Francis turned to her. "Rose," he said, "I'm sorry. I can't go with you. I've got to stay with Mama. I can't leave her by herself all day."

Brigid could have cried. It had been months since there had been an outing, and she so wanted Francis to be with her now. She said nothing. It would do no good.

"Yes," said Rose, and she nodded her head with a sigh. "You may have a point. Brigid and I will be fine, won't we, Brigid?" and she turned her thinness round to look at Brigid, silent in the back of the car. "Have you a nice game you could play while we go?"

"Yes, Rose," said Brigid, but she did not look at Francis. "I have my Travel Ludo, from Christmas."

"Good. You'll be occupied then. On you go, Francis."

"Thank, you, Rose," said Francis, and then he stopped, and his face looked brighter. "I know," he said. "Take Ned."

"Ned?" said Rose. "Nobody said Ned was here."

No one could have said, except Brigid, and she had no

intention of telling that to anyone.

"No, he's here," said Francis, scanning the road for traffic. "Look," he said, opening the door. "There he is behind the hedge. Ned!"

And there he was, as always, Ned Silver, silently watching.

"Well," said Rose, "I thought he was still away at school. I don't think I'll ask him why he's not. I may not want to know."

Francis got out and spoke quietly to Ned.

Rose, through the window, called: "Ned? Will you check inside? And if it is all right, you can come."

There was no need to check. Mrs Mulvey, polishing the brasses at the front door, waved down, "Please take him, Miss Durrant," she called. "You'd be doing me a favour," and before Brigid knew what was happening, Ned Silver was in the back of the car with her, yet again, and all she could see of Francis was a pair of long legs sprinting up the passage.

It was a silent journey. Ned was no substitute for Francis. Unlike Brigid, he did try at first to make conversation with Rose, asking her if Uncle Conor would be meeting them. Rose said he would not, and something that was like a steel barrier entered the car between the children and Rose, so that after that everyone stayed quiet, even through the drumlins and the green summer lanes. Halfway, Brigid did try to get Ned to play Travel Ludo with her, but he looked at it and at her with such disdain that she lost heart and put it away.

Only when they saw the sea did Brigid, almost in spite of herself, utter a sound of satisfaction. She asked if she could roll down the window, and she inhaled the salt air and took in the soft grey of the horizon, and the lonely call of the circling birds. She did not notice until they were past it that the car had not gone to her grandfather's house.

"Aren't we . . . ?" she began.

Rose drove on, steadily. "Your grandfather is walking out to meet us where the road ends," she said. "He says he is going to take us to the house at the edge of the world."

"But how . . . ?"

Ned dug his finger, sharply, in Brigid's arm. "That, perhaps?" and he pointed to a telephone box, near her grandfather's distant house. "Unless it was carrier pigeon. Or, I know, Pony Express. 'Davy . . .'" he began to sing, and Brigid, raising her hand to give him one good whack, met Rose's warning eyes in the mirror. She dropped her hand, and looked stonily out of the window.

"It wasn't carrier pigeon, Ned," she heard Rose say. "And it wasn't Pony Express, and that will be enough from you. Anyway, don't you think it will be pleasant to be by the sea on this nice day?"

"But, won't Granda be worrying about Daddy?" Brigid asked, turning back from the window.

She looked again at Rose's mirror eyes, and the hint of warning was still there.

"Not if we take his mind off it," she said. "Your Aunt Laetitia doesn't finish up at her school until tomorrow, and we can have a good day out with your granda, can't we?"

No Laetitia? Brigid, her spirits lifting, nodded her head.

Where the road ended, they did indeed see the tall figure, in his black hat. Brigid thought, with a stab, of the day her father drove them to the hospital, and his hat and Granda's hat had nodded and bobbed at each other all the way over and all the way home. Now, her father was in the hospital himself, and Granda was here, standing like a traffic policeman – like Mr Doughty and Mr Steele. Brigid shut out those names: she was going to the sea, and she would think of nothing else.

The car stopped, releasing a silence where the sky became a wider blue, the crying of the birds more intense, and the smell of seaweed and salt still stronger and more enticing. The children tumbled out of the car, and were greeted with handshakes from Brigid's grandfather.

"Well," he said, "this is an expected pleasure! I'm sorry that I have no picnic, but I am afraid I didn't tell Laetitia where I was going. Enough on her mind. She'll think I am out for a walk when she gets in."

"We didn't expect a picnic, Mr Arthur," said Rose. "Did we, children?"

Ned and Brigid exchanged eyes, and it was clear to Brigid that he, like her, had rather expected a picnic: but they shook their heads, for once united.

In a straggling line, at varying speeds, they began to make their way across the grassy bank above the sea. In the distance they could see the little house.

"What news?" said Brigid's grandfather to Rose.

"None yet," she said, and Brigid could feel the careful reticence of her voice. "A little later, I'll phone from the telephone box near your house, if I may."

"The one you telephoned from, Granda," said Brigid.

"Good girl," said her grandfather, "to work that out."

"I worked it out, really," said Ned.

"Good boy, then, too," said the grandfather, "though it might have been more gallant to leave a lady's word unchallenged."

Ned bit his lip, and Brigid felt a small rush of triumph. She thought, that's for Davy Crockett, and missed the beginning of something Rose was asking.

"I didn't want to involve my daughter in any anxiety," she heard her grandfather say. "She knows that there is . . . concern, and I am leaving it there for the moment."

Brigid did not understand what he was leaving where, but she said nothing. Ned had been put in his place, and it was enough now to concentrate on the rocks and tufts of the bank, clambering over a place where there once had been a path and now was none.

As they climbed, however, it seemed to get harder, and Brigid saw her grandfather reach his hand more than once to Rose. "I am sorry, Miss Durrant," he said. "I'm so used to clambering about here myself, I forget what it must be like for a lady."

Brigid thought, indignantly: two ladies.

"Oh, Mr Arthur," said Rose, "I'm almost ashamed to say

how much I am enjoying myself, just being away from, well, everything."

"We could have gone by the lane," said Mr Arthur, "but it is very muddy . . . and your shoes . . ."

"Are wrong, I know," Rose said, with a slight laugh. "I should have worn walking shoes. I don't know what I was thinking . . . Oh!" and she stopped, as the gable of the little house came suddenly into view, above a cove that seemed to be simmering green-blue, throwing up arcs of white spray.

Brigid and Ned, almost colliding, stopped where they stood.

"The Churn Rock," said Brigid's grandfather, proudly. "I promised this to you, children. Do you remember?" They did. "My wife used to say she used to lie awake as a girl, listening to the sound of the sea at night, and the lost sound of sirens, and the beam of the lighthouse . . . See over there?" and they did, indeed, see the lonely tower on a distant rock. "It made her afraid, she said, till morning came."

Brigid took her grandfather's hand: she understood that fear. She felt him turn to Ned, "Smugglers came here too, you know. That little cove over there," and he pointed to a shallow inlet to the left, "that's called Jack's Point."

"Jack's Point," repeated Ned, and Brigid saw his eyes look far away.

Then her grandfather put up his hand: Brigid thought again of Mr Steele and Mr Doughty. "Now, children, make a chain," he said, "because I don't want anybody falling in. It may not look it, but it's treacherous. The last submarine to be sunk in the First War went down there. There are ships and fishing boats and God knows what else beneath that water, and I don't want any of us to join them. Hold on tight."

In her mind Brigid saw pictures: a child in the night, the sea's high waves, far out at sea a creaking rigger tossed in a storm. She held tightly with one hand to her grandfather. The other she raised to be taken by Rose. The noise of the water and the crying of the seabirds filled her ears: it was impossible to speak as they passed above the inlet. Damp spray settled on their hair and faces, and the taste of it sat in their mouths. Brigid was terrified and exhilarated all at once, and Ned seemed lost in his own secret world.

Then they turned a corner and, quite suddenly, there was quiet. A small stone wall led to a sheltered place, mossy and grassy, and there was a little mound of stone, like a beehive.

"What's that, Granda?" asked Brigid.

"Ned, don't climb in there," said her grandfather, his hand suddenly firm on Ned's arm. "That's a corbelled pigsty and, believe it or not, is a listed building. It's a very ancient structure. No, there are no pigs now," he said, as Ned's face looked the question, "though I shouldn't be surprised if there weren't the odd ghost."

Ned, peering, said scornfully: "I see no ghosts."

Then Rose's quiet voice spoke: "I'm not so sure," she said.

They all turned to look at her and, receiving no response, followed her eyes. Above them, at the gable of the house, dark against the light, stood a figure, quite still. Brigid's heart pulled tight: perhaps it was a ghost, angered at their having come back to the deserted house. How lonely and grey the poor house looked – no smoke from the chimney, the front door locked for years, the garden forlorn and abandoned, and a tall sentinel standing by the blank gable. In spite of herself, Brigid took hold of Ned Silver's arm, and he did not pull away. Together, they moved a little backward.

Then the figure stepped forward, and she saw that it was Cornelius Todd. Confusion swept over her. Why was he here? He had not been seen since Easter. No one but Ned had even mentioned him, and only Ned seemed happy to see him now. "Uncle Conor!" he cried, pulling forward, but Brigid held on to his arm, restraining him, for no reason that she could articulate.

"Ssh," she said. "Rose."

Rose, white and a little unsteady, her hand on the arm Brigid's grandfather offered, moved carefully across the stony grass, towards her former fiancé. Brigid, standing by the wall with Ned, saw her grandfather lift his hat in greeting, yet she saw, too, an unusual stiffness in his bearing. She noted that he did not release his hold on Rose's arm. Brigid heard only "called to see" and "telephone" and "no response" and "came myself", but she could not hear more without going forward, and some dim fear, something she could not explain, held her back.

Ned, by her side, pulled on her arm. "Come over here," he said, and his voice was urgent. Brigid, still watching the adults, allowed herself to be led backward. "Look," he said, and now he sounded really excited. "There's this ledge, and we can look right into the water. It's like a cave." His hand was on her arm, and he felt strong as Francis. She glanced again over her shoulder. The adults were engrossed: no one would miss them for a moment. She took Ned's hand, and they stepped out onto the edge of the rock. He was right. It was wonderful, the prow of a pirate ship, water around them and beneath them, spray salting their faces and, yet, they were sheltered from the noise, the hissing boom at once far away and close, hypnotically close beneath them.

Throughout her life, Brigid could never explain, even to herself, what happened next. One moment she and Ned were safely placed in a crevice of the rocks, close together and yet separate. The next, his arm was clasped around her, his face beside hers, his eyes deep as the sea and bright with sudden terror; a wall of white water was wrapping them in cold salt spray, and they were slipping, and falling, and gasping all at once. The next thing she knew was a pumping silence that was heavy and green, echoed by a pounding that was inside her head. Above her was black darkness like rocks and a wet, wavering blue sky. She opened her mouth, calling "*Mama!*" but water rushed in, salty and choking, and no sound came out. She tried again: "*Francis!*" No sound, more salt, more water, more rushing and pounding inside her ears, her whole head bursting, unable to breathe. She flailed and kicked, the weight of her clothes and her shoes pulling her down, but she kicked, and kicked again, until she broke the surface of the water, and the sky was blue and still, and there were dark figures above her, and she heard a voice cry "*Brigid!*" out into the wind. It was Rose, spinning above Brigid's reach, her arms out.

Another cry sounded, without words. That was her granda. In the same instant, beneath and around the other cries, she heard: "*Myra! Oh God!*" Then, she slid beneath to the green gasping and the salt and the pounding, and the blue above wavered again, and darkness like an octopus enfolded her, and arms and legs that must be hers were flailing, not able any more to rise above the green waving ceiling, slowing down, giving way. And then, through the opaque swirling rush, her heaviness was lifted, a great sodden weight, straight out of the water, and a sharp slippery warmth came up beneath her.

When she opened her salt-stung eyes, she was propped against a rock. Beside her was Ned Silver, wet, his hair flat against his face, gasping as she was gasping, and beside them both knelt Uncle Conor, soaked, his coat gone, his shirt clinging to his back, coughing and gasping too. Rose, her face white and pinched, wrapped warmth around Brigid. It smelt of tobacco and tweed, like Uncle Conor. She was very cold. Leaning against Rose's skirt, she could see that Rose had put her arms round her front, and yet she could not feel them. Her grandfather stood with his hands hanging loosely by his sides, his eyes on Cornelius. He was breathing as if he had been running.

Through her body, Brigid felt the vibration of Rose's voice: "Myra?" she said. "Myra, Cornelius?"

Cornelius, hunkered still on the rock, looked up at her, his mouth slightly open.

"Rose, I . . ."

"My mum," Brigid heard, the voice not that of Rose or Cornelius, but Ned Silver, small, white and hunched against the rock beside her.

Below them, the sea churned and spat, and the day had turned to mizzling rain.

"Quite," said Rose, and it was clear the conversation was at an end. She began to ease Brigid to her feet. "Mr Arthur, you have had a shock, and these children are wet and cold. We must get you all into the car."

"Mine," said Cornelius, and his voice was strong again. "Go up through the field. Mine's at the gate." Rose lifted her hand as if to protest, but Cornelius extended his own and caught it. "Please," he said. "It's too far down the way you came, and no one's fit for it."

Rose, drawing back her hand as if she had been stung, lifted Brigid to her feet, and helped her pick her way across the grass and stones. They climbed past the silent pigsty, empty of beasts and ghosts, past the closed-up house that they would not now explore, past the haggard, past the trough where the horse had drunk, along the path walked by all the generations of that deserted farm, through the long grass of neglect, until they reached the gate, tied up with rope to a white pillar like the pillars at faraway Tullybroughan. Then, tired and slow and sleepy, and no longer at all sure where she was, Brigid felt herself lifted into a car she did not know, Ned at her side. Rose was between them, her arms round them both, her grandfather was in front, and Cornelius in the driver's seat, and he was slowly, slowly, turning the car in the narrow lane, and then they were bumping along under green, thorny branches, and there was a beating and a scratching against the roof, and then they were on a smooth road, and the bumping stopped. No one spoke. The children shivered, and the car smelt of damp and salt and seaweed.

As they came to the edge of the little town, Brigid heard Rose, her voice as cold as the seawater she still tasted: "If you would be so kind as to leave me here, I will drop Mr Arthur off and take the children home."

"Please," Brigid heard her grandfather say, his hat turning from the front seat, "do, please, come into my house and get the children warmed before you set out. And, we can telephone to the city from outside the door."

For a moment, Rose was quiet again. The car purred easily on the smooth surface, Cornelius drove steadily, eyes ahead, intent on the road, saying nothing, his face set like stone.

Rose drew in her breath. "Yes, Mr Arthur," she said then. "Perhaps that would be best. Though, thanks to Mr Todd, I already know something of what is happening."

Brigid thought: Uncle Conor is Mr Todd again. And what is happening? She said: "What is happening, Rose?"

Rose, beside her, with silent Ned nestled in on her other side, breathed in again: Brigid felt it suck in and go out, like the tide she had just been in, all through the coldness of her body. "Your daddy has to stay in hospital, Brigid. He isn't too well."

It was not possible for Brigid to feel colder, yet she felt a new shiver go through her. "For how long?" she said.

Rose did not reply at once. "I don't know that, Brigid. I'm sorry."

Her words fell like snow upon Brigid's heart, and she said nothing more until they had gone through the village, and drawn up outside her grandfather's house and everyone, including Cornelius, had got out of the car. On the doorstep stood Laetitia, her hands to her face and Brigid, cold and shocked though she was, could not help but be glad when Laetitia took both children to the kitchen, pulled off the wet things, wrapped them in towels and rubbed their skin until they were dry and warm, and the shivering had almost stopped. She took some clothes out of the ironing basket, a man's shirt and some trousers of her own, and she made Ned put them on and roll up the sleeves and the legs, and pull the belt of the trousers tight, and she told Brigid she would get her something from the hot press. This was a Laetitia Brigid had never seen yet, dazed as she was, she did not even think to wonder at it. This new Laetitia sat the children close beside the range, warm for cooking, gave them hot, sweet tea, and then, saying she would just go and find something for Brigid to put on, she left the kitchen.

Wrapped in blankets, the children sat at opposite sides of the warm stove and looked at each other. The pile of wet clothes steamed gently on the clotheshorse.

For a time, neither spoke, then: "Myra," said Ned. "He said 'Myra'."

Your mama, thought Brigid.

"It was him," Ned said. "It must have been him all along."

Brigid said: "All along what?"

"The note, stupid . . . I thought it was Laurence she was running after, but it must have been Uncle . . . it must have been Conor. It must have been him. I'm sorry, Brigid. I'm sorry about falling in, too."

Brigid shook her head. "It's all right," she said, though she did not really understand what he meant. "But, what happened in the water? Did Uncle Conor save us? Is that what happened?"

It was already like a dream.

"He's not our uncle, Brigid," said Ned, shaking his head in his turn. "But I thought he was my friend. I thought he was like . . . you know, Davy Crockett, like a hero." His face was very young, as if he were younger than Brigid, and she felt sorry.

"I might let you wear my Davy Crockett hat when we . . ." began Brigid, and then, from under his blanket, Ned lifted his hand. It was still white, almost blue, but there were traces of pink in the skin as he lifted it.

"*Hsssttt*," he said.

Outside the window, they heard voices.

"Please," floated Rose's voice, low but clear, "I have enough to cope with, and I want to telephone my sister. Please step out of my way."

"Rose," said Cornelius, coaxing, penitent, and Brigid pictured him standing in Rose's way, blocking out the light in that way he had, big and dark with his crooked tooth and his hooded, sleepy eyes, and his coat that smelled of tobacco and spice. "Rose, please."

"Myra Silver," said Rose. "You called Myra Silver's name,

276

when the children were going under the water. Not my niece's name. Not even Myra Silver's son's name. *Her* name. *Her* name. Get out of my way, please."

Ned had frozen, his hand still in the air. The pink was leaving his fingers.

"Rose!" said Cornelius Todd's voice, and Brigid could hear its urgent pleading. "You're wrong. You are wrong. She . . . I knew her when we were young, long before you, long before she was married. I knew her as Myra Moore, just as the Arthurs did. She sang. You know I grew up near here. I . . . took her out once or twice, years ago. That's all."

"Oh," said Rose, and her voice was like ice. "That's all? That's why you called out her name when you saw her son and my niece about to drown?"

Brigid heard Cornelius sigh, and the dark shadow outside the window shifted. She imagined Rose trying to walk round him. She imagined him blocking her way.

"All right. All right. She . . . well, she got in touch with me when the marriage to Silver began to go wrong. She – she wrote to me when she was in Scotland, and I went and met her to try to help, but that was all. I tried to help, and I couldn't, because she . . . wanted more from me than I could give. And then she took the ferry for home, and she never made it. Rose, what can I say? She wanted from me what I can give to no one but you. She was in despair, she turned to me, and I couldn't help her. You think I don't have to live with that?"

In the shadowy window, there was silence, but no movement.

"Oh Rose," he said, and his voice, though soft, was a resonance through the cold air, "you know there's nothing I would not give up for you. God, I've already done it. I've turned my back on everything I believed in, my whole commitment to a cause that is . . . I . . . Rose!" The shadows on the window grew, lessened, and grew. "Rose! She didn't mean anything to me."

His voice had grown louder, stronger, and Brigid, in spite of herself, stood up and, trailing her blanket, shuffled to the window to try to see what was happening, but the windows had thick bubbled glass, like her father's glasses. She remembered him then; and for a moment, she could not hear or think, and her mind went blank, and her ears heard nothing, and her eyes could not see for salt and mist. When she came back to herself, rubbing her eyes, pulling the blanket round her, she saw that the shadow was gone from the window.

The door from the hall opened. Brigid turned, as Laetitia came in, her arms full of clothes: "These will have to . . . God almighty . . . where's that child?"

Brigid looked behind her to where Ned had been, to see an empty chair, and where his wet shoes had been, a damp spot on the tiles. Behind that, the back door stood open, swinging on its hinges as if it, too, had been taken by surprise.

Chapter 25: Angel

Ned was gone. There was no sign of him in the house, the little garden, or the road outside. He was not to be found in the village. Cornelius Todd drove again out to the deserted farm, but Ned was not there, either.

When he came back with this news, his hands helpless at his sides, Rose stood up. "That's enough," she said. "I'm leaving. I have to get Brigid home. I think Mr Todd, having caused the disturbance, is quite capable of finding Mrs Silver's boy by himself."

There was silence. Brigid expected to hear Laetitia or her grandfather, or Cornelius himself, say something, but for a long moment no one spoke. They seemed too stunned to deal with anything more.

Then Laetitia who, to Brigid's surprise, had voiced no complaint, became all quiet efficiency, packing bags, locking windows: "He will have to find him," she said, with unusual calm. "We have our own troubles to see to. But, Rose, we need to go and get your car first. Mine's not big enough for everybody. I'll take you over there now. Pop, you get your coat, and get ready. We'll not be long."

Brigid saw Cornelius sit suddenly down on a hard, upright chair, passing his hand over his forehead. No one else looked near him. Her grandfather, ignoring his daughter's command,

279

stood by the window, quite still, gazing out beyond the sky and the sea, as if he were already somewhere else. Only Rose, suddenly hard-edged, disturbed Brigid. She was not sure she was comfortable with this new Rose, unsmilingly opening the door, getting into Laetitia's car and disappearing with hardly a word. Yet, as Laetitia had said, they were back very quickly, and it struck Brigid that she must have driven very fast indeed, because it seemed to have taken them much longer in Rose's little car. She had no chance to ask anyone about it before Rose, still unsmiling, bundled her into the car, shook hands with the Arthurs, made her thanks and her goodbyes and drove away, all without a word to Cornelius.

A second car followed them from the house. Laetitia drove her own, small and neat like Rose's, but newer, shinier and, yes, faster. This was a different Laetitia again. With her father in the front seat, his hand raised in greeting, she passed swiftly by them at the edge of the town, leaving Rose and Brigid to follow behind at Rose's steadier pace.

It was not until after they had disappeared that Rose finally spoke. "I'm sorry, Brigid," she said. "I don't mean to seem as if I don't care about Ned Silver. I do. He's just not my priority at the moment. In any case, C – Mr Todd will find him. He won't have gone far."

There was that Mr Todd again: not Cornelius, certainly not Uncle Conor. Brigid slid a sideways glance at Rose. Beneath her collar, no sparkle danced on the hollow bones of her neck, and on her finger there was no ring.

"I don't know what priority means, Rose," she said.

"I'm sorry, Brigid. You're so advanced in many ways, I tend to . . . Well. You'll have to be quite advanced now, I'm afraid." She paused.

Brigid felt a beating in her chest, like wings.

"Your father is very unwell. The operation showed that the illness lay beyond his eyes, deep in his brain. Do you understand?"

Brigid said: "He gets headaches when he wakes up. He told me on Saturday. But they always go away."

Her eyes on the road, Rose nodded. "Yes, but you see, they were a sign that something was very wrong. It's a great pity he didn't tell anyone in time – and, no, you couldn't have prevented anything by telling about the headaches when he told you. It was already too late."

Too late, Brigid thought. Too late for what?

"But he'll get better?"

The answer came like the water round the rocks, cold and suffocating in her mouth and her ears.

"I don't know, Brigid," she heard Rose say, her eyes still straight ahead. "We have to wait and see."

They were out of the village, turning slowly away from the shining and treacherous sea. The edge of Brigid's eye caught pinks and yellows of clouds above, the sunlit flash of seabirds on waves and a shingled shore, but she did not look back. Like Rose, she kept her eyes straight ahead, as the land settled into its comforting mounds, the egg-like drumlins, the people-seeming trees.

"Rose," she said, "tell me what is in my daddy's brain."

Rose answered directly. "It's called a tumour, and it has grown behind his eyes. It's like a ball, and it has made him unable to see, and it has given him headaches."

Brigid began to understand. "It made him different," she said. "It made him cross, and he forgot things he never forgot. It made him like a dream I had: he was Not-Daddy, and Mama was Not-Mama. They were all the Not-people. Rose, I think I dream straight."

Rose drew in breath, and let it out, slowly. "I'd be sorry to think so, Brigid," she said.

Brigid opened her mouth to tell Rose of the dream she had where Tullybroughan was a ruin, then closed it again. She remembered what Michael said: no one wanted to know about dreaming straight.

They drove on to the city, swinging in short, then longer curves into wider roads, the houses more frequent, serried in ranks, the car curving gradually away from the drumlins and the fields, until they were back at the edge of the city, under Brigid's own mountain, calm and blue behind the house, and the Friday Tree in all its summer fullness, just as if her father did not have a ball growing behind his eyes.

The house folded round them without a sound. Even Dicky was silent in his cage. Brigid's grandfather sat at the table in the sitting room, his head down, not speaking. Yet, he motioned Brigid to him as she came in, and set her on his knee, just as Laetitia came in. She carried a pot of tea, and a plate of sandwiches.

"You should get a new car," she said to Rose, without rancour. "I got here long ago."

Rose said nothing: her eyes rested on the corner by the window, where Francis sat by himself, looking at nothing.

There were so many people in the room, but no Mama, and no Daddy.

"Where is Mama?" Brigid asked her grandfather, in a whisper.

"At the hospital," he said, his voice low as hers.

The telephone rang, deep and muffled in the dark cloakroom. Surprisingly quickly, Brigid's grandfather rose from his seat, easing Brigid to the floor, and stepped into the hall. Brigid heard him, even through the closed door, shouting into it as if he were in a high wind: "Hello? Grace? Hello?"

"Brigid, come over here to me," said Rose, "and you, too, Francis."

One from the corner, one from the window, they went over, a deepening silence all about them, and they waited.

"Sit here on my knee, Brigid. Francis, come in here beside me."

They did as Rose said, hearing nothing but their own breathing, and the clink of the cup Laetitia moved to and from her mouth. Yet, she was not drinking the tea. She was simply lifting the cup up and down, up and down, and each time she raised it the teaspoon slid into the well of the saucer.

From the hall came monosyllables: "Yes. I see. I will."

The door opened. Rose tightened her arm round Brigid, and held Francis so close that Brigid could feel the heat of his body as well as her own. Her grandfather stood in the doorway, his arms hanging as they had when she and Ned were pulled out of the water.

"Gone," he said. He put his hand over his eyes, and leaned against the wall. "Gone," he said again.

"Who?" Brigid said, twisting round and taking Rose's face in her hands. The skin did not move as quickly as the bones, and a red mark spread where she caught Rose's cheek.

"Who is gone? Is it Mama? Where?"

"No," said Rose, gently taking Brigid's hands from her face. "Not your mama. Your daddy."

She stopped, and Brigid saw Laetitia replace the cup in the saucer, and sit then, like a statue, like long-forgotten Miss Chalk.

Rose said: "God took your daddy home to live with him."

Brigid felt her head drop, as if her neck could no longer hold it and, as it did, she saw Francis' head shoot up and back, as if he had been struck in the face. Brigid looked up at Rose.

"But this is his home," said Brigid. "With us. Here."

The silence grew larger, filled the whole house. No one broke it, not Laetitia or Rose, not Francis or Granda Arthur. Not even Dicky made a sound, and yet there was a sound like sobbing, but it was so far inside Brigid's head that she did not know whose it was.

Time then stopped measuring itself in hours and minutes, and went into a rhythm that did not have day or night, but was like water, like the green water that had swirled round Brigid as she fought to breathe at the Churn Rock. Everyone moved like dreamers. One minute they seemed to be at the house, then they were in the hospital, the same hospital where Brigid had been, where Mama had been, and they were standing looking down, and somebody – Michael, in his Sunday suit that he wore for Easter – was holding Brigid up, looking down at a figure that seemed like her father, but was cold, with a sharp nose and closed eyes and a pale, straight mouth. This Not-Daddy was utterly still; he was haughty, removed, his face a little puzzled as though there was a question he was trying to answer. His hands were clasped round black rosary beads, but when she touched his fingers, they were hard and stiff. His face, too, was chill to her lips. Even his greying hair lay still and lifeless. Brigid thought: he is not there. She kissed his coldness anyway, and Michael lifted her down, and placed her beside her mother, pale and remote as Mary the Mother of God. Beside her stood Rose. Laetitia was the only person who cried. Her grandfather stood by in silence, tall and spare and puzzled in his face as Brigid was inside, as her father seemed in his box.

Time stretched out, day into night into day, and Brigid thought it would go on like this for ever, that this was life now, all the people, and her father in the box, and from morning to night tea and sandwiches and muffled voices, and candle wax, and blinds closed, and the clocks all stopped.

She could not bear it when the men came into the pale room and put a lid over the shiny wood of the box. Standing by Francis, remembering the waters over her head, she said: "How will he breathe?"

Francis said: "He doesn't need to, any more."

Brigid looked at him in disbelief. In the water, when she could not breathe, it was all she could think about, all she longed to do. How could he not need to breathe? She wanted to ask, but all the people then began to pray, over and over, the words and the pleas and the petitions she had heard at Mass and in school, all to the God who had taken her father away. They spoke now, in one low voice, but Brigid was silent. She slipped from the room, and no one noticed.

She wandered the house, looking at his books on the shelf,

and his hat on the hat stand, and his shoes in the cloakroom, waiting for him as she was waiting for him. She saw his handwriting – "*From your daddy*" – on the book he had bought her last October, and her heart lifted. Then she remembered: he would not write to her anything again. His hands were still now, wrapped round his black rosary.

The people came out from the room, in a line, as if they were at school. Brigid watched them. They extended their hands and they shook their heads. They were sorry for Mrs Arthur's trouble, and the children, God bless them. It was like a sad party, and everywhere there were people sitting in groups, darkly clad, nodding and sighing, talking about their father and the good man he was, and people placing their hands on Brigid's head and shaking theirs again, and telling Francis he was the man of the house now. Mr Doughty came and he too was sorry for Mrs Arthur's trouble, and the children, God bless them, and he said Mr Steele was out now looking for young Silver, and they would find him, the clip, and he spoke to Rose, too, and Brigid heard him say Ned's name.

Mrs Mulvey came from next door, and Brigid saw her shake her head. "No sign," she said. "No sign yet, all last night or today," and to Rose, she heard her say, "No, indeed, it was not your fault. Nobody could watch him, nobody on this earth could watch that child – like mercury, and his father not here, never here, God knows. Only for Mr Todd I don't know what I'd . . ." and she went away, shaking her head.

Cornelius Todd came, and Brigid saw him run his hand though his hair as he looked down at his friend. She heard him say "*A Mhuiris, a chara,*" and saw him bend his head. Rose did not come into the room when he was there. Brigid heard her say, to Brigid's grandfather: "No, he hasn't found him, and the police haven't either. God knows where he has gone, and I can't even think with all of this . . ." Brigid's heart lifted again: she thought Rose was talking about her father, that he was not really gone. Then she heard her grandfather say, "Young Silver'll turn up.

We'll get him back," and he patted Rose's hand, and Brigid knew in despair it was only Ned Silver they were talking about.

Isobel was not there. Isobel did not come, and Brigid thought: unreliable.

They were at the church, then, its tall spire tolling out long mournful notes, sad as night on the bright July day. Far off, in the hills, there were drums. The Twelfth of July was coming. Bees droned in the bushes outside as they waited for the coffin to be brought in. One buzzed loudly in the church, louder and more urgent than the priest's sad voice. Brigid heard prayers, and more prayers but, above her, outside the colours of the window and the impassive statues, the summer birds sang as if her father had not died. She saw faces she knew: Mr Doughty but not Mr Steele, Uncle Conor. She thought for a moment that made her stomach turn over that she saw George Bailey. It looked like him, standing in half-shadow, his tall thin form, his kind face, his dark hair; she could remember the deep skies that were his eyes from the day he took her home. She longed to be back there, anywhere but here.

Just when it could not get worse, it got worse, and the box was lifted by men in black coats. Francis stood by his mother, in his school blazer and, at last, long trousers. Next, they were outside. Far away they heard children playing, and the flowers outside the church were bright in their beds, yellow and red and pink. Brigid, in the sea of dark people, stood with her family.

Then all the men at the funeral, including her grandfather, Francis and Michael, walked a little behind the hearse, followed by cars, slow as walking. Brigid sat with her mother, Rose and Laetitia in the first car. They went past the houses, and when they came to theirs, every car stopped. Brigid's mother opened the car door then, took her by the hand and led her out, followed by Rose and Laetitia.

"Why are we getting out, Mama?" said Brigid, watching the black car sliding away. "Why are we not going, too?"

"Ladies don't," her mother said.

They stood outside the gate, and the slow procession moved on, down past the post office and the barracks, down to the big gates of the cemetery. From their gate, Brigid and her mother and Rose and Laetitia saw the snaking line of cars vanish, one by one, into the silent graveyard.

Somewhere far off, just as they turned to go in the gate, Brigid heard a sharp cracking sound, like a firework. Everyone stopped.

"What was that?" said Rose, reaching for her sister's arm.

Brigid's mother shook her head.

"It was for all the world like a gunshot," said Laetitia.

Rose scanned the skies. "But where did it come from?" She turned round, on one heel, her hand outstretched. "From there," and she pointed to the trees, "or the cemetery? I can't tell."

"Oh, God," said Laetitia, beginning to weep. "I can take no more, and my poor brother just dead."

Brigid's mother tightened her hold on Brigid's hand. "No need for histrionics, Laetitia," she said. "It was probably nothing. A car backfiring."

They went into the house. It was very quiet, blinds still drawn, clocks still stopped. Dicky, his head under his wing, stood still on his perch. Brigid climbed the stairs to the bathroom, Blessed Oliver watching her all along the corridor, there and back. She kept her eyes away from the closed door of her parents' bedroom. She did not want to remember that her father was not there. All through the house, she saw the places he would never be again. His chair in the sitting room sat empty. On the mat, discarded, kicked to one side, the morning paper he would never read. Though she had wanted all the people milling through the house to go away, Brigid felt suddenly afraid of this silence, of the absence like a presence, weighing on her like a stone. She wanted to be out of it.

She slid through the kitchen and out to the brightness of the birds in the garden and the trees in the plot. The blackcurrants were out, and she was even glad to see the wasps about the yellow broom tree. She did not care if they stung her: they could sting away. Anything was better, even the wicked buzzing of a wasp was better than the silence and the candle wax and the darkness of the prayers. She leaned on the fence between the plot and their garden, right into the corner beside the Silvers' house. High in the sky, the sun sat bright. One cloud, floating past the top of the house, settled over the cemetery where her father was. At the back of the plot the Friday Tree shimmered its leaves, the other trees waving to its lead: and for a second Brigid felt a reminder of happiness.

Then, in the quiet, she thought she heard a sound, a rustling. There it was again. Someone was there. She spun round, but she could see no one: then, "Brigid," said a voice at her left, low and soft. It was a man's voice, and she knew it, but she could not think how.

"Brigid," it said again, "get back to your house."

She craned her neck to the left, and saw a face she knew, half-hidden by the bushes.

"George," she said, and something like joy shot through her. She was not surprised. "I knew you'd come back. I thought I saw you today at Mass."

He nodded, sadly. "I went for your father. He was a good man, Brigid. Will you go inside, now, please?"

Brigid felt her eyes fill, but she shook her head. "Not till you tell me where you went. You disappeared. No one believed you were there. No one at all. Unless, maybe Francis."

She heard an impatient sigh. She had heard plenty of those: she stood her ground.

"I'd tell you, Brigid, but I haven't time. And it's dangerous. You shouldn't be out here at all."

"You're out here," said Brigid, reasonably. "Just tell me why. Then I'll go in."

Another rapid sigh.

"Quickly, then," he said. "Listen. That day, I just wanted to see you home, but I didn't want anyone to see me. Do you understand? Same today. But I can't take you home, today, because I have to wait for a signal that it's safe to go. Now, please go in. Please!"

Brigid understood signals. "A smoke signal?" she said.

"A smo– ? No. Not that sort."

"Sometimes I saw smoke at the Friday Tree. Up there." She pointed to it. "It's shaped like Friday."

"Is it?" said George. "That was probably me. I hid out under that tree last autumn, when I had to get away from some people I used to . . . work with." He looked about him again, anxiously, as if the people were there. "I don't any more, so they don't like me, and they're after me."

"I saw smoke not long ago," said Brigid. "Was that you?"

"No," said George Bailey, and he looked up at the Friday Tree again. "I hid in a house once winter came. But listen, Brigid. Someone fired a shot at me just now, from up there. The Friday Tree. Did you not hear it?"

"I heard something," said Brigid.

"Then you know why I've got to get away."

"To Bedford Falls?" persisted Brigid.

"To Bedf–? Yes . . . yes, there," said George, and he looked about him, anxiously. "They're expecting me."

Brigid took this in.

"Will you go now, Brigid, please?" said George. "He might shoot again."

"Does he have a real gun, like Mr Doughty and Mr Steele?"

He nodded, showing her his hand. It was bleeding from a long graze,

"Come in," said Brigid. "Come into the house. Mama will make that better."

George shook his head. He smiled, though his face looked sad. "I can't," he said. "I . . ." Suddenly he pulled back out of sight. "Brigid!" he said. "Keep in! Hide yourself."

Brigid flattened herself into the bushes, her blurred sight just able to make out a shaking in the undergrowth below the Friday

Tree. She saw a movement, then another, and a small figure and some distance from him, a man's. A head like a seal shot out from the undergrowth, and she heard a loud report, and then the head like a seal disappeared, and the small figure disappeared, but then it got up and ran towards her, and she saw that it was Ned Silver, bedraggled, matted, but alive and running, stumbling through the carrots and the cabbages.

"That's Ned Silver!" whispered Brigid. "We thought he was lost, all last night and the night before!"

George Bailey caught him, shivering and small, and Ned, half-crying, began to struggle.

"Don't, Ned," said Brigid. "It's George Bailey. He won't hurt you."

"I won't," said George. "I won't hurt you. Didn't you sometimes come up where I had my hideout?"

Ned, dirty and wide-eyed, but shivering less, nodded. He said, "Yes. Was that yours? I thought it was the other one's . . ." and he looked over his shoulder. "He has a gun. I saw him creeping . . ."

"He'll not creep far now," said George. "Someone has hit him." He put his hands under Ned's ribs. "Are you sure you're not hurt?" he said.

Ned shook his head.

George nodded, and lifted him into his own garden, the blood from his hand leaving a smear on Ned's already dirty clothes, her grandfather's shirt and Laetitia's trousers. It seemed a long time since Brigid had seen him pull the belt tight, in the house in Lecale.

"Will you keep my secret?" said George. "I haven't hurt anyone. And I'm going away now."

"Don't go, George!" said Brigid. "Everyone goes away."

"I've told you. I have to," he said, simply. "Look over there."

Brigid could make out, near the Friday Tree, the greenish black of a policeman's uniform, with a glinting, smoking darkness in his hand that must be a gun, pointing at something down in the long grass.

"I think it's Mr Steele . . . but I don't know . . ." said Brigid, and a terrible thought struck her. "Oh, George, did he shoot that man?"

"He did," said George, grimly. "It's a wonder he didn't hit the child."

"Oh, George, then go, go!" urged Brigid. "He might shoot you too! Go, before he gets down here!"

"He's not coming down here," said George. "Look. He's gone off in the opposite direction."

Brigid glanced across. He was right.

Still, George did not move, and stood looking at Ned.

"I won't say," said Ned. "I promise," and, dirty and dishevelled, he swivelled and ran through the garden as only Ned Silver could do – until Brigid heard a scuffling and, to her horror, the voice of a man.

"Whoa, there!" it said.

On different sides of the fence, Brigid and George, flattening themselves into the bushes, looked through the leaves.

Inside the Silvers' garden, Cornelius Todd was holding the struggling boy. "Ned," they heard him say. "Stop kicking. Now." Cornelius looked up to the bushes. Without raising his voice, he said, his tone almost conversational: "You'd better go now. I can't cover for you any more. It's as safe as it's going to get. And, Brigid, you should be inside."

Brigid and George locked eyes.

"He does that," whispered Brigid. "He just appears out of nowhere."

George did not answer.

"I am going, Conor," she heard him say. "Thank you for coming. You'd better get out of here, too," but when she turned to see what Uncle Conor would do, she was astonished to find he was already gone, and Ned too. Her mother had been right. Uncle Conor was just like the Cheshire Cat.

"You heard him," said George, above her head. "That was my signal. Time I wasn't here. But Brigid? Tell no one," he said.

"Especially not Isobel."

"I wouldn't tell Isobel anything," said Brigid, adding, in spite of herself, "but why especially not her?"

He was already half-turned away. "The man with the gun is her brother," he said, and, as Brigid stood taking this in, George suddenly stopped, turned back and, reaching into his pocket, handed her a piece of paper, worn and creased. "Take this," he said. "It's a prayer. Say it for me when I'm gone. Get your brother to read it if you can't. You can tell him about me. But no one else. Promise?"

"I promise," said Brigid. "But, where are you going?"

"I told you," he said, and he was already moving away through the bushes, his voice growing faint. "Bedford Falls."

Chapter 26: Brother and Sister

In the days that followed the funeral, silence settled over the house. All who had come to mourn the untimely death of Maurice Arthur resumed their own lives. The bustle and noise, confusion and discussion, ritual and solemnity, all ceased. Brigid did not hear even the sound of tears, her own or anyone else's. The house held only emptiness. In her room, she wrapped brown paper round an empty matchbox, and placed it in the centre of the theatre. No plays were imagined or performed. Marianne, her audience and critic, sat still and expressionless on the dressing table.

Yet, outside, the summer beckoned and, despite herself, a morning came when Brigid longed to be part of it. The sun was high in the sky, but she was still in pyjamas: no one told her these days to get dressed, to have breakfast, or to occupy herself. No Daddy read from the papers. No Mama talked of the baby God might send, or had not sent. There was no more Isobel, no Rose, not even Uncle Conor or Ned Silver. There was no Granda, no Laetitia, no George Bailey. The house held three lonely people and a budgerigar, and suddenly, that sunny morning, Brigid had had enough.

"I'm going up to the garden," she announced to Marianne, silent and unresponsive on the dressing table. "You look after things here." She took herself downstairs, running her hand along the banister, swinging as she had been forbidden to do on the newel post at the end. Here, a long time ago, Francis had cowered in fear at her cowgirl suit and her gun. That was the day her parents had come back to them, their voices floating from the sitting room. Now that room, like the hall, though filled with morning sunshine, lay still. One window sat slightly open, the curtain moving slowly in the summer breeze. No one had thought to close it. Shafts of light caught dust-motes that nobody would brush away. In the dining room stood the table where her father had lain in his box the night before the funeral. Brigid closed her mind: she would not have that memory.

She went to see Dicky and lifted the cover from his cage. He sat with his head under his wing: one dark, wary eye looked out. With a little trepidation, Brigid opened the cage, and reached her finger to scratch his head.

"Hello, Dicky," she said.

Dicky looked straight at her with his black, gleaming eye. "Hello, Dicky," he said, his voice cracked and croaking.

Brigid felt her mouth drop open and, filled with amazement, she turned and ran from the room, round the banister, up the stairs, down the long corridor under Blessed Oliver, and into the new silence of Francis' room. He was sitting on his bed and, like her, he was in pyjamas. In front of him sat an old book she had often seen on his shelves, and on the open page she saw the words: "*Brother and Sister*." He looked up, but he did not seem surprised to see her.

"Brigid," he said, "I was just going to get you. I want to show you someth–"

"Francis," she cried, hardly able to take the time to tell him. "Come downstairs. Dicky's talking!"

Francis, eyes wide as her own, swung his legs down from the bed and took off along the corridor, downstairs and into the kitchen, Brigid scrambling after him. Breathless, tumbling over each other, they arrived to an empty room: the door of the cage lay open as Brigid had left it, but there was no Dicky. They stopped, and Brigid, her heart pounding, saw what had happened.

"Oh, Francis," she cried, "the window was open. I've let him get out!"

He took her arm. "It's all right," he said, though she could hear his heart, loud as her own. "He's done this before. We know where he'll be."

"The Friday Tree?" said Brigid.

Francis nodded. He was already on his way out the door. "Are you coming?"

"Yes . . . but Francis, the Friday Tree was where that man . . ."

"Brigid, it's still the same tree. Are you coming?"

Still in pyjamas and slippers, unwashed and dishevelled, Francis and Brigid ran out through the kitchen, the back yard, up the steps and along the path as they had done so often the previous summer. Now, Brigid could keep up more easily, and she could climb over the fence without help. She remembered to pull a docken leaf against the nettle stings, and did not say a word when the nettles inevitably brushed her.

Though the morning was bright, there was no one in the plot. Neither Mr Doughty nor Mr Steele had been there since the day of the funeral, and the young vegetables that had survived the running and the trampling, feathery tops of carrots and lush potato plants, waved about unattended, parting easily for the children. At the top of the plot, the Friday Tree stood above them, its fresh summer green an invitation to climb.

"Dicky!" called Francis, softly.

"Dicky!" cried Brigid.

"Oh, not loudly, Brigid," said Francis, and his voice was filled with anxiety. "Don't frighten him."

They stopped, and listened. They heard songbirds and whirring insects, far away a dog barked in crazy joy, but they did not hear Dicky. Brigid looked at Francis' face, creased with anxiety.

"Francis," she said. "I don't think he's here."

Francis looked up through the leaves, and held on to a slender branch. "He's here," he said. "We just have to be patient." He folded his legs under him, and sat down on the patch of pale grass where the camp had been.

"Francis," said Brigid, "that's where –"

"I know," said Francis. "It doesn't matter now. He won't be back."

Brigid did not know whether Francis meant the man with the gun, or Ned Silver.

"Where is he now?" she said.

"I don't know. Prison, maybe."

"I meant Ned," said Brigid.

"I don't know where he is now," said Francis. "With his father, I suppose."

Brigid looked back towards the houses, theirs and the Silvers'. Both seemed cold, bent down with shut eyes. Brigid shivered. "Imagine him getting here by himself. Where was he, all that night? Two nights! Do you think he was cold?"

Francis shook his head. "I don't think so: it's not really cold at night. It would have been different if it had been later on. It's how he got here I don't understand."

Brigid thought of George Bailey, here all through the cold nights of autumn, and felt a stab of remorse for their comfort while he hid here in the plot. She spread her hands, and stretched out her feet. Her legs were really long: she could stretch them out almost as far as Francis' knees.

"Can I show you something, Francis?"

"What?"

She took out the paper George had given her. "Someone gave me this, the day of the . . . the day Daddy . . ."

"What is it?"

"It's a prayer but I can't make out the writing. Can you?"

He took the paper, and scanned it briefly. "It's a prayer to the Angel Raphael. Who did you say gave it to you? Someone at the funeral?"

George was at the funeral. He had told her so. Brigid said: "Yes, someone at the funeral."

"Well, it's quite long. Look, I'll read out the important bit for you, all right?"

He lifted it up to read and, for a moment, Brigid saw her father, and the paper, and all the mornings that were gone. "'*Raphael*,'" he read, "'*lead us to those we are waiting for, those who are waiting for us. Raphael, Angel of Happy Meeting, lead us by the hand towards those we are looking for.*'" He put it down, his face puzzled. "Who did you say gave this to you?"

Brigid said, simply: "George Bailey."

Francis looked up at her. "George Bailey. From Bedford Falls?"

"Going to Bedford Falls. He was leaving for there. He gave me that, and he said I was to get you to read it for me and tell you it was from him, but not to tell anyone else he was there."

Francis said nothing, but his face softened and cleared. "Ah, the man in the plot. He was the man who brought you home, that nobody saw?"

"He was George Bailey," said Brigid, firmly.

Francis nodded. "George Bailey, then."

Brigid remembered the man with the head like a seal, creeping through the undergrowth, the man who had shot George's hand. "When he came," she said, thinking back, "Mr Doughty or Mr Steele, I mean – but I don't know which – do you think he came looking for George? Or did he know someone else was there? Isobel's brother? Or Ned?"

Francis shook his head. "I don't think they would have fired shots if they had known there was a child there."

"But they would at Isobel's brother? Mr Doughty or Mr Steele?"

"Mr Doughty was at the funeral. I think it was Mr Steele who was here."

Brigid thought of Mr Doughty, who had always given them rhubarb and cabbage; Mr Steele had not. Steely, Ned called him:

that was what he was, and he never stopped. It made sense that he was in the plot, with guns and shooting, and it made sense that Mr Doughty made time to be kind.

"Brigid," said Francis, breaking her reverie. "There's something I should tell you. I met the man in the plot, too."

"You met George Bailey?"

"Yes, I . . ."

There was a sound in the undergrowth.

"Stay still," said Francis.

The sound came closer: peering out, Brigid saw a dark figure and, suddenly, close to, very close to her, she saw a man. Her heart began to bang against her ribs. The leaves parted: Mr Doughty's face peered through, and Brigid felt her own relief and that of Francis ripple through their bodies.

"What's this?" he said, quietly. "Cowboys and Indians again? Don't you think we've had enough goings-on?"

Francis stood up. "Mr Doughty," he said, "we're sorry. It's our budgie. He got out, and we came to get him down . . . but he hasn't . . . We're sorry."

Brigid stood up beside Francis, her hand on his arm. "It's my fault, Mr Doughty," she said. "I let Dicky get out."

Mr Doughty crouched down beside them. He did not look angry. His face was round and red, and he looked too hot. He put out his hands, joined and softly cupped.

"Look here," he said, and his voice was gentle. "Look what I found when I was coming into the plot." In his hands lay a still little ball, feathers green and black and white, little hand-like claws curled gently in the big man's hand, a long black tail lying along his wrist.

Francis was the first to speak, his voice higher than usual, and faster. "Is he dead, Mr Doughty?"

Mr Doughty shook his head. "Stunned, I think. He must have flown into a branch and knocked himself out. Here . . ."

He reached his hands to Francis who, very carefully, took Dicky into his own.

Mr Doughty, watching the children, seemed thoughtful. "How is your mammy?" he said as he got to his feet.

Brigid turned to Francis. He was looking down at Dicky, stroking his feathers, and did not raise his eyes. "She . . . she's still in bed," she said. "I think she's very tired, Mr Doughty. She sleeps a lot."

Mr Doughty looked the children up and down. "Judging by your rig, you sleep a lot, too," and he laughed without sound, which made both children, looking down at their pyjamas, laugh a little themselves. "You know," he said, and he had stopped laughing, "you shouldn't be in here."

They hung their heads.

"I think you should be escorted home by a member of the Royal Ulster Constabulary," he said, and now he was more serious. "I want to tell you something, and I want you to listen. We have a fair idea there was another man here for a time, and you shouldn't be out in this place by yourselves. Look at poor young Silver, the narrow escape he had."

Brigid and Francis looked at each other in alarm.

"Please, Mr Doughty, don't tell Mama we came out here," said Brigid.

"I think," said Mr Doughty, unexpectedly, "that I could do with a cup of tea, which I am quite prepared to make, if you would be so kind as to bring me through the back door."

Then he took Brigid's hand and, motioning Francis before him, walked back with them through the plot. Without ceremony, he lifted them both over the fence, stepped back, pulled some young carrots, and early rhubarb, handed them to Brigid over the fence in his old way, then swung his own long legs easily over the fence and walked down the garden with the children.

It was strange to be in the garden with a policeman, strange to see him bend his head through the back door, stranger still to see him roll up his sleeves, wash his hands at the sink, and fill the kettle. It was strange, and it was comforting. He moved quietly about the kitchen, found bread and toasted it, discovered milk and put it in a jug, got a tray and arranged a cup, saucer, plate and jug, poured tea into the teapot, placed it on the tray and held out the whole thing to Francis. "Are you a big enough man to take that up to your mammy?"

Francis looked down at Dicky, quiet in his hands.

"Give the birdie to your sister," said Mr Doughty.

Brigid found herself cupping the faintly trembling form of their little bird, as Francis walked carefully into the hall, the tray balanced, his knees slightly bent.

"Tell your mammy I was passing, and came in for a cup of tea," said Mr Doughty. "Don't let on I made it."

Francis smiled, though his eyes did not. He said, "Yes, Mr Doughty," and carried on through the hall.

Mr Doughty placed more cups and saucers on the table, put toast before Brigid, and fixed her a cup of hot, sweet and sugary tea, like Rose's tea at Tullybroughan, like Laetitia's after Brigid fell in the water. Mr Doughty sat down beside her, smelling of the garden and the plot and, for almost the first time since the funeral, Brigid felt safe. She looked at the toast, uneaten, before her, but she felt no hunger.

Mr Doughty took it and cut it up into fingers. "Soldiers," he said. "Eat some for me, there's a good girlie," and at the familiar endearment, Brigid felt a prickling start up behind her eyes, and tears she did not want fell hot on her face and on the table.

Before she knew it, she was lifted up and was sitting on Mr Doughty's knee, comfortable as her grandfather's. Slowly, she relaxed against the beating of his heart. "Mr Doughty," she said, so quietly that she did not know if she spoke at all, "what happened to Ned Silver?"

"Ah, poor little Silver," said Mr Doughty. "He got a bad shock, out there in the plot. That character."

Brigid wondered for a moment which character he meant. "Isobel's brother?" she said, carefully, and felt Mr Doughty nod.

"He'll trouble no one for a long time," he said, "because he's in prison, and there he'll stay, I hope."

"I'm glad," said Brigid. And she was, simply and without complication. He had frightened her and now, like a bad dream, he was gone.

"Aye, well you might be," said Mr Doughty. "He was one bad article. And it may be a while before you see your Isobel."

I don't want to see her, thought Brigid. "Where has she gone, Mr Doughty?"

"We don't know where she's got to. There's no sign of her."

"But did she do something bad?"

"Well, maybe not . . . you could say she tried to help her brother and, while that may not have been wise, or even right, it's not hard to understand, is it?"

Brigid thought. "No," she said.

Francis came back in.

"All well, son?" said Mr Doughty.

"Yes, thank you," said Francis, and sat down at Mr Doughty's other side.

"Well," Mr Doughty continued, "Isobel. She brought him food in the plot. I saw her do that, and I saw you looking from your garden. I suppose many a sister might have brought her brother food. But there was more. We believe she was hiding him in a house all winter. She put about a story that her brother was home from England, and needed looking after, which was at best a half-truth."

"I . . ." Brigid did not know Isobel had hidden her brother in a house all winter, but she imagined Francis, hunted, camping out of doors without shelter or food, like George Bailey, and Ned Silver. She said: "I would bring Francis food."

Glancing at him for approval, she was surprised to see Francis flush, and hang his head.

"Aye," said Mr Doughty, and Brigid noticed he looked rather long at Francis as he spoke, "I'm sure you would. I don't find that bit hard to understand but, the thing is, her brother was an escaped criminal, and she knew that. All the same, I don't like it, women in court and in jails and . . . ah, that poor Ellis woman across the water . . ." He frowned, and looked down, drumming his hands on the table, then he stopped, and cleared his throat. "In any case," he said, "as things stand, I doubt if it will go very far at all."

Brigid remembered George Bailey's view of Isobel, but she could not break her promise to George and tell Mr Doughty. "Isobel is unreliable," she said.

"That's a big word for a small girl," said Mr Doughty, raising his cup.

"It's Mama's word, Mr Doughty. But, Ned Silver, where is he? What happened to him?"

"Mr Doughty?" said Francis suddenly, and both Brigid, put out, and the policeman, not at all so, turned to him expectantly.

"What is it, son?"

"I . . ."

"Take your time," said Mr Doughty, and his voice was very calm. "What's on your mind?"

"Nothing, Mr Doughty," said Francis. "I'm sorry if I interrupted. You were going to tell us about Ned?"

Mr Doughty shifted in his seat, and Brigid took this as a sign to go back to hers. She climbed down, and sat at the table beside him, turning towards him, her hands beneath her chin. He thought a long time before he spoke.

"That wee boy, you know, lost his mother a few years ago."

Brigid nodded. "We know. The *Princess Victoria*."

"Yes. That's right. Anyway, the wee fellow was either sent away to school or left alone with a housekeeper and . . . well, it wasn't fair on him. I used to see him in the garden, looking up at your windows, always by himself. We brought him to the barracks the odd time, John Steele and myself, and we made him tea. So, he wasn't afraid when we talked to him after that business in the plot. He's not a bad child."

Brigid felt a sort of pity for Ned, waiting for them in the garden. Then she thought: did he tell about George? Did he keep his promise? Mr Doughty ran his hand over his head.

"He couldn't tell us much, though. Didn't seem to remember who he saw, or what happened."

Brigid thought: good for Ned.

"He was very shocked. And anyhow, we had caught the fellow with the gun and . . . for other reasons . . . we didn't press him. You know Mrs Silver knew your father's family from before she was married?"

Brigid said: "Yes. She was Myra Moore. She knew our granda – and our almost-uncle Laurence."

"She would have done. I gather she was always looking for friends."

Brigid said: "But . . . Mr Doughty . . . if she had Mr Silver, and Ned . . . why was she lonely? Why did she need Uncle Conor to be her friend, if she had them?"

He shook his head. "That's the bit nobody can understand, least of all the child. It's all he wanted to talk about in the station. You could say Mrs Silver didn't have her husband near her. Still, you'd think maybe she could have gone with him to wherever he was. Or, she could have spent her time with her own child. Most women would, it seems to me." He shook his head again, and poured more tea for Brigid and Francis, then for himself. He heaped sugar into his cup, and stirred it, and then he pushed the bowl towards Brigid. "There was a lot of talk at the time. I don't know. I doubt if anybody knows. It was a nine-day wonder. Then she was dead, and poor young Silver was packed off to school. And that didn't work out very well, as we know. If he didn't escape, he was expelled, and he was an expert at both."

"What happened after he left Granda's?" said Brigid.

"He seems to have found his way up here. He wouldn't tell us. My guess is he climbed on to the back of a lorry, judging by the state of him. Dangerous for any child."

Brigid thought: not that one, but she did not say so.

"Anyway, he got back here, but he didn't go home. He hid in the plot and, God forgive me, with all that was going on, I didn't find him. Nor did John Steele. Not to mention that housekeeper. There's another one shouldn't be in charge of a child." He put his cup down and shook his head. "He had little more than a blanket he got from somewhere, and clothes too big for him, and shoes stiff with damp."

"Our aunt, in Lecale," said Brigid. "She gave him the clothes and the blanket."

"Was that it? It's a miracle he didn't get pneumonia, or worse, outside in the night air. Characters running about the plot. And we only got one of them." Mr Doughty got up. "We'll need to toast more bread. Anyway, young Silver is with his father at the moment, and I gather he's going to be all right. He's a hardy soul, for all he looks so frail." He lifted a slice of bread from its wrapper, then paused again. "The strange thing is: Mr Silver should have been on the *Princess Victoria* himself that day."

"Why was he not?" Brigid asked. "Mrs Silver mightn't have been so lonely if he had gone. She might have talked to him instead of Laurence. She said she had lost somebody: was it him she had lost?"

Mr Doughty shrugged his shoulders. "Maybe. The Silvers were both booked on that boat. Mrs Silver was singing at something in Scotland – was it to do with Burns Night? I think it was. Anyway, he was to go up there for this concert or whatever it was and come over home with her, I suppose to patch the whole thing up. Who knows? Then, for whatever reason – his work, maybe? – he cancelled his booking a day or two before, and she was on her own."

That's when she asked Uncle Conor to go and see her, Brigid thought, and then she asked him for something he could only give to Rose, and he wouldn't give it. She thought this, but she did not say it.

"And she asked Laurence to meet her on the boat," said Francis, suddenly, "and then they both died."

"Yes," said Mr Doughty, and his voice changed. "More's the pity. It was a long way to ask someone to come just so that she could talk about the troubles she had brought on herself."

"Where's Mr Silver, now, Mr Doughty?" Francis asked.

"Still in Egypt, I believe. It's hot out there at the moment, and I don't mean the weather."

"My granda said it was shaping up to be hot round the border towns," said Brigid.

Mr Doughty sat back in his chair, and looked long at Brigid. "Did he, now?" he said. "Well, you can tell him from me, next time you see him, he's not wrong. It'll be another hot Twelfth, if I'm not mistaken."

"Is Ned with his father?" Francis said.

"I believe so," said Mr Doughty. "He should be anyway. He should be with his father."

"Mr Silver told Ned that Catholics are riddled," Brigid said.

"Riddled?"

"Riddled with something . . . super-something."

"Superstition?" Mr Doughty laughed, a great, hearty laugh. "Well, I'm not. And I'm a Catholic, like you. So's John Steele, as a matter of fact."

There was a sound in the hall, and the door was pushed open. The children's mother came in, carrying a tray. She wore her blue dressing-gown: Brigid had a fleeting memory of Christmas morning.

"Mr Doughty, what must you think of us?" she said. "I'm so sorry. We're at sixes and sevens here."

"Mrs Arthur," he said, scraping the chair as he got to his feet, "forgive me. I was talking to the children outside, and I invited myself in for a cup of tea. I hope you don't mind."

Good Mr Doughty had not given away their secret. He pulled out a chair for the children's mother and sat down beside her.

"Mr Doughty," she said, "we have been a little out of events the last while. Francis has told me your news of Isobel and her brother. What of my sis– . . . my late husband's friend, Cornelius Todd?"

Mr Doughty sat up straight in the chair. "Ah. Cornelius Todd.

Well, Mrs Arthur, I don't want to trouble you about this at the moment. I remember he was, as you say, a friend of your late husband. It makes me sorry to tell you that Cornelius Todd has . . . connections, to the IRA."

She put down her cup, almost missing the saucer. "Jesus, Mary and Joseph," she said, and let her head drop.

"Mrs Arthur," said the policeman. "I'm off duty at the moment. I'm here as a neighbour. Let's not distress ourselves about it. Maybe, another time, we'll talk of it."

"His father was involved, the time of the Civil War. He was very much against Partition. That's all I ever knew," said the children's mother, almost to herself. "I know Rose worried in case . . . and my brother had doubts . . . but Maurice and my father-in-law always said Cornelius had more sense . . . and I'm sure he promised Rose he'd keep away from . . . I don't know. Truly, I don't know. Maurice could tell you more about him, but Maurice . . ."

"There's nothing to tell, Mrs Arthur," he said. "We knew all we needed to know, long before. We were watching him, ever since those bad boys tried to bomb the barracks in England last autumn. Todd had been involved, and so, as we now know, was the man we caught in the plot."

"Yes," she said. "Isobel's brother. How I was deceived in that girl."

"Indeed. But for a long time, it seems, Cornelius Todd has had no involvement, beyond visiting prisoners, which is not a crime, and attending gatherings in public places, which is not yet a crime. He seems not to have been a part of this latest business. I'm sorry for your sister. She's a lovely young lady."

Mrs Arthur lifted her head. To Brigid, she looked like Mama again. "Thank you, Mr Doughty. As it happens, my sister had already broken her engagement to Cornelius Todd some little time ago. He is nothing to her now, or to us."

Mr Doughty bowed his head. "For your sister's sake, and for yours, I'm glad. But I meant that I was sorry that she had to learn of his involvement." He stood up. "How's the little birdie coming on?" he said, and stroked Brigid's hand.

"I think he's –" Brigid began.

"Brigid," said her mother, "go and put that bird back in its cage. I don't know why you –"

"She was showing him to me, Mrs Arthur. It was my fault," said Mr Doughty and Brigid, in that moment, gave him a corner of her heart.

They walked him to the front door, Brigid keeping her hand over Dicky.

Mr Doughty stopped in the hall. He was going home, he said, to his daughter for his dinner, and in the afternoon he would come and do some work in the plot. "I was wondering," he added, "if this young man would like to help me? I could do with a hand in the plot." He looked down at Francis, and placed one hand on his head.

Brigid, left out, was not pleased.

Francis turned his head to look at his mother. "Mama?" he said.

"Would you like that, Francis?" she said.

"I would," he said. "But what about Brigid?"

Mr Doughty said: "Would you like to, as well, Miss?"

"Could I watch?" asked Brigid and, to her surprise, everyone laughed.

Her mother said: "Brigid can watch, or she can help me make rock cakes for later. Rose is coming back to stay for a while, and I think Granda Arthur is coming up to town today on the bus. We can all have tea."

Brigid nodded. "Mr Doughty too?" she asked.

"Of course. But first," said her mother, "some of us, myself included, need to get dressed." She opened the door, and the summer light streamed in. "I must put up the curtain," she said, and then, as Mr Doughty stepped through the doorway, she placed her hand on his arm. "Mr Doughty," she said, and her voice dropped, "I don't want my sister to run the risk of meeting

. . . anyone she doesn't want to. You know who I . . ."

Mr Doughty looked down at his feet. "As far as I know, Mrs Arthur," he said, "she'll meet no one. Cornelius Todd hasn't been seen since the day of the funeral. He seems to have left Northern Ireland. And, I'm afraid, it's going to be left at that."

"But, Mr Doughty," said Mrs Arthur, "Isobel . . . she was in our employment. Won't we all be involved in questions about the whole thing, now that the funeral is . . ."

"Mrs Arthur," said Mr Doughty, "Isobel is gone. Her brother is behind bars. Nothing will happen to involve you or your family."

"Are you sure?" she said.

"Yes," said Mr Doughty. "I am. It's because of young Silver . . . or, more to the point, because of his father, and the work he is doing out in Egypt."

"You mean . . . ?"

"I mean, our instruction is that neither the government in London, nor anyone connected with it, is to be left open to embarrassment. Because of Silver's position, it's thought best not to risk scandal."

"Suez," said Mrs Arthur.

Mr Doughty nodded. "Yes. Suez. You'll hear no more of this business, and we have to close the book. The fellow that we know caused trouble is back behind bars. I wish we could have had a word with that other character, whoever he was, because I know I saw someone else there last autumn – and I would have liked to catch Todd, too, before he took off." He looked at the children, first Brigid, then Francis, and said nothing for a moment. "But I didn't," he continued, "and now I can do no more. Do you know, Mrs Arthur, I think across the water they don't care what goes on here. They don't care what we do to one another, so long as they're not embarrassed before the world. Suez matters to them – we don't." He sighed again. "Well. On another bit. Good morning to you all, and I'll be happy to join you later on."

At the foot of the stairs, Brigid exchanged glances with Francis. She was not sorry about Isobel. She had always had mixed feelings about Uncle Conor – but never to see him again, his broad shoulders and his crooked smile? Francis' face showed the same uncertainty, yet neither said anything, until suddenly Francis left Brigid's side, and stepped in front of Mr Doughty. The big man stopped.

"Mr Doughty," said Francis, "there is something I have to tell you."

Mr Doughty said nothing. Motionless, he waited.

Something cold gripped Brigid's heart.

"Francis," she said, but Francis only looked quickly at her, anxious and flushed, and turned back to Mr Doughty.

"I brought food to someone in the plot," he said.

"Did you, son?" said Mr Doughty, but he did not sound cross, or even surprised.

"He was hiding. He didn't do any harm to anyone. He told me about it one day. I was off school. I was – I hadn't been well, and then I was allowed to go up the garden. And he was in the plot, and . . . we got talking, and he told me the whole thing, how he got involved with the IRA because he thought it was for the good of Ireland."

Ireland, thought Brigid. Not Ireland again.

"But he wouldn't do what Isobel's brother wanted, all the bombings and the guns. He left the IRA, and came home here. He didn't want to have any more to do with it. He wanted to have a normal life, like us. He was a friend of . . . of our father."

"Francis," cried his mother. "What do you mean? Your father had nothing to do with those men."

"No, I know, I didn't mean . . ." said Francis, and he turned to face her. "But he was a friend of Daddy long ago, before all these bombings in England, when they used to speak Irish and talk about Parnell. Like Uncle Conor," and Francis lifted his head, almost defiantly. "Uncle Conor was part of it, really part of it, but he was still Daddy's friend."

His mother said nothing. She bit her lip, and her face grew pale.

"But I know Daddy didn't have anything to do with all that," said Francis, "because I asked the man in the plot about that, about Daddy. And he told me, straight, that Daddy said men with families couldn't afford the luxury of politics beyond their own fireside. 'Render to Caesar,' he said Daddy said."

Wanly, his mother smiled. "He did like to say that, especially when clients complained about the amount of tax they had to pay. But yes, Francis, I see what you mean."

"Tell us what happened your friend in the plot, Francis," said Mr Doughty, evenly.

My friend, thought Brigid, with irritation. George Bailey is *my* friend.

"He came over here after the bombings in England, because he knew if he got arrested he would be blamed, even though he had left before all that started. Uncle Conor tried to help him, he said, but there was only so much he could do."

"Yes," said Mr Doughty, drily. "I'm sure."

"I think he really did," said Francis, his brow furrowing. "But Isobel's brother had run here too, and when he found out George was in the town, he set out to find him. George was sure he meant to kill him, in case he told on the others. He tried, and then George had to get away."

"George?" said Mr Doughty, and now he did sound surprised.

"George Bailey," said Francis, almost with impatience. "Brigid calls him that."

"It's his name," said Brigid indignantly. "And, as well, nobody was supposed to know about George. It was meant to be a secret."

Francis looked at her and sighed. "Brigid," he said, "I've thought about this. We have to let Mr Doughty know what happened, especially if George didn't do anything."

"He didn't," said Mr Doughty. "You needn't worry: you've

broken no confidence. I did know there was a man those fellows were after, but I didn't know why, and you've helped me with another bit of the jigsaw."

What jigsaw, thought Brigid.

"I still would have liked to talk to him, though," said Mr Doughty, thoughtfully. "Perhaps, when we are in the plot, you can fill in a few more of the details, Francis."

Francis looked uncertain, and silence fell.

"You needn't be afraid, son," said Mr Doughty. "If he is the man I think, then we know he was in the clear and, as I told you, he's well gone by now."

Brigid felt first relief, then sadness. Well gone meant she would never see George Bailey again.

"Well, now," said Mr Doughty, "this will never get the work done. Mrs Arthur, you have two fine children there, and you can be proud of them."

"Thank you, Mr Doughty," said their mother, and she placed a hand on each of their shoulders.

"I'll see you all later on," he said and, with a wave of his hand he walked thoughtfully away.

"Goodbye, Mr Doughty," they called together, as he lifted his hand in farewell.

Francis said: "Till this afternoon!" He was no longer flushed, and his head was high.

"And rock cakes, Mr Doughty!" added Brigid, to be sure of his return.

She made to lift her hand to wave, and remembered that she was still holding Dicky.

While their mother stood at the door, Brigid followed Francis into the kitchen, and Francis opened Dicky's cage. He held out his hands, and Brigid carefully opened hers. Dicky lay in her hand and, as they looked, he opened his black eye.

"Hello, Dicky," said Francis, softly, but Dicky said nothing. "Are you sure he spoke that time, Brigid?"

"I am sure," said Brigid. "He said: 'Hello, Dicky'."

311

"Well, he's not saying anything now," said Francis. "Maybe he's still concussed. Give him over to me. I'll tell him about Suez. That'll bring him round."

"Tell me, too," said Brigid, opening her hands, "because I don't know what that was all about, and I'd like to know why you never told me you knew George Bailey."

In the end, Francis did not tell her any of it that day because, at the moment of passing to him, Dicky suddenly moved his head, spread his left wing, pushed away from Brigid's hand and flew out of her palm. Awkwardly at first, then with growing assurance, he circled the room, past the ceiling light, round and round.

"Francis! Close the windows," Brigid cried. "He'll get out again. Francis!"

Francis, his eyes alight, shook his head. "He won't," he said. "He won't go far, will you, Dicky?"

And Dicky, as if in reply, called back from the ceiling, "*Hello, Dicky! Hello, Dicky!*"

Brigid clasped Francis in delight. "I told you, Francis," she cried. "I told you!"

Francis held out his arms to Brigid, as if they were about to dance, and swung her round, Dicky circling above them. "*Absolument pure,*" he said, and lifted her up, swinging her high above his head, as if she too were a bird; and she spread her arms wide, like feathered wings. "*Absolument pure,*" he said again, and Brigid, spinning in the air, laughed aloud.

Acknowledgements

This book has been a long while in the making. Thirty-odd years ago, before circumstance took me into the academic world, David Marcus awarded me a prize at Listowel, published my work in *New Irish Writing* and shortlisted me for a Hennessy award. Ten years ago, he suggested that I write a novel. That tireless champion of Irish writing accepted no excuses. It took some years, and was set aside many times, but it was written, and David was its first reader. In sadness at his final illness and death, I set the novel aside once more.

Just last year, I went back to *The Friday Tree* and gave it to my agent, Paul Feldstein. Paul took over, submitting it to Poolbeg, the very firm, founded by David Marcus with Philip McDermott in 1976, which had published my work on Michael McLaverty over twenty years ago. That fact was unknown to Poolbeg's present dynamic leader, Paula Campbell, when she accepted it as the first title in the exciting launch of Ward River Press, and she and her marvellous team set to work. I cannot adequately thank Paul Feldstein and Paula Campbell for their immediate faith in the novel. I thank with admiration my meticulous editor at Poolbeg, Gaye Shortland, for her patience, humour and unwavering focus; and I want to mention also those first careful and helpfully critical readers, my daughter Judith and my friends Bernadette McLean and Paul Shevlin; and, always, my son John who, however much he has to do himself, takes time to keep me calm.

In addition to David Marcus, to whom the book is dedicated, I must express my gratitude to my other early mentors, no longer here, who set me on my way in the writing of fiction: Sam Hanna Bell, author of *December Bride*, who awarded me a prize for the first story I wrote; Michael McLaverty, one of our greats, who told me I could do it; and another, whom McLaverty famously fostered, Seamus Heaney, for a lifetime's friendship and inspiration.

To two other QUB mentors, Professors John Cronin and Ronnie Buchanan, I owe much for their continued friendship and advice; and to two extraordinary women writers, Jennifer Johnston and Edna O'Brien, both of whom are still at the height of their powers, and took time to encourage me by reading and commenting on early work, I extend my gratitude.

A special debt of thanks is due to Jim Fitzpatrick, Chairman of the *Irish News*, for kind permission to quote from contemporary accounts published in that most valuable resource, and to Libraries NI for permission to make copies from its newspaper archive.

Interview with the Author

How did you come to write the book?

It was suggested to me ten years ago by David Marcus, whom Seamus Heaney named for his encouragement of writers "the Blessed Marcus". It took me a while to do as David asked, because I was at the time still involved in the academic world and the writing of literary criticism but, gradually, over the next few years, with many stops and starts, it was completed. Again, as Seamus Heaney also wisely pointed out, the important thing with writing is "getting started, keeping going – and getting started again". I think the starting again is the hardest, and perhaps the most important.

Where did the idea come from?

I grew up in Northern Ireland, and after some years working and living in Dublin from the mid-1970s until the early 1980s, returned to live in Belfast, where I have my home today. With the distance that living away from the place of birth brings, I grew increasingly aware of something subconsciously absorbed, a sense that the trouble we had experienced in the North in the late 1960s had not, as newspapers and television seemed to be telling us, suddenly burst upon an unsuspecting, peaceful and law-abiding society. The 1950s in the North was quiet only on the surface. A visit to Belfast's excellent Newspaper Library confirmed that there was a prolonged bombing campaign by the IRA in the mid-1950s, starting in England and then moving to the North; while at the same time, long before the well-known Garvaghy Road incidents, 12,000 Orangemen repeatedly insisted on their right to walk, on what was at the time described as a "hot Twelfth", through a largely nationalist area in County Down. Everything was in place, ready to erupt, long before 1968.

Why did you decide to write about 1955–1956 rather than the other years leading up to 1968?

I think things are at their most interesting, historically and imaginatively, before the defining moments have taken place. In 1955, for example, the Suez crisis had not yet happened, and the Hungarian revolution had not taken place. There was still a sense that the Second World War, still comparatively recent in the minds of people, would serve as a reminder that something so horrific must never happen again. In Belfast, because there had been the Blitz in 1941, bombed-out buildings still stood as a kind of warning. I stop the novel before the imminent crises I allude to, at home and around the world, become too serious to be dismissed. I suppose I wanted to suggest – within the fictional world I had created – that the desire for peace might yet prevail.

Apart from documented political events, to what extent are the events in the novel based on reality?

The tragedy of the foundering of the *Princess Victoria* in January 1953 did happen, with the loss of many lives. Davy Crockett, or rather the actor who played him in the

Disney film, did visit Robbs' department store in Belfast in April 1956 – a fact which was not revealed to me or my siblings at the time, or we would certainly have clamoured to be there. He was, in fact, delayed by some hours, according to contemporary newspaper reports, firstly because Customs at the border were suspicious of his eighteenth-century musket, and then because some Queen's University students tried to kidnap him as a rag stunt. There was indeed a riot when he did not turn up, and it interests me to consider that the very children who may have been there would have been just the age to become the students who demonstrated and marched in 1968 at the outset of the real eruption of what became known as "the Troubles".

Why did you use these real events?

I hoped they would root the novel in reality, and allow me to let my imagination move round the margins.

What is the significance of the title?

I really did believe the seven trees at the back of our house were the shapes and colours of the days of the week. I later discovered I was not the only one, by any means, to ascribe colours and shapes to the days of the week. Nobody else agrees with my colours and shapes, however, which just goes to show how wrong people can be!

Why the epigraph from the Brothers Grimm?

The tales of the Brothers Grimm come from folktales which, as we know, are often terrifying. They did not sweeten their tales for children, and the originals of the stories – as documented, for example, in Iona and Peter Opie's *The Classic Fairy Tales* – are grim indeed: children, abandoned or betrayed by those who have charge of them, have to face the world early, and learn not only the virtues of courage and honesty, but also, all too often, the arts of cunning and duplicity. For Brigid and Francis, though they have good, caring parents and some kindly relatives and friends, the world beyond these is far from safe. There is always, in their experience, a distance between adults and children, as in the world of the Grimms. School, in particular, is not child-friendly, and there is no gradual introduction as happens today. The children go from the cocoon of home and family into an alien world, where they are expected to be little adults in training, and to act accordingly. Like the children in the Grimms' story, they decide to look out for one another, and, like the children in the Grimms' story, when they do go forth into the wide world, it is the smaller, apparently weaker sister who adapts more quickly to the requirements of a fairly ruthless society, while the older brother is shown to be unexpectedly vulnerable.

Would you like to take a trip back to 1955?

I would: though it might be a mistake. It could be like the scene in Thornton Wilder's *Our Town*, where the recently dead Emily is offered the chance to return for one day to any day she likes from her life. She is warned, however, not to choose an important day. Not heeding the warning, she selects a birthday. The intensity of the emotion she feels overwhelms her, and she sees why she was warned to choose a day of no significance, because that, however insignificant, would in itself be so hard to bear that she might not be able to cope. A day of any importance, as she discovers, is so intolerable that she begs to leave. If I did go back, therefore, it would have to be the dullest day imaginable.

You have published in the creative field before, mainly with the short story. Beyond that, your writing has been in the field of

non-fiction, often academic. **Are there great differences in approach?**

The main difference is that in fiction, creative speculation is not only allowed, but is necessary. In non-fiction, as in the historical and literary research I carried out for my book on Jane Austen's nieces in Ireland, *May, Lou and Cass*, there is no room for speculation. It is essential to keep to recoverable fact. In the case of that book, however, the facts were so extraordinary that there was no room or need for speculation. The training of the academic, all the same, is very valuable for a fiction-writer. Any historical references must be checked carefully, and though the imagination may be at play, there must still be geographical and historical consistency.

Thinking again about the creative aspect, are your characters entirely fictional, or based on people known or encountered?

We did have a green budgerigar called Dicky. He was exactly as described in the book, and he did once fly up to the Friday Tree, underneath which my eldest brother sat patiently until Dicky felt like coming down. It took some time. For the rest, they take their characteristics from a number of people. I had three brothers, two still living, and I have a sister; I have a son and daughter, and eleven nieces and nephews. Brigid's character began through observation of quite a few small girls, including, here and there, my remembered self, though I am certainly not Brigid. I would never have got up to half the things she does, however much I might have liked to. The character of Francis, though indeed drawn from more than one source, is largely based on that of my eldest brother Seamus, who was as every bit as clever, good and kind a brother as Francis. Ned Silver walked in one day – from nowhere – when I had finished the first draft. He was called Harry in those days, until

A.M. Homes used the name in her recent novel *May We Be Forgiven,* and he had to become Ned. His opening line, "Why don't you kill her then?" was directly borrowed from a casual remark made by one of my siblings' children to another. It was so casually shocking – and so wickedly funny to those who heard and related it – that it lodged in my mind. The other characters are largely composites. I did once know an enigmatic man who, in his own words "fought with Collins, then fought *with* Collins", and had a fund of extraordinary stories about the past. Remembering him gave me the idea for Cornelius Todd.

Did the fictional creations become real in your mind?

They did, and those who made it to the end are still there, getting on with their lives.

Did they act unexpectedly or did you always know what they would do?

Well, Ned, as I mentioned, walked in fully-fledged one day. I never quite knew what he would do until he did it, which is a wonderful feeling when writing fiction. To me, it means the thing is working, really alive. As the book progressed, I found they all had their own agendas, to a certain extent, and I began to sympathise with Flann O'Brien's beleaguered author in his *At Swim-Two-Birds,* whose characters don't want to do anything he has planned for them, and go off in all sorts of directions every time he goes to sleep. I had quite a job bringing some of them into line; sometimes, though, like Ned, they knew better than I did what they were going to do.

Do you have any favourites among the characters?

Francis has to be a favourite for me, and that scapegrace,

Ned, who is, under it all, a rather lonely and neglected child. I think Rose, the children's aunt, is the quiet heroine of the book. She never falters, and she puts everyone's welfare before her own.

You said that, now the book is finished, your characters are still "getting on with their lives". Do you intend to write up their later history?

I do know their later history and may write it up at some point, though I think not straight away.

Do you have your next project in mind?

I do, and am working on it even as we speak – but I think it's best not to talk too much about plans until there is something to show for them. Someone, I can't remember who, once said "You can talk it or you can write it". I think, in my case, it's generally better to write it first.

Discussion Topics:
The Friday Tree

1. The novel is set in 1955–56. How different does life seem today? For adults? For children? Would any of the aspects of 1955–56 be recognisable?

2. Was the sense of danger in the 1950s palpable outside Northern Ireland?

3. The Davy Crockett incident was repeated throughout the UK. Do you think the fact of these near-riots might have a special resonance in Ulster?

4. The *Princess Victoria* went down in a terrible storm in January 1953. In what ways is that experience of communal loss after disaster echoed or repeated in the present day?

5. Newspapers feature throughout the novel. To what extent do they serve a similar function today?

6. The landscape of rural Ireland seems relatively unspoiled in 1955–56. How much of that remains today in Ireland?

7. Is life today, supplemented by digital technology and rapid travel, better or more difficult than in 1955?

8. The novel makes reference to the celebration of our traditional calendar customs. Hallowe'en and Christmas aside, have any of these celebrations continued to the present day?

9. To what extent does the Plot have metaphorical significance in the novel?

10. Is there a clear villain in the novel?

11. Is there an identifiable hero or heroine?

12. Which character stays most in the reader's mind?

13. What is the main difference in the children's understanding of life at the beginning and end of the book?

14. How well does the author convey to us the world as perceived by a child?

15. Most of the adults in the novel make every effort to protect the children from the adult world. Is it a mistake to do so?

16. Which adult in the novel understands the mind of a child best?

17. Discuss the role of Francis in his relationship with Brigid.

18. Cornelius Todd is a complex and mysterious character, who elicits widely differing reactions from the other characters. Why is this?

19. What, do you think, is the significance of the epigraph from the Brothers Grimm?

≋ WARD RIVER PRESS
titles coming 2014

Ruby's Tuesday **by Gillian Binchy**
coming Spring.

The Last Goodbye **by Caroline Finnerty**
coming Spring.

Sing Me to Sleep **by Helen Moorhouse**
coming Spring.

Into the Night Sky **by Caroline Finnerty**
coming Autumn.

The House Where it Happened **by Martina Devlin**
coming Autumn.

Levi's Gift **by Jennifer Burke**
coming Autumn.